CENTRE STAGE
SECOND EDITION

Mathew Clausen

Consultant: Samantha Kosky

PEARSON
Heinemann

Sydney, Melbourne, Brisbane, Perth, Adelaide
and associated companies around the world

This book is dedicated to Eileen, Norman and Annabelle

Pearson Heinemann

An imprint of Pearson Australia
(a division of Pearson Australia Group Pty Ltd)
20 Thackray Road, Port Melbourne, Victoria 3207
PO Box 460, Port Melbourne, Victoria 3207
www.pearson.com.au

© Mathew Clausen 2004
First published 2004 by Heinemann
2012 2011 2010 2009
12 11 10 9 8 7 6

Copying for educational purposes
The Australian *Copyright Act 1968* (the Act) allows a maximum of one chapter or 10% of this book, whichever is the greater, to be copied by any educational institution for its educational purposes provided that that educational institution (or the body that administers it) has given a remuneration notice to Copyright Agency Limited (CAL) under the Act.

For details of the CAL licence for educational institutions contact Copyright Agency Limited (www.copyright.com.au).

Copying for other purposes
Except as permitted under the Act, for example any fair dealing for the purposes of study, research, criticism or review, no part of this book may be reproduced, stored in a retrieval system, or transmitted in any form or by any means without prior written permission. All enquiries should be made to the publisher at the address above.

Copying of the blackline master pages
The purchasing educational institution and its staff are permitted to make copies of the pages marked as blackline master pages, beyond their rights under the Act, provided that: 1. the number of copies does not exceed the number reasonably required by the educational institution to satisfy their teaching purposes; 2. copies are made only by reprographic means (photocopying), not by electronic/digital means, nor stored nor transmitted; 3. copies are not sold or lent; 4. every copy made clearly shows the footnote (e.g. 'Copyright © Pearson Australia 2009. This sheet may be photocopied for non-commercial classroom use').

For those pages not marked as blackline masters pages the normal copying limits in the Act, as described above, apply.

Publisher: Cathy Panozzo
Editors: Susan Lee and Astrid Judge
Designer: Sarah Hazell
Text and cover designer: Gerry Theoharis
Cover illustration: Jeff Raglus
Illustrations: Gregory Roberts
Photograph researcher: Jan Calderwood

Typeset in Berling 11/13 by Palmer Higgs Pty Ltd
Prepress by Digital Imaging Group (DIG)
Printed in Malaysia (CTP - LSP)

National Library of Australia
cataloguing-in-publication data:

Clausen, Mathew.
Centre stage : creating, performing and interpreting drama.
2nd ed.
Includes index.
For secondary school students.
ISBN 978 1 74081 337 2
1. Drama - Textbooks. 2. Acting - Textbooks I. Title.
792.028

Pearson Australia Group Pty Ltd 40 004 245 943

The selection of Internet addresses (URLs) given in this book were valid at the time of publication and chosen as being appropriate for use as a secondary education research tool. However, due to the dynamic nature of the Internet, some addresses may have changed, may have ceased to exist since publication, or may inadvertently link to sites with content that could be considered offensive or inappropriate. While the author and publisher regret any inconvenience this may cause readers, no responsibility for any such changes or unforeseeable errors can be accepted by either the author or the publisher.

Neither the publisher nor the author can accept responsibility for injury that may be sustained when conducting any of the activities described in this book. The decision to undertake an activity is the responsibility of the teacher. Factors such as group size, and students' ability levels and experience should be taken into account.

Contents

Introduction
    To the Student   vi
    To the Teacher   vi
    About the Author   vi
    About the Consultant   vi
    Acknowledgments   vii
National Profile Statements and Outcomes for Drama, Levels 5 and 6   viii
New South Wales Outcomes for Drama and Cross-curriculum Content, Stages 4 and 5   ix

Part One — Creating and Performing Drama

Chapter 1   The Performer's Tools: Body and Voice   2
    1.1   Warm-ups   3
    1.2   Mime: Creating Illusion Through Use of the Body   6
    1.3   Body Language: Expression, Gesture and Interpretation   9
    1.4   Voice in Performance   14
    1.5   Performance Task: *The Lake*   20

Chapter 2   Improvisation: Spontaneous Performance   25
    2.1   An Overview of Improvisation   26
    2.2   The Skills of Improvisation   27
    2.3   Character Types and Status in Improvisation   33
    2.4   The Elements of Drama   35
    2.5   Improvisation Exercises   38
    2.6   Performance Task: Improvisation   41

Chapter 3   Playbuilding: Devised Performance   44
    3.1   Steps in Playbuilding   45
    3.2   Playbuilding Structures   47
    3.3   Creating and Controlling Focus   50
    3.4   Scene Transitions   52
    3.5   Creating a Character   56
    3.6   Stage Spaces and the Audience   58
    3.7   Performance Task: Creating a Play   61

Part Two — Interpreting Drama

Chapter 4 Scripts: Interpretation and Presentation 70
- 4.1 The Director 71
- 4.2 The Stage Manager 72
- 4.3 Script Detective Work and Stanislavski's System 74
- 4.4 Rehearsing and Performing Scripts 81
- 4.5 Directorial Concept and the Elements of Production 85
- 4.6 The Designers 89
- 4.7 Performance Task: Interpreting Script 93

Chapter 5 Writing a Review: Analysing and Evaluating Performance 103
- 5.1 Steps in Reviewing a Live Performance 104
- 5.2 Evaluating the Components of a Live Performance 106
- 5.3 Written Task: Review of a Performance 109

Part Three — Dramatic Forms and Performance Styles

Chapter 6 Melodrama: Just for the Thrill 114
- 6.1 An Overview of Melodrama 115
- 6.2 Plot and Dramatic Structure in Melodrama 117
- 6.3 Characters in Melodrama 118
- 6.4 The Melodrama Acting Style 119
- 6.5 Staging in Melodrama 124
- 6.6 Performance Task: Time Running Out 126

Chapter 7 Comedy: It's All in the … Timing 129
- 7.1 An Overview of Comedy in Performance 130
- 7.2 Slapstick: Physical Comedy 131
- 7.3 Character in Slapstick Comedy 136
- 7.4 Parody: Imitation and Exaggeration 140
- 7.5 Performance Task: Don't Slip on the Soap! 143

Chapter 8 Mask: Disguising and Revealing 147
- 8.1 An Overview of Mask 148
- 8.2 Neutral Masks: Creating Individual Character 149
- 8.3 Half Mask and Chorus Work: Creating Group Character 153
- 8.4 African Mask Performance 158
- 8.5 Performance Task: Mask Ritual 162

Chapter 9		Non-Realistic Theatre: Visions, Dreams and Symbols	**167**
	9.1	An Overview of Non-Realistic Theatre	168
	9.2	Dreams and the Subconscious	169
	9.3	Expressionist Theatre	174
	9.4	Performance Task: Non-Realistic Theatre	181

Chapter 10		Playback Theatre and Documentary Drama: Interpreting True Stories	**185**
	10.1	Playback Theatre	186
	10.2	Documentary Drama	193
	10.3	Performance Task: Documentary Drama	199

Chapter 11		Physical Theatre: Roll Up, Roll Up!	**202**
	11.1	Legs on the Wall: A Physical Theatre Company	203
	11.2	Physical Theatre Exercises	205
	11.3	Performing a Physical Theatre Script	210
	11.4	Performance Task: Physical Theatre	216

Chapter 12		Scripted Drama: Writing Australian Plays	**219**
	12.1	Exploring Australian Culture and Identity	220
	12.2	Hannie Rayson: An Approach to Script Writing	223
	12.3	Aboriginal Scripted Drama	235
	12.4	Writing Your Own Scripted Drama	241
	12.5	Script Writing Task: Australian Drama	245

Part Four Appendixes

Appendix 1	The Logbook	250
Appendix 2	Rehearsal Log Sheet	259
Appendix 3	Performance Self-assessment Sheet	261
Appendix 4	Audience Evaluation Sheet	263
Appendix 5	Lighting Cue Sheet	265
Appendix 6	Sound Cue Sheet	266
Appendix 7	Make-up Design Sheet	267
Appendix 8	Costume Design Sheet	268

Glossary	269
Useful Resources	276
Index	277

Introduction

To the Student

Drama is a special area of study where you, the student, become the performer: the instrument that expresses ideas and feelings through dramatic action to an audience. *Centre Stage* is written to help you discover, explore and develop the ways you can create, perform and appreciate drama. *Centre Stage* can be used in every lesson and offers opportunities for you to utilise your creativity, imagination, ideas and skills to create interesting and entertaining drama.

At the back of the book in the appendixes section you will find some material to help with your drama work. The appendixes include guidelines for how to write logbook entries, and some examples of these. There are also samples of a self-evaluation sheet, an audience evaluation sheet, sound and lighting cue sheets, as well as costume and make-up design sheets. A glossary of drama and theatre terms can also be found at the end of the book. You will find these resources useful in a number of ways.

So, good luck with your journey into the world of drama and theatre. Have fun and enjoy.

To the Teacher

Centre Stage is designed to provide students with a two-year course in Drama that addresses the Drama statements and outcomes for levels 5 and 6 in the *National Curriculum Profile for Australian Schools*. Part 1 provides an extensive introduction to various aspects of drama practice. It covers voice and movement work, improvisation and playbuilding. Part 2 examines and explores script work and the elements of production; it also looks at review writing. Part 3 explores the techniques and conventions of different forms and styles of performance. *Centre Stage* allows students to develop knowledge, skills and understanding progressively, but also allows for chapters to be treated as discrete units of work.

Recounting, researching and evaluating are strongly encouraged in each chapter as a means of developing an appreciation and understanding of drama as well as underpinning the process of making, performing and appreciating drama.

Performance tasks are provided for each topic to determine student achievement of the stated outcomes. The performance tasks draw on the skills and understanding students have gained in their exploration of the topics. Each performance task has a specific evaluation sheet. The evaluation sheets are photocopiable, and allow the teacher and students to identify achievement of outcomes through particular performance task criteria. The comments section at the end of the evaluation sheet allows for description of achievement as well as advice for the ongoing development of skills and understanding.

Support for this text is available by going to the Heinemann World Wide Website. Throughout the text the hi.com.au icon (see left) appears in the margin. This icon indicates useful, carefully selected websites at: **pearson.com.au/schools**. Please note that the location and content of the listed websites were valid at the time of printing.

About the Author

Mathew Clausen has fifteen years' experience teaching Drama to primary and secondary students in Victoria and New South Wales; he has taught both VCE Drama and HSC 2 Unit Drama courses. Mathew completed his Bachelor of Education at Melbourne State College, and established the community theatre company Instant Theatre, which was committed to performing new and established Australian works. Mathew is also one of the founding members of the Melbourne Playback Theatre group and taught at the National Theatre Drama School. Currently Mathew is Drama Coordinator at Loreto Kirribilli, New South Wales, where he has been responsible for the introduction of Drama to the curriculum. He is also a Senior Marker of HSC Drama Design Projects and a writer of education notes for the Sydney Opera House's education program.

About the Consultant

Samantha Kosky is currently Drama Coordinator at Newington College, New South Wales. Samantha is an experienced reviewer of resource material for secondary Drama and English students. She has thirteen years' experience teaching Drama and English in both government and private schools, and has been involved in middle and senior school Drama syllabus development. Samantha has tutored at regional and state Drama camps, is an experienced director and has marked HSC Drama in New South Wales since the course's introduction. She is currently an active member of the Drama Committee for the Association of Independent Schools.

Acknowledgments

Many thanks to Samantha for her advice, wisdom and sense of humour; and to Catherine De Tullio for her advice on the melodrama chapter.

Many thanks to members of the Legs on the Wall theatre company for their generosity and permission to use material appearing in Chapter 11; thanks in particular to Artistic Director Debra Iris Batton, General Manager Michelle Vickers and core ensemble members Rowan Marchingo and Alexandra

Mathew Clausen

The publisher and author would like to thank Helen Wilde, Debbie Wall, David Van Vuuren, Bronwyn Farrawell, Bev Omerod, Noel Chamberlain and Ken Barrett for their detailed and helpful reviews of the first edition; and Mathew Brown, Peter Cox and Clair Simpson for their detailed and constructive feedback of the second edition.

The author wishes to acknowledge Brad Haseman and John O'Toole for their explanation of the elements of drama in their book *Dramawise* (Heinemann, Melbourne, 1987). Also, the list of lazzi on page 135 has been adapted from *Acting in Person and Style* by J. L. Crawford, C. Hurst and M. Lugering (Brown and Benchmark, Sydney, 1995).

The author and publisher would like to thank the following for granting their permission to reproduce copyright material:

Photographs and realia:

Arena Theatre Company/Rosemary Myers, p. 45; Arts Management/Barrie Kosky/Kate Gollings, p. 176; Jenni Carbins, p. 92; Centre National de la Photographie, p. 12; Chunky Move/Gideon Obozarnec, p. 10; Sophie Clausen, p. 74; Mat Clausen p. 25; Company B Belvoir Street Theatre/Marco Bok, p. 2; Company B Belvoir Theatre/Heidrun Lohr, pp. 44, 71, 103, 129, 185; Mike Curtain/Gayle MacGregor, p. 91; Branco Gaica/Gavan Swift, p. 90; Guthrie Theatre, Minneapolis, p. 148; Great Southern Stock, p. 165; Bryce Hallett, p. 104; *TV Soap* magazine, No. 17, Nov. 2003, p. 144; Richard Jeziorny, p. 89; Tony Kishawi, p. 149; Legs on the Wall Theatre Company/Daniel Bereholak, p. 202; Chris Lilley, p. 130; Mary Evans Picture Library, p. 125; Conrad Page, p. 211; Lyn Pierse/Theatresports (registered trademark) Down Under p. 27; photolibrary.com p. 62; Hanni Rayson, p. 224; Jacque Robinson, p. 186; Sydney Opera House/Peter Holderness, p.119; Sydney Theatre Company/Peter Holderness, p. 114; Sydney Theatre Company/Tracy Schramm p. 70, 149; The Bridgeman Art Library/Nasjonalgalleriet, p. 175; The Melbourne Theatre Company/Geraldine Turner/Jeff Busby, p. 219; JenniferWest/W.A.A.P.A., p. 14; Dallas Winmar/Malcolm Cross, p. 236.

Extracts:

Brown and Benchmark, Sydney, 1995, for the lazzi in Chapter 7, adapted from *Acting in Person and Style*, by J. L. Crawford, C. Hurst and M. Lugering; Mathew Clausen for permission to reproduce the script 'Dana and Lee'; Mathew Clausen and Paige Kilponen for the Prompt copy in Chapter 4; P. P. Craney for permission to reproduce scene 13 of *Home*, commissioned by Shopfront Youth Theatre for Young People; Currency Press Pty Ltd for permission to reproduce extract from *Dinkum Assorted* by Linda Aronson; Currency Press for permission to reproduce extract from *Wild Rice*, by Huong Nguyen Phi Hai, Pat Rix and Geoff Crowhurst; Currency Press for permission to reproduce extract from *Inheritance* by Hannie Rayson; Currency Press for permission to reproduce extract from *Aliwa!* by Dallas Winmar; extracts from *AQA GCSE Drama* by Price, Morton and Thomson. Reprinted by permission of Harcourt Education Ltd; extracts from *The Hairy Ape*, from *The Hairy Ape and all God's Chillun Got Wings*, Nick Hern Books and Royal National Theatre, London, 1993; Legs on the Wall for extracts from *Runners Up*; W. W. Norton and Co for extract from *A Dream Play* by Strindberg, 1975; The Peters Fraser and Dunlop Group Limited on behalf of Roger McGough, for the poem 'The Lake' by Roger McGough from *Words and Beyond*, published by Heinemann Educational Australia, 1987; Tomas Transtronmer for poem 'Solitude'; Katie Wright for her review of the performance of *The Tempest* by William Shakespeare, by Bell Shakespeare Company, Sydney Opera House.

Every effort has been made to trace and acknowledge copyright material. The author and publisher would welcome any information from people who believe they own copyright material in this book.

National Profile Statements and Outcomes for Drama, Levels 5 and 6

Level 5 Outcomes	Chapter				
Creating, Making and Presenting	1	2	3	4	5
Exploring and developing ideas Uses starting points such as observation, experience and research to express ideas and feelings.	✓	✓	✓	✓	
Using skills, techniques and processes Structures drama by organising drama elements and applying appropriate skills, techniques and processes.	✓	✓	✓	✓	
Presenting Plans, selects and modifies presentations for particular occasions, taking into account factors such as purpose, space, materials and equipment.	✓	✓	✓	✓	
Arts Criticism and Aesthetics Uses appropriate language to describe the ways drama is organised to express ideas and feelings.	✓	✓	✓	✓	✓
Past and Present Contexts Shows an understanding of the ways drama is made within particular cultural and historic contexts.	✓	✓	✓	✓	✓

Level 6 Outcomes	Chapter				
Creating, Making and Presenting	6	7	8	9	10
Exploring and developing ideas Explores the drama of different cultures to generate and develop ideas for drama.	✓	✓	✓	✓	✓
Using skills, techniques and processes Uses drama elements, skills, techniques and processes to structure drama appropriate to chosen styles and forms.	✓	✓	✓	✓	✓
Presenting Rehearses, presents and promotes drama in ways appropriate for specific audiences.	✓	✓	✓	✓	✓
Arts Criticism and Aesthetics Identifies, analyses and interprets drama and discusses responses to it.	✓	✓	✓	✓	✓
Past and Present Contexts Shows an understanding of drama from different social and cultural groups, demonstrating an understanding of histories and traditions.	✓	✓	✓	✓	✓

New South Wales Outcomes for Drama and Cross-curriculum Content, Stages 4 and 5

Stage 4 Outcomes	Chapter											
	1	2	3	4	5	6	7	8	9	10	11	12
Making												
4.1.1 Identifies and explores the elements of drama to develop belief and clarity in character, role, situation and action.		✓	✓	✓								
4.1.2 Improvises and playbuilds through group-devised processes.	✓	✓	✓									
4.1.3 Devises and enacts drama using scripted and unscripted material.		✓	✓	✓								
4.1.4 Explores a range of ways to structure dramatic work in collaboration with others.		✓	✓									
Performing												
4.2.1 Uses performance skills to communicate dramatic meaning.	✓	✓	✓									
4.2.2 Experiments with performance spaces and production elements appropriate to purpose and audience.	✓	✓	✓	✓		✓		✓				
4.2.3 Explores and uses aspects of dramatic forms, performance styles, theatrical conventions and technologies to create dramatic meaning.		✓	✓	✓		✓	✓					
Evaluating												
4.3.1 Identifies and describes elements of drama, dramatic forms, performance styles, techniques and conventions in drama.	✓	✓	✓	✓	✓	✓	✓	✓	✓	✓	✓	✓
4.3.2 Recognises the function of drama and theatre in reflecting social and cultural aspects of human experience.	✓	✓	✓	✓	✓	✓	✓	✓	✓	✓	✓	✓
4.3.3 Describes the contribution of individuals and groups in drama using relevant drama terminology.	✓	✓	✓	✓	✓	✓	✓	✓	✓	✓	✓	✓
Stage 5 Outcomes												
Making												
5.1.1 Manipulates the elements of drama to create belief, clarity and tension in character, role, situation and action.		✓	✓			✓		✓	✓	✓	✓	✓
5.1.2 Contributes, selects, develops and structures ideas in improvisation and playbuilding.		✓	✓			✓	✓	✓	✓	✓	✓	
5.1.3 Devises, interprets and enacts drama using scripted and unscripted material or text.			✓			✓	✓	✓	✓	✓	✓	✓
5.1.4 Explores, structures and refines ideas using dramatic forms, performance styles, dramatic techniques, theatrical conventions and technologies.						✓	✓	✓	✓	✓	✓	✓

Stage 5 Outcomes (continued)	Chapter											
	1	2	3	4	5	6	7	8	9	10	11	12
Performing												
5.2.1 Applies acting and performance techniques expressively and collaboratively to communicate dramatic meaning.			✓			✓	✓	✓	✓	✓	✓	
5.2.2 Selects and uses performance spaces, theatre conventions and production elements appropriate to purpose and audience.		✓	✓			✓	✓	✓	✓	✓	✓	✓
5.2.3 Employs a variety of dramatic forms, performance styles, dramatic techniques, theatrical conventions and technologies to create dramatic meaning.						✓	✓	✓	✓	✓	✓	✓
Evaluating												
5.3.1 Responds to, reflects on and evaluates elements of drama, dramatic forms, performance styles, dramatic techniques and theatrical conventions.	✓	✓	✓	✓	✓	✓	✓	✓	✓	✓	✓	✓
5.3.2 Analyses the contemporary and historical contexts of drama.	✓	✓	✓	✓	✓	✓	✓	✓	✓	✓	✓	✓
5.3.3 Analyses and evaluates the contribution of individuals and groups to processes and to drama using relevant drama concepts and terminology.	✓	✓	✓	✓	✓	✓	✓	✓	✓	✓	✓	✓
Cross-curriculum Content												
Information and Communication Technologies (ICT)			✓	✓	✓	✓	✓	✓	✓			✓
Work, Employment and Enterprise	✓	✓	✓	✓	✓	✓		✓	✓	✓	✓	✓
Aboriginal and Indigenous			✓					✓				✓
Civics and Citizenship			✓			✓						✓
Difference and Diversity	✓	✓	✓	✓	✓	✓	✓	✓	✓	✓	✓	✓
Environment	✓	✓	✓			✓				✓	✓	✓
Gender			✓	✓	✓	✓	✓	✓	✓	✓	✓	✓
Key Competencies	✓	✓	✓	✓	✓	✓	✓	✓	✓	✓	✓	✓
Literacy	✓	✓	✓	✓	✓	✓	✓	✓	✓	✓	✓	✓
Multicultural			✓	✓				✓		✓	✓	✓
Numeracy	✓			✓	✓	✓	✓				✓	

Creating and Performing Drama

Chapter 1 — The Performer's Tools: Body and Voice

Chapter 2 — Improvisation: Spontaneous Performance

Chapter 3 — Playbuilding: Devised Performance

Chapter 1

The Performer's Tools: Body and Voice

Why Study Body and Voice?

The two most essential elements of drama and theatre are the performer and the audience. The interaction between the two creates the unique experience that we know as live performance. One cannot exist without the other.

In live performance, the performer is the instrument of expression and uses mental, physical and vocal skills to engage the audience. Dancers spend hours developing flexibility, stamina, strength, balance and control to assist in their creative expression through dance. The performer also must develop mental, physical and vocal skills to help create interesting and powerful drama. In the first four units of this chapter you will explore and develop the skills of body and voice for performance work. In the final unit of this chapter you will utilise these skills in a performance work that you devise.

This chapter is divided into the following units:

1.1 Warm-ups
1.2 Mime: Creating Illusion Through Use of the Body
1.3 Body Language: Expression, Gesture and Interpretation
1.4 Voice in Performance
1.5 Performance Task: *The Lake*

Outcomes

In this chapter you will:

- explore and identify the expressive potential of the body and voice
- select and incorporate mime, movement and voice into performance work
- incorporate your ideas and feelings to shape performance work
- use a variety of starting points to devise performance work
- explain and discuss how the performer's use of movement and vocal dynamics contributes to performance work.

Tyler Coppin in *Steve Martin's WASP with the Zig-Zag Woman and Patter for the Floating Lady*. Courtesy of Company B Belvoir. Photograph by Marco Bok.

1.1 Warm-ups

Read The Purpose of Warm-ups

Warm-ups have several purposes:

- to prevent injury from strained muscles or ligaments
- to help the performer relax; to relieve mental and physical tension
- to help the performer prepare both mentally and physically for performance work
- to maximise the expressive potential of the body by drawing on the energy of the performer.

The following warm-up exercises will help you prepare for class work and performance work. You do not need to practise all these exercises. You may try only one or two and come back to the others at another time. The exercises are divided into two categories:

- **Physical exercises**. These are good for encouraging alertness, building a sense of working as a team, and creating energy.
- **Centring exercises**. These are good for posture, releasing tension, and developing the ability to create and sustain concentration, belief and focus.

Exercise Warm-ups

Physical Exercises

1 Stretch

Stretch different parts of your body by trying the following exercises. For each exercise you must stretch as hard as you can, without straining yourself.

- Stand between two imaginary pillars and try to push them over.
- Reach for a $50 note stuck to the ceiling. Imagine that your feet are glued to the floor.
- Lie on the floor. Imagine you have ropes tied to your wrists and ankles, and you are being stretched in four directions.
- Hug yourself as hard as you can.

2 Roll, Stretch, Jump and Electric Shock

First, the class practises each of the following movements: a roll, a stretch, a jump and an 'electric shock' which involves you pretending your body has been given a blast of electricity. On the signal from the teacher, the class begins to walk through the space, maintaining an equal distance between group members.

The group explores different ways of moving through the space, for example on toes, backwards, sideways and leaping. At any point the teacher may call 'roll', 'stretch', 'jump' or 'electric shock'. The group responds instantly to the request and then returns to moving through the room, maintaining an equal distance between group members. You can play this as an elimination game in which the last person to complete either roll, stretch, jump or electric shock is required to sit down.

3 Everybody Do This!

Each person in the group takes a turn at giving the group a warm-up exercise. For example, a student may run backwards or perform a stretch or star jumps. As they perform their exercise the student calls out 'Everybody do this!', and the remainder of the group copies that person.

4 Move as Though

Find a place in the room to stand on your own. Your teacher will call out the following instructions. You are to respond to the instructions as quickly as you can. Don't interact with others.

- Move as though you are made of jelly.
- Move as though you are made of molten metal.
- Move as though you are made of crystal.
- Move as though you are made of snow.
- Move as though you are made of fire.
- Move as though you are made of sloppy mud.
- Move as though you are made of mist.
- Move as though you are made of brittle twigs.

5 No Walking

In this exercise you have to find ways of moving through the room without walking. Once you have tried ways of moving through the room on your own, find a partner and explore how two people can work together to move through the room without walking. Some ways of moving include crawling, sliding, tiptoeing, running, rolling, leaping, spinning and jumping.

Challenge

In groups of four, five or six, continue to explore moving through the room without walking. Create a way of moving from one side of the room to the other by combining a series of different ways of moving.

Write and Discuss

1. What benefit do you feel the warm-ups have in preparing you for drama work?
2. Write down one or two other exercises that you think would be beneficial in preparing a performer for physical work. Explain why.
3. Make up your own warm-up activity. Your activity can be for an individual, a small group or the whole class. Describe your warm-up in your logbook and justify its purpose and benefits. Be prepared to teach it to your class.

Centring Exercises

Centring involves aligning the posture of the body so that we are standing straight and feel balanced. We all have our own personal way of standing that makes us feel comfortable. It may be putting our weight on one leg or folding our arms across our chest. In performance, because we are pretending to be other people and things, we need to be able find a starting point that prepares us for performing. Centring helps our bodies to obtain a neutral starting point for acting work. It also creates a sense of stability because our weight is balanced over a central point. Once we are centred we are:

- physically prepared for any movement work
- mentally prepared because we are more focused, which allows us to be more engaged with the character and the performance.

1 *Spine Roll*

To achieve a sense of 'centre' it is helpful to use the spine as an indicator of where our centre is located. This exercise helps to prepare the performer by removing tension from the neck and shoulders as well as correcting posture. Unbalanced posture can create unnecessary tension in the body.

The group stands in a circle. Stand with your feet under your hips. Look straight ahead and keep your arms by your side. Count to seven and as you do slowly drop your head forward on to your chest. Feel the weight of your head and allow this weight to 'unroll' your spine as you slowly bend towards the floor. It is very important that you bend your knees when you are halfway down so that you don't strain your lower back. Once you have reached the hanging position, swing your torso gently from side to side to make sure your neck, head and arms are completely relaxed.

Once you have checked how relaxed you are, reverse the process and roll upwards, starting with the tail bone of your spine. Your head should remain hanging until your body is in a standing position. Then let your head drift up over seven counts. Once you come to a standing position, hold this final position before you relax.

Being focused means we are able to concentrate without being distracted.

Stand in a circle as a group. Stand in a way you feel most comfortable. Close your eyes and make mental notes regarding the way you stand. Complete the Spine Roll exercise. When finished, hold the final position. Make mental notes and compare the differences between your own way of standing and the way you stand once you have completed a Spine Roll.

2 Pendulum

Stand with your feet slightly apart and with your arms hanging by your side. Begin a very gentle rocking motion. Rock forward on to your toes and backward on to your heels. It is important that you only rock forward and backward as far as is comfortable without stumbling or falling. Increase the size of the forward and backward rocking motion. Once you reach a comfortable angle, begin to reduce the size of the rocking motion until the movement has almost stopped. It is useful to close your eyes at this point to gain a sense of where your centre of balance is. Once you come to a complete stop, hold the stillness for a moment.

1.2 Mime: Creating Illusion Through Use of the Body

'The ultimate goal of performers' movement training is the integration of mind, body and spirit.'

Jean Sabatine, dance and movement teacher

Read What Is Mime?

Mime is a form of performance that uses body language, gesture and movement to create the illusion of objects, people and locations in an empty space. It is usually performed without the use of voice. A mime artist may train solely in the art form of mime for several years, developing skills that help their ability to create illusion.

Exercise: Mime

The following exercises explore some of the basic skills of effective mime. When practising mime, be aware of maintaining a strong level of focus, energy and control over your movements. This will make your mime work more engaging.

1 Isolation of Body Parts
In preparation for this exercise it is a good idea to undertake some relaxation and stretching exercises. This exercise involves exploring the movement potential of each body part, including your ability to bend, stretch, rotate and tense.

2 Pulling Faces
Facial expression is an important part of communicating in mime. Pull faces and explore the movement potential of your facial muscles. Use your jaw, eyes and eyebrows to create as many expressions as you can. Work with a partner and stand opposite them. Take turns in mirroring each other's facial expressions.

3 Eye–Hand Coordination
One of the keys to creating the illusion of smaller objects in mime is the use of eye–hand coordination. We tend to look at an object before we pick it up.

Imagine you have a hand-sized object in front of you. Make sure you look at the object first and see it clearly in your mind. Sometimes thinking of an object from your home helps to make the object seem clearer. Pick up and use the object, imagining its weight, shape and texture. Make sure your hands accurately represent the shape of the object. Imaginary objects you might explore are a matchbox, a yo-yo or a calculator.

4 Showing Weight and Quality
Imagine you have three boxes in front of you. One is neatly packed and filled with clothes; one is badly packed and filled with crystal; and one is falling apart and filled with books. Pick up each box and put it back down again. Make sure you clearly communicate the relative weight and quality of each box.

5 Showing Length
Work with a partner. Imagine you are both picking up a lengthy object, such as oars from a rowing shed, or a ladder. With your partner, carry the object around the room. You will need to pay close attention to maintaining the distance between you and your partner to achieve the illusion of a set length.

6 Maintaining the Illusion
It is important to remember that whenever you establish an object or item of furniture in mime that the audience will not forget the position of the object and how it is used. Make mental notes of marks on the walls and floor, for example, to help you remember the correct position of mimed doors, windows and items of furniture.

Establish the positions of the following. Everyone should take a turn using the mimed window and curtains to see if the positions of the objects and how they are used is maintained.

- Mime opening a door that slides to the left, then walk through it and close it behind you.
- Open a set of curtains, then open the window behind the curtains. Leave the position of the curtains and the window for the next person to adjust. The skill required here is to closely observe the position of the curtains and the window so that when you enter the scene you maintain the illusion.

7 Mime Role-Plays

Work with a partner and mime the following exercises. Consider how you can manipulate the elements of movement in your mimed role-plays to help achieve effect.

- **Two house painters.** One is on the roof and one is on the ground. A pulley system carries up heavy cans of paint and lowers empty cans of paint.
- **Two landscape gardeners.** You each have a wheelbarrow that you fill with bricks and then push from one end of the garden to the other. The path you use winds and twists.
- **Two kite flyers.** It is a very windy day. The kites threaten to be blown away by the wind and eventually get tangled in the air.
- **Two vets.** You are holding down an angry cat and trying to administer an injection.

Vocal sound effects can be an entertaining addition to your mime performance.

Present Mime Role-Play

In groups of three, devise your own mime situation to show to the class. Decide on characters, location and a simple story-line. Make sure you include a range of objects that explore your ability to use space, to show size, weight and length, and to maintain the illusion.

Write and Discuss

1. Outline the steps that you and your partner took to prepare the mime role-play.
2. Evaluate one group's presentation, discussing how they made their story clear through the use of mime.
3. Evaluate how well one performer used mime to portray the various qualities of an object, such as its size, weight and moving parts. In your discussion, include examples of how they used movement and facial expression to add to and enhance effective communication in mime.
4. Evaluate your own performance. Discuss your ability to mime weight and size and to maintain illusion.
5. Comment on how others in your group assisted you in maintaining illusion.

Refer to Appendixes 1, 3 and 4 for help with your logbook entries. The appendixes provide you with guidelines for evaluating your own performance work and the work of others.

1.3 Body Language: Expression, Gesture and Interpretation

Read — What Is Body Language?

Human communication involves the whole body, not just words. Experts believe that verbal communication accounts for only 25 per cent of communication between humans. The message we give through physical poses, gestures and facial expressions is called 'body language'. A performer's body language not only gives us information about their character's personality, it also provides us with information about their character's relationships with other characters.

A gesture is a significant movement of part of the body, such as a limb, that is intended to gain a response from one or more people. Some gestures have a universal meaning; others have a meaning that is specific to a culture. A single gesture may or may not mean anything: it is the general sequence of signals and the situation in which they occur that is informative.

Practitioner Profile

Gideon Obozarnec
Artistic Director and Choreographer of Chunky Move

Gideon Obozarnec studied at the Australian Ballet School, and after graduating in 1987 he danced with the Queensland Ballet and the Sydney Dance Company. Gideon has choreographed for all the leading Australian dance companies, as well as choreographing five works for Nederland Dans Theatre.

Whether it's straight acting, caricature, clowning or dancing, it is always the language of the body where the audience looks for truth and integrity. Conviction in your performance lies in the understanding and mastering of your body.

Dance with a kind of physical theatre interests me because although its impact on an audience is much more subtle than words its stories and fiction penetrate past the rational into the more personal and emotional recesses of people's imaginations. It is in this [intersection] where the viewer forms a bond with the performer. Without this, there is no reason to go beyond written text. You could just give it to them in writing.

Exercise Body Language

1 Body Signals
Find frozen poses and gestures to communicate the following emotions:
- boredom
- victory
- nervousness
- confusion.

2 Body Messages
Use movements that finish in a frozen position to indicate the meaning of each of the following statements:
- 'Come here quickly.'
- 'I don't know.'
- 'Get away from me.'
- 'Sit next to me.'
- 'Something isn't right.'
- 'I think I'm lost.'
- 'I'm not quite sure, but I think I smell gas.'

Write and Discuss

1. Using your own words, write a definition of 'body language'.
2. Draw or describe what your body language may be if you were feeling embarrassed.
3. Draw or describe what your body and face may do if you were feeling defensive.
4. When you want to impress someone, what body language do you use?
5. Undertake research using your library, the Internet and your family and friends to see if you can find one example of how our body language is interpreted differently in other cultures.

3 Snapshots

Take a frozen position to communicate the following characters in the following situations:

- A young child looks enviously at another child's toy.
- A scientist makes an amazing breakthrough in the laboratory.
- An Olympic athlete at the end of a sprint realises he or she has just missed out on first place.
- A scuba diver sees a shark in the distance.
- A shop assistant is caught stealing money by the manager.
- A teenager gets on a fast and furious ride at the amusement park.
- The same teenager gets off the ride at the amusement park.
- An elderly person finds their new seedlings have been trampled.
- A teenager pretends to like a disappointing birthday present.

4 Tableaux

In groups of four, devise three of your own tableaux. Each pose should show four characters in a particular situation. Show your tableaux to the class and see if they can interpret the characters and situations you are trying to communicate.

A tableau is like a picture or photograph of a group of people; it is arranged in a way that is visually appealing and communicates information about the characters and the story. The plural of the word 'tableau' is 'tableaux'.

5 Crowd Response

A line of four or five chairs is placed in front of the class. The chairs will represent a row of seats at a specific public venue. Four or five volunteers are chosen from the class and sit in the seats. Your teacher provides the volunteers with a location and a running commentary. For example, your teacher may place you in a cinema watching a tragic love story. As your teacher describes the different stages of the film (such as the lovers meeting, then the lovers fighting) your facial reactions and body language change according to the information that is given.

Some possible situations you could try are a football match, a stadium concert, a bizarre theatre performance and a lecture.

Hint

Augusto Boal is a South American theatre practitioner. He developed the Theatre of the Oppressed, which is a form of theatre that involves the audience in the performance and allows them to find solutions to problems. Boal's book, *Games for Actors and Non-Actors*, contains an excellent range of physical exercises.

6 Great Game of Power

Augusto Boal (see margin) developed an exercise that explores how power and status can be exercised through body language, and the use of space and levels. This exercise also explores how performers and their use of levels and space can be visually striking.

- Place six chairs, one table and a bottle in the centre of the room. Individuals volunteer to arrange the furniture to make the bottle the most powerful object in the tableau.
- In the next step of the Great Game of Power you need to include six volunteers in the tableau. A seventh volunteer arranges the chairs, table, bottle and participants to make one volunteer appear more powerful than the others. This step can be repeated several times by choosing different volunteers to create new arrangements.

Write and Discuss

1. Discuss the ways in which tableaux can be a simple but effective tool for performance work.
2. Describe how the performers used effective body language to communicate power or lack of power.
3. Which tableaux most clearly showed an object or person as the most powerful? Why?
4. Which tableaux appealed to you? Describe why you found them appealing. In your response discuss the use of levels and space; the relationships between characters; and the facial expressions and posture of the performers.

Robert Doisneau, *Paris by Night*

Present: Interpreting Body Language

Use the photo on page 12, or a group photo of your own, to prepare a short, mimed role-play in groups. Your performance will show the characters in the moments before the photo was taken. In your preparations, explore the body language of the different characters and the way the characters relate to one another. Your role-play must start with a tableau that you devise. It must finish with a tableau showing the positions of the characters in the photo.

Write and Discuss

1. Pick three characters from the photo provided or from your own photo. Interpret the predominant emotion or reaction of each character. Explain how each character's body language and facial expression helped you with your interpretation.
2. Describe how you used body language, levels and space to convey your character's relationship to other characters.
3. Describe any discoveries you made about the character you played while you explored their way of walking and using gestures.
4. Choose one group's tableau. Give your interpretation of two characters and describe their personality types. Base your interpretation on the body language of the characters in the tableau.
5. Choose the group which performed the most visually appealing tableau. Discuss how this group used levels and space to make their tableau appealing.

The Performer's Tools: Body and Voice

1.4 Voice in Performance

'Make what you say remarkable to the hearer.'

**Cicely Berry, Head of Voice,
National Theatre, London**

Practitioner Profile

Jennifer West

Voice Coach, Western Australian Academy of Performing Arts

With film and television offering more regular work than theatre, many actors forget voice warm-ups, and when they return to the stage they find they have lost vocal power and flexibility. It is vital that you warm up your voice every day (twenty minutes is fine). It is especially important to do voice warm-ups before you work with text.

There are three initial areas to approach:

1. *Release tension in the shoulders, jaw, neck and upper chest. This allows the voice to drop into its natural position and opens chest resonance.*
2. *Expand the ribcage and do deep abdominal breathing to support sound.*
3. *Drop the back of the tongue and lift the soft palate to open the back of the throat. This frees sound and reduces nasality.*

Read Training the Voice

You have just completed exercises that focus on the expressive potential of the performer's body. You will now explore the expressive potential of the voice. Although some of the following exercises will focus purely on warming up the voice and exploring its expressive ability, most will include a combination of the use of movement and vocal dynamics.

There are four areas of vocal dynamics that a performer needs to consider and develop. You can be assessed on these in performance so it is wise to ensure you understand what each involves.

You will explore the area of delivery in Unit 4.3, p. 70, in the Building Your Character exercise.

The exercises below will explore each of these areas:

Articulation. This involves using the mouth, tongue and lips to create and shape sounds. A performer with good articulation speaks clearly and is easily understood.

Projection. This involves projecting the voice, without straining, so that you can be heard easily from a distance.

Delivery. This involves making your voice varied and expressive.

Breathing. This involves the ability to inhale deeply and control exhalation.

Exercise: Breathing

1 Finding the Diaphragm Muscle

Lie on your back on the floor. Place your hands on your stomach and consciously breathe in to the lowest part of your lungs. Exhale. Breath in again, then exhale. See if you can feel your diaphragm muscle working to bring in air and to control the release of air.

If you feel dizzy or lightheaded rest for a moment because you have probably absorbed too much oxygen too quickly.

2 Controlling the Release of Breath

Stare at a spot on the ceiling. Take in a deep breath, then blow a steady stream of air towards that spot. Take another breath. Slowly release air towards the same spot, but see if you can control the release of air over ten counts. By gently pulling in your stomach muscles you will be able to control how quickly your diaphragm relaxes. This allows you to control the release of air.

Practise this every day and see if you can control the release of air over twenty counts or more.

3 Increasing Lung Capacity

Stand with your arms in front of you, palms together. Take in a deep breath. Concentrate on drawing air to the very bottom of your lungs. As you inhale, raise both arms out to either side until they are up above your head. Let your arms cross each other and continue down to either side. Exhale as you do this.

When your arms are above your head, hold them there for a second and take in a little more air in a couple of breaths. Hold the air for a second and then release the air quickly while lowering your arms to your sides.

Read: Projecting Not Shouting

Developing the ability to project your voice means developing your ability to be heard *without* having to shout. The voice needs a lot of air to create a full sound and to carry a sound for a period of time, so your ability to breathe deeply is very important. This is especially valuable if you need to deliver long sentences and don't want to run out of breath. It is important to remember that projecting the voice involves a combination of:

- thoughts that help you 'send' your voice to the point you wish it to go
- physical exercises that help develop your ability to project
- the use of resonators to help give the voice volume (see the hint on page 16).

Exercise Projection

Exercises 1 and 2 prepare the voice for projection. Exercises 3, 4 and 5 explore the ability of the voice to project.

1 Bear's Yawn and Stretch

Imagine you are a huge Russian bear waking from a deep hibernation. Have a yawn and stretch. Yawn and stretch again, but this time exaggerate the stretching and yawning sound.

2 Sighing

- Imagine you are feeling unhappy. Breathe in, then sigh without using the voice to create a sigh sound. Repeat the sigh, but this time add a little voice to the sigh sound.
- Imagine you have just seen a baby perform a 'cute' trick. Repeat the sigh and add full voice to the sigh sound.
- Imagine you are a wildlife officer demonstrating calls of nocturnal animals. Repeat the full-voiced sigh and make the sigh sound slide up and down in pitch.

3 Projecting to a Point

Lie on your back and find a spot on the ceiling on which to focus. Breathe in, then sigh. Repeat this, adding more sound to each sigh. Imagine the sound you will create is like a torch beam that you will shine on a specific point on the ceiling. Turn the sigh sound into an 'aaah' sound. Always aim your voice at the same spot. With each 'aaah' sound, slide up and down the scale.

4 Pillar of Sound

Stand in a circle. As a class, complete the Spine Roll exercise (see p. 5) to help align posture and release tension. When you come to a standing position, all class members should focus their attention on an imaginary, clear cylinder that is in the centre of the circle and reaches from the floor to the ceiling. All class members will direct any sound towards the cylinder.

- The class begins by taking three slow, deep breaths.
- The class takes another breath, and then sighs.
- The class takes a breath, and then begins to hum.
- The class should 'scatter breathe', meaning that the constant sound is maintained by each person taking a breath and continuing to hum in their own time.
- Concentrate on making the sound resonate on your lips and cheekbones.
- The class finds its own pitch.
- On the given signal from your teacher, all class members drop their jaws open to send an 'aaah' sound to the imaginary cylinder. Imagine that the energy of your voice is rushing up the cylinder to the ceiling. Maintain the sound for a period of three minutes; then let the class find its own finishing point.

Hint

A resonator is a hollow cavity in the body that helps amplify sound. For example, the nasal cavities and mouth act as resonators. To understand how a resonator works, imagine going into a big, empty hall and talking. Often you will hear your voice echo. Hard surfaces bounce sound waves back to the listener. Our resonators use hard surfaces in the body to amplify sound. If we warm up physically, relax and breathe before voice work we help open the resonators and encourage better sound quality.

Challenge

Explore different vowel sounds. Time how long you can project the vowel sound before you run out of breath.

Hint

Shouting is NOT projecting. If your throat tickles or is sore during these exercises, you are straining your throat. Stop and check that you are relaxed.

Challenge

The class repeats the Pillar of Sound exercise but experiments with different pitches to create harmonies. In this exercise, closing your eyes helps you to focus on pitch.

5 Gunshots

Stand and place your hand on your stomach to detect the movement of the diaphragm muscle as it helps to create this sound. Find a fixed point in the room to which you will 'send' your voice. Practise saying the following sounds but use the 'jumping' action of your diaphragm muscle to help push the sound to a fixed point in the room. The sounds are 'hey', 'ho', 'ha' and 'hee'. Using the 'h' sound also helps to work the diaphragm muscle. Imagine that each sound is like a bullet heading to a particular point in the room.

On a given signal, turn to a new spot in the room and deliver a different gunshot sound. Repeat this until you have completed a 360 degree turn. Stand in a circle and send gunshots around the circle as quickly as you can. Everyone MUST send the gunshot to the centre of the circle.

Read: Articulation, Vocal Dynamics and the Shaping of Sound

Articulation exercises help work the muscles of the mouth, tongue and throat. If these muscles are not strengthened, our ability to articulate is hampered because the voice becomes muffled and unclear. Vocal dynamics can also be manipulated by considering the following:

- **Pace.** How fast or slow sound is.
- **Rhythm.** The pattern in which sounds, or qualities of sounds, are repeated.
- **Pitch.** How high or low sound is.
- **Volume.** How loud or soft sound is.
- **Pauses.** Breaks or silences between sounds.
- **Emphasis.** The stress placed on certain words or syllables.
- **Tone.** The emotion or attitude behind the meaning of words.

Exercise: Articulation, Vocal Dynamics and the Shaping of Sound

1 Mirror Facial

Stand opposite a partner and mirror the following:

- Open your mouth as wide as you can.
- Close your mouth as small as you can.
- Stretch your tongue to your nose, to either side of your mouth and to your chin. See if you can make your tongue touch all four points in a circular motion.
- Stick out your tongue.
- Curl your tongue into a sausage shape.

2 Vowels and Consonants

- Vowel sounds are created by altering the shape of the mouth. Roll through the vowel sounds in this sequence: 'a', 'e', 'i', 'o' and 'u'. Try each vowel sound and alternate between a short sound and a long sound, for example 'ah' (short) and 'aaaah' (long).
- Sounds that are created by the lips and by using a push of air are called 'plosives'. Sounds that use the back of the throat are called 'gutturals'. Explore the sounds 'puh', 'buh', 'tuh', 'duh',

'kuh' and 'guh'. Consider how your lips, tongue and teeth are used to create these sounds.

3 Sound and Action

As a class, create the following sounds simultaneously. Your teacher will give you the signal to make each sound.

- an explosion
- a motorbike racing
- a clock ticking and then chiming twelve
- a modem connecting to a server
- a circular saw cutting through wood
- a respirator or a heart monitor in a hospital.

4 Soundscapes

As a class, create a soundscape of a particular environment. Each member of the class finds somewhere to sit or lie in the space. He or she then contributes sounds to create a particular location or environment. It is helpful to close your eyes for this exercise and listen to the sounds of others. Start with only a few sounds; the group leader may choose individuals one at a time. Other individuals are added as the soundscape takes shape. Some examples of soundscapes are a rainforest, ocean depths, a busy street corner, a farmyard, a building site and an orchestra tuning before a recital.

Write and Discuss

1. Describe your experiences in trying each of the voice exercises. Identify the exercises you found most challenging. Give reasons for your answer.
2. Make four suggestions for how you could improve your use of voice in performance.
3. List and explain the seven aspects of vocal dynamics.
4. Think of two possible soundscapes you could create: for example, a busy restaurant or the zoo at feeding time. Explain how you could manipulate vocal dynamics to create your soundscape.

Present Living Objects

In this task you will incorporate movement and sound to heighten the abstract qualities of objects. An abstract quality is something we cannot feel, see or touch, for example impatience or laziness. By heightening the abstract qualities of objects, we are able to make an object more distinctive and interesting in performance. For example, a group of three people may be a couch and use their bodies to look slumped and heavy. They may move from side to side in a slow rhythm and pause occasionally. The group could also use their voices to make groaning sounds and sighs. They may also create the occasional 'ping' sound to

Object	Defining quality	Use of movement	Use of sound
Clock tower	Eerie	Swaying, regular, rhythmic movements to indicate the hands of the clock; be mechanical figures.	Whispering; ticking; wind blowing; slow and heavy clock chime.
Autoteller	Faulty	Stiff, mechanical movements, some out of time and erratic.	Sound words such as 'buzz', 'whirr', 'click', 'boing', 'plink' and 'klunk'.

indicate a broken spring. Through the use of physical and vocal dynamics we gain a clear picture of a couch, and through the communication of its abstract qualities we know it is old and worn.

Complete a table in your logbooks listing a range of landmarks and objects, such as machines. Indicate the main quality of each, for example 'old', 'new', 'fast', 'slick', 'damaged', 'sharp' or 'bright'. Also indicate how you could use movement and sound to help portray the object and its quality. The table above gives a couple of examples to help you get started.

Form groups of six and share your lists of objects. Choose one object from the list of each person in your group to present to the class. Although you will have some idea of what to do in terms of sound and movement you will discover more as you rehearse your presentation. Consider how you can manipulate movement and vocal dynamics to heighten your representation of the defining qualities of your chosen objects.

Write and Discuss

1. Pick two objects presented by two different groups. List the strengths of these presentations. Consider how movement was used to clearly represent the object, the interaction of group members, the use of levels and space, and the use of sound. Make any suggestions for improvement. Be specific with your advice. For example:

   The group that performed the eerie clock tower worked well together. They used people as gargoyles; and they used people and levels to create the height of the tower. They made the hands of the clock look bent and broken. Some group members needed to stretch their arms up more fully to give the impression of the height of the tower. I think they needed to make the sound of wind blowing more intense because it was too soft and it seemed gentle rather than frightening.

2. Discuss your findings above with the class.

1.5 Performance Task: The Lake

Read The Task

In this task a poem is used as the basis for performance. *The Lake* by Roger McGough comments on how humans can endanger the environment through neglect. The poet uses a powerful and sometimes comic image of dangerous and hungry underwater pigs. The pigs symbolise greed, pollution and the environmental consequences of carelessness by humans. At the end of the poem, the pigs, who feed on the waste left by humans, threaten to consume humans.

You are to devise a performance that explores the consequences of human neglect on the environment. You may choose to incorporate the whole poem or part of the poem in your performance; alternatively you may use the poem as a starting point for your own ideas.

Some ideas for your performance include:

- performing the poem
- writing and performing your own poem that explores environmental issues
- devising a performance piece that shows incidents that lead up to the polluting of the lake
- devising a performance piece that is titled *The Lake: Part 2*
- basing your performance on another resource that comments on the same issue, such as a newspaper article, a song or a picture.

Each performance will need to include the following:

- the use of vocal dynamics to create atmospheric sound and sound effects, including consideration of rhythm and repetition
- exaggerated and stylised movement, including consideration of rhythm, repetition and control
- examples of mime
- examples of people being objects that have distinct qualities
- two tableaux, one at the beginning and one at the end of your performance.

Prepare Preparing to Perform

Read *The Lake*. After you have read the poem, complete the exercises, and the Write and Discuss section; then read the evaluation sheet. Remember to draw on your understanding of body and voice from the exercises you have completed in this chapter. This understanding will help you to make effective decisions in the creating and making of your performance work.

The Lake

For years there have been no fish in the lake.
People hurrying through the park avoid it
like the plague. Birds steer clear
and the sedge of course has withered.
Trees lean away from it,
and at night it reflects, not the moon,
but the blackness of its own depths.
There are no fish in the lake.
But there is life there. There is life…

Underwater pigs glide between reefs of coral debris.
They love it here. They breed and multiply
in sties hollowed out of the mud
and lined with mattresses and bedsprings.
They live on dead fish and rotting things,
drowned pets, plastic and assorted excreta.
Rusty cans they like the best.
Holding them in webbed trotters
their teeth tear easily through the tin,
and poking in a snout, they noisily suck out
the putrid matter within.

There are no fish in the lake.
But there is life there. There is life…

For on certain evenings after dark
shoals of pigs surface
and look out at the houses near the park.
Where, in bathrooms,
children feed stale bread to plastic ducks,
and in attics,
toy yachts have long since run aground.

Where, in living rooms,
anglers dangle their lines on patterned carpets,
and bemoan the fate of the ones that got away.

Down on the lake, piggy eyes glisten.
They have acquired a taste for flesh.
They are licking their lips. Listen…

            Roger McGough

Sedge: waterside plants that resemble dry grass.

Debris: rubble, ruins or wreckage.

Sties: holding pens for pigs.

Excreta: excreted matter, such as sweat and urine.

Putrid: revolting, smelly or rotting.

Shoal: a great number of fish swimming together.

Anglers: people who fish.
Bemoan: mourn.

Exercise: Creating Images

Use the following exercises to explore the ways of representing the different images, characters and objects described in *The Lake*.

- In small groups, use your bodies to create a pile of objects that have been discarded by humans. Use vocal sound and movement to portray the quality of the object you represent.
- Move about the room as the underwater pigs. Explore how they may move. Express their eating rituals through the use of mime. Add vocal sounds to communicate the character of the pigs.
- In groups of ten, create the lake that 'reflects, not the moon, but the blackness of its own depths'. Use movement and vocal sound.

Write and Discuss

1. What is the mood, or feeling, conveyed by the poem? What images help to communicate the mood of the poem?
2. List the objects in the poem. Describe how you would create these objects and their qualities. In your description, include choices regarding use of vocal sound, movement and tableaux.

Evaluate: Performance Checklist

You and your teacher will evaluate your work individually using a list of criteria. These criteria relate to your achievement in this task. Some criteria will relate to the achievement of the group. The criteria are listed on the evaluation sheet at the end of this chapter and will be used to evaluate your ability to:

- incorporate movement and mime to effectively communicate character and/or object
- incorporate rhythm and repetition in voice and/or movement for effect
- integrate movement and vocal sound to portray objects and their qualities
- create effective tableaux, including powerful use of space and levels
- work effectively as part of an ensemble
- select, modify and link aspects of your drama into a coherent and polished performance.

Hint: Refer to Appendix 2 for some guidance on the rehearsal process.

Write and Discuss

Arts Criticism and Aesthetics

1. Refer to the criteria on the evaluation sheet (p. 24). Use these to evaluate one other group presentation. Be detailed in your analysis, using examples to support your evaluation.
2. Evaluate your own performance within your group. Offer suggestions for how you could make your performance even more successful.

Past and Present Contexts

3. Draw on your experiences of preparing and performing *The Lake* to discuss the importance of mime, movement, body language and vocal dynamics in performance. Include in your answer an explanation of how your choices in these areas helped to effectively communicate the issues presented in the poem.
4. Imagine your are teaching a drama class. Explain to the class why the study of movement and vocal dynamics is important.

Refer to Appendixes 1, 3 and 4 for help with your logbook entries. The appendixes provide you with guidelines for evaluating your own performance work and the work of others.

Evaluation Sheet
Chapter 1 The Performer's Tools: Body and Voice

Performance Task: *The Lake*

Student: _____ Teacher: _____

Related Outcomes

By completing this task you should be able to:
- select and incorporate mime, movement and voice into performance work
- incorporate your ideas and feelings to shape performance work
- use a variety of starting points for performance work
- explain and discuss how the performer's use of movement and vocal dynamics contributes to performance work.

Criteria	Level of Achievement			
	Beginning	Consolidating	Mastering	Excelling
Exploring and Developing Ideas Have you prepared for your performance by: • incorporating in your performance your ideas on the issue of 'the environment'? • including resources from your own research? • recording all planning, rehearsals and decisions in writing? • completing Write and Discuss questions as required?				
Using Skills, Techniques and Processes Have you selected and included the skills of voice and movement by: • effectively communicating character and/or object through the use of movement and mime? • incorporating voice to suit character and to create mood? • effectively incorporating rhythm and repetition in voice and/or movement? • portraying objects and their qualities?				
Presenting Have you planned, selected and modified your presentation by: • considering the available space and how it can be used to suit your purpose? • structuring and linking aspects of the drama into a coherent and polished performance?				

Comments: _____

_____

_____

_____

_____

Chapter 2

Improvisation: Spontaneous Performance

Why Study Improvisation?

Improvisation is both an entertaining form of performance, and a valuable tool for exploring and developing drama work. Improvisation requires a performer to think quickly and to be inventive and imaginative. It is also an important element in the process of playbuilding because it allows the performer to explore character and ideas through action. The improvisation activities in this chapter are excellent preparation for the playbuilding tasks in Chapter 3 (pages 61–8).

This chapter is divided into the following units:

2.1 An Overview of Improvisation

2.2 The Skills of Improvisation

2.3 Character Types and Status in Improvisation

2.4 The Elements of Drama

2.5 Improvisation Exercises

2.6 Performance Task: Improvisation

Outcomes

In this chapter you will:
- explore and utilise the skills of improvisation
- identify the elements of drama and incorporate them in improvisations
- create and sustain character types in improvisations
- contribute and incorporate your own ideas to create improvised performance work.

2.1 An Overview of Improvisation

> 'Switch off the no-saying intellect and welcome the unconscious as a friend: it will lead you to places you never dreamed of, and produce results more "original" than anything you could achieve by aiming at originality.'
>
> Irving Wardle, theatre writer

Improvisation has been used as a training tool in health, employment and education to help participants gain a greater understanding of people and the way they behave.

Read Improvisation in Performance

Becoming a successful improvisation performer requires the development of skills to create powerful, entertaining and interesting improvisations. Regular practice and evaluation will also encourage:

- the ability to be creative and imaginative spontaneously
- the ability to work cooperatively with other performers
- an understanding of the elements of dramatic situation.

Improvisation has been an aspect of many forms of Western and non-Western performance for centuries. During the mid 1960s, improvisation became a very popular tool for training performers and creating performance work. This loose, informal style of theatre reflected the changes in society's attitudes and values at the time. The Pram Factory in Melbourne and the Nimrod Theatre in Sydney produced plays that reflected the influence of these changes in society and the arts. Writers, performers and directors began to experiment with new forms of theatre. Famous Australian playwrights, such as Jack Hibberd and David Williamson, refined plays that had been developed in workshop improvisations.

When engaged in improvisation, the performer is very 'audience aware'. Although the performer is focused on being a character in a situation, he or she is constantly aware of audience reactions; these help the performer make the best decisions for the outcome of the performance. An Italian form of comic, improvised performance, known as commedia dell'arte, relies on stock character types and improvisation to develop comic moments. Commedia dell'arte performers encourage audience reaction by directly playing to the audience.

2.2 The Skills of Improvisation

Practitioner Profile

Lyn Pierse

Author of Theatresports® Down Under

Lyn Pierse graduated from the National Institute of Dramatic Art (NIDA) in 1983. She is a veteran Theatresports® champion, and as a National Coach pioneered its teaching in Australia, New Zealand and Japan. She has appeared on radio and in theatre, film and television, including as Sister Mary Leonard on ABC TV's 'Big Gig'. Lyn teaches improvisation at NIDA and stand-up comedy at the Actors' Centre. She is a guest teacher at schools, universities and teacher training institutions throughout Australia. Her book, *Theatresports® Down Under*, is in its second edition.

The Skills of Improvisation

You can develop a number of skills to improve your effectiveness as an improvisation performer. Although each skill is looked at separately, it is important to remember that in performance all skills are drawn on simultaneously.

As you practise the exercises for each skill, be prepared for your teacher to 'side coach' you. Your teacher may encourage you to accept an offer, or to extend or advance a situation. Try to incorporate your teacher's advice without dropping character or stopping the action. You may find your teacher offers a lot of side coaching when you first try these exercises. As you gain confidence with each skill, your teacher will reduce the amount of side coaching.

Read ### Skill 1: Spontaneity

Spontaneity is the ability to 'act on the spot', without hesitation. It requires the performer to provide ideas during performance that help the drama to move forward. The ability to be spontaneous in performance, to act without hesitation, helps maintain the pace and tension of the improvisation.

Lyn Pierse's book, *Theatresports® Down Under*, is recommended as an excellent reference for improvisation work.

Keith Johnstone, author of the well-known book *Impro: Improvisation and the Theatre*, believes that when we improvise our fears of being rejected or failing make us 'edit' many of our good ideas. This makes us hesitate, therefore interrupting the flow of the performance. He suggests that you 'do' before you think. This is being spontaneous; it will give the most honest and often the most appropriate response.

Exercise Spontaneity

Challenge

Stand and physically represent the words as you say them by creating a shape with your body. Try increasing the number of people working together. Each person in the group takes a turn calling out a word, and the entire group creates a statue or tableau to represent the word called.

1 Word Association

In pairs, sit opposite each other. In turn, each person says a word in quick succession. The aim is to keep going for as long as possible without laughing or hesitating.

2 *Instant* Romeo and Juliet

In this exercise a well-known Shakespearean play has been chosen as the basis for some improvised situations. The use of known characters from a known story helps you 'do' without thinking and hesitating. You will act as specific characters from the play in particular situations. Sometimes you will be asked to be an object. You may be required to use voice and sound. Try not to discuss what you do, and aim to complete the task as quickly as possible. Your teacher will give you a time limit of five or ten seconds to complete each activity.

- In pairs, become a chef and assistant chef preparing the food for the Capulet ball. Discuss the menu.
- In groups of eight, create a tableau that shows the opposing families in Verona: the Capulets and Montagues. Two people must represent Juliet (a Capulet) and Romeo (a Montague) showing their opposition to the feud.
- In groups of three, become Mr Montague and two palace cleaners. It is the morning after the ball, and Mr Montague is coping with the mess. The cleaners gossip about Romeo and Juliet.
- In pairs, become Juliet and the nurse. The nurse is reminiscing and giving Juliet advice on love.
- In groups of six, become the balcony on which Juliet stood when talking with Romeo.
- In pairs, become Romeo and Juliet in the balcony scene. Romeo is on the balcony and Juliet has a new and different speech to deliver to Romeo.
- In groups of four, come up with five titles of 'advice' books for Romeo and Juliet.
- Become the friar in his chambers, making his medicines. He tries some medicines on himself, with incredible results.
- In groups of ten, create the interior of the Capulet family tomb. Use sound to heighten the atmosphere.

Hint

Reminiscing is fondly remembering the past.

Write and Discuss

1. Which situations worked best for you? Why?
2. Which situations did not work well for you? Why?
3. Did you find it difficult to be spontaneous? Can you remember the sorts of thoughts you had when you hesitated? Can you think of ways to counter the hesitant thoughts?
4. Did you tend to initiate in an improvisation or did you wait for others to contribute first? Why?
5. Is it more important to lead or to follow? Why?

Read — Skill 2: Making Offers

Making offers is the ability of the actor to be imaginative, make positive and active contributions to the development of the plot, and establish characters, location and time. An offer may be verbal or physical. An example of a verbal offer is to say, 'Quickly, I think they're on the window ledge!' A physical offer may be a performer using mime to signal to another performer to follow them and walk quietly. Alternatively, a physical offer could be to become an inanimate object that another performer can use.

Hint

A good improvisation actor is always looking for opportunities to make offers that will benefit the overall improvisation.

Exercise — Making Offers

1 Physical Offers

In pairs, improvise short scenes in which one partner makes a physical offer without dialogue. The other person accepts the offer, using speech if they choose, and the scene is quickly brought to a resolution. For example, the first person may make a physical offer by raising both arms above their head. Their partner accepts the offer by saying, 'Stick 'em up!' Then the second person makes a new physical offer to start a new situation.

2 World Adventure

In pairs, pretend you are exploring the globe. Take it in turns to make suggestions about the next step in your adventure. You can make verbal or physical offers. For example:

A Let's go to the Taj Mahal in India by submarine!

The pair improvises getting to and being at the Taj Mahal. B then mimes hopping on a dog sled.

A Some healthy looking huskies you've got there.

B I only train the best. Let's get to the glacier before sunset!

The action then moves to the new location.

Hint

Improvising can be intimidating, especially when you don't know what is going to happen next. Be open to new possibilities and opportunities; take risks. Resist the desire to control what is happening; trust your fellow performers.

Challenge

Try this Word by Word exercise with four people. The four people divide into pairs to create two characters. Put these characters in a situation: for example, they could act out a job interview or perhaps a shop assistant serving a customer. The challenge in this exercise is for the four performers to yield to each other to create conversation that flows smoothly between the two characters.

Read

Skill 3: Yielding

'Yielding' is the ability of the performer to 'give way' to another performer's offer without blocking. In a sense it is like saying 'yes' to your fellow performers.

Exercise

Yielding

1 Word by Word

Work with a partner. You are going to work together to create one character. You will do this by taking turns to say words that when joined together create sentences. Stand shoulder to shoulder and put your inside arm around your partner's waist. You are only allowed to speak one word at a time. For example, the two of you could say, 'The - window - is - dirty - and - needs - cleaning.' You must speak in first person. For example, you should say, 'I - like - that - chair' not 'We - like - that - chair'. Move through the room together, describing objects and furnishings.

2 Postie

This exercise works best when the group watches one pair at a time. Work with a partner. Stand shoulder to shoulder, as you did in the previous exercise. A letter will be delivered by a volunteer from the group. The character opens the door to receive the letter and then reads out the letter's imaginary contents. The letter's contents are created while you and your partner read the letter out loud, one word at a time.

3 Knock-knock, Ring-ring, Yoo-hoo

This is an exercise to be performed in front of the class. A central character is at home. He or she deals with the interruptions of people who knock at the front door or telephone and with neighbours who call over the back fence. One volunteer stands to one side of the performing area as one of the characters who will knock at the door. Another volunteer stands to the other side as one of the characters who will make a phone call. A third volunteer becomes one of the neighbours who calls 'Yoo-hoo' over the fence.

The challenge is for the central character to yield to the offers made by those who knock, ring or call over the back fence. The volunteers can be as many different characters as they like. It is wise to start slowly, but to increase the frequency of interruptions as the person in the centre becomes more confident in yielding to the offers presented. It is also possible for each character to knock, ring or call 'Yoo-hoo' more than once. This helps to build up several plot lines.

> ### Write and Discuss
> 1. Define 'yielding' and explain its purpose in improvisation.
> 2. In what ways did you yield to or cooperate with your partner?
> 3. Did you have difficulty in yielding to your partner? How could you improve in this area? Support your answer with examples.

Read ## Skill 4: Focus

The skill of focus is demonstrated when a performer concentrates their attention on a person, object or event. It is like funnelling the audience's attention to a particular point. Often the point of focus is indicated to the audience through the performer's use of their eyes. A strong use of focus helps to determine what the improvisation is about (see also Chapter 3, page 50).

- The subject of the focus can vary; for example, it may be an object, a person or a group of people.
- The position of the focus can also vary; it may be close to you, slightly distant from you or far away from you.

Exercise ## Focus

1 Focus Using Objects
You will need a collection of assorted props for this exercise. Work with a partner and choose one object. Improvise a situation that uses the object as the point of focus. You can pick up the object and use it in a variety of ways, but it must always remain the point of focus.

2 Changing Focus
Sometimes the focus of a situation will change during the improvisation. A performer in improvisation needs to be able to yield to the change of focus.

- Divide into groups of three. Choose an object.
- One member of the group begins to improvise a situation in which the object is the focus of the situation.
- The second performer joins the situation. The first performer widens their focus to include the second performer. Both performers focus on the object.
- The third performer enters the scene and stands at a distance from the pair.
- The first two performers shift their focus away from the object to the third performer.
- The scene continues with a focus on the third performer and is then brought to a conclusion.

Challenge

Once the focus has included the third performer, reverse the order of focus: going back to two performers and the object, and finishing with one performer and the object.

Write and Discuss

1. Explain how the improvisation games you played today have helped you understand the importance of the skill of focus. Comment on any discoveries you made regarding strong offers and effective use of focus. Give examples from your own improvisation work to support your answers.

Read ## Skill 5: Extending and Advancing the Action

The skill of 'extending' requires the performer to embellish, elaborate and fill out information. The skill of 'advancing' pushes the story along to the next stage. Extending and advancing can be achieved both physically and verbally. For example, in an improvisation, a murderer sharpens a knife. The murderer repeatedly holds up the knife to the light, testing its razor edge. Here the performer is extending the moment by making the knife seem more dangerous and threatening. The victim then advances the narrative by saying, 'I'll tell you everything. Just untie these ropes and take me to the warehouse.' The murderer cannot refuse this offer, and the story moves on to the next stage.

Exercise ## Extending and Advancing

Challenge

Create some of your own situations where you demonstrate the skills of advancing and extending. Present these to the class.

1 Extending and Advancing Actions

Individually, begin to mime a simple action, for example opening a can of pet food. When you hear your teacher call the command 'Extend' you must continue with your activity, but focus on making more of the particular moment. In the example of opening the can of pet food, you could extend the moment by focusing your attention on the action of attaching the can opener to the can. When you hear 'Advance' called out you progress the opening of the can to its next stage, for example turning the handle on the can opener. When you hear 'Extend', the turning of the handle of the can opener becomes more difficult. Repeat both 'Extend' and 'Advance' alternately until the activity is finished.

Challenge

With a partner, follow the Extending and Advancing Stories exercise as described, but this time perform as much of the story as you can by including physical reactions, and by using sound and mime.

2 Extending and Advancing Stories

Divide into pairs and choose to be A or B. A begins by telling an imaginary story. B interrupts the story at points and asks for more information. Once A has extended the story by giving more information, A then proceeds with the story. For example, A may say, 'One day I was walking along the beach and found a chain.' B asks questions to extend the information, such as 'What did it look like?', 'What was it made of?' and 'Did it have any special markings?' A responds by yielding to the question. A then advances the story. For example, A may say, 'As I picked up the chain, someone grabbed my wrist.' B then asks another question to extend the narrative, and so on.

Write and Discuss

1. Write the skills of improvisation down the left-hand side of a blank page. Leave a gap of about ten lines between each skill. Explain how you felt you achieved in each skill. Reflect on the exercises in which you participated.
2. Which skill areas do you feel best demonstrate your strengths in improvisation?
3. Which skill areas do you feel are challenges for you? Offer suggestions for how you could improve in these areas.
4. Explain the importance of each skill in creating a successful improvisation. Give examples from your class work to justify your response. Here is a sample logbook entry to help you:

'I have just realised how important advancing and extending are as improvisation skills. We have practised these skills over two lessons. Extending allows the performer to make the most of the moment. Joe and I were improvising a struggle to get his character's pet dog into the back of a car. The more we struggled the more the audience laughed. When we felt the joke was over, we advanced by deciding to walk the dog to the vet.'

2.3 Character Types and Status in Improvisation

Read Character Types and Status

In certain types of improvisations you may be given information about a character, while at other times you may be asked to create a character on the spot. To make improvisations interesting it is important to stretch the imagination to create a range of character types rather than relying on predictable characters. This approach gives characters greater complexity, or dimension. For example, a mum who is cooking in the kitchen could be changed to a mum who is packing to fly to China to oversee the building of a single-span bridge. A dad sitting in his chair not saying much and reading the paper could be changed to a dad who illustrates children's storybooks and is also practising to be an opera singer.

In improvisation you also need to be aware of the status relationship between your character and other characters. A character's status, or sense of power, often influences the way they behave. For example, a person who feels they are in charge may be more of a leader and may give instructions to other characters. A character of low status may be unsure in a situation and ask for assistance or advice. Audiences especially enjoy watching situations where the status of a character is changed.

Exercise Character Types and Status

1 Character Brainstorm

Name and age	Occupation	Hobbies	Achievements	Status
Karol Kana, thirty-eight years	Stockbroker	Surf-lifesaving	Mother of five happy children	High
Steve Nguyen, twenty years	Demolition expert	Raising Persian cats	Invented the 'safe' explosive	Low

Divide into groups of four. Create six interesting and unusual character types. Use the table above as an example.

- Choose four character types from the lists you created. Stand as a line, shoulder to shoulder, in front of the class.
- Each person must introduce themselves to the class as their character by telling their name, age, occupation, hobbies and achievements.

2 Status Pairs

Divide into pairs and choose one of the following status relationships:

- parent and child
- employer and employee
- teacher and student
- pop star and fan.

With your partner, improvise a situation that explores the expected status relationship between the two characters. Although these are familiar situations, remember to try to devise characters that are interesting types rather than predictable stereotypes. Once you have performed in one of the listed situations, choose another and swap the status role that each person played. This will provide each performer with an opportunity to experience being characters of high and low status.

3 Reversing Status

Divide into pairs and choose two characters. In this exercise the expected status relationship of characters is reversed. For example, a parent character is low status and the child is high status. The child takes on high status responsibilities, such as giving advice and permission to go out.

Write and Discuss

1. How did you use your body language to communicate your character's relative status?
2. Describe one character you played in the exercises you have just completed. Identify the features of your character that you felt made them unusual and interesting.
3. Why is it important to create complex characters in improvisation?

2.4 The Elements of Drama

 ## Read Explanation of the Elements of Drama

All interesting drama requires certain elements to be engaging and entertaining for the audience. Each of the elements of drama is outlined on pages 36–37. An example of a plot has been included to help illustrate how each element of drama works in performance. Although the illustration outlines each element separately, it is important to remember that they work together simultaneously in performance. Read and discuss the explanation of the elements of drama in preparation for your performance task in Unit 2.6 (pages 41–43).

Understanding the elements of drama and how they work together to create dramatic meaning helps the performer create powerful and interesting drama.

The Element

Role and Character. The who?
Example: Three scientists.

Situation. The what?
Example: Three scientists search for a small, almost extinct creature whose saliva is believed to contain incredible medicinal properties.

Focus. The focus is the central event, theme, issue or problem. Example: The scientists safely capture the small creature and help it to survive. This allows its saliva to be used to make a wonder drug, which will save humankind.

Language, Sound and Movement. How the characters and story are expressed, including the use of verbal language, vocal sounds, body language and movement. Example: The scientists use medical jargon to show their knowledge. Their body language shows the status relationship between the scientists. Their movements are hurried to indicate the urgency of the task.

Moment. Key moments in the performance help to punctuate the tempo. This helps to build dramatic tension. Example: Just as the scientists feel they will not find the creature, they discover evidence in the bushes at the bottom of the volcano that it is somewhere nearby. This moment heightens their excitement that their plan may be realised.

  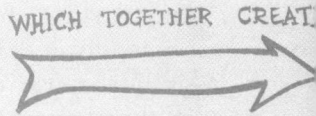

Symbol and Atmosphere.
Symbols include objects, signs, flags, settings, gestures and language. They are used in drama to represent issues and themes, and to help establish atmosphere. Example: The volcano that threatens to erupt could symbolise the danger that humankind faces if the scientists do not succeed in making the wonder drug.

Creating and Performing Drama

# of Drama

Tension. Tension is created when the characters overcome obstacles. This drives the situation and is directed by the focus. The tension can create comic moments as well as serious moments. Example: The scientists search for the creature at a volcano. It threatens to erupt, which may prevent the scientists from safely capturing the creature and saving it from extinction. We anticipate a disastrous moment as time runs out. This tension pushes the characters and the situation to the climax.

DIRECTED BY

Place and Time. The where? This includes the past, present, future, setting, indoors or outdoors, time of day and season. Example: A volcanic crater that is steamy, hot, noisy, uncomfortable and dangerous, and that threatens to erupt.

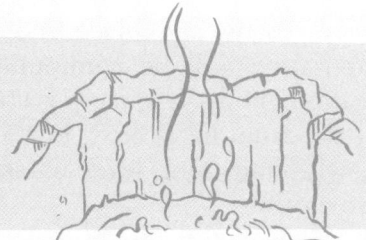 

Dramatic Structure. The framework through which the content is presented. Example: The story of the scientists is presented with a linear narrative that is performed in a realistic style.

Space. How the space and spatial design is used to visually communicate relationships between characters, and between characters and the environment. Example: The performers travel around the whole stage area to communicate the journey to the volcano. Ramps and boxes are used to create the edge of the crater.

Rhythm. The manipulation of timing through pace and tempo. Example: The scientists slow the pace of their movements as they scale the side of the volcano; this helps to build tension. Or the scientists increase the pace of their search to build energy and excitement.

Dramatic Meaning. All the elements of drama combined create dramatic meaning. Example: In the story of the scientists the dramatic meaning may be interpreted as people's potential to work together to overcome difficulties.

AND

Audience Engagement. This is how the performer manipulates the actor–audience relationship to achieve a specific response. Example: The performers act using a 'fourth wall' approach to help the audience believe in the characters and the situation.

Improvisation: Spontaneous Performance

2.5 Improvisation Exercises

Read Improvisation and the Elements of Drama

The following improvisation exercises are designed to test and challenge your improvisation skills. They also require you to demonstrate an understanding of the elements of drama, because you will need to spontaneously establish characters, situation, tension, focus, and place and time. The meaning of your improvisation will be communicated through your use of imagination, body language, gesture and voice. This may seem a little daunting at first, but after practising these exercises you will find your level of skill will improve, as will your improvisations.

Exercise Improvise!

Hint

Don't expect that all situations will work well straight away. Be patient: the more you practise, the more skilled you become.

Hint

Be prepared for side coaching from your teacher. The side coaching will help improve the improvisation and requires you to listen to the coaching tips while still performing.

Work carefully through each of the following exercises. Each exercise should be explored over an extended period of time. This will allow you to focus on improving your incorporation of improvisation skills and the elements of drama. It is also recommended that you revisit different improvisation exercises in later Drama lessons alongside your use of improvisation as part of the process of creating and making performance work.

1 Improvisation Tag

- One person stands in front of the group and mimes an activity. When it is clear what the person is doing, your teacher calls 'Freeze'.
- Another volunteer joins that person and makes an offer to introduce an entirely new situation, using the frozen position of the first person as the starting point.
- After the pair have improvised for a while your teacher calls 'Freeze' and the pair freeze the action.
- Another volunteer from the group taps one of the frozen pair on the shoulder and that person sits down.
- The frozen position of the remaining person is the stimulus for a new situation. The volunteer observes the frozen position and creates a new situation by making a verbal or physical offer.
- The scene continues until your teacher calls 'Freeze', then a new volunteer is chosen.

2 Space Jump!

Form groups of four.

- One performer begins a mimed activity in front of the class. It is best if the activity is very physical. At any time, your teacher calls 'Space jump!' and the performer freezes.
- A second performer uses the frozen position of the first performer to create new characters in a new situation. At any time, your teacher calls 'Space jump!' and the performers freeze.
- A third volunteer joins them and once again an entirely new situation is created from the frozen positions of the first two performers. After the three have improvised for a while, your teacher calls 'Space jump!' and the performers freeze.
- A fourth volunteer joins the three performers and once again an entirely new situation is created from the frozen position of the three performers. After the four have improvised for a while, your teacher calls 'Space jump!' and the performers freeze.
- The fourth person leaves the scene and the three remaining players return to the scene they played previously. However, they must use their frozen positions as the starting point for the scene they are returning to.
- After the group have improvised for a short while your teacher calls out 'Space jump!' and the group freezes.
- The third person now leaves the group and the remaining pair return to the scene they played before but use the current frozen position as the starting point.
- After the pair have improvised for a short while your teacher calls out 'Space jump!' and the pair freeze. The second person leaves the performance area. The remaining person uses their frozen position to return to the first situation and brings the scene to a conclusion.

3 Hidden Objective

The group is given a situation. Each performer is given a hidden objective on a slip of paper. During the improvisation, each performer must attempt to achieve their objective in the least obvious way by the end of the improvisation. The audience is then asked to identify each character's objective.

4 Whose Line Is It?

Each class member writes down lines on slips of paper. They can be statements or questions. These lines are only to be revealed during the performance. Two performers select two or three slips of paper each and are given a location. During the improvisation, the performers must include the lines on the slips of paper they selected. They must yield to the content and implications of each line, and extend and advance the action accordingly. It is good to warn your fellow performer that you are about to include a line by introducing it somehow. For instance, you might precede the line with 'So I said to her/him ...' or 'I asked for a newspaper and he replied ...'

Read: Improvisation Locations, Situations and Characters

The following table gives some sample locations, situations and characters that you can use in your improvisation practice. Choose from across the three categories.

Locations	Situations	Characters
A singles' dinner for six	Solving a riddle	An overweight politician
A teachers' self-defence class	Looking for love	A radio announcer who specialises in 'love song dedications'
A 'hens' night'	Selling a new product	
A ferry captain's birthday party	Revealing a secret	A clairvoyant
A duck pond at the botanical gardens	Chasing a criminal	A footballer
	Spying on a foreign agent	A scientist
The wrong room	Building a house	A sailor
Customs at London Airport	Creating a fragrance	A university student
A photographer's darkroom	Planning a holiday	A bachelor
A change room at a swimming pool	Learning a hobby	A music video host
	Auditioning for a television show	A goldminer
An ostrich farm		
On the deck of the *Titanic*	Speaking to the deceased	A survivor of a shipwreck
A fireworks factory	Shearing sheep	An Eskimo
Climbing a bridge	Painting a mural	An eccentric artist
A feathers, sequins and football convention	Repairing a car	A matchmaker
	Diving for treasure	A cowardly rebel
A crocodile farm	Removing a splinter	A busybody
A parent training camp		
A shell appreciation meeting		A mind-reader

Write and Discuss

1. Which exercises did you enjoy most? Why?
2. Did you have difficulty finding ways to end improvisations confidently? Make suggestions for how you could improve in this area.
3. Describe two characters you found unusual and interesting from one of the exercises you observed.
4. Explain how you feel you have improved in any of the skill areas of improvisation.
5. Is teamwork important in improvisation? Explain why.

2.6 Performance Task: Improvisation

Read — The Task

In this task, you and your teacher will evaluate your ability as an improvisation performer. You will need to draw on the skills of spontaneity, making offers, yielding, focus, and extending and advancing.

You will also show your understanding of the elements of drama by completing a preparation task in groups. The preparation task will provide a list of ideas to use for the performance task. Your teacher will choose ideas from this list for you to use as the basis for your improvisation.

Prepare — Creating and Making an Improvisation

Complete the following steps to prepare for the improvisation performance task.

Step 1. Divide into groups of four.
Step 2. Each group is given one of the following elements of drama:

- characters
- situation
- focus
- time and place

Step 3. Each group is to create and write six options for their element of drama. The options need to be written down so they are not forgotten. Use the table of examples below to help you in your preparation.
Step 4. Share your ideas with the members of your class or write all the ideas on a whiteboard or blackboard to create one central table.

Element of Drama	Possible option
Characters	• Two deep-sea divers • A family of ants • Three backpackers in India
Situation	• Travelling on an overseas holiday • Moving into a new house • Donating blood
Focus	• To crack the secret code • To reveal a secret • To ask someone on a date
Time and place	• Early morning on a mountain top • Under a spaceship in 2100 • In a well at night

Present ## Improvisation

Your teacher will now give your group of four a selection of ideas chosen from the table generated by the class.

During the improvisation you are to:
- include all the ideas that your teacher has selected
- establish a clear situation
- establish and build tension
- use appropriate language and movement.

Evaluate ## Performance Checklist

You and your teacher will evaluate your work individually, using a list of criteria. These criteria relate to your achievement in this task. Some criteria will relate to the achievement of the group. The criteria are listed on the evaluation sheet at the end of the chapter and will be used to evaluate your ability to:

- create an interesting character type
- be spontaneous and make useful and appropriate offers
- yield
- advance and extend the action
- manipulate vocal dynamics and movement effectively to suit character and/or object
- work successfully as an ensemble
- build tension in your improvisation
- bring the improvisation to a conclusion.

Hint

Refer to Appendixes 1, 3 and 4 for help with your logbook entries. The appendixes provide you with guidelines for evaluating your own performance work and the work of others.

Write and Discuss

Arts Criticism and Aesthetics

1. Write an evaluation of your achievement in your improvisation. Use the Performance Checklist above to help you identify your strengths and the areas in which you could improve.

2. Write an evaluation of one other member of your group, using the Performance Checklist above. Let the person read and respond to your comments.

3. Write an evaluation of a group whose improvisation you felt was strong. Discuss the development of plot, characters and tension, and how the focus was maintained. Did the group arrive at an effective ending? Why was the ending effective?

Past and Present Contexts

4. Offer three reasons that you feel explain why improvisation is seen as an essential component of a performer's training. In your answer, consider the benefits of utilising improvisation both in rehearsal and in performance.

Performance Task: Improvisation

Student: _____ Teacher: _____

Related Outcomes

By completing this task you should be able to:
- explore and utilise the skills of improvisation
- incorporate the elements of drama in improvisations
- create and sustain character types in improvisations
- contribute and incorporate your own ideas to create improvised performance work.

Criteria	Level of Achievement			
	Beginning	Consolidating	Mastering	Excelling
Exploring and Developing Ideas Have you prepared for your performance by: • contributing your own ideas? • completing Write and Discuss questions as required?				
Using Skills, Techniques and Processes Have you selected and included the skills of improvisation, vocal dynamics and movement by: • effectively communicating role/character and/or object through the use of movement and mime? • incorporating an effective use of vocal dynamics? • being spontaneous and making useful and appropriate offers? • yielding to the offers of other performers? • extending and advancing the action?				
Presenting Have you demonstrated skill in working as an ensemble by: • considering the available space and how it can be used to suit your purpose? • drawing together the elements of drama to create a coherent performance? • building tension? • bringing the improvisation to an appropriate conclusion?				

Comments: _____
_____
_____
_____

Chapter 3

Playbuilding: Devised Performance

Why Study Playbuilding?

Playbuilding is a process whereby a play is devised and rehearsed over a period of time, and is then performed for a specific audience. The process of playbuilding involves the refining of the plot, themes, characters and staging. Your work in Chapters 1 and 2 has provided you with skills in the areas of vocal dynamics, movement, character types, improvisation and the elements of drama. In this chapter you will draw on and extend these skills in your building of plays. You will also consider more closely the creation and development of character; and learn how audience seating arrangements can be shaped to suit the purpose of the performance.

This chapter is divided into the following units:

3.1 Steps in Playbuilding

3.2 Playbuilding Structures

3.3 Creating and Controlling Focus

3.4 Scene Transitions

3.5 Creating a Character

3.6 Stage Spaces and the Audience

3.7 Performance Task: Creating a Play

Outcomes

In this chapter you will:

- apply the steps of playbuilding, from research to performance
- draw on a range of starting points for playbuilding
- contribute ideas, feelings and experiences to the process of playbuilding
- consider the actor–audience relationship and select stage spaces to suit playbuilding tasks
- create and develop characters using character biographies
- include and manipulate selected theatrical techniques in performance tasks
- create effective scene transitions.

Hugo Weaving and Geoffrey Rush in *The Alchemist*, Company B Belvoir, 1997. Photograph by Heidrun Löhr.

3.1 Steps in Playbuilding

'Playbuilt plays are powerful. Each member of the group contributes in some way to the development of the presentation; the final performance reflects the creativity and energy of all its members.'
Carole Tarlington and Wendy Michaels, **Building Plays**

Practitioner Profile

Rosemary Myers
Artistic Director, Arena Theatre Company, Melbourne

Here Rosemary describes her approach to playbuilding:

My process of developing new performance work is highly collaborative and can involve working with composers, film-makers and choreographers. I like to create multidisciplined work that celebrates the reshaping of our cultural expression in the age of techno science; like a rock concert with a story set in a contemporary art gallery, utilising fast editing, image saturation and symbols to create a sensation more like advertising or pop video than traditional Western performance. I think the best theatre is marked by a strong directorial vision that communicates in ways other than just spoken word.

Hint

Using any resource as a starting point requires you to use your imagination. It also requires research, going to the library or using the Internet to find out more information. So allow yourself ample time to do research that will assist you to create people, events and locations.

Read ## The Process of Playbuilding

The steps below provide a guideline for building plays. When you reach the performance tasks at the end of this chapter, refer back to these steps to help you build your play. Following these steps will help you to manage your rehearsal time and make the most of your playbuilding.

1 Select a Starting Point

Choose a source of inspiration. Possible resources are personal stories, photos, poetry, songs, oral histories, objects, symbols, art works, themes, people and events from history, and people and events from other cultures.

Playbuilding: Devised Performance

Your understanding of improvisation and the elements of drama will be helpful for your playbuilding. Revise Chapter 2 to refresh your memory.

It is important to write and record all the steps in your playbuilding. This not only gives you a sense of direction but also provides you with material to reflect on as the piece develops.

You can use your chosen resource in a number of ways, for example:

- as a starting point for ideas. The resource is not directly referred to or included in the performance.
- as a symbol to 'background' the main story and to highlight issues or themes.
- as a prop in the performance and as the focus of the performance.

2 Identify the Purpose or Intention

Consider whether you want your performance to entertain, inform, question or provoke. For example, the intention of your performance might be 'to explore the theme of friendship'.

3 Make Decisions

- Consider the intention of the performance and how the arrangement of the audience seating can help achieve the purpose.
- Consider the style of performance. For example, is it a comedy or drama; is it realistic or non-realistic?
- Consider how the elements of drama can be manipulated (see Unit 2.4, pages 35–37).
- Consider how the narrative is structured. For example, will it be linear or non-linear?

4 Create and Rehearse

Brainstorm ideas. Use improvisation to explore and rehearse ideas. Refine the development of tension and highlight the climactic moment by manipulating timing and pace. Heighten particular moments by refining the use of theatrical techniques, such as flashback, tableau, sound and stylised movement. Identify creative and imaginative ways to transition between scenes.

5 Perform

Perform to a selected audience.

6 Evaluate

Evaluate your performance, both individually and as a class.

3.2 Playbuilding Structures

Selecting a Playbuilding Structure

Playbuilding is your opportunity to create an original performance. Before you begin rehearsing it is important to consider the options you have for creating the structure of your performance. The structure of your performance is the framework through which the content of the drama is presented. Preparing a structure will help make the intention of your piece clear to the audience.

As a group, you should consider the type of playbuilding structure you wish to adopt as the basis of your performance. There are two types of playbuilt structures to choose from: narrative and montage.

Read Narrative Playbuilding

A narrative structure tells a story. The events of the story are linked by cause and effect, and usually lead to a climactic moment. A narrative structure can be either linear or non-linear.

Linear Narrative

A linear narrative tells a story in chronological order. It has a plot line that carries the action forward. A standard plot line will have one or more protagonists, a distinct climactic moment and a resolution.

Exercise *Analysing Narrative*

Divide into groups of three or four. As a group create a list of three or four linear narratives from plays, novels or films. Identify the protagonist/s and the antagonist/s. Choose one narrative. Break the narrative into the following three sections:

- an 'exposition' in which the characters, place and time, and tension are established;
- a 'crisis', or 'complication', in which conflict and tension are heightened; and
- a 'resolution' in which an outcome is reached.

Hint

A 'protagonist' is the central character in a play. There may be more than one protagonist. An 'antagonist' is the character who forces the protagonist into action.

Non-linear Narrative

Like a linear narrative, a non-linear narrative also tells a story, but in a non-linear narrative the events are not presented in chronological order. The non-linear narrative employs flashbacks or flash-forwards to tell the story.

Exercise *Non-linear Role-Play*

Divide into groups of four. Devise a short role-play that incorporates the use of either flashback or flash-forward, or both techniques. Your plot should still have a narrative structure, so although you flash forwards and backwards in time there should still be a central narrative that moves to a climactic moment. Some ideas for role-plays are:

1 A deep-sea diver recalls diving on a dangerous shipwreck.
2 A group is having a party on the beach. The role-play then flashes forwards to the present day; at the same beach an important discovery is made.
3 A child and their grandparent are trapped temporarily in a location of your choice. The role-play flashes back to the past and forwards to the future at various points.

Read ## Montage Playbuilding

The montage playbuilt performance explores a central theme, issue or subject through the use of short, self-contained scenes. These scenes, or episodes, give the montage playbuilt performance an episodic quality. Each scene is independent of the others; however, the scenes are unified by their exploration of a theme, issue or subject. Each scene in a montage playbuilt piece has its own timing and thrust. But the pace and energy of the overall performance also works towards a clear climactic moment.

Montage Role-Play

In preparation for this role-play you will need to create a mind map on a page in your logbook. Choose one of the words from the following list. Brainstorm as many images, situations and characters as you can related to the word you've chosen. Then, using stylised movement, soundscapes or tableaux, create a series of short scenes of contrasting styles to represent your ideas.

Oxygen, reflection, egg, camouflage, balloons, desert, honesty, black, seasons, opposites, voyage, community, plots, hunger

Hint

Whether you choose a narrative or a montage structure for your playbuilt performance it is important for the playbuilt performance to progress from a starting point to a climactic moment. A consideration of how you manipulate the elements of drama (see Unit 2.4, page 35) will help you achieve this.

Dramatic Forms, Dramatic Conventions and Performance Style

Read ## Dramatic Forms

In the history of drama and theatre there have been many different dramatic forms. These include: Realism, Expressionism, commedia dell' arte, melodrama, Epic Theatre, Ancient Greek drama, Absurdism, mime, Restoration comedy, physical theatre, and so on. During your study of drama you will examine many of these dramatic forms in detail.

48 Creating and Performing Drama

Each dramatic form springs from a particular place and time. The form is unique because it is based upon a specific structure, subject matter, acting style, actor–audience relationship, or use of production elements.

Dramatic Conventions

Within each dramatic form you will find particular dramatic conventions. These are the typical features of the form; you will see these conventions used repeatedly in theatre and drama of the same form. For example, a Shakespearian play will contain a 'soliloquy', in which a character talks to himself or herself, or reveals his or her thoughts without addressing a listener. A soliloquy is a dramatic convention typical of the Shakespearian form of drama. In the commedia dell'arte form of theatre performers wear comic half-masks to portray stock characters; this is a dramatic convention typical of the commedia form.

DEVELOPING A PLAYBUILT PERFORMANCE

Begin with an idea

Choose from
NARRATIVE (LINEAR OR NON-LINEAR) OR MONTAGE

Consider
DRAMATIC FORM

Commedia dell'arte, Pantomime, Mime, Epic Theatre, Ancient Greek drama, Restoration comedy, Symbolism, Melodrama, Kabuki, Realism, Absurdism, Aboriginal ritual, Expressionism, Vaudeville, Shakespearian drama, Puppetry, etc.

Select and incorporate
DRAMATIC TECHNIQUES AND CONVENTIONS

Narration, Exaggerated movement, Asides, Soliloquy, Projected signs, Mime, Actors moving amongst the audience, Mask, Playing to the audience, Political song, Transformation, Tableaux, Extended silences, Changing character in view of the audience, Slow motion, Stock characters, Fourth wall, etc.

Consider/Remember
THE ELEMENTS OF DRAMA

Role and character, plus *situation*, are directed by *focus*, driven by *tension*, made explicit in *place and time*, through *dramatic structure*, and the use of *language, sound and movement, moment, space, rhythm*, to evoke *symbol and atmosphere*, which together create *dramatic meaning* and *audience engagement*.

Create your
PERFORMANCE STYLE

Read ## Performance Style

The final, polished theatrical performance has its own performance style. This style is a result of the many decisions that have been made regarding the use of dramatic forms and conventions. And your own ideas also affect the performance style. For example, you may choose to use the conventions of melodrama—asides, music to accompany the entrance of characters, cheers and boos from the audience—but perform your playbuilt piece in the style of a parody of a contemporary television soap opera.

The form or style you adopt for your playbuilt piece will depend on a variety of factors. You do not need to limit yourself to one form or style of performance. In fact, it is likely you will borrow from a range of dramatic forms and performance styles to create your playbuilt piece.

3.3 Creating and Controlling Focus

Focus is important in drama. For the performer, having a good sense of focus means being able to concentrate and remain in character, both when rehearsing and when performing. Through a skilled use of focus a performer can help the audience sustain belief in his or her performance. A good sense of focus also enables the performer to work effectively as part of an ensemble.

In terms of the overall dramatic action being presented, an effective use of focus directs the audience's attention to specific moments in the action. When rehearsing it is important to plan the focus of the dramatic action, especially at key moments. This will prevent the action from becoming unclear.

Exercise ## Focus Role-Play

Read through the following list of examples of how focus is established in performance. Then divide into groups of five or six. Prepare a short role-play of five minutes in length in which three of the methods of establishing focus are incorporated. Present your role-play to the class.

- Space—Focus can be established according to where performers are positioned in the space (for example, upstage, downstage, centre stage, on levels, in groups or individually).
- Gesture—A gesture can concentrate attention (for example,

Creating and Performing Drama

pointing, facing a particular direction, touching, waving, putting your hand up or wiping your brow).

- Eye contact—Focus can be established using eye contact (for example, one performer looks at another, one performer is looked at by all the others, two groups of performers look at each other, one performer looks at an audience member).
- Contrast—Focus can be achieved by contrasting images (for example, all performers are in darkness except one who is in light, all performers move except one who is still, all performers move in slow motion except one who moves quickly).
- Language and voice—Focus can be achieved through the selection of who is speaking, what they say and how it is delivered (for example, a tour guide speaks in a serious tone to a tour group, warning them of the dangers of an unstable cliff edge).

 ## Working as an Ensemble to Establish Focus

When playbuilding as a group, it is important to develop a strong collaborative relationship among group members. This will help make all aspects of the performance, including establishing focus, more effective.

By undertaking lots of improvisation work and practical activities together, you will learn to collaborate and establish a strong ensemble.

The chorus exercises provided in Chapter 8, Unit 8.3, are designed to improve the use of pace, tempo and timing in an ensemble. The exercises also encourage participants to establish a strong sense of focus. You do not need to use mask with these exercises.

 ## Establishing Ensemble Focus

1 The First Step

As a group, spread out evenly around the space. The whole group is to take a first step together at the same time. There are no cues or signals for this. Try to focus on sensing the exact moment for taking the step.

2 Controlling Pace

As a group, spread out evenly around the space. As in the previous exercise, the group is to take a first step together. The group continues walking and builds pace until everyone breaks into a run. The group then reduces the pace until reaching a standstill all at the same time.

3 Rhythm and Peripheral Cues

Imagine a public location that will allow each member of the class to have a specific role. Each performer creates a character to suit the location. Each character has their own private activity which will move them from one point in the space to another. All characters start performing their activities at the same time. The activities start slowly, with a low level of energy, then build

In ensemble work the contribution of every member is equally valued. There are no individual stars, and then extras. Every part is as important as another.

in intensity and pace, and finally slow until the performers all freeze at the same time. Try the following variations:

- Each person in the group is given a number. The characters start performing their activities as their number is called, either in sequence or randomly. Repeat.
- Individual characters choose when to start and finish.

4 Three Up, Two Down

Five performers stand in a line, leaving a gap between each person. Each performer remains focused throughout the exercise. Finding a spot to look at can help establish this. When the exercise commences any person can crouch down or stand when they feel the impulse to. There can be only three people standing and two crouching at any moment. Try not to develop a pattern or pre-empt what the group is going to do. Remain focused, trust your instincts and respond accordingly.

Write and Discuss

1. Using examples from your own performance work explain the two meanings of the term 'focus'.
2. Choose two of the following means of creating focus: space, gesture, eye contact, contrast, language and voice. For each of the two methods you have chosen, outline in point form a dramatic moment which illustrates the use of this method. Share your ideas with the class. Choose three or four examples from those provided by the class and perform them.

3.4 Scene Transitions

Read Scene Transitions

Scene transitions should not be seen as a break in a performance but as an integral way of adding to the performance. Scene changes can be achieved in a variety of ways depending on the dramatic form of the performance, the performance space and the availability of technology. A poor scene transition interrupts the flow of the performance. The following lists describe some techniques that can be used for scene transitions.

Performer-Based Scene Transitions

- A narrator addresses the audience while set and/or actors are changed.
- Actors remain on the stage, and transform their physical shapes and positions, to create new characters in a new place and time.
- Actors enter the stage area or exit to the offstage area.
- Actors change costume in front of the audience.

Elements of Production Scene Transitions

- Blackout of lights—Scenery is changed and performers move while lights are out.
- Cross-fade of lights—One lighting state fades down while another fades up.
- Curtains open or close.
- Change of scenery (for example, flying in backdrops, flats, revolves, trucking of sets, changes in projected imagery or use of film footage).

Hint

'Flying in' a backdrop means the backdrop is lowered from the fly tower above the stage. A 'revolve' is a mechanised, circular area built into the stage floor; it revolves to change the scene of a play. 'Trucking' sets involves moving them onstage from the wings by placing them on special mechanised platforms with wheels.

Transformation

Most classroom performances require students to remain in the performance space and not exit from the room. For this reason classroom performances require you to create imaginative and original scene changes. A theatrical technique that can be employed to make scene changes effective is transformation.

The technique of transformation has evolved from the work of many theatre practitioners. One key practitioner was the Polish theatre director Jerzy Grotowski (1933–1999). His theatre sought to create plays that had strong social and political messages. He devised the term 'Poor Theatre' to describe what he thought was true theatre, focused on actors in a space using their skills to create the world of the drama without expensive sets, lighting or costumes.

Transformation is an effective dramatic technique for creating scene transitions. The technique requires the performer to use his or her expressive movement and voice skills; and to manipulate energy, rhythm, timing and space. Using transformation for scene transitions often requires a group of performers to work as an ensemble. There are endless ways of creating scene transitions using transformation, for example:

- Snap transformations—in which all performers change position instantaneously
- Cross-fade transformations—in which performers use slow and controlled movements to merge from one character and setting to another
- Transformations accompanied by a regular or irregular rhythm
- Transformations with or without sound.

Hint

Improvisation Tag and Space Jump! (see Chapter 2, pages 38–39) are good improvisation games for developing skills in transformation.

Hint

At their best transformations are ingenious, and entertaining for audiences. They seem to magically create new characters and places even though the performers have not left the stage.

Exercises: Transformation

1 Transforming Objects in a Circle

Sit in a circle as a class. Your teacher will give you an object, such as a piece of fabric or rope, to pass around the circle. Each person transforms the object by reshaping it and using it in a way that indicates a new object.

2 Transforming Objects in Groups

Divide into groups of three. Each group requires one chair and one piece of fabric. Using people and objects, each group is to create a tableau to illustrate the following titles.

- Victory
- Peak Hour
- Drought
- Adrift

Your teacher will give you ten counts to transform from the first tableau to the next tableau. It is important that members of the group make and yield to offers from one another so that the tableau is transformed without discussion.

3 Transformation Using Sound and Rhythm

Devise two short, self-contained scenes that explore one of the following words.

- Trust
- Balance
- Pressure
- Escape

Consider how you will use a combination of sound and rhythm to create transitions from one scene to another. The choice of rhythm and sound will need to have some relationship to the overall subject, or to the scene that has just ended or is just about to be shown.

4 Scene Transitions Using Transformation

Divide into groups of five or more. Choose one of the following situations to practise transformation in creating scene changes.

- One performer plays a girl getting ready for her school dance. Other performers are items of furniture in the girl's bedroom. As the girl gets up from her chair and moves downstage, the other performers establish the rhythm of the music at the dance and transform their positions to become new characters.
- A scene in an office. All performers freeze. One character takes off a jacket and puts on a windcheater. As the character makes this costume change, the other performers create a soundscape of wind and waves. They also snap transform, one at a time, into surfers at a beach.
- Four supporters at the football are cheering for their team. On the scoring of a goal they freeze. Using vocal sound and movement, they snap transform from the football to a building site.

Read ## Motifs

A motif is an image or moment of action that is repeated throughout a performance. Although a pattern is established, the nature of the motif may change slightly each time it occurs. A motif reinforces a symbol or message and it is a powerful tool for creating focus. Motifs can be used effectively as playbuilding scene transitions. For example, a play that explores the issue of refugees may have scenes set in two countries; these scenes could be linked by scene transformations using a recurring motif of a refugee boat on its journey.

Devising Three Scenes Linked by Motif

Divide into groups of four. Create a short linear narrative that uses a standard three-scene format. In other words, include a beginning to establish characters and situation, a middle in which a problem or conflict is encountered, and a resolution. Link the three scenes by moments of transformation. Experiment with any of the types of transformation you have explored in the previous exercises, including the use of motif.

Write and Discuss

1. What is transformation?
2. Describe and evaluate two examples of successful transformation that you have observed in your class work. Identify how space, rhythm, timing, and physical and vocal skills, were used to achieve the transformation. Here is an example of how you might respond:

   'Today we watched all the group performances. Each group was given the title "Circus" as a starting point. Adrian, Sally, Courtenay and Lily showed the best use of transformation. Their scene transitions moved smoothly between scenes in the big top and scenes in the clown's caravan. The group used slow-motion movement, and humming and whispering, to help show that the scenes in the big top were in the clown's imagination. He wants to be the star of the show and dreams of how he can become famous. The group's use of timing and control of movement was excellent, especially as they synchronised the slow motion. The scene transitions and use of transformation were as enjoyable to watch as the scenes themselves.'

3. What is a motif? Provide your own example of a motif and explain how it could be used in scene transformations. Alternatively, explain how you have observed a motif being used in the work of others.
4. Research the work of Grotowski. Summarise his beliefs on theatre and performance. Discuss his aims, perceptions of successful performance and the desired actor–audience relationship.

3.5 Creating a Character

Read Role and Character

In your drama performance work you will play both roles and characters. To play a role you need only have basic information about it. For example, a role may be defined simply as 'the mother', 'the policewoman', 'the politician' or 'the citizen of the town'. Roles can be important in performance because they help the audience to focus on themes and issues. Roles also help to move the plot forward by being vehicles for providing important information, advice or points of view. A role may be small but the performer still needs to apply a skilled use of vocal dynamics, movement, energy and focus to play the role well.

Characterisation is the development of a role into a character. The performer will have much more knowledge about the personality and life experiences of a character they play. The performer can discover information about a character by engaging in written exercises, drawing on personal experiences and analysing the script.

Hint

A character biography provides the performer with all the important information about the character. The information includes who the character is and why they behave the way they do.

Read The Character Biography

In the performance tasks at the end of this chapter you will be required to develop characters over a period of time. This provides an excellent opportunity to create more complex and detailed characters.

The following exercises explore how to create an original character using a character biography. The character you create may be based on someone you observe or may come from a picture you have seen in a book or magazine. The character needs to be original, so avoid choosing a famous identity or someone you know. Use the character biography writing exercises below to begin your creation of an original character.

Hint

The more you know about your character, the more interesting and truthful your character will be in performance.

Exercise Creating a Character

1 Character Details

Write down all the essential details about your character. Include the following:

- personal details, such as age, occupation, nationality, star sign, address, languages spoken, education, hobbies and family details
- physical description, such as weight, height, colouring, distinguishing features, clothing and accessories.

Creating and Performing Drama

2 Asking Questions

Ask questions of the character to learn more about their personality and how they may behave in certain situations. Often the way we behave is due to what we believe about the world, ourselves and others. Write answers to the following questions. As you write your answers you will need to think as the character to gain the best responses.

- In social situations I am _____ because I _____
- My relationship with my parents is _____ because _____
- My favourite film is _____ because _____
- I would never _____ because _____
- I used to _____ but now I _____ because _____
- The most frightening experience I ever had was _____
- My ambition in life is to _____
- I think the world is a _____ place because _____
- I believe true happiness is _____

Hint

In your playbuilt performance you may play a number of roles. These roles are important as they can represent different points of view. They can also establish relationships between the people, ideas and environment being presented in the performance.

Write and Discuss

1. Write your own questions for your character to answer. Write questions that you feel will help you develop a deeper understanding of your character. Share these with the class.
2. Ask group members to suggest other questions. Write down the questions that you feel would be useful in the development of your character.

Exercise Being the Character

In the following exercises you will need to use the character that you have already established in the Creating a Character exercises above. These exercises will help you to sustain and develop your character. They will also help you to establish a strong sense of belief.

1 A Day in the Life

Start with a relaxation exercise and imagine your character clearly. Find a position to show your character in bed in the early hours of the morning. On the signal from the teacher you are to wake as the character. Begin by acting out the character's morning routine. If you need to, include imaginary family members who are part of the morning routine. On a given signal, your teacher will ask you to freeze and move the character forward in time by a few hours. Take up a new position and show the character in a new situation and performing a new activity. This continues until the character returns to bed at the end of the day.

Hint

The skill of spontaneity is needed for the character-building Hot Seat exercise. You may be asked questions that surprise you because they may involve providing information about your character that you have not considered before. Answer the questions as quickly as you can. If you hesitate you will drop out of character.

2 Character Phone Call

Place your character in a situation where they have access to a telephone. Begin by acting as the character in the location. Give the character an activity in which they are involved. After working for a short time on the activity, the character makes a telephone call. The performer must use the character's voice when speaking to the imaginary caller, as they improvise the conversation out loud. Once the conversation is finished the character returns to their activity. On a given signal, the character hears the phone ring, answers the call and improvises another conversation.

3 Hot Seat

One volunteer sits in front of the class as their character. The class asks the character questions about the character's life and past experiences. The aim of this exercise is to help the performer learn more about their character; not to intimidate the character or point out inconsistencies in their answers.

Write and Discuss

1. Describe any new information you discovered about your character after completing the exercises.
2. Write several diary entries for your character. Describe particular events and explore your character's reactions to them.
3. What is a role? Why are roles important?
4. How does a performer establish a strong sense of belief when playing a character?

3.6 Stage Spaces and the Audience

Read ## Considering the Audience

When devising performances it is necessary to consider two important factors:

- **Stage spaces.** Where is the play to be performed?
- **Audience arrangement.** Where will the audience be placed in relation to the performance?

  To answer these questions you will need to consider:

- the type of play to be performed
- the availability and suitability of a venue
- audience comfort and their ability to see; also known as consideration of sight-lines.

Read ## Choosing Audience Seating Arrangements for a Purpose

The way you seat the audience has a direct impact on their appreciation of the performance. Some of the earliest performances had the audience sit in an arena format, that is in a full circle around the performers. No scenery was used. The seating of an audience in an arena format focuses the attention of the audience to a central point. Being able to see other audience members encourages a stronger sense of 'sharing' an experience. This awareness of other audience members encourages energy and excitement.

Playwrights of tragedies and comedies in ancient Greece explored the power of 'background' and began to add basic scenery to enhance the action in their plays. The semicircular shape of the tiered amphitheatres gave a perfect view of the actors, but also allowed the audience to look beyond the acting area to the views of the mountains and countryside. The once-complete circle had been broken to allow for the inclusion of scenery. It is thought that the view of the mountains and countryside helped the audience imagine battles, the gods on Mount Olympus and the relevance of the play to their own homeland.

Today, theatre groups still experiment with audience seating to achieve certain effects. Many outdoor performances use an Environment performer–audience arrangement where the performers are among the audience and/or the audience moves to different locations for different scenes.

An example of an interesting use of audience in modern performance was in a production devised by Theatre Works, a Melbourne theatre group. In their performance *Storming Mont Albert by Tram*, the audience sat on an actual tram destined for the suburb of Mont Albert, as though they were normal passengers. As the play progressed, performers playing characters got on the tram at different stops and acted out scenes from the play. The performers indirectly involved the audience in the action and used familiar characters and situations for comic effect.

Write and Discuss

1. Why might performers choose to stage their play on a tram? What impact would this decision have on the relationship between the audience and the performers?

Read ## Types of Theatre Spaces

Some examples of types of theatre spaces are illustrated on the following page.

To remember stage left and stage right, always remember that stage left and stage right are from the actor's point of view.

Playbuilding: Devised Performance

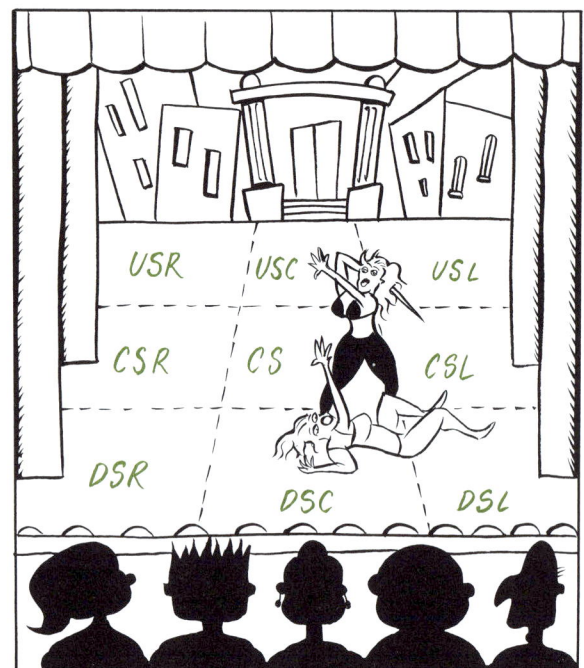

Proscenium. The proscenium stage is rectangular in shape and is divided into nine areas. In the illustration above each area is labelled with an identification code. USC stands for upstage centre, DSL for downstage left, CS for centre stage, and so on. These codes are a useful form of shorthand for performers, directors and stage crew. The areas above and to the sides of the stage are hidden by the proscenium arch and the wings.

Environment. This type of audience arrangement varies from performance to performance, depending on the requirements. Raised platforms, rostra, wagons, gangways, catwalks and other performance areas are arranged in a performance space so the audience feel they are within or surrounded by the action. This type of arrangement also allows for movement of the audience from one location to another.

Theatre-in-the-round. This type of stage is divided into thirteen areas. This audience arrangement focuses the attention of the audience to the centre of the arena and encourages the audience to 'share' the experience.

Thrust. The thrust stage takes the action into the audience by using an extension to the proscenium stage that makes the audience feel closer to the action.

Write and Discuss

1. Draw audience arrangements for the following performances. Be imaginative in your ideas for where the play is performed (it need not be performed in a traditional theatre) and how the audience are seated. Remember to consider the age of the audience and their comfort. Explain why you think your choice would be effective.
   - a performance for primary school students about road safety
   - a serious, realistic drama set in a living room
   - a rock musical about the French Revolution
   - a Shakespearian play set in a forest.
2. Explain how you think your choices for audience arrangement would suit the purpose of each performance and would make the performance more interesting for the audience.

Hint

A proscenium stage often slopes upwards from front to back, which explains the terms 'upstage' and 'downstage'.

3.7 Performance Task: Creating a Play

Read An Overview of the Performance Tasks

In this unit you are given a choice of three performance tasks. Each task allows for the creation of character and situation, and will require you to incorporate planning and research. You will also need to meet particular performance requirements and include theatrical techniques to heighten aspects of your performance. In these performance tasks it is recommended that you work in groups of no more than five people. Groups that are larger can slow down the planning process and will not provide as many opportunities for developed characters. You will need to time your performance so that it meets the guidelines set by your teacher.

Choose Selecting a Playbuilding Task

Read the outline for each of the three performance task options. Choose the task that most interests you. Note, if you choose Performance Task 3, you will need to complete a special preparation task.

Performance Task 1: Something Supernatural

Read ## The Task

In groups, devise a performance that uses the title 'Something Supernatural' as its basis. In your play, one or more characters are involved in a supernatural experience, such as a ghostly visitation, a prophecy that comes true or an unexplained happening. The supernatural experience has a powerful effect on the character(s) and creates a dramatic change in their lives. This change may be positive or negative.

The following resources are provided as assistance. You can decide whether to use them directly or indirectly in your performance.

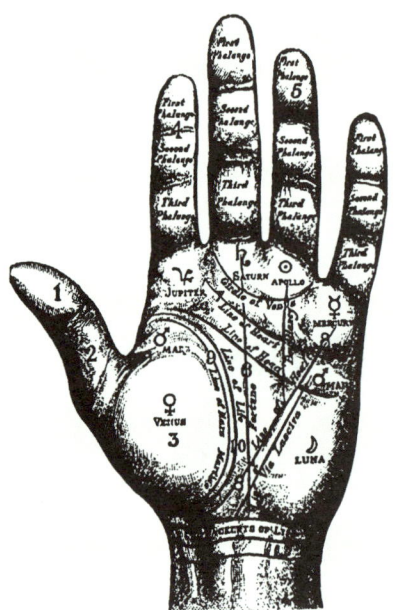

In your performance, you need to include:

- characters that have been developed using character biographies
- an audience arrangement that you devise or one you have chosen from the examples on page 60
- the dramatic technique of stylised movement and vocal sounds to highlight the supernatural experiences of the characters.

Performance Task 2: Journey

Read

The Task

Devise a performance that uses the theme of 'journey' as a starting point. Your play will be about one or more characters on a journey. The journey could be one of exploration, escape or discovery. Your performance will show three different locations and the way the characters travel to each location. It will also show how your characters are affected by their experiences on the journey. Some characters may change significantly because of their experiences; some may not change at all.

The resources on this page are provided as assistance. You can decide whether to use them directly or indirectly in your performance.

Incorporate the following in your playbuilding:

- a journey set in Australia
- a group of original characters who may or may not know each other
- for each character, a 'hidden' objective that they reveal by the end of the play
- the use of contrasting locations
- an audience arrangement that you devise or that is chosen from the examples given on page 60
- the dramatic technique of slow motion to highlight an important moment.

You may show the characters travelling from one location to another. Find a way to 'compress' the travelling time so that the bulk of the play's action occurs at each location.

Tourists of Australia: The Essential Guide

The key to finding Australian tourists is always water. Check waterfalls, rivers, and of course, beaches. Those in search of young tourists should not stray far from coastal southern Australia and rarely far from major urban centres... Key identification aids: any vehicle towing a caravan, any vehicle towing or carrying a boat, any fully-equipped 4WD vehicle, any bus that looks like it is lived in, generally anyone making a lot of noise.

'Where to Find Tourists in Australia', http://www.esat.kuleuven.ac.be/~martin/tourists.html

Playbuilding: Devised Performance

Performance Task 3: A New Beginning

Read ## The Task

Work in groups to devise a performance that incorporates the theme of 'a new beginning'. It may be set in any place and in any time, but a character or a group of characters must face 'a new beginning'.

- The new beginning may have happened suddenly or it may have been known about for some time.
- The new beginning may have been eagerly anticipated.
- The new beginning may have been anticipated with fear.

In your play the characters are at the start of the new beginning and set about dealing with the change to their lives. As the play progresses, we learn more about how each character copes with the adjustment to the new beginning. In the course of your play we also learn more about the characters' past experiences.

The resources on the following page are provided as assistance. You can decide whether to use them directly or indirectly in your performance.

Incorporate the following in your playbuilding:

- a group of characters who are affected by the new beginning
- the use of recorded music at the beginning and end of your play to help establish mood and atmosphere
- an audience arrangement that you devise or that is chosen from the examples given on page 60
- the theatrical technique of flashback; include no more than four flashbacks to help explain each character's past.

Prepare ## Performance Task 3: Flashbacks

In a flashback we step back in time momentarily and are informed about an incident in the past that helps us understand what is happening in the present. You will need to consider how, in your performance, you make the transition from the present to the past in a way that does not interrupt the performance's flow.

Here are three examples of how you can incorporate flashbacks in your performance:

- Freeze the action and quickly take up a new position showing the characters in the past situation; then continue performing. Repeat this procedure to return to the present.
- Have characters walk from one area of the stage to another to indicate a different place and time.
- If you have access to technical equipment, use lighting changes or music to bridge the changes between flashbacks and the present time.

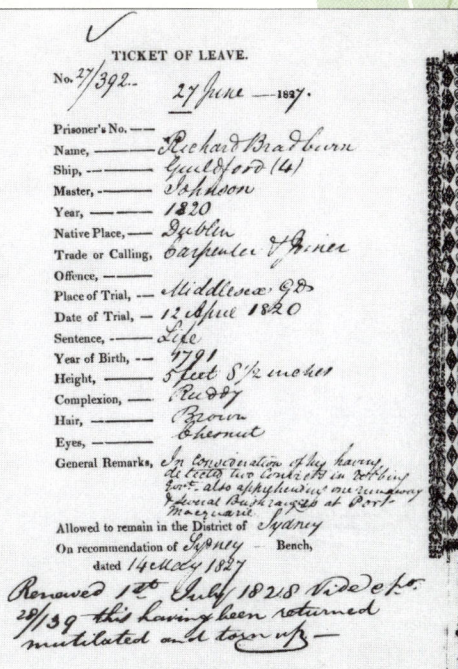

600m. SEE TWO MEN WALK INTO HISTORY

In two hours, 14 minutes, yesterday, Neil Armstrong and Edwin Aldrin opened a new world before the wondering eyes of the estimated 600m. people watching them from Earth.

The watchers saw the shadowy figure of Armstong make the first step on to the moon's surface—perhaps the most significant single event of the century—and Edwin Aldrin follow him soon after.

160 Years of the Sydney Morning Herald: *Major News Stories, 1831–1990*

Read ## Preparing for Performance Tasks 1, 2 or 3

Revise the steps in playbuilding in Unit 3.1 (pages 45–46). The tasks in the Write and Discuss section on page 66 will assist you in completing the playbuilding steps.

Write and Discuss

1. Identify the purpose of your performance.
2. Brainstorm ideas for climactic moments, points of tension and conflict.
3. Brainstorm ideas for the characters and develop your character by completing a character biography.
4. Brainstorm ideas for situations. Consider the elements of drama (see page 35) in your notes and discussions.
5. Brainstorm ideas for how you can incorporate the required dramatic technique in your performance.
6. Consider how you may seat your audience to achieve your purpose. Create your own audience arrangement or choose an audience arrangement from the examples on page 60.

Rehearse: Exploring, Developing and Selecting

- Use improvisation to explore characters and situations.
- Develop your character using the character biography and the character exercises outlined on pages 56–8.
- Explore the use of space, considering your chosen audience arrangement.
- Explore how the use of levels can add impact to your performance.
- Refine and rehearse the scenes, and the scene transitions, to achieve a coherent and polished performance.

Evaluate: Performance Checklist

You and your teacher will evaluate your work individually, using a list of criteria. These criteria relate to your achievement in this task. Some criteria will relate to the achievement of the group. The criteria are listed on the evaluation sheet at the end of this chapter and will be used to evaluate your ability to:

- portray character/role through considered use of voice and movement
- sustain and develop character in performance
- research and prepare a playbuilt performance
- include any required dramatic technique
- evaluate your own work and the work of others
- structure and link aspects of your drama into a coherent and polished performance.

Write and Discuss

Arts Criticism and Aesthetics

1. Choose one character from one other group; it should be a character which you feel was particularly convincing. Identify the reasons why you feel the performance was convincing.

2. Did your performance demonstrate the use of effective scene transitions? Give reasons for your success or lack of success in this area. Offer suggestions for how you could improve your creation of scene transitions.

3. What was the climactic moment of your piece? How did you make this moment stand out for the audience?

4. Describe how you incorporated the required theatrical technique in your performance. What effect did you want to achieve through the inclusion of this technique?

5. Make suggestions you feel would improve your use of rehearsal time in future playbuilding tasks.

6. Imagine you are redirecting one group. Outline the difficulties you observed in the staging of their performance. Offer suggestions for improvement.

7. Evaluate one group and their use of scene transitions. Using drama terminology, explain how they achieved their transitions and whether or not the transitions were effective.

Past and Present Contexts

8. Imagine you are a performer working with people who have no previous drama experience. Outline how improvisation has been used in the past as a tool for playbuilding. Use examples from your own playbuilding to explain how improvisation is valuable in rehearsals.

9. Research a form of theatre or style of performance that uses a non-proscenium stage space for a specific purpose. For example, you might look at the theatre of Jerzy Grotowski, Augustus Boal or Circus Oz. Report your findings to the class.

Hint

Refer to Appendixes 1, 3 and 4 for help with your logbook entries. The appendixes provide you with guidelines for evaluating your own performance work and the work of others.

Performance Task: Creating a Play, No. ___

Student: _____ Teacher: _____

Related Outcomes

By completing this task you should be able to:
- apply steps in playbuilding from research to performance
- draw on a range of starting points for playbuilding
- contribute ideas, feelings and experiences to the process of playbuilding
- consider the actor–audience relationship and select stage spaces to suit playbuilding tasks
- create and develop characters using character biographies
- include and manipulate selected dramatic techniques in performance tasks
- create effective scene transitions.

Criteria	Level of Achievement			
	Beginning	Consolidating	Mastering	Excelling
Exploring and Developing Ideas Have you prepared for your performance by: • recording and planning rehearsals and decisions in your logbook? • completing a character biography? • completing Write and Discuss questions as required?				
Using Skills, Techniques and Processes Have you selected and incorporated performance skills and the elements of drama by: • representing character/role through effective use of vocal dynamics? • representing character/role through effective use of body language and movement? • sustaining and developing character/role? • establishing tension and clearly identifying the climactic moment? • incorporating the dramatic technique described in the outline of the performance task?				
Presenting Have you planned, selected and modified your presentation by: • considering the available space and how it can be used to suit your purpose? • structuring and linking aspects of the drama into a coherent and polished performance?				

Comments: _____
_____
_____
_____

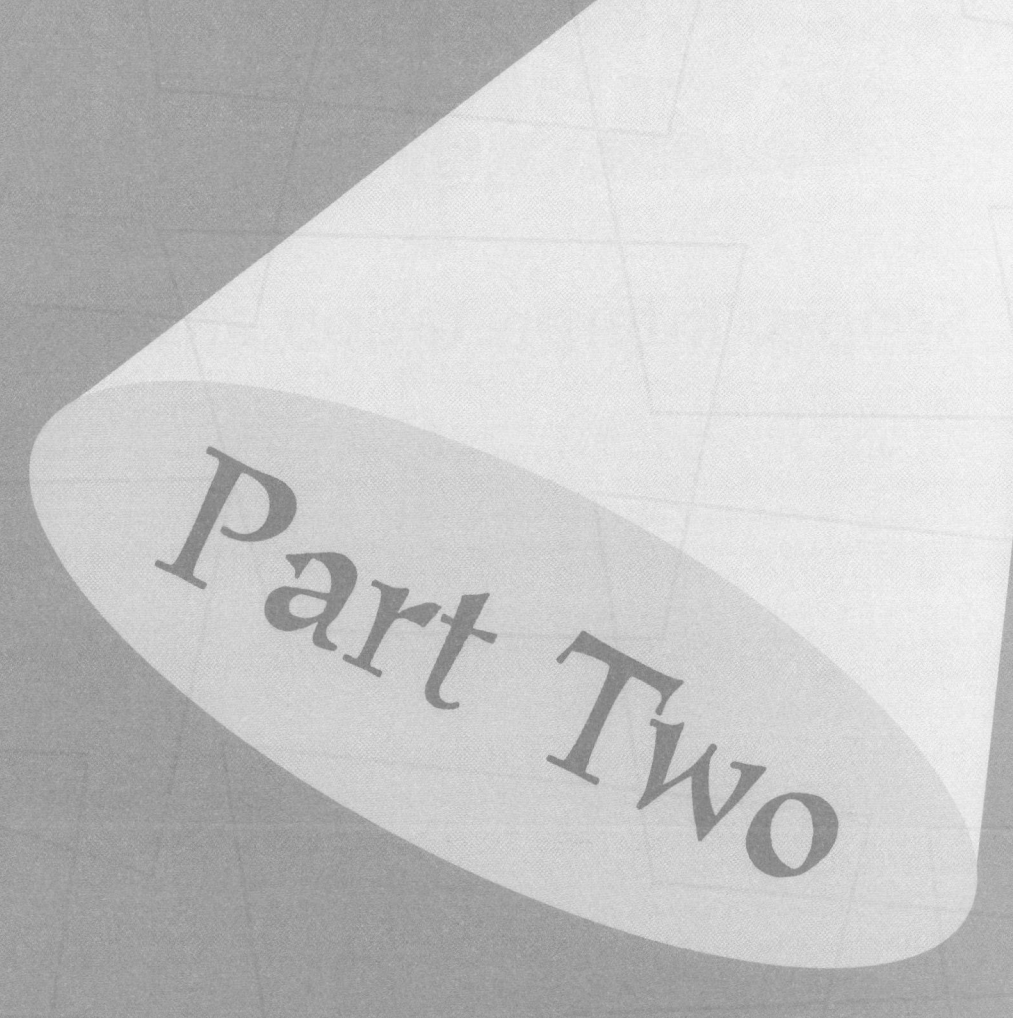

Part Two

Interpreting Drama

Chapter 4   Scripts: Interpretation and Presentation

Chapter 5   Writing a Review: Analysing and Evaluating Performance

Chapter 4

Scripts: Interpretation and Presentation

Why Study Scripts?

Working with scripts is a process of discovery. A polished performance of a script is the end product of analysis and rehearsals. These processes help the director, the performers and the production team develop an understanding of the script and explore creative opportunities for its presentation. Studying the methods of script interpretation and presentation will develop our ability to read, interpret and perform scripts.

This chapter is divided into the following units:

- **4.1** The Director
- **4.2** The Stage Manager
- **4.3** Script Detective Work and Stanislavski's System
- **4.4** Rehearsing and Performing Scripts
- **4.5** The Directorial Concept and the Elements of Production
- **4.6** The Designers
- **4.7** Performance Task: Interpreting Script

Outcomes

In this chapter you will:

- explore and consider the collaborative roles of the director, the performer and the production team in the interpretation and performance of scripts
- create a prompt copy for use in rehearsals and performance
- explore and apply a method of analysing a script for meaning, character development and effective presentation
- interpret and present a scripted performance.

Leeanna Walsman, Sandy Gore and Vanessa Dowling in *Chasing the Dragon*, Sydney Theatre Company, 1998. Photograph by Tracey Schramm.

4.1 The Director

> *'Actors are in the habit of putting their attention only on the roles assigned to them... This is a mistake... It is very important that the performer senses the production as a whole, its entire intent... Then, by itself, the part given to you will become clear.'*
>
> Stanislavski

Practitioner Profile

Neil Armfield
Artistic Director of Company B, Belvoir St Theatre

In addition to his current role as Artistic Director of Company B, Belvoir St Theatre, Neil Armfield has directed for the State Theatre Company of South Australia, the Australian Opera and television. After his acclaimed production of *Cloudstreet*, Neil wrote:

> We realised that there was such a hunger in our audience for stories that reveal our relationship with each other and with the land on which we live, that explore our need to belong, our need for security and the embrace of the family. I'm reminded now of the power that theatre has to define, to remake the world. And for us that is an awesome responsibility and an extraordinary privilege.

Aaron Blabey and Neil Armfield in rehearsal for Company B Belvoir's production of *As You Like It*, 1999. Photograph by Heidrun Löhr.

Read: The Director's Role

The role of the director is a relatively 'new' occupation. Prior to the end of the nineteenth century, the director in theatre was virtually non-existent. The term 'actor–manager' or 'stage manager' was given to the person or actor who was responsible for organising the performance. Today some of the director's tasks and responsibilities are as follows:

- They negotiate with producers and theatre companies about the choice of production, the possible casting and the selection of the production team.
- They interpret the script and develop a directorial concept, which is recorded in the director's production brief (see Unit 4.5 for more details). The concept explains the director's overall vision of

Hint

A good director leads, directs and instructs the performers but also allows the performers to make their own discoveries.

Hint

Blocking involves making decisions about how each scene appears on stage. It also involves directing actors to assist them with their positions, entrances, exits and moves, for example.

the play and will include consideration of themes, issues, characters, lighting, costume, sound, set and style of performance. It will also contain a copy of the script with explanatory notes, sketches and ideas.

- They complete a detailed unit breakdown (see Unit 4.3, pages 74–80) and analysis of script, including careful consideration of the elements of drama (see Unit 2.4, pages 35–7).
- They lead a group of actors and the production team through a process to performance.
- They block the action of the play.

Write and Discuss

1. Work with a partner. Research a theatre director and prepare a brief chronological biography to present to the class. Include the director's personal details, the plays they have directed and their major contributions to theatre and drama. Some directors to choose from are Gale Edwards, David Berthold, Wesley Enoch, Simon Phillips and Michael Kantor.
2. What kind of leader do you think a director should be? To answer this question you may use your recollections of previous performances where you have been directed.
3. Research directing by interviewing a theatre director. He or she may be the director of a school production, amateur theatre production or a professional production. Ask questions that will help you understand the role and responsibilities of the director. Also ask questions about the director's approach to working with actors, and the process they apply to create their directorial concept.

4.2 The Stage Manager

Read Managing a Performance

The stage manager plays a central role in the presentation of performance work. They oversee and coordinate all the various elements of a production. Some of the stage manager's duties are:

- attend all rehearsals and assemble the prompt copy
- include in the prompt copy a full copy of the script, including detailed notes on actors' movements, scene changes and sound and lighting cues

72 Interpreting Drama

- record details of blocking, set changes, lighting and sound cues in columns on a page opposite a page of script
- use a code to ensure the efficient recording of sound and lighting cues, moves of actors and the positions of set items
- use the prompt copy during the performances to call cues and ensure that all the elements of the production run smoothly.

The example of a prompt copy (see below) shows how the cues are written to correspond with the dialogue and stage directions in the script. The use of aerial diagrams in the action column shows the movements of actors in the scene.

The following information will be found on pages in the front or back of the prompt copy:

- **A costume breakdown.** A list of all the actors/characters and the costumes they wear.
- **A props list.** A list of all the props used in the performance, where they are to be placed, who uses them, and in which act and scene they are used.
- **Pre-show setting list.** Outlines what needs to be checked and in place before a show can start.
- **Scene chart.** Charts which actors are in which scenes.
- **Contact list.** A list of the names and addresses of all people involved in the performance.

Hint

During rehearsals, notes on blocking are made in the action column of the prompt copy. Lighting, sound and technical cues are added during the final weeks of rehearsal when the theatre is available and the set and equipment have been installed.

Hint

Set items as well as actors' positions and moves can be indicated by using letters and arrows.

Props	Sound = SFX	Light = LFX	Action
Cissy: bouquet DSR **Margaret:** camera USL **Lisa, Helena:** confetti	• Standby SFX cue 17 (*Wedding March* and cheering) • SFX 17 cue GO	• Standby, followspot CS • Standby LFX cue 24 (full light) • Followspot GO: follow Cissy to DSC	• Actors in position at doors to stairs USR and USL • Cissy Onstage DSR
Scene 13 *Sound of* The Wedding March *and cheering. A spotlight comes up CS. Cissy dives into the spotlight and catches bouquet. As she clutches it to her chest, full lights come up to reveal Margaret, Jeanette, Lisa, Helena and Kat waving and yelling to the departing couple.* **Margaret** (*Taking photos*) Oh Jeanette! Look at Cissy, she's so excited. **Jeanette** Yes, always a bridesmaid though. (*Jeanette and Margaret exit. Kat goes to Cissy.*) **Kat** Good catch, Ciss. **Cissy** Sarah said she'd aim for me. (*Felix enters.*) **Felix** Hi. **Kat** Hi.	• SFX cue 17 FADE OUT	• LFX cue 24 GO X-fade (full light up, followspot down)	Stairs ↖ ↗ Stairs L+H J+M Kat ↓ → Cissy Audience • Jean and Marg. exit USL; Kat to CS • Felix enters USR

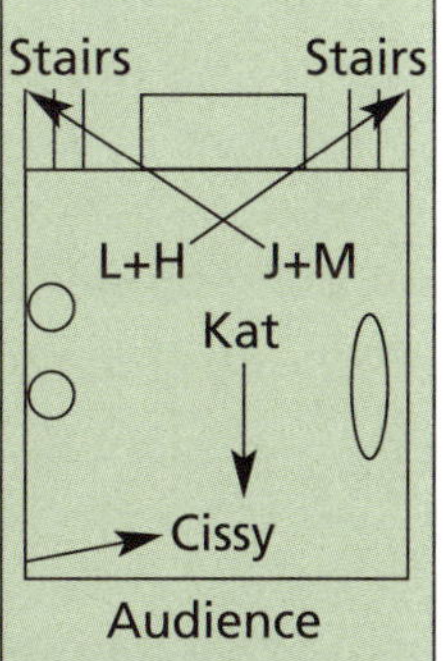

Practitioner Profile

Sophie Clausen
Freelance Production Coordinator and Stage Manager

Sophie is a graduate of the National Institute of Dramatic Art (NIDA) Production Course. She has worked as a stage manager and production coordinator both in Australia and the United Kingdom. She has worked with the Adelaide Festival, Skylark Theatre, and most recently the Melbourne Theatre Company.

I began working in theatre on a voluntary basis through school and with a theatre company. I studied the production course at NIDA, which gave me a broad and extensive understanding of theatre and technical production, with substantial hands-on experience. A stage manager needs strong organisational, time management and people skills. Although stage managers give a special focus to the technical aspects of a production, they need to understand all the elements of a production. They need to keep their cool under pressure, and be practical, communicative and appreciative. A stage manager needs to appreciate the importance of maintaining a safe and supportive environment to enable the director and performers to discover and create.

4.3 Script Detective Work and Stanislavski's System

Read Looking for Clues

In this unit you will undertake exercises that are the first steps in preparing a script for rehearsal and performance. You will:

- read and rehearse a script
- prepare a prompt copy
- develop your understanding of character, incorporating aspects of Stanislavski's System for actors
- work as both director and performer.

Interpreting Drama

Read: The Birth of Realism

A number of developments at the end of the nineteenth century encouraged a change in the way people thought about theatre and acting. One important influence that encouraged change was the development of psychology as a field of study. This branch of science aimed to create a better understanding of the human mind and of personality. This greater understanding influenced the way characters were written about and performed.

Constantin Stanislavski was a Russian performer–director who worked with the Moscow Art Theatre in the early 1900s. He reacted against the 'artificial' acting of the nineteenth century (see the coverage of melodrama in Chapter 6, pages 114–128). Stanislavksi believed that actors should achieve psychological truth in their performances. He devised a series of techniques to help performers create believable characters. These techniques are known as 'the System'. Stanislavski is also known as the founder of the dramatic form termed 'Realism'. Realism attempts to re-create life on stage using realistic settings, lighting, sounds and characters. The theatre term 'the fourth wall' comes from the style of Realism and refers to a proscenium arch stage and the 'invisible' fourth wall the audience looks through to observe the lives of the characters on stage.

The proscenium arch is the 'picture frame' around the proscenium arch stage. The arch and wings hide the backstage area and heighten the illusion of real life on stage.

To study the whole System in depth would take a very long time. We will only look at some important aspects of the System as part of your script detective work. You will be able to develop your understanding in later years of study.

Exercise: Script Detective

The four exercises below take you through the initial exploration and analysis of a script. They incorporate the following aspects of Stanislavski's System: given circumstances, character objectives and building character. The script that has been selected is realistic in style. In your script detective work you will look for clues to help you understand the characters and the scene. Clues can be found in the stage directions and the dialogue.

- **The stage directions.** These are the written instructions to the actor and director. They usually appear in italics.
- **Dialogue.** The main source of information is the dialogue. It will help provide information about the story of the play, and the characters, setting, themes and issues. To complete the script detective work successfully you must carry out all the exercises and complete them in the sequence presented. To complete all these exercises will take more than one session.

Hint

Although a script is provided, you can use the following exercises to work with any script.

Prepare ## Creating a Prompt Copy

To prepare for these exercises, photocopy the script provided and paste it into your logbook (see the example on page 73). Paste the page of script on the left-hand side of an open double page. Divide the right-hand page into three columns: one for sound cues; one for light cues; and one for action and staging. Leave a few blank pages before or after your script to write your responses to the questions in the Step 1 and Step 3 exercises.

Read ## Step 1 Finding the Given Circumstances

Divide into pairs and read through the *Dana and Lee* script below. Alternatively, you could have two volunteers read the parts to the class. Use this first reading to gain an overview of the characters and the situation. As well as playing one particular part, for the purposes of this exercise you also need to think as the director of the script, so you need to use your imagination to try to picture what this script may look like in performance.

Exercise ## The Given Circumstances

After you have read the *Dana and Lee* script, use the following questions to help determine the given circumstances associated with the character you are playing: 'Where am I?', 'What time of day is it?', 'What is the season?', 'Who is here with me?', and, 'Why am I here?' Write your responses in your prompt copy.

Dana and Lee

(**Lee** *sits down and opens his backpack. He pulls out a book and begins to flick through the pages.* **Dana** *approaches from behind. She is eating and quickly finishes the last mouthful. She wipes any stray crumbs from her lips and then wipes her hand on her pants. She hesitates for a moment. She approaches* **Lee** *and sits at the far end of the bench.* **Lee** *is aware of* **Dana**'s *presence but does not look up from his book.*)

Unit 1
Title: The First Try
Sub-objectives:
Lee: To be left alone.
Dana: To get Lee's attention.

Dana Studying?
Lee   What?
Dana Studying? I wouldn't do that in public.
Lee   I'm not studying. *(Pause.)* I'm sort of busy. Do you mind?
Dana Sorry!

Unit 2
Title: The Second Attempt
Sub-objectives:
Lee: To be left alone.
Dana: To get Lee to talk to her.

Dana *(Silence. She moves closer to* **Lee** *and pulls out a stick of gum from her pocket. She offers a piece to* **Lee**.) Gum? *(He shakes his head.* **Dana** *moves closer again.)* Are you going to Vic's on Saturday?
Lee   No. *(He turns away from her.* **Dana** *moves away momentarily. Silence.)*

76 Interpreting Drama

Dana (*She moves closer to him and looks over his shoulder at the book.*) Planning to make a movie?

Lee Can't you take a hint? Listen! Stop hassling me.

Dana What?

Lee You've been hanging around like a bad smell for days. Everywhere I go, you're there. It's giving me the creeps.

Dana I haven't been following you, if that's what you're implying. It's just coincidence. It's not as though this place is big enough to get lost in. What's your problem anyway. You're acting a bit paranoid. (*She moves away from him.*) I only wanted to talk.

Lee Yeah, right! (*He packs the book into his backpack and goes to leave.*)

Dana Where are you going?

Lee Anywhere you're not.

Dana Lee…

Lee Look, I don't want you to come near me, look at me or speak to me. Get it?

Dana Listen, drop kick. You're not that special. Do you think I'd purposely waste my time trying to get a bit of attention from Mr Freeze? You're so arrogant. Typical boy's reaction. Maybe I'm trying to do you a favour. It's not as though you couldn't do with a few friends at the moment. (*There is a long, uncomfortable silence.* **Dana** *tries a different approach.*)

How long do you think you can keep avoiding me?

Lee What?

Dana I know all about it. It's not such a big deal.

Lee What are you talking about?

Dana I spoke to your mum.

Lee Mum?

Dana Yeah, she rang me. I know what happened at your old school. Said she was worried about you. She said not to mention it, but I reckon the sooner you realise people care about you and are worried about you the better. She thought I could help. We were good friends once, remember?

Lee I wish she'd mind her own business.

Dana She only means well.

Lee I know, but she doesn't understand that it just makes things worse. I can deal with it on my own.

Dana I don't think you can. (*Pause.*) What's the big deal. No-one knows what really happened anyway. People love a bit of scandal and gossip. If they don't know the truth, they make it up. They'll forget about it sooner or later.

Lee You don't get it, do you? They won't! There'll always be questions and those stupid whispers. People look at me like I'm a freak. Sometimes I wish I could get as far away from here as possible.

Dana And what use would that be? *(Pause.)* You already give out the 'back off' messages, the way you keep hanging out on your own and dwelling on it. You need to get out more. Losing it all the time doesn't help either. It lets people see how touchy you are. If you keep fighting back you give them ammunition. I know what it's like. *(Pause.)* Everyone makes mistakes. *(Pause.)* I've watched you clinging to that 'mood' all term like you want it to be part of you, and I know you're not like that. *(A long pause. Silence.)* Okay, I'll go. I'm obviously annoying you. (**Dana** *goes to leave.*)

Lee What happened, I can deal with. Wrong place, wrong time I guess. All I wanted was a clean start. But I think my reputation got here a long time before I did. *(Pause.)* Life sucks.

Dana *(Pause.)* Maybe. (**Dana** *waits and then goes to leave.*)

Lee *(Pause.)* Maybe what?

Dana Nothing.

Lee Great advice. *(Pause.)* Sorry.

Dana You're pushing it, Lee.

Lee I said sorry! *(A long pause.)*

Dana Have you got any plans for Friday? *(Pause.)* Yes or no?

Lee *(Pause.)* Friday?

Dana Do you want to see *Time* on Friday? I hear it's pretty wild. *(Pause.)* At least in a film I won't be able to talk to you.

Lee What makes me think that's almost impossible? Sorry. Again.

Dana Bell's gone. I've got double dance now and I'm not going to wait around for your answer.

Lee *(Pause.)* Look, I just think I need…

Dana I reckon you think too much. It's not such a hard decision. Yes or no?

Lee Friday? I want to see that. *(A long pause.)* Can I let you know?

Dana *(She starts to exit.)* Look, let's just say seven o'clock out the front. If you're there you're there, if you're not you're not.

Lee Okay, sure.

Dana I've really got to go. See you.

(**Dana** *exits and* **Lee** *sits down. He thinks for a moment. And then, remembering the time, grabs his backpack and hurries offstage.*)

Read ## Step 2 Unit Breakdown: Finding Character Objectives

The 'objective' is what the character wants to achieve. Sometimes the character can have more than one objective, and sometimes the character does not achieve their objectives. Objectives can be explicit or hidden. A character's objective is what motivates them to behave the way they do. Examples of objectives are to win the game, to marry, to keep things the way they have always been, to get the job, to persuade and to deceive.

Stanislavski believed that each character in a play aims to achieve their 'super objective'. To achieve their super objective, the character needs to achieve sub-objectives in each scene of the play. The steps a character takes to achieve sub-objectives can be found in script units.

Exercise ## Finding Units and Sub-Objectives

A unit breakdown shows the building blocks of a script. The building blocks give an overview of the way tension is used in the script and can also be used to help identify character objectives. Each unit contains a distinct moment of action, an idea, point or issue being discussed.

Follow the steps below to complete a unit breakdown of the *Dana and Lee* script. The first two units have been done for you.

- Using a pencil, draw a line after the line of dialogue or stage direction that you feel ends a unit.
- Label the unit with a title that you feel sums up what the unit is about, for example 'You Don't Love Me', 'The Plan' or 'Mum's Worries'.
- Identify your character's objective in each unit (the sub-objective) and identify the character's overall objective in the scene.
- Identify one unit in the script that you feel contains the climactic moment. Pick the precise moment or 'beat' in the rhythm that you feel is the climactic moment. Justify your choice.

Hint

Beginnings and ends of units are indicated by entrances and exits of characters, changes in conversation, or changes in action, mood or tension.

Read ## Step 3 Second Reading: Building Your Character

Read the *Dana and Lee* script a second time, and then begin to perform as the characters in the situation. This requires the partial adoption of the characters by considering the use of body language and voice, delivery of lines and staging. In this second reading, also consider how the progression of units helps to build tension and leads to the climactic moment.

Scripts: Interpretation and Presentation 79

Hint

The sort of language the character uses can provide you with information about the character's personality, situation and background.

Write and Discuss

Once you have finished a performed reading, complete the following questions and tasks to help develop your understanding of your character. Record your responses in your prompt copy.

1. What sort of language does your character use? For example, does the character use formal or informal language?
2. What does the rhythm of the character's speech tell you about the energy of the character? Can you find examples from the script?
3. Subtext is the meaning behind a line. Sometimes the meaning is obvious; at other times it is more subtle. In performance, our selective use of body language and timing helps to make the subtext more apparent to the audience. What thoughts lie behind your character's lines? What body language, gestures, pose and mannerisms, for example, will you use to communicate the character's subtext?
4. Are there any pauses in the character's dialogue? If so, what thoughts lie behind the pauses? How long should the pause(s) be held? Why? What impact do the pauses have on the mood and atmosphere of the script?
5. What do other characters say about each other? What does this information tell you about the characters?
6. What is the character's status in relation to the other characters? What evidence from the script can you find to support your opinion?
7. Complete a detailed character biography (see Unit 3.5, pages 56–8). Begin the biography by using the information about your character that is contained in the script. Then add information of your own.

4.4 Rehearsing and Performing Scripts

Read — Rehearsing and Performing

The exercises you completed in Unit 4.3 (pages 74–80) are the three steps you need to complete before you rehearse and perform scripts. To refresh your memory, they are listed below:

- **Step 1.** Finding the given circumstances.
- **Step 2.** Unit breakdown: Finding character objectives.
- **Step 3.** Second reading: Building your character.

The remaining steps are:

- **Step 4.** Rehearsals: Exploring and testing ideas.
- **Step 5.** Performance: Being the character.
- **Step 6.** Evaluation: Looking for improvement.

In Steps 4 to 6 you will explore the following aspects of Stanislavski's System: relaxation, emotion memory, 'the magic if', and concentration.

Read — Step 4 Rehearsals: Exploring and Testing Ideas

The rehearsal process involves the following stages:

- Continue to read and rehearse the script. Record all blocking in the action column of your prompt copy. Include decisions for hand props, movements, positions of actors, delivery of dialogue, character objectives, the building of tension to the climactic moment, and so on.
- Explore how the use of space and levels can add meaning to your performance. For example, how can the status of the characters be emphasised by using levels and/or distances from other characters?
- Improvise situations that show the characters 'outside' the time and place indicated in the script.
- Continue to develop your character by adding to the character biography. You can also incorporate the following techniques from Stanislavski's System: relaxation, emotion memory and 'the magic if' (see page 82).
- Memorise lines once all decisions have been made.
- Make final refinements to blocking, lighting, sound and performance work.

Hint

It is important to develop the habit of writing notes during rehearsals. These notes can be used to reflect on your character work and the general interpretation of the script. You should use a pencil for notations on your script so that corrections and alterations can be made easily.

Hint

It is best to leave the memorising of lines until last because the way you deliver a line depends on your interaction with other actors. It also depends on consideration of important factors. If you learn your lines too soon, it is difficult to change the way the line is said later.

Hint

Repetition is the best way to memorise lines. You should only memorise small chunks of script at a time. It is also helpful to imagine the situation the character is in as you memorise the line.

Hint

Methods of relaxation have been used for centuries to help people not only relieve tension but achieve in particular areas. Today many professional sporting clubs employ sports psychologists who use relaxation and visualisation techniques to help players perform well. Relaxation has the same benefits for performers who would like to improve their performance work.

- Complete a technical rehearsal. This is where the focus is placed on the movement of scene changes and the light and sound cues. Finalise cues in the prompt copy.
- Complete a dress rehearsal. This is where you perform with all the required elements and without interruption, as though it is the actual performance.

Exercise Techniques from Stanislavski's System

Relaxation

Relaxation is an ideal technique to use in conjunction with 'the magic if' and emotion memory exercises to develop character. When we are relaxed, our imagination is heightened, helping us recall and create feelings and sensations.

Lie on the floor and progressively tense and release different body parts. Breathe in as you tense the muscles, and exhale as you relax them. When you are completely relaxed, imagine you are the character in various situations. Use your imagination to explore the character's feelings and thoughts.

Emotion Memory

Emotion memory requires you to recall memories of the emotions you felt when you were in a situation that is similar to the situation the character is in. For example, you may be playing the role of a character who is lost in a strange city. In this instance you should recall a time when you were lost to help evoke the feelings associated with the experience of being lost.

'The Magic If'

You may have to play a character in a situation that is outside your own life experience. The question 'What if…?' helps you to play your character truthfully by utilising the power of the imagination to vividly create experiences and feelings. By asking this question you are putting yourself in an imaginary situation and determining how you would react. For example, you may never have been first in a race. Asking yourself 'What if I won a race?' leads you to ask questions such as 'How would I feel?' or 'What would I do at the moment I crossed the finish line?'

Read Step 5 Performance: Being the Character

In the script work in this chapter you have looked at the style of Realism. This style attempts to re-create life on stage. The performers in a realistic play need to use their skills of concentration and focus to become absorbed in the character and reduce their awareness of the audience. Stanislavski believed that in realistic acting the performer is 90 per cent being the character and 10 per cent aware as the performer. Stanislavski believed that, to achieve this, the performer needed to concentrate and focus their attention to help them become more deeply involved in their character.

Exercise: Concentration

Concentration is the ability of the performer to maintain their involvement in their character and the performance by ignoring external and internal distractions. An external distraction may be a distant noise outside the performing area or an unexpected event that happens on stage. An internal distraction is where the mind wanders from pretending to be the character in the situation and instead thinks about other things. If the performer is totally engaged in the performance and the character, and resists being distracted, the audience will be more convinced that the performance is truthful.

Stanislavski used an exercise called 'Circles of Attention' to explain how concentration is maintained in performance.

Circles of Attention

Work with a partner. Create two characters and set them in an improvised situation within a room of your choosing. At the beginning of the improvisation, their circle of attention should encompass the whole of the performance area. The performers utilise the skill of concentration to limit their awareness of the audience and to maintain focus. On a given signal from the group leader, the circle of attention becomes smaller until it is only a small area around the two actors.

Example: The circle of attention encompasses the whole performance space. Two people are inside an art gallery. The circle of attention reduces. The two visitors examine a large glass cabinet of pottery work. The circle of attention reduces even further. The two visitors examine a program of art works, looking for the name of an artist.

Challenge

During the Circles of Attention exercise, audience members can occasionally cough, stand or move to a different seat. The performers are to ignore these distractions and maintain their concentration by focusing on the situation.

Scripts: Interpretation and Presentation

Step 6 Evaluation: Looking for Improvement

After you have performed, it is important to evaluate the performance. In theatre jargon this is also known as the 'post mortem'. This is an opportunity for the director, the performers and the production team to consider the strengths of the performance and the areas for improvement. Often the post mortem helps to build a deeper understanding of the play and its message.

Dana and Lee

Continue developing the *Dana and Lee* script (pages 76–78) to performance by completing the requirements for Steps 4 to 6. You will need to:

- rehearse the script with your partner; based on the information you have discovered, incorporate decisions about character, setting and how the scene is played
- include the use of sound and lighting, if you have access to equipment
- write all your cues in your prompt copy so that the lighting and sound operators are able to follow your instructions
- present your interpretation to the class.

Hint

Memorise all your lines. This will make your performance of the script more enjoyable to watch. Reading a script limits the performer's ability to use body language and be absorbed in the character.

Write and Discuss

Use the following tasks to evaluate your work and the work of others.

1. Briefly describe the process you went through to gain an understanding of the *Dana and Lee* script.
2. Outline any discoveries you made about the characters or the situation.
3. Compare your interpretation of the script with one other interpretation. What were the similarities and differences? Can you offer an explanation for the differences in interpretation?
4. Compare your character interpretation with a class member who played the same character as you. What were the similarities and differences? Can you offer an explanation for the differences in interpretation?
5. Describe how one interpretation of *Dana and Lee* best demonstrated an understanding of the building of tension to the climactic moment. How was this achieved? In your discussion refer to the use of rhythm, pace, timing and energy.

4.5 Directorial Concept and the Elements of Production

Directorial Concept

The 'directorial concept' is the director's vision for the play. The concept will include consideration of:
- the characters, setting and era of the play
- the message, themes and issues of the play
- the performance space
- the target audience
- the elements of production.

The designers of costume, set, lighting and sound work closely with the director to realise the directorial concept in the staging of a production. The designers use the directorial concept as the basis for their designs.

The Elements of Production

The 'elements of production' in a performance are:
- lighting
- sound
- set
- costume.

These elements of production serve an important function in the performance of a play. Through the power of symbol, they help to convey information about atmosphere, themes and character.

The designers of set and costume will consider the following basic design elements and principles when formulating their ideas.

- **Design Elements**: line and its direction, shape, texture, proportion, colour, tone and size.
- **Design Principles**: dominance, balance, harmony, contrast, variety, radiation, gradation, repetition, symmetry, asymmetry.

Each designer will consider their own particular requirements in their initial planning. The factors to be considered as part of each design discipline are as follows.

- **Costume Design**: Costumes required, types of garments, colours, textures, accessories, patterns on fabric, comfort and practicality for the performers.
- **Set Design**: The stage space, use of vertical and horizontal lines, use of angles, use of shapes (circles, squares, and so on), colour, texture, levels, furniture, entrances and exits, locations of the action, symbolic images.
- **Lighting Design**: Use of light and shadow, sense of warmth or coolness, colour, pattern, highlight, silhouette, spotlighting, washes.

- **Sound Design**: Use of recorded music, sound effects, soundscapes, voice-overs, live music, percussion.

Write and Discuss

Refer to the design websites listed for this chapter at **hi.com.au/centrestage**. Visit some of these websites and select one costume or set design that is illustrated on the site. Copy the image to a Word document. Then type a dot-point list that evaluates your chosen design. Although you may not know the play for which the design is intended, comment on the designer's use of the design elements and principals. Explain how the design may help establish atmosphere, communicate character or work symbolically.

Read *Summer of the Aliens* by Louis Nowra

The following example provides a description of a production and demonstrates how the elements of production evolve from the directorial concept.

Synopsis

Louis Nowra's play *Summer of the Aliens* opens with the older Lewis as narrator. He takes us back into his memories as a boy growing up in Broadmeadows, Victoria. The young Lewis has an active imagination and indulges his obsession with flying saucers to escape from the harsher realities of his world.

Social, Historical and Political Context

The play is set in Australia in the early 1960s. This was a frightening time for the world, as America, believing in the threat of Communism, was on the verge of bombing Cuba during what was known as the Cuban missile crisis. Australia was also dealing with the impact of the many new immigrants who were arriving from Europe during this period to begin a new life. Despite its dark background and some disturbing moments the play is funny, provocative and moving; it will appeal to a broad audience.

Broadmeadows is a northern suburb of Melbourne. In the 1960s it was largely made up of paddocks with a few housing estates.

Intention and Performance Style

The play is about a rite of passage from youth to adulthood. The use of a realistic acting style will encourage the audience to consider the issues of racism, sexuality, and abuse, as believable characters will encourage empathy. At points in the action the older Lewis will speak to his younger self. This dramatic technique will help the audience identify with the changes Lewis goes through.

Although the play will be realistic in acting style, the set will be symbolic to show that what we see on stage are the memories of the older Lewis. The performances of some of the other characters will be stylised to help convey the young Lewis's perspective.

Performance Space

The play will be performed in a 250-seat auditorium with a thrust stage.

Set Design

The set is intended to look artificial. The stage floor is raked and will be covered in dry grass to represent the paddocks of Broadmeadows. A large cyclorama will be lit in certain colours to show times of day. At its base will be three miniature houses to suggest the rest of the housing estate. The housing estate where the young Lewis lives must seem vast, empty, dull and monotonous. The people who live there seem out of place. Three clouds will be painted on the cyclorama and they are intended to look artificial. It is summer so everything must look hot and dry. Lewis's house is represented by only one room, the kitchen. It will be decorated in the style of the 1960s. The colours of lemon yellow and pastel pink will give it a homely feel.

Costume Design

The period is important. The costumes will be researched and designed to be as suggestive of the early 1960s as possible. Hair styles should also be typical of the period. Performers will have their hair styled or wear wigs as appropriate. Research will be conducted to see how make-up was applied during this period. Each character will be distinguished by the colour and tone of their costume. The costumes will have a hint of roughness about them to indicate the characters' economic situations. The angel costumes will look impressive but homemade. They will look more powerful under certain lighting.

Lighting Design

The general lighting will be composed of strong washes in straw colour and in blue. Lewis's house will be lit by profile spots (see Glossary) to isolate scenes in that location. Other areas will also be isolated for certain scenes. There will be two shades of blue gels used for the floods on the cyclorama to indicate day and night. The fading of lights on the cyclorama will be very important for establishing mood. Special lighting effects include the flying saucer effect, fibre optic lights for the miniature houses and a fire effect for the final scene of the play.

Sound Design

The play includes a few radio announcements from the period; these will have to be researched. Sound effects include budgie noises, wind, rain, thunder, crickets and cicadas. Music from the era is required in some scenes. Some atmospheric sounds and music will be specially composed by the designer for certain scenes. The atmosphere at certain moments should be gripping.

Exercise: Theatre Design Project

Create a set and/or costume design using the software program Stagestruck. Choose a play to design for. If designing a set focus on two particular scenes in the play; if designing a costume focus on two characters. If you do not have time to read a full-length play, choose a one-act play or a play you have studied in another subject.

Before you choose particular scenes or characters to design for, create a directorial concept for your play. Use the following questions to help you.

- **Performance Style**. What style will the play be performed in? Why?
- **Themes and Issues**. What are the themes and messages of the play?
- **Target Audience**. Who is the target audience and why is this play appropriate for them?
- **Performance Space**. Where will the play be performed? Why is this an appropriate space for your performance?
- **Set Design**. Which scenes will you design a set for? What are the locations of the scenes? What is the predominant mood or atmosphere of the play? How can colour, shape, scale of set pieces, and so on, help establish symbol and atmosphere?
- **Costume Design**. Which characters will you design costume for? What are the features of each character's personality? How will colour, garment and texture portray personality? What are the dramatic needs of the characters in each scene and how will the costume design support these? Consider time period, season, occupation, and so on.

Write and Discuss

Visit the website of Melbourne's Arena Theatre Company at: **hi.com.au/centrestage**. View the images and video clips of the performances and read the descriptions of the productions. Identify some of the features of set, costume and multimedia used in an Arena Theatre Company performance. Who is the target audience for this company?

4.6 The Designers

Read

Putting It All Together

We have already looked at the role of the director, the stage manager and the performer in the interpretation and performance of scripts. In this unit we will further examine the roles of the production team, who are an essential component in realising the directorial concept. Although each area contributes its own creative ideas, all areas are united by the directorial concept. This collaboration between the director and the designers helps to ensure the final production has a sense of unity and cohesion. The main responsibilities of each role are listed under each production area.

Hint

Professional directors rarely make decisions about set, costume, lighting and sound in isolation. Often the development of the directorial concept is a collaborative effort, involving all the designers.

Practitioner Profile

Richard Jeziorny
Freelance Set Designer

Richard graduated from the National Institute of Dramatic Art in 1981, completing a Diploma of Design. He has worked for theatre, film and television. Richard is currently designing *Urban Dream Capsule* for the Festival de Theatre des Ameriques in Montreal, Canada, and for the London International Festival of Theatre.

Designing for the theatre is not an isolated creative act. Ideas emerge from a detailed study of the text, and from research and intense discussions with the creative team. In workshops I have given with actors, dancers and musicians, we are constantly amazed at the similarity of language we use. We talk about 'line' in visual terms but also as the connection between two points (in the text, on the floor and in the space). We talk about mass, space and shape (the shape of a piece of music and of the body of a scene). We talk about colour and texture, of rhythm and symmetry and of proportion, focus and unity. Making theatre is about a keen observation of life in all its detail and absurdity, and a transfer of this observation to the stage.

Scripts: Interpretation and Presentation

Read Set Designer

- Considers the appearance and style of the set, taking into account the requirements of the directorial concept.
- Considers the use of colour, texture and shape and how they will work with the designs for costume and lighting.
- Considers practical issues, such as the venue, the size of the performing area, the entrances and exits of actors and the ease of scene changes.
- Provides 1:25 scale drawings and a three-dimensional model of the set.

Read Lighting and Sound Designer

- Designs lighting and sound to suit the requirements of the directorial concept.
- Considers practical lighting issues, such as whether the actors can be seen and whether special effects are achievable.
- Considers practical sound issues such as the coordination of technical equipment and the use of microphones.
- Finds and records all the necessary music, sounds and sound effects.

Practitioner Profile

Gavan Swift

Lighting Designer

Gavan Swift graduated from the National Institute of Dramatic Art in 1994. He has designed lighting for many productions, including *Steel City*, *The John Wayne Principle*, *Little Shop of Horrors* and *The Winter's Tale*.

> *The basic purpose of lighting in theatre is illumination. If we can't see what is happening, then the lighting has failed the production. To carry this point further, what we do not light is as important as what we do light. Lighting is a selective art, where the lighting designer chooses what the audience will and will not see. He or she uses the lighting to tell the audience where to look, what time of day it is, what the mood is and where the scene takes place. The role of the lighting designer is to work with the director, set designer, costume designer and actors to create appropriately designed lighting that forms a creative and integral part of the production.*

Interpreting Drama

- Selects lanterns and colours of gels, and considers how they contribute to mood and atmosphere; assesses the effect of lighting on set and costume designs.
- Prepares a 1:25 scale drawing of all lamps and their positions.
- Assists the director to make artistic decisions about lighting states and lighting changes.
- Provides a running cue sheet of all lighting and sound cues.

A lighting state contains particular lamps that are set at certain levels. There can be several lighting states within one scene.

Costume Designer

- Designs costumes to suit the requirements of the directorial concept; considers, for example, the period and the style of performance.
- Considers practical issues, such as fitting of costumes, costume changes and whether the actors can move freely in the costumes.
- Makes artistic decisions in consultation with the director, such as choice of fabric, fabric colours and style of costumes.
- Prepares and presents renderings of all costumes for all characters.
- Constructs costumes that need to be specially made.

A costume 'rendering' is an illustration of a costume design. The rendering can be presented as a sketch, collage, watercolour or computer-aided design. The rendering will include annotations on how the costume is constructed, and may be accompanied with samples of fabrics and colours.

Practitioner Profile

Gayle MacGregor

Wardrobe Coordinator, Queensland Theatre Company

Gayle began working for the Queensland Theatre Company while at fashion college. She worked as a casual machinist and is now wardrobe supervisor.

How a costume fits, restricts or enhances movement is critical to the actor's performance. Rehearsal costumes are essential because they allow the director and actor to make final decisions about the costume's suitability. Wardrobe is then able to build the costume to the director's, designer's and actor's needs.

Correct training in the area of theatre costuming is essential. It is rare to find an apprenticeship or on-the-job training. My advice to those wishing to make a career out of theatre costume would be to learn tact, diplomacy and patience. Listen to your actors, because building a good working relationship with them from day one of rehearsal will make your life a lot easier further down the track and make each production more rewarding.

Read Publicity and Marketing Coordinator

- Coordinates the design of posters and publicity materials with reference to the directorial concept.
- Works with graphic designers, printers, media and distribution agencies.
- Checks spelling and information details on all copy.
- Devises innovative ways to publicise the performance, including functions, previews and charity events.
- Coordinates the design and content of the program.
- Writes press releases to help promote the sale of tickets for performances.

Practitioner Profile

Jenni Carbins
Freelance Marketing Consultant

Once marketing manager in charge of building the image of Company B Belvoir in Sydney, Jenni now has a broad range of clients across the cultural and entertainment industries.

Marketing the arts is unlike any other form of product marketing. While most products are sold after extensive research into consumer needs, promoting the arts begins with a person's artistic vision and it is up to the arts marketer to find an audience.

It is therefore important to accurately interpret what happens on the stage—through graphics and other communication tools, such as promotional material, media releases and direct-mail campaigns—in order to attract a sector of the population that will appreciate the work. Although the bottom line is 'bums on seats', the marketer also considers developing new audiences so a production that challenges society's perceptions is experienced by the widest—not only the biggest—audience possible.

4.7 Performance Task: Interpreting Script

Read — The Task

In pairs or small groups, you are to prepare a script and perform it for an audience. You are to find your own script or use one of the scripts provided at the end of this chapter. Performing arts bookshops and script websites are good sources for finding scripts. Try to avoid using film scripts as these often need to be adapted substantially to make them appropriate for live performance. For successful completion of this performance task you are required to:

- choose a script
- prepare a prompt copy
- include, in the front of the prompt copy, written answers to script detective work (see Unit 4.3, pages 74–80)
- clearly describe your directorial concept. This will include a discussion of how the elements of production—set, lighting, costume and sound—will be unified.
- use sketches and include samples of colours and fabrics, for example, to help illustrate your ideas
- follow the steps in rehearsing and performing a scene (see Unit 4.4, pages 81–84)
- record all your responses in your prompt copy
- give a short, verbal presentation to the class that summarises your directorial concept for the script and how you would perform it if you had access to a full production team.

Hint

You may like to think of how your set or costume designs could be used in a symbolic way to help establish mood and atmosphere, and to convey some of the broader issues of the script.

Prepare — Rehearsing and Performing Script

Follow the steps below to prepare for the performance task.

1. Choose a script and cast the roles.
2. Paste a copy of the script into your logbook. Use the example of the prompt copy in Unit 4.2 (page 73). Even if you do not have access to sound and lighting equipment, you can record your creative ideas for sound effects and lighting cues. Remember to leave pages for the written responses.
3. Follow the script detective steps (see Unit 4.3, pages 74–80).
4. Follow the rehearsing and performing scripts steps (see Unit 4.4, pages 81–84).
5. Write a character biography for your character.
6. Write a point-form directorial concept for the extract you choose to perform. Your concept will identify themes and issues, as well as the predominant atmosphere. Your concept will also explain how costume, set, lighting and sound will help to communicate themes and issues.

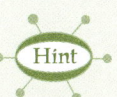

Hint

When rehearsing, it is important to remain focused as the character. Consciously engage yourself as the character in the scene and with the other character. This will encourage more truthful interaction between you and the other performer.

Scripts: Interpretation and Presentation

The prompt copy will be assessed in terms of:
- presentation and layout
- inclusion of required elements
- degree of sophistication in interpretation of the script.

Evaluate

Performance Checklist

You and your teacher will evaluate your work individually using a list of criteria. These criteria relate to your achievements in this task. Some criteria will relate to the achievement of the group. The criteria are listed on the evaluation sheet at the end of this chapter and will be used to evaluate your ability to:

- sustain and develop character in performance
- select and incorporate voice that is suitable for character
- select and incorporate effective body language and movement
- effectively use the performance space
- develop a script into a coherent performance
- make suitable choices for lighting, sound and costume.

Hint

If you are planning to use lighting or sound refer to Appendixes 5 and 6 for sample lighting and sound cue sheets. Appendixes 7 and 8 provide guidelines for designing make-up and costumes.

Read

Home

Characters: 1 female, 2 male

The play *Home* was commisssioned by Shopfront Youth Theatre for Young People; it was written by P. P. Cranney. The play explores the concept of 'home' through two story-lines: that of a girl who runs away from her home and that of two refugees to Australia.

Merinda and Ali are brother and sister; they have escaped their war torn country without their parents and family. They are staying with their uncle in Australia. Ali is having difficulty adjusting to his new home and is still affected by memories of war. His sister Merinda has adapted more quickly and wants to belong to her new country. In this scene, Ali and Merinda come into conflict over Sammy, a boy Merinda has met.

Scene 13
Homelands #5: Uncle's Place

(In a bedroom in their uncle's flat, **Ali** *and* **Merinda** *are sleeping in separate single beds. We can hear traffic noise—one particular loud backfire causes* **Ali** *to start thrashing about in his bed as if in a nightmare.* **Merinda** *gets up, crosses to his bedside and tries to soothe him.)*

Merinda   It's all right, Ali, it's all right! It's only the traffic. Sleep, my brother, sleep. Everything's all right.

*(***Ali*** drifts back to a more peaceful sleep.)*

(To audience) Our mother writes to us—finally! The situation has not improved back home. Stay in Australia as long as you can, she says. She gives us an address of an uncle who we have never

94 Interpreting Drama

met. He lets us move into his tiny flat in a block of redbrick units near a busy road. I'd become used to the silence of the bush that surrounded the barracks, and here the noise of the traffic, night and day, makes it difficult for me to sleep. At least I don't suffer the nightmares that torture Ali more and more.

(She leaves her sleeping brother, and begins to quietly get ready for the day. It is now morning: as **Merinda** *energetically prepares for school and work,* **Ali** *rises sluggishly, without enthusiasm for the new day. He turns on the TV and slumps down in front of it.)*

Merinda What will you do today, Ali?

Ali The same as I did yesterday and the day before that: I'll wait.

Merinda But we have no idea when the war might end. (*No response*) Mum wouldn't say that it is too dangerous to come home if it wasn't true.

Ali She says that to protect us—we should be there to protect her.

Merinda There's nothing we can do. If you would accept that, if you would try to learn English, or get a job, instead of just sitting all day watching (*TV*).

Ali Watching our homeland being destroyed—bombed and burnt to the ground. Our people being killed.

Merinda We can do nothing.

Ali Then that's all I'm doing. Leave me alone.

Merinda But it's not good for you to just sit and—

Ali I'm sick of your nagging and whining.

Merinda Ali, please …

Ali Shut up!

(Maybe he kicks or throws something. **Merinda** *is silenced by the depth of his anger. She continues to prepare to go out.)*

Merinda I'll be going straight from school to work tonight. I'm on the late shift, you and uncle will have to feed yourselves.

*(***Ali** *doesn't reply.)*

There is plenty in the fridge … *(Still no reply)* See you later.

*(***Merinda** *leaves.* **Ali** *flicks the remote control at the TV.)*

News Report NATO continued its air strikes against the besieged city overnight despite growing concerns about mounting civilian casualties …

A passenger train carrying up to three hundred civilian commuters, including children …

Outside the capital, Government forces clashed with Liberation Army rebels in a bloody confrontation …

*(The news fades out [or under] the sounds of the battle we have heard before in the earlier 'War Zone' scene. The room becomes a battlefield; we are in the War Zone again. Perhaps among the other images there is the image of **Ali** and **Merinda**'s **Mother** being pushed around and assaulted by soldiers. The War Zone sound effects crescendo, **Ali** hurls the remote control at the TV, goes into his bedroom and throws himself on his bed. The War Zone effects fade out.)*

*(Later that night, **Merinda** enters the flat with a boy, **Sammy**. **Sammy** waits by the entrance. **Merinda** enters the bedroom. **Ali** stirs in his bed.)*

Ali Merinda?

Merinda Sorry to wake you. Have you eaten yet?

Ali I'm not hungry.

Merinda Uncle?

Ali Probably at the club. Poker machines! ... What are you doing? It's late. Who's that out there with you?

Merinda I have no class in the morning. I'm going to the movies with a friend.

Ali You brought someone here?

Merinda Yes, I've brought a friend home. We're going to see a film.

Ali You think so, eh? If it's one of those Australian girls, I don't think you'll be going anywhere.

*(**Ali** sees **Sammy** waiting. **Merinda** follows out.)*

Merinda Ali, Sammy's not a girl ...

Sammy Not the last time I looked anyway.

Merinda Ali, this is Sammy.

Sammy Hello, Ali, nice to meet you.

*(**Sammy** puts out his hand, but **Ali** does not take it. **Ali** directs most of the following to **Merinda**.)*

Ali He speaks—

Merinda Our language, yes. And his English is good too.

Sammy 'How are you going, mate.'

*(**Sammy** and **Merinda** laugh.)*

Merinda Sammy works with me at McDonalds.

Sammy Yeah, take my word for it: don't eat there unless it's an emergency—and even then think twice!

Ali Why have you brought him here—into our home?

Merinda So this is your home now—good, you must be feeling better.

Ali I'm not joking. Why have you brought him here?

Merinda He's taking me to the movies. *(To **Sammy**)* I'm ready, let's go.

Sammy Listen, Ali, it's really ... *(all right)*

Ali That's not our language he speaks.

Merinda Yes, it is—it's the same as ours.

Ali Where are you from?

Merinda Ali, he's been in Australia five years …
Ali I asked where is he from? That accent—from the North.
Sammy Originally, my people—(*came from*)
Ali Your people are slaughtering our people.
Merinda Ali, don't say such stupid things.
Ali We are exiled in this stupid country because your people are killing our people—my father, my family.
Merinda No, Ali, please, don't talk like this.
Sammy Our family came to Australia, too, because we were driven out by war.
Ali A war that your people started.
Merinda Sammy didn't start the war. People like us don't make wars. Governments make the wars.
Ali How could you bring this person to this house. If you don't care about my feelings—
Merinda I do care about—
Ali (*Over her*) If you don't care about my feelings, think of your uncle—you know he lost his family, his homeland, because of these people …
Sammy Merinda, I'd better go—
Merinda Wait, we're going together, to the movies.
(**Ali** *pulls his sister back.*)
Ali You're not going anywhere with scum like this.
Merinda Ali!
Sammy Ali, you better take it easy.
Ali Get out of here—get out of here now!
(**Ali** *pushes* **Sammy** *back toward the door.* **Sammy** *would like to retaliate, but doesn't for* **Merinda***'s sake.*)
Sammy I'll go now, Merinda. This was a mistake.
Merinda No, please, wait—
Sammy I'll see you at work tomorrow.
Ali Merinda will not be returning to work.
(**Sammy** *goes.* **Merinda** *pulls away from* **Ali**.)
Merinda Ali, how could you? You are not my father! You can't do this to me!
Ali I'm glad your father is not here to be shamed by you like this.
Merinda My father shamed?
Ali Yes, to see you become friends—become lovers maybe—with people who want to kill us, drive us from our own land.
Merinda Sammy and his family came here before this war. They were driven out of their homeland by another war. Sammy has nothing to do with what is happening to us.
Ali His people—his people right now are waging war on us.

Merinda	Sammy is not waging war on us. We are in Australia now. We are not at war in Australia.
Ali	I am telling you—you will not have anything to do with his kind——is that clear?
Merinda	And you say I shame our father? My father's soul was never as bitter and poisoned as yours. You're the one who shames our father's memory.

(**Ali** *hits her across the face, shocking himself as he does so.* **Merinda** *does not retaliate—she picks up her things and leaves the flat, perhaps chasing after* **Sammy**. **Ali** *does not attempt to stop her or follow her.*)

(**Ali** *stands alone. The sound effects of the War Zone fade up and out.*)

Read ## *Dinkum Assorted* by Linda Aronson

Characters: 3 female (2 main parts; 1 minor)

Dinkum Assorted by Linda Aronson is set in an Australian country town in the mid 1940s. The women at the local Dinkum biscuit factory have taken the places of their husbands and boyfriends who have gone to fight in the war. Connie and Joan both work in the factory.

Connie is an immigrant from Manchester in England. She works as the tea lady and is unpopular with the other women because they believe she is a spy for the management. Joan has arrived in the town to escape from her husband. She wants a divorce, and with Connie's help begins a custody battle for her daughter, Helen. As an outsider, Joan is also unpopular with the women in the factory who see her 'city ways' as a bit snobbish. Connie has given Joan accommodation and has become attached to her. She hopes Joan will bring her daughter to live in the town. In this scene Connie discovers Joan has other plans, which involve Douglas, a man she has met in the town and formed a relationship with. Millie, who plays a minor role in this extract, is another worker in the factory.

Scene Six

(*The factory dayroom.* **Joan** *is on the phone to* **Douglas**, *in Sydney.*)

Joan	Yes, I'm still here. (*Angrily*) No, you listen … well, I left everything for you! (*Anxiously*) How can I believe that, Douglas? How can I?
Millie	(*off*) Coming, Mrs Barron!
Joan	Look, I can't talk …
Connie	(*off*) Hurry up, slowcoach.
Joan	I have to go. I'll write. Tonight! Come to you tonight! How can I, Douglas? I have to go.

(*She hurriedly hangs up, shaken.* **Connie** *enters with the trolley.*)

Connie	What are you doing still here? Look at the time, you're supposed to be at the solicitors!

Joan I'll go later, then I can help you get things ready for tomorrow …

Connie (*Irritably*) Look, I was organising refreshments for big board meetings before you could wipe your nose. Go and get your coat. (*Uncomfortably*) And here.

(She gets out an envelope, and hands it to **Joan**, *who opens it. It contains banknotes.)*

Joan I can't keep taking this!

Connie It's not for you, it's for Helen. If we want her back you're going to have to fight …

Joan I don't know whether I want to fight! Not this way, not in the courts …

*(***Connie** *looks at her in amazement which instantly turns to irritation. She begins vigorously cleaning the trolley.)*

Connie (*Irritably*) This is no time for soul-searching. Pull yourself together—she's your child and you're responsible for her! And you can get home earlier tonight, I nearly burnt the bottom out of a saucepan keeping supper hot for you …

(Pause.)

Joan Connie, I've told you, I don't want supper made for me.

Connie Oh, you're high and mighty for someone who can hardly pay their rent!

Joan I just don't want supper thank you very much, it's very kind of you, but I—

Connie (*Furiously*) Don't have it then, no skin off my nose, bloody Lady Muck!

Joan I didn't ask you to do all these things for me …

*(***Connie** *stares at her.)*

Connie You've had another letter from him, haven't you, that's what's wrong with you.

Joan Nothing is wrong with me.

Connie From Douglas! From the boyfriend!

Joan I'm not discussing my personal life here …

Connie You fool! They're putting him up to it. It's a trap! They want proof for the court case! If you put one foot out of line they'll take that child!

Joan I'm not discussing this.

(They confront each other.)

Connie (*Menacingly*) Go to that solicitor.

Joan Leave me alone, Connie!

Connie You're going to him! You're going to the boyfriend's!

Joan No, I'm not!

Connie You'll lose the child! They'll take her away! They'll have all the proof they need!

Joan   I am only going for a few days, I'll be back!

Connie   You won't be back!

Joan   Well, what's the point? She hates me! They've turned her against me. He's all I've got left.

Connie   You've got a daughter.

Joan   For my whole life people have been telling me I'm worthless, he makes me feel worth something, he wants me!

Connie   *(Savagely)* I tell you what he wants!

(She jerks her head to indicate the Americans.)

He wants the same thing they all want, standing up in doorways and down dark alleys!

Joan   Stop it!

Connie   Except they're more honest, they go to prostitutes! They're men! This is a war! In a month you'll be out on the street with nothing!

Joan   You know nothing about it. It's nothing to do with you!

Connie   Nothing to do with me! I gave you my savings!

Joan   Oh yes, money, I thought we'd come to money; here you are!

*(She hands over the envelope **Connie** gave her earlier and proceeds to count out extra money.)*

Here, and … three, four, four pounds ten, five, five pounds, six, and I'll send the rest on!

*(**Connie** turns away, upset. She is almost in tears.)*

Connie   Joan …

(Pause.)

Joan   Perhaps if you'd cared more about people and less about money you'd have a few more friends in this town. I've got a right to some happiness. He wants me, and I need to feel wanted, I'm not ashamed of that.

Connie   And you aren't wanted?

(Pause.)

Joan   I'll send for the things I've left.

Connie   Will you send for Helen, too? She's like a bit of luggage to you, isn't she?

Joan   Don't you dare say that!

Connie   *(Overlapping)* Carted about, dumped, brought out when you feel like it!

Joan   I love her.

Connie   You love yourself!

Joan   I've got a right to some freedom!

*(**Millie** enters.)*

Connie   Oh yes! You're very big on rights! Well, you listen to me, you selfish bitch, there's no such

thing as freedom. Freedom's paid for like everything else in this world …
(She breaks off, unable to believe how easily she's been duped. Pause.)

Joan   I didn't plan it to be like this, Connie. I'm grateful to you for all you've done.
(Pause.)

Connie   *(Savagely)* Are you? Are you? Well, good for you.
*(They stare at each other. **Connie** exits.)*

Write and Discuss

Arts Criticism and Aesthetics

1. Discuss how successful you felt you were in using the six steps in rehearsing and performing scripts. In which steps did you feel you made the most progress? Why?

2. Identify the strengths of your prompt copy. In which areas could you improve?

3. Evaluate your performance, considering the performance criteria listed on the evaluation sheet on page 102.

4. Describe one performance you enjoyed. Pick key moments that you remember and explain why you felt those moments were successful. Consider the performers' use of voice, body language, focus, timing and character portrayal.

5. If you have seen several different pairs performing the same script extract, compare one strong performance with another. Discuss the similarities and differences between the performances, and the effectiveness of the choices made.

Past and Present Contexts

6. Describe how the exercises from Stanislavski's System assisted you in preparing your script. In your discussion, explain the value and purpose of Stanislavski's System both for the performer and the audience.

7. Imagine you are a director. Choose a play, novel or film you will stage. Explain in point form your ideas for costume, lighting, set, sound and marketing. Include sketches and diagrams where possible.

Refer to Appendixes 1, 3 and 4 for help with your logbook entries. The appendixes provide you with guidelines for evaluating your own performance work and the work of others.

Scripts: Interpretation and Presentation

Evaluation Sheet — Chapter 4 Scripts: Interpretation and Presentation

Performance Task: Interpreting Script

Student: _____ Teacher: _____

Related Outcomes

By completing this task you should be able to:
- create a prompt copy for use in rehearsals and performance
- articulate a directorial concept for your script performance
- explore a method of analysing a script for meaning, character development and effective presentation
- interpret and present a scripted performance
- explore the use of the elements of production in the interpretation of a script.

Criteria	Level of Achievement			
	Beginning	Consolidating	Mastering	Excelling
Exploring and Developing Ideas Have you recorded your analysis and rehearsal process by: • completing a legible prompt copy that is annotated and divided into units; and shows blocking, lighting and sound cues? • recording all research and rehearsal notes? • completing a character biography? • completing Write and Discuss questions as required?				
Using Skills, Techniques and Processes Have you selected and incorporated the skills of voice, movement and character work by: • sustaining and developing character in performance? • using vocal dynamics that are suitable for the character? • using body language and movement in a way that helps to communicate the character?				
Presenting Have you planned, selected and modified your presentation by: • making effective decisions regarding the stage action and the use of space? • presenting a performance that is coherent and well-rehearsed? • presenting a directorial concept that includes consideration of the elements of production?				

Comments: _____
_____
_____
_____

© Mathew Clausen

Chapter 5

Writing a Review: Analysing and Evaluating Performance

Why Study Review Writing?

In this chapter you will focus on writing a review of a performance. You have already begun to develop skills as a critic of performance through your reflection on your own performance work and the performance work of others. When you review a performance and make evaluations about its strengths and weaknesses, you are challenging, confirming and clarifying your understanding and appreciation of performance. This knowledge and understanding can then be applied to improve your own performance work.

This chapter is divided into the following units:

5.1 Steps in Reviewing a Live Performance
5.2 Evaluating the Components of a Performance
5.3 Written Task: Review of a Performance

Outcomes

In this chapter you will:
- identify particular elements of a performance for evaluation
- identify the strengths and weaknesses of a performance
- appreciate how the elements of a production work together in a performance
- incorporate examples from a performance to support judgments
- select and incorporate appropriate language to discuss ideas
- use computer technology to publish a review of a performance.

Cate Blanchett, Don Reid, Gillian Jones and Ralph Cotterill in *The Seagull*, Company B Belvoir, 1997. Photograph by Heidrun Löhr.

5.1 Steps in Reviewing a Live Performance

Practitioner Profile

Bryce Hallett
Senior Drama Critic, **Sydney Morning Herald**

Bryce Hallett began reviewing drama and music theatre in 1994 when he was Melbourne Arts Editor of the *Australian*. He is a judge for Sydney's Critics Choice Awards.

Curiosity, a love of drama—preferably on the stage—and a respect for those whose job it is to entertain, are central to the critic's role. Sitting in judgment of a play is, of course, subjective. But evaluating a performance requires an appreciation of many disciplines—voice, movement, mime, direction, scenery, costumes, sound and lighting—and of the theatre's potential to create 'magic' when some or all of the elements are united.

It is contemporary practice that design elements do not overwhelm, distract or unnecessarily intrude. Generally, a production's look (that is the set, costumes and lighting) should be in service, rather than command, of the text or script.

Apart from a keen interest in theatre and a desire to champion the original and the new, the reviewer's great strength lies in writing: an ability to communicate ideas; engage the reader; and offer insights into the weird, wonderful, and fantastic worlds on stage.

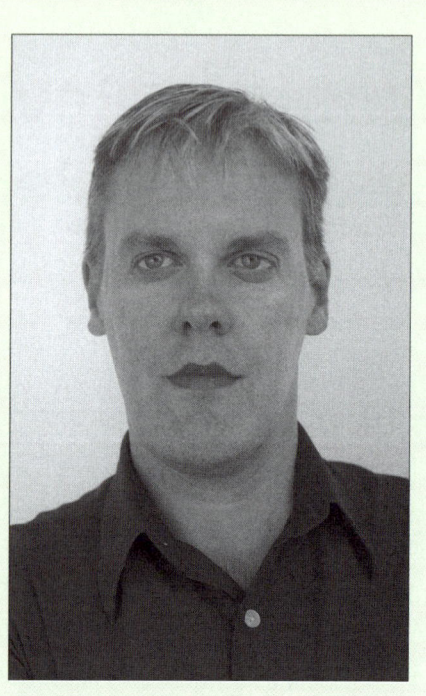

Hint

Some theatre groups offer discussion time with the audience after the performance. If you are writing a review, this is an excellent opportunity to clarify any questions you may have about the performance.

Read **Step 1: Watching a Performance**

To write a review you need to choose a performance to attend. Performances to see could include:

- a local school or community production
- a visiting performer or theatre group
- your own school production
- a professional theatre production.

Step 2: Noting Your First Impressions

After watching a performance, you will have quite a strong sense of whether or not it was effective. This is usually reinforced through your feelings of whether or not you were engaged, moved, excited or disinterested in the performance. Sometimes, using a rating scale first helps you to determine your overall initial impression. You can then be more specific about where the strengths and weaknesses are. For example, you may give a performance a rating of 7 out of 10. You then need to explain why you could not give the performance a rating of 10 out of 10. It might have been the acting, the overall flow of the performance, the script and/or the use of sound and lighting.

Hint

It is a good idea to make notes about a performance either during it or shortly after you have seen it. This will help you to remember the points you want to include in your review.

Step 3: Writing the Review

Whatever your feelings about a performance, it is important to articulate your opinions clearly and to support your point of view with evidence. Writing a more detailed analysis of a performance gives you the opportunity to be specific about the particular elements of a performance and whether you thought they were strong or weak. The elements of a performance to consider in your review are:

- plot
- acting
- direction
- interpretation of the script
- set design
- costume design
- lighting
- sound
- use and choice of performance space.

Write and Discuss

Imagine that you are a theatre reviewer for a newspaper and answer the following questions:

1. What criteria would you use to determine the success of each element in a performance?
2. What criteria would you use to determine how well each element complemented the overall performance?
3. List and explain three qualities that you feel a good reviewer needs to have to be successful.

Hint

When writing your review avoid using the first person 'I'. By using the third person your review seems more objective. For example, instead of writing 'I thought the lighting helped to create the sombre mood' rephrase your sentence to read 'The lighting helped to create the sombre mood'.

5.2 Evaluating the Components of a Live Performance

Read ## Structuring a Review

Use the following points as a guideline for what you may include in your review.

1 Write an introduction
In your opening paragraph you need to include:
- the name of the play you are reviewing
- the name of the playwright
- the theatre where the performance was held
- the date of the performance

If you choose you may also indicate your overall impression of the play.

2 Summarise the Plot and Story; Identify the Performance Style
Briefly summarise the plot and story. The skill in this section of your review lies in your ability to reduce the whole story to a brief, summarised version, usually one paragraph in length. You do not need to include all the details, just the main events. The following example is for a linear narrative performed in a realistic style.

- **Plot.** This is the actual action that happens on stage. For example: The play is set in a Tasmanian coastal town over one evening. A couple, who lost one of their sons in a boating accident some years ago, are visited by a mysterious survivor of the boating accident. The survivor has important news about the death of the son.

- **Story.** This involves more than what happens on stage. The story includes information about the characters and the situation that has occurred *outside* the actual action on stage and is often revealed in the exposition. For example: During the play, the couple reveal that their son was involved in gambling and crime. They also give information about the aftermath of the boating accident: the effect it had on the town and that confidential documents about the investigation into the accident went missing.

3 Discuss the Themes and Issues
Outline the themes and issues that you feel were important in the play. The themes and issues carry the message of the play and are important in helping the audience gain meaning from the performance. For example: the couple learn to accept the death of their son through the visit of the boating accident's survivor. The themes and issues of the play are guilt, accepting loss, injustice and confronting the past.

Hint

Some performances you see may not use a linear narrative or be performed in a realistic style. For these performances you should summarise the key moments of the performance rather than providing a summary of the plot.

Hint

The 'exposition' is the information that is given through character dialogue and action at the beginning of the play; it helps to tell the story.

You should also discuss your impression of the directorial concept in your review. Comment on the director's interpretation of the play, and how the choice of dramatic form and performance style helps to communicate the play's themes and issues.

4 *Evaluate the Performers*

Evaluate the success of the performers in playing their characters. You should be familiar with the sorts of areas to comment on because you have been assessed in these areas yourself. Choose two performers to evaluate.

Ask the following questions for each performer:

- How well did they use body language to express their character? Give two examples.
- Were their movements and gestures appropriate for their character?
- How well did they use their voice to express their character and deliver lines? Was their use of voice appropriate for their character?
- Were there any key moments in the performance that provide good examples of the performer's ability to portray character/role? Identify one or two key moments.
- Did they seem to blend with the action of the performance or did they stand out? Was this a positive or negative in the performance? Why?
- How focused did they seem during their performance?
- How convincing did the performer seem in their portrayal of their character?

5 *Comment on the Use of the Elements of Production*

Discuss how effective you think the use of sound, lighting, set and costume were in the performance. You may also comment on how these production elements were used symbolically in the performance.

Ask yourself the following questions:

- Were the costumes suitable for the characters? How did the choice of colours and designs suit the overall look of the performance?
- Was the set an effective use of the space? Why? Was the set easy for actors to manoeuvre around? In terms of colour and layout, did its design enhance the performance? How?
- Were the visual elements of costume and set unified in any way? Was contrast used for effect? Was there a symbolic use of shape, colour or texture to convey meaning, or to create atmosphere?
- How did the elements of production support the directorial concept?
- Did the lighting make the actors visible?
- Was special lighting used at any time for particular effect? How did this special lighting add to the success of the performance?

- Did the use of live or recorded sound enhance the performance? How?
- How did lighting and sound establish location and create atmosphere?

6 Sum Up the Overall Success of the Play

In the concluding paragraph you need to do more than just repeat what you have already written. You need to look at all the elements you have previously analysed and come to a decision about the overall success of the production. Often it is helpful to read a copy of the script of the play you have seen. This helps you to understand and comment on the way in which the play has been interpreted by the director and performers.

Before you write the conclusion, consider the following:

- Refer to the rating out of 10 that you gave the performance. After consideration of each of the performance elements, do you still feel that this is a fair rating? Why or why not?
- Which aspects of the performance were strongest? Why?
- Which aspects of the performance were weakest? Why?
- Did any particular performance element seem to overshadow others? How?
- Can you make any suggestions for improvement?
- Create a title that sums up your impression of the play, as well as the comments and tone of your review. Your title needs to be engaging so consider the use of puns or alliteration.

5.3 Written Task: Review of a Performance

Read — The Task

You are to write, edit and publish a review of a live performance. The review will explore and discuss the components of a performance, as outlined in Unit 5.2 (pages 106–108). The word length of the review will be set by your teacher.

Prepare — Creating and Making a Review

Your planning for this activity will be assisted by reviewing the steps listed in Unit 5.1 (pages 104–105) and by reading the sample review provided at the end of Unit 5.3.

In your review, include discussion of:

- plot and story
- themes and issues
- actors' performances of their characters
- elements of production and how they contribute to dramatic meaning.

Remember to conclude your discussion with an overall opinion and evaluation.

Evaluate — Review Checklist

You and your teacher will evaluate your work individually, using a list of criteria. These criteria relate to your achievement in this task. These criteria are listed on the evaluation sheet at the end of this chapter and will be used to evaluate your ability to:

- respond to each of the areas of a performance that need to be evaluated
- write a detailed and analytical response
- include examples from the production to illustrate and support your judgments
- write in an articulate and sophisticated manner appropriate for theatre criticism
- present ideas using a coherent and clear structure
- draft, edit and publish your review incorporating a headline and graphics.

Write and Discuss

Arts Criticism and Aesthetics

1. Once you have written your review, reread it. Look for ways to improve the communication of your ideas. Write a second draft.
2. Read another person's review. Write comments about the strength of the review. Discuss your responses with the person who wrote the review.
3. Give your review to someone else to read and ask them to make notes on your review. Discuss their comments. Write a final draft.

Read **Sample Review**

TEMPTING SHAKESPEARE
by William Shakespeare

Bell Shakespeare Company
Sydney Opera House

The Bell Shakespeare Company's most recent production, *The Tempest* directed by Jim Sharman, is a real triumph. It is a slick, contemporary adaptation; though very true to the original text.

It is the story of Prospero, former Duke of Milan, who is overthrown and exiled by his brother and his enemy, the King of Naples. He and his daughter have lived for many years on a small, magical island. Prospero has developed his skills of magic and uses them to command the brutes and spirits of the island.

Fate crosses Prospero's path when a ship carrying his brother and the King of Naples sails near the island. Prospero uses his powers to summon a tempest to sink the ship and wash ashore its inhabitants, where he hopes to confront his enemies. His daughter, Miranda, falls in love with the King's son, Ferdinand. In another sideplot, the King's brother, Sebastian, and Prospero's treacherous brother, Antonio, are plotting to kill the King. All is reconciled by the end of the play and the world's harmony is restored.

The character of Prospero is the most complex in the play, and the most important. It is his story and, although he is not always the focus, he is almost always present onstage, observing the events. It is due to his actions that the events of the story take place. His motivation is his desire for resolution. Despite his brother's crimes against him, Prospero does not seek revenge. His prolonged exile on the island has not only allowed him to perfect the art of magic, it has helped him grow wise.

John Bell's interpretation of Prospero was sensitive and engaging. His performance was subtle and controlled: an effective technique to portray this particular character. He revealed the many aspects of Prospero's character without being heavy-handed or obvious. Bell, as Prospero, was onstage through much of the play as an ever-present observer. When he was part of the action, Bell maintained a balance between Prospero's heightened expression of emotions and his dignified restraint. Bell adopted a deep and resonant vocal tone and a calm, even delivery to convey Prospero's intelligence and wisdom. The gestures and movements chosen were dignified and characteristic of a man who has come to terms with his life and has learnt acceptance. He carried himself with dignity and serenity. Bell's interpretation of Prospero as such a man blended well with the overall mood of the play.

Paula Arundell's realisation of Ariel was fresh and vibrant. Ariel is a spirit and is usually portrayed as male. Ariel is the humble servant of Prospero and, unlike the disobedient Caliban, obeys Prospero's every command in the hope that he may one day free her. This is the driving force of the character. She is good-natured and cheerful, and always enthusiastic as she embarks on any mission. Arundell brought a fresh slant to this character. Her movements and facial expressions communicated a refreshing youthfulness. Her interpretation of the character also conveyed a contemporary edge through Ariel's mischievous playfulness. Arundell also succeeded in communicating the more serious motivation behind the character. She maintained an energetic performance throughout and her musical items were carried off flawlessly. Her gestures and expressions were large, often childlike, and she moved about the stage with an ethereal sense of lightness. Her gestures were indicative of Ariel's happy nature. Yet, in sombre scenes, such as those in which she talks to Prospero about the prospect of being set free, Arundell was able to capture the more serious emotions behind Ariel's playful facade.

The set design is one of the most impressive features of the play and, from the opening scene, it creates a powerful impact. At the start of the play we see a boat being battered by a strong storm. Finally it sinks, washing its passengers ashore. What is so amazing about this scene is that it is played out on little more than a perspex platform. The lighting is such, however, that the audience is plummeted straight into the scene very effectively, without the use of a realistic set. The set's simplicity is versatile enough to represent various parts of the island: from Caliban's primitive cave to Prospero's book-filled home.

The lighting, which was very effective and important in creating the atmosphere, complemented the stage design.

The costumes were designed to evoke a quality of storybook fantasy; looking as if they had come from a child's dress-up box, with many different styles being flung together. Some characters were dressed in period costume, some in contemporary clothes.

The production was a mixture of realistic and non-realistic style, which suited the play's dreamlike quality. The use of song and slow-motion sequences added to the dreamlike atmosphere and the non-realistic style of performance. The director, Jim Sharman, also employed a technique where his actors remained in view, sitting to the sides of the acting area. Here the actor's role was passive, as though observing the action. This further added to the sense of a childlike fantasy story. Sharman also placed the live musician, Tyrone Landau, onstage, in among the action. It was as if the director wanted to tell the story of *The Tempest* in a simple way, and his actors were like toys that were the means by which he was able to do this.

The production moved smoothly through both dramatic and comic situations and moments. Sharman's direction was extremely successful in conveying the magic and energy of the play without making it appear childish or tacky. It was, overall, a very enjoyable production and one of the Bell Shakespeare Company's most successful to date.

Katie Wright
(940 words)

Evaluation Sheet — Chapter 5 Writing a Review: Analysing and Evaluating Performance

Written Task: Review of a Performance

Student: .... Teacher: ....

Related Outcomes
By completing this task you should be able to:
- identify particular elements of a performance for evaluation
- identify the strengths and weaknesses of a performance
- appreciate how the elements of a performance work together
- use examples from a performance to support opinions
- use appropriate language to discuss ideas
- use computer technology to publish a review of a performance.

Criteria	Level of Achievement			
	Beginning	Consolidating	Mastering	Excelling

Criticism and Aesthetics
Have you communicated an understanding of the overall play by:
• summarising the plot and story?
• describing and explaining the themes and issues?
• describing the directorial concept, its appropriateness and effectiveness?
• using examples to support your opinions?
Have you considered the actors' interpretation of character by:
• evaluating the actors' performances of their characters?
• using examples to support your judgments?
Have you considered the impact of the production elements on the overall performance by:
• commenting on the impact of:
  – set
  – costume
  – lighting
  – sound?
• using examples to support your opinions?
Have you expressed your ideas well by:
• using appropriate language and terminology?
• creating a well-structured review that is clear, sophisticated and articulate?
• presenting a word-processed review that includes a title and graphic?				

Comments: _____
_____
_____
_____
_____
_____

Interpreting Drama © Mathew Clausen

Dramatic Forms and Performance Styles

Chapter 6 — Melodrama: Just for the Thrill

Chapter 7 — Comedy: It's All in the …Timing

Chapter 8 — Mask: Disguising and Revealing

Chapter 9 — Non-Realistic Theatre: Visions, Dreams and Symbols

Chapter 10 — Playback Theatre and Documentary Drama: Interpreting True Stories

Chapter 11 — Physical Theatre: Roll Up! Roll Up!

Chapter 12 — Scripted Drama: Writing Australian Plays

Chapter 6

Melodrama: Just for the Thrill

Why Study Melodrama?

Melodrama was once one of the most popular forms of theatrical entertainment and reached the peak of its popularity in the mid to late nineteenth century. Melodrama has its own particular types of plots, characters and situations. Studying melodrama helps to identify the influences of melodrama plots and characters in popular entertainment today, including action and adventure films and soap operas. Studying melodrama also helps improve our understanding of the history of theatre and equips us with more skills to use in performance work.

This chapter is divided into the following units:

- **6.1** An Overview of Melodrama
- **6.2** Plot and Dramatic Structure in Melodrama
- **6.3** Characters in Melodrama
- **6.4** The Melodrama Acting Style
- **6.5** Staging in Melodrama
- **6.6** Performance Task: Time Running Out

Outcomes:

In this chapter you will:

- investigate the origins and conventions of melodrama in Australia
- explore and express a range of stock characters from traditional melodrama
- select and explore the use of vocal dynamics and movement to portray melodrama characters
- explore and practise the acting conventions of traditional melodrama
- create and manipulate tension through the melodrama plot device of 'time running out'.

John Hargraves and Lynette Cullen in *The Sunny South*, Sydney Theatre Company, 1980. Photograph by Peter Holderness.

6.1 An Overview of Melodrama

'[When studying nineteenth-century theatre] it is necessary to start with melodrama and the means of production because they defined and contained all nineteenth-century theatre; for a century melodrama remained the most popular form of entertainment.'

Michael R. Booth

A Brief History of Melodrama

Melodrama developed into a theatrical form in about 1800, thanks to the French playwright René de Pixérécourt. It was a reaction against the theatre of the Restoration period of the late 1600s.

Melodrama was also influenced by the development of a new style in art, music and literature, called Romanticism, through which people began to express their feelings in art. Melodrama was emotional theatre, and the melodrama plays of this period were tales of suffering, suspense, romance and evil deeds.

Live music was incorporated in melodrama performances to heighten the emotions of scenes and was also used to indicate character entrances. Melodrama relied on full use of theatrical devices, special effects and dramatic scene changes, all aimed at thrilling and moving an audience.

Melodrama in Australia

The first Australian melodrama was written in Tasmania in 1834 and was called *The Bushrangers*. This play reflects our early convict history and romanticises the escape of a convict, Mathew Brady, and a number of other prisoners from the Macquarie Harbour penal settlement in Tasmania.

Most early Australian melodramas were adaptations of European plays. Later, in the nineteenth century, clearly identifiable Australian settings and characters were established. Typical characters included:

- Bushrangers.
- Gold prospectors (also known as 'diggers').
- Currency lads and lasses. These were young male and female characters who were notable for being born in Australia. They reflected a freshness and independence that differed from their European counterparts, especially the currency lasses. The Australian heroine could ride, shoot and

swim; she was a complete departure from the vulnerable, sweet, weak heroines of European melodrama.
- Bumbling Irish policemen for comic relief.
- Aboriginal companions.
- New chums. These were immigrants to Australia, usually from England, who were seen as being naïve about the way of life in Australia.

Read: The Actor–Manager

Actor–managers were in charge of their theatre companies and usually played the lead male role. The most famous Australian actor–managers were George Darrell, Alfred Dampier and Dan Barry. They included some Australian stories in the plays they performed; although plays from overseas playwrights were considered more popular than Australian plays.

The most popular Australian melodramas used the legend of Ned Kelly as the basis for the plot. One notable Australian melodrama is *Robbery Under Arms*, by Alfred Dampier and Garnet Walch, which blends a little of Victor Hugo's *Les Miserables* with the Ned Kelly story. It was produced in 1890, and although Kelly was hanged in 1881, the memory of his death was still fresh in the audience's minds. By 1914, the popularity of melodramas had faded due to the invention of motion pictures. In the period from 1834 to 1914, Australia had produced some 600 melodramas.

Read: What Is a Melodrama Convention?

Identifying the conventions of a theatre style involves highlighting the distinctive aspects that make it different from other styles. The conventions of melodrama will be identified and explored in Units 6.2 to 6.5 (pages 117–125) and cover:
- plot and dramatic structure (how the play is put together)
- characters
- acting style
- staging.

Write and Discuss

1. Research entertainment, particularly theatre, in Australia during the period 1850–1900. Report your findings to the class.
2. Imagine that you are an actor–manager. Write a diary entry in which you describe a scene from a melodrama you have performed in.

6.2 Plot and Dramatic Structure in Melodrama

Read

The Melodrama Plot and Dramatic Structure

The main purpose of melodramas was not credibility, but the capacity to ignite the audience's reactions. The basic moral behind melodramas was the struggle between *good* and *evil*, and the re-establishment of a morally correct and just society. Each play relied on extreme situations and extreme states of being, for example justice versus revenge, honesty versus dishonesty, and innocence versus corruption. A traditional melodrama plot would include the following three elements:

- **Provocation.** In melodrama, a provocation is the initial cause for setting the action in motion; very often it is the jealousy or greed of a wicked character. For example, the evil landowner wants to marry the innocent daughter; otherwise he will evict her poor family from the property.
- **Pangs.** The pangs are the sufferings of the good and innocent characters who are in conflict with the evil. For example, the distressed daughter reluctantly agrees to marry the evil landowner to help save her family.
- **Penalty.** The penalty is that suffered by the wicked character for his evil ways in a last-minute reversal of fortune. For example, the hero arrives to save the day and reveals that the evil landowner had originally taken ownership of the land by deceiving the daughter's drunken father, who is in fact the rightful owner.

Hint

Melodramas also incorporated the use of topical jokes, comic interludes and slapstick to attract audiences.

Hint

Slapstick is an energetic and physical form of comedy that can include falling, tripping, hiding, dropping things, bumbling and chasing for comic effect.

Write and Discuss

1. To get an idea of the impact that melodramas had on nineteenth-century audiences, consider some of your favourite action or adventure films. Which features of them do you like in particular? Discuss and record these features.
2. What similarities are there between your favourite action and adventure films, and melodrama?

6.3 Characters in Melodrama

Hint

Melodrama actors often played the same character type in all melodrama plays. In Australia, the actor–manager would often play the role of the hero.

Read ## Melodrama 'Stock Characters'

The characters in melodramas were not supposed to be lifelike, but they had to be identifiable types. These sorts of characters were standard and audiences expected to see types with which they were familiar. These types of characters are often referred to as 'stock characters'.

The stock melodrama characters are the:

- **Hero.** Handsome, strong, brave, honest and reliable. Status: middle class or higher.
- **Heroine.** Beautiful, courageous, innocent and vulnerable. Status: middle class or higher.
- **Villain.** Cunning, without morals, dishonest, cruel and evil. Status: middle class or higher.
- **Villain's accomplice.** Usually provides comic relief because he is the bumbling sidekick. Status: lower class.
- **Faithful servant.** Also provides comic relief, and also does the dirty work. He usually discovers evidence against the villain. Status: lower class.
- **Maidservant.** A female character who is lively and who flirts with the faithful servant. Status: lower class.

Write and Discuss

1. Find two pictures of characters from adventure, superhero or action films that you think are good examples of the types of melodrama characters listed above. Use movie magazines, the Internet and your library to help in your research.
2. Underneath each picture, write a list of the personal qualities you feel best describe the character, according to the list of melodrama character types.
3. Share your findings with the class.

6.4 The Melodrama Acting Style

The Sunny South, Sydney Theatre Company, 1980. Photograph by Peter Holderness.

Read The Melodrama Acting Style

The melodrama acting style requires the use of strong facial expressions, large movements and gestures, and a clear and well-projected delivery of lines. This was considered the norm for actors in nineteenth-century melodramas. This style of acting seems unusual today, but audiences of this period took this form of theatre seriously and would see the highly dramatic and meaningful gesture as part of a great actor's success.

Melodrama actors concentrated on 'showing' emotions more than feeling them. They were skilled in the use of facial expression and heightened body language to show particular emotions. Inflections in the voice and the use of gestures also gave the audience cues to react by either booing or cheering. We also need to remember that the actors felt that big gestures, exaggerated expressions and the use of full voice were needed to reach the back corners of the large theatres as well as rise above the noise of the audience.

Read Melodrama and the Australian Audience

By the end of the nineteenth century, Australia's population was concentrated largely in city centres. The discovery of gold encouraged an increase in population and an expansion of the major cities. New theatres were built and these could hold large audiences.

In Australia, theatres were initially operated under strong government control because they were regarded as dangerous places that encouraged crime. Performances attracted large audiences. The audiences were unruly and reflected a mixture of upper, middle and lower classes. The upper section of the theatre seating was often full of drunk young men who delighted in calling out to the actors on stage. It was not uncommon for most of the audience to be under the influence of alcohol as they watched the performance. Spectators hissed, threw fruit and rioted when actors forgot lines. Actors encouraged audience interaction by often ad-libbing lines and telling bawdy jokes. They also encouraged audience members to cheer the hero and to boo and hiss the villain. Audible gasps of shock, horror and surprise would be heard at moments of excitement and tension in the performance.

Write and Discuss

1. Explain how being aware of the audience and playing to the audience may influence the melodrama actor's use of vocal dynamics and movement.

Exercise: Melodrama Acting Style: Demonstrating Emotion

Challenge
Repeat the exercise and, each time you hold a pose, include a sound or word that you feel adds to your interpretation.

Walk through the room, and on the signal from your teacher hold a pose for one of the following emotional states. Do not use sound. Focus your energy on communicating the emotional state through every part of your body, including your face. Repeat the exercise until you have practised all the following emotional states: evilness, innocence, courage, laziness, vulnerability, defiance, repentance, haughtiness, desperation, grief, lovesickness, territoriality and cruelty. Divide into two groups; show each person in your group four emotional states.

Write and Discuss

1. Identify the individuals who you feel portrayed particular emotional states well. Describe how they used body language to make their demonstration effective.
2. Explain three ways in which you feel you could use body language effectively to demonstrate emotion.

Exercise: Morrochesi's Acting Exercises

The famous nineteenth-century actor Antonio Morrochesi believed that there was a mimed action that corresponded to every word in a performance. Morrochesi was one of the first people to write a handbook for actors. In this book he had instructions for how actors should play various emotions and psychological states, such as love, jealousy, rage, anger, passion and insanity. Often an actor would use these gestures without even thinking. The following examples are from Morrochesi's book on acting.

Rage
Take off your hat, put it on, press it down in place, throw it on the ground, pick it up and tear it to pieces. Stride up and down restlessly: sometimes in a straight line, sometimes turning sharply. Every now and then run your hands through your hair. Unbutton your shirt and pause for a moment here and there. Bang hard with your fist on the furniture. Turn chairs upside down. Smash vases and crockery. Bang your fist against the back of your neck. Open and close doors. Throw yourself into a chair, bounce up and down on it, and then jump to your feet again.

Pride
Set one arm crossways over the breast; the other resting with the back of the hand on the hip and the elbow thrust forward. Hold your head high.

Exercise: Melodrama Character Types

Now you have begun to explore body language and movement in the melodrama acting style, it is time to explore some stock melodrama character types.

1 Melodrama Character Addition
In Unit 6.3 (p. 118) we explored the stock melodrama characters. Three of the common melodrama character types, and their qualities, are the:
- **Hero.** Brave, honest, fair-minded and strong.
- **Villain.** Deceitful, evil, cruel, sneaky, sly and untrustworthy.
- **Heroine.** Virtuous, sweet, innocent, vulnerable, honest and trustworthy.

Use the following steps to create these three melodrama character types:
- Adopt a frozen pose.
- Add a walk or stride that clearly represents the character's personality.
- Add a mannerism or gesture that is representative of the character's personality.
- Add a sound, word or phrase that you feel represents the character's personality.

Explore physical and vocal portrayals of the following Australian melodrama characters. Use the steps listed to build each character.
- **The digger (a gold prospector).** Rough, loyal, fair-minded and honest.
- **The Australian heroine.** Strong, feminine, confident and outspoken.
- **The evil bushranger.** Rough, cunning, ruthless and cruel.

Present Playing to the Audience

Each person in the class chooses a melodrama character they enjoyed playing. Each person presents their character in front of the class. The class cheers or boos the character accordingly. The performer should be aware of the audience's reactions and improvise the character's response.

Write and Discuss

Pick two characters that you felt were strong representations of the character types. Describe how the performers used the following drama skills to create an effective character type: body language, gesture, vocal dynamics and focus.

Hint

Refer to Unit 1.4 (pages 14–19) and undertake two voice warm-up exercises before you start the following exercises.

Exercise Melodrama Character and Vocal Dynamics

Saying lines in the melodrama acting style requires the use of emphasis. This can be achieved by choosing certain words or syllables to say in a special way. Emphasis can also be achieved through consideration of the elements of vocal dynamics: pace, rhythm, pitch, volume and pauses.

1 Melodrama Character Lines

Try saying the following lines, adding special emphasis where letters are in upper case. As you practise, find a mimed action for the words you emphasise. The lines should be said with full emotion and at full voice.

Challenge

Repeat these lines, but add a 'roll' to all the underlined 'R' sounds.

Heroine I am INnocent. You are so cr<u>O</u>OOEL *(cruel)*.

Hero YOU have entered this home like a WOOLF *(wolf)* and TORN from her mother's arms the HOPE of her old age. I should SEEEZ *(sieze)* you by the throat, and DASH you P<u>R</u>OSTRATE to the earth, as TOO FOWEL *(foul)* a carcass to walk erect and MOCK the name of man.

Heroine No mother, I canNOT marry Charles. It would <u>BR</u>EAK my heart to do so and I would surely DIE!

Hero I STE<u>R</u>-<u>R</u>UCK *(struck)* him down.

122 Dramatic Forms and Performance Styles

Write and Discuss

1. Identify the dominant emotion that each character is feeling for each line they say.
2. Describe the body gestures and facial expressions you used to help communicate the emotion of each line.
3. Describe how one other group member delivered their line in a way that you felt met the requirements of the melodrama acting style. Comment specifically on their use of body language and vocal dynamics.
4. Why did melodrama performers use stylised voice and movement to portray their characters?

2 Asides

In an aside a character speaks directly to the audience to reveal a thought or plan that is kept secret from the other characters. The performer's delivery of an aside should establish a feeling of secrecy and draw the audience's focus from the general action to the performer delivering the aside.

Try performing the following villain's aside, which reveals his secret thoughts. To add to the feeling of secrecy, put a hand to one side of your mouth, with the fingers together and the palm cupped and facing down. Try to pick the words that need to be emphasised.

The villain's aside precedes a line where he pretends he is sorry for what he has done and refuses to kill the defenceless hero. This will require a swift change of body language, vocal delivery and facial expression: from the delivery of the aside to the delivery of the line.

Villain *(Aside)* First I shall gain his confidence, then I shall take what is rightly mine!

The actor playing the villain changes the emotion that is portrayed by altering body language and vocal delivery.

(To the hero) No! Too much of your blood is upon my head! Be justly revenged: take mine!

Write and Discuss

1. When delivering the aside how did you use body language and voice to create a feeling of secrecy and to manipulate the character's relationship with the audience?
2. How did you change your use of body language and voice from the delivery of the aside to the delivery of the line to the hero?

3 *Melodrama Character Lines*

Divide into pairs. Write one line for each of the following characters: hero, villain and heroine. On a piece of paper, indicate which character says the line and whether or not it is an aside, and underline any words or syllables for emphasis. Put all the lines written by all pairs into a hat or box. Everyone takes a line from the hat and is given a couple of minutes to practise their line. Each person then delivers their line, with appropriate character body language, gesture and use of emphasis.

Present Modern Melodrama

In pairs, choose one of the following situations to present to the class.

- Trying to persuade a parent to let you go out.
- Being caught by a teacher and punished.
- Two lovers on a date telling each other how in love they are.
- A bully caught picking on a student and saved by the school sports hero or heroine.

The situation should be short. The emphasis in this exercise is the use of melodramatic body language and the use of melodramatic delivery set in a contemporary situation. Plan and rehearse your scene before you present it to the class.

6.5 Staging in Melodrama

Read What Did Melodramas Look Like?

Melodramas in the late 1800s had the benefit of being staged in theatres with the machinery and equipment to create the required elaborate settings and effects. Fly towers and counterweight systems allowed backdrops and scenery to be hidden and revealed from the area above the stage. Scenic artists created familiar, local settings for Australian melodramas. Their aim was to re-create settings as accurately as possible. The increased use of electric stage lighting, rather than gas lighting, also added to the visual effects.

This cross-section of a stage shows the treadmills and moving panorama used to stage a horse race.

Sensation Melodramas

By the late 1800s a particular type of melodrama called 'Sensation Melodrama' had gained popularity. In Sensation Melodramas, the highlight of the performance was the moment of sensation when some disaster or catastrophe would occur, be it a flood, avalanche, fire, earthquake, explosion, death or murder along with other general mayhem. The originator of Sensation Melodrama, Dion Boucicault, had real fire engines extinguish a real fire set in an apartment building in his production of *The Poor of New York*.

Australian melodramas reflected this trend. In *The Sunny South*, by George Darrell, a train is derailed on stage and in *Robbery Under Arms*, by Alfred Dampier, a stagecoach is driven onto the stage and is hijacked by bushrangers. Another performance in Melbourne re-created a horse race by having horses run across the stage, out one side door of the theatre, up the lane behind the theatre and in through the other side door—all to give the realistic impression of a horse race at high speed.

Write and Discuss

1. List three famous, popular blockbuster films or stage musicals that use spectacular effects.
2. Describe the spectacular effects used in the performances you listed above. What did they add to the dramatic impact of the performance?
3. What is a Sensation Melodrama?

6.6 Performance Task: Time Running Out

Hint

Melodramas used live music to heighten the atmosphere of the performance. You may like to incorporate an appropriate piece of music to accompany your performance. Movie soundtracks are a good source.

Hint

It is helpful for the audience to boo or cheer appropriately during the performance. This will encourage the performers to play to the audience.

Read The Task

In groups, devise a climactic scene from a melodrama. The scene should be a climactic moment where the hero rescues the heroine from the evil clutches of the villain. The moment should use the device of 'time running out' to add tension to the scene. You could use a stopwatch or a visible clock with a second hand to give you a genuine feeling of having to rescue someone quickly. Just remember not to rush the action. In fact, sometimes it is better to slow the action almost completely at the climactic moment so it seems that time hangs in the air. This is usually the moment when we think the hero is about to die and all is lost. For example:

- The heroine is tied to the train track. The hero and villain struggle as the train approaches.
- The heroine dangles from a frayed rope over a cliff face. The flame of a burning candle threatens to break the rope.
- The heroine is trapped in a burning house and the door is locked from the outside.

You must also include the use of asides in your performance, as well as the use of distinct poses and gestures to express the emotion of the character's lines. In performance you must play to the audience and encourage their reactions to particular events on stage.

Prepare Creating and Making a Melodrama

- Brainstorm characters and situations. You may think of examples from adventure or action films.
- Consider how dialogue can use emphasis to suit the melodrama acting style.
- Identify the climactic moment.
- Consider ways you can build tension through the use of sound effects.
- Consider ways you can control the building of tension through the action of the scene.

Evaluate Performance Checklist

You and your teacher will evaluate your work individually, using a list of criteria. These criteria relate to your achievement in this task. Some criteria will relate to the achievement of the group.

Dramatic Forms and Performance Styles

The criteria are listed on the evaluation sheet at the end of this chapter and will be used to evaluate your ability to:

- select and incorporate body language and movement in the melodrama acting style
- select and incorporate voice in a melodrama acting style
- sustain and develop character in performance
- select and incorporate stylised body language to express the emotion of character lines
- include and deliver asides
- manipulate the actor–audience relationship to encourage the audience's involvement
- create and control tension
- highlight the climactic moment
- incorporate your knowledge and understanding of melodrama into your own performance work.

Building tension works best if you start your performance at a moderate pace and with a moderate level of intensity, and build the pace and intensity as you move toward the climactic moment.

Write and Discuss

Arts Criticism and Aesthetics

1. Evaluate one group. Describe their strengths in the use of body language.
2. How did the group create and maintain tension in their performance?
3. Evaluate your own presentation. Outline your strengths in the melodrama acting style. Use examples from your own performance to support your evaluation.
4. Evaluate your ability to include awareness of your audience into your melodrama performance. Describe examples where you or another performer interacted with the audience to heighten the performance.

Past and Present Contexts

5. Give two examples of how melodrama has influenced popular entertainment today. Draw a table that shows a comparison between melodrama and your examples. Include in the table comparisons of character, plot, settings and acting style.
6. What made Australian melodrama different to European melodrama?
7. Describe the kind of actor–audience relationship you would expect at a melodrama performance.
8. Why were melodramas so popular in the late nineteenth century? Research the social beliefs, politics and entertainment of this period to help write your answer.

Refer to Appendixes 1, 3 and 4 for help with your logbook entries. The appendixes provide you with guidelines for evaluating your own performance work and the work of others.

Performance Task: Time Running Out

Student: _____ Teacher: _____

Related Outcomes

By completing this task you should be able to:
- explore and express a range of stock characters from traditional melodrama
- select and explore the use of vocal dynamics and movement to portray melodrama characters
- explore and practise the acting conventions of traditional melodrama
- create and manipulate tension through the melodrama plot device of 'time running out'.

Criteria	Level of Achievement			
	Beginning	Consolidating	Mastering	Excelling
Exploring and Developing Ideas Have you prepared for your performance by: • considering and incorporating the plot conventions of melodrama? • recording and planning rehearsals and decisions in your logbook? • completing Write and Discuss questions as required?				
Using Skills, Techniques and Processes Have you incorporated melodrama acting conventions by: • creating a stock melodrama character type? • delivering lines with appropriate emphasis on certain words? • using asides to communicate your character's thoughts? • playing to the audience to encourage their involvement? • representing your character's personality through appropriate choice of body language and movement? • incorporating suitable body language to show the emotion of your character's lines? • sustaining and developing character in performance?				
Presenting Have you rehearsed and presented a performance for a specific audience by: • incorporating the conventions of melodrama? • structuring the drama into a coherent and polished performance using effective scene transitions? • manipulating and maintaining tension?				

Comments: _____
_____
_____

Evaluation Sheet — Chapter 6 Melodrama: Just for the Thrill

Dramatic Forms and Performance Styles © Mathew Clausen

Chapter 7

Comedy: It's All in the…Timing

Why Study Comedy?

Comedy is a unique and distinctive genre with an extensive history. It has evolved into a wide range of forms and styles. By studying comedy we are able to appreciate the skills and techniques that help create comedy. We can employ these skills in the creation of performance work.

This chapter explores two styles of comedy—slapstick and parody—and is divided into the following units:

- 7.1 An Overview of Comedy in Performance
- 7.2 Slapstick: Physical Comedy
- 7.3 Character in Slapstick Comedy
- 7.4 Parody: Imitation and Exaggeration
- 7.5 Performance Task: Don't Slip on the Soap!

Outcomes

In this chapter you will:

- perform physical comedy, including a slip, a trip and a fall
- explore and demonstrate how status relationships between characters create comedy
- utilise the skills of imitation and exaggeration to create parody
- explore and discuss ways in which comedy can contribute to performance work.

Irene Waugh, Christine Douglas and Grant Smith in *'Love Burns'* and *'Trouble in Tahiti'*, Company B Belvoir and OzOpera, 1998. Photograph by Heidrun Löhr.

7.1 An Overview of Comedy in Performance

'The joke of life is the fall of dignity.'
Mack Sennett, American silent movie producer

Practitioner Profile

Chris Lilley
Comedy Writer, Actor, Stand-up Comedian and Voice Artist

Chris Lilley is currently working on a sketch comedy show for the Seven Network called 'Fast Food'. This follows on from his recent work as a writer–performer on Seven's sketch comedy series 'Big Bite'. Chris regularly performs stand-up comedy and does voice-over work.

Chris's interest in comedy began at high school, impersonating teachers and putting on end-of-year revues. He then became involved in university theatre and comedy revues, and began working as a stand-up comedian. Chris has made several short films based on characters he has created himself over the years. These films led to him being asked to join the cast of 'Big Bite'; his involvement with the show has given him the opportunity to further develop his characters for television.

Read ## Comedy in Performance

Although the intention of comedies is to amuse, they often use serious issues to explore the lighter side of human experience. Some famous comic plays have included plots that are about war, husbands being unfaithful to their wives, or people not telling the truth. Comedies are also often about trivial and day-to-day matters. In these comedies, characters create problems for themselves and others through their own foolishness. It is also fairly common for comedies to have a happy ending, in which all wrongs are made right.

Comedies have a positive psychological benefit for the audience. The laughter created by comedy not only releases tension,

130 Dramatic Forms and Performance Styles

but also helps us to view awkward and difficult situations less seriously. In a sense it is almost a relief that someone else is in the predicament, and not us. Television situation comedies exploit the fact that we gain immense enjoyment from identifying with and observing others in difficult situations.

Comedies have been written in a wide variety of performance styles. Some of these include Restoration comedy, commedia dell'arte, black comedy, farce and satire.

Write and Discuss

1. Research one of the comic forms listed above. Report your findings to the class.
2. List some of your favourite comic films and television programs.
3. Describe two characters from the films and television programs you have selected. Find one or two reasons why they are comic.

7.2 Slapstick: Physical Comedy

Read — An Overview of Slapstick

'Slapstick' is a term used to describe a style of comedy that incorporates falling, hitting, tripping, balancing, breaking, chasing and hiding to create humour. It places emphasis on showing comedy rather than creating comedy through dialogue. Television programs that use home videos of people in situations where accidents occur are a good example of how slapstick humour still appeals to audiences today. As the audience watches someone trip or fall, they are both laughing at and identifying with the individual's loss of dignity. The audience also responds to the timing, or the surprise and shock of the moment. Whereas the

Hint

A 'slapstick' is literally a prop bat made of two hinged sticks that slap sharply together when the bat is used to hit someone. This gives the illusion of hitting someone with a stick, without actually hurting the actor. The slapstick is a staple gag of the Italian masked comedy commedia dell'arte.

home videos are about real mishaps, slapstick is about creating the illusion of mishaps.

The term 'timing' refers to the ability of the performer to incorporate an underlying rhythm that governs when particular events best occur in a comic routine. If you have ever had the experience of telling a joke well, you have used timing effectively. If you pause unnecessarily long before the punch line, you lose the momentum of the joke and consequently the humour 'falls flat'.

Write and Discuss

1. List any television comedy programs you have seen that include the use of slapstick humour.
2. Describe three slapstick moments from one of these programs that you particularly enjoyed.
3. Explain why you enjoyed these moments.

Exercise Slapstick Comedy

Timing is 'sensed' during the improvising of situations, and is developed and rehearsed once a successful comic moment is discovered. During these exercises, be aware of the timing of the comic moments and how this can influence your work. After you have completed all the slapstick exercises, select and show examples of slapstick work to the class.

1 Trip

Walk through the room. At a given signal from your teacher, quickly push the ball of either your left or right foot into the floor and use this point as the imaginary object you are tripping over. As you push the ball of your foot into the floor, you need to stumble forward and then regain your composure. The size of the stumble will indicate to the audience the size of the object. After you have tripped, continue walking and look behind you with a confused expression, to try to see what it was you tripped over.

Hint

Complete an extensive physical warm-up (see Unit 1.1, pages 3–6) before you undertake the slapstick exercises.

Challenge

Try tripping over several objects of different sizes one after the other. Leave variations in the distance between each trip.
For example, you may start with one trip, walk a few metres and then complete three trips in quick succession. This challenge will test your use of timing.

2 Slip

Walk through the room. At a given signal from your teacher, allow either the right or the left leg to suddenly rise up, almost like a soft kick. You should wobble slightly, and lean backwards to give a sense of losing your balance. Continue walking and look behind you to see the imaginary item you slipped on.

As in the Challenge for the previous exercise, complete a series of slips varying the distances between them.

3 Side Fall

Stand upright in a space free from furniture. If you have mats, it is advisable to use these as you practise this exercise. A fall to the side involves several steps:

- Bend knees together while leaning slightly to the side you want to fall to.
- Allow your body to completely relax, as if you are about to faint.
- As you begin the fall, continue to deepen the bend of the knees and increase the lean to one side.
- As you fall, begin to bring both arms up above your head so that they will lie along the floor above your head when you complete the fall.
- The first body parts to make contact with the fall should be the upper thigh and the side of the buttock. Your head should rest against the arm that is outstretched along the floor.

Do not try 'dead falls', which are falls directly face down or backwards. These are highly skilled falls and require special training. They can be dangerous without proper supervision.

Hint

It is important to remember that the reaction of the character immediately after the moment of collision is highly important to the potential humour of the moment.

4 Collide

Work with a partner. Try the following collisions between two people. To create the illusion of a full-force collision you need to determine with your partner beforehand the precise moment of collision. In rehearsal, walk towards your partner at normal speed, and at the point of contact 'pull back' so the physical contact with your partner is not delivered with full force. The illusion of a real collision is dependent on your sense of timing and the way in which you both react to the collision.

Surprise Back and Front Collision. Creep backwards towards your partner, pretending you are sneaking through a house at night. First, count the number of steps it would take to reach each other. When you practise, count each step out loud until you are confident. The characters need to react in fright and shock at the moment of collision. You could also try a surprise front collision by having two characters absorbed in reading a newspaper as they walk towards each other. Use your peripheral vision to judge the distance from each other and the right moment for the point of collision.

Collide and Drop. Use two trays with plastic cups and bowls. Pretend to be two busy waiters serving customers. Find a moment where the two waiters have a front collision while holding their trays. As the collision occurs you can add the catching of cups or an exaggerated letting go of the tray and its contents to make the moment more powerful.

5 Stuck

Pretend you get your hand or foot stuck in a bucket, biscuit jar or some other container. You may be painting a room and accidentally step into the bucket or be stealing lollies from a jar. Try to remove the container, showing enormous effort and strain but no success.

Hint

The double take is performed very quickly. Practise slowly at first and then increase the speed of the reactions.

6 Double Take

A double take involves looking at an object or other characters twice: the first time quickly and with less notice taken, and the second time for longer and with more notice taken. Pretend you are walking down a street and see a very surprising sight. Maybe it is a large spider or a magnificent pair of shoes that you have always wanted. Walk past the imaginary object or character and look once quickly, but don't pay much attention to what you see. In the split second following the first look, it dawns on you that what you have seen is worth looking at a second time. Look at the object again, but for longer and with an appropriate reaction.

Write and Discuss

1. Which exercises did you feel worked most effectively for you? Why?
2. Describe one good example of the use of timing.
3. Make suggestions for how you could improve your work in each of the exercises.

7 Lazzi

'Lazzi', or 'comic accidents', originated in the improvised performances of commedia dell'arte. Lazzi (plural of 'lazzo') are comic moments that use physical, visual humour, and utilise the improvisation skill of extending, which was covered in Unit 2.2 (page 32). Practise the following lazzi. Present your favourite lazzo to the class once you have tried them all.

- Accidentally sit on a basket of eggs.
- Squirt water in your eye at the drinking fountain.
- Carry a pie and fall into it.
- Drop ice-cream on your lap.
- Spill hot coffee on your lap.
- Sit on a cactus.
- Accidentally rinse your mouth with shaving lotion.
- Get your tie caught in an electric beater.
- Hold sour milk in your cheeks while you look for a place to spit.
- Kick yourself in the shin while dancing.
- Miss the nail while hammering and hit your thumb.
- Step on a drawing pin.
- Have soap in your eyes while you search for a towel.
- Pour fuel on a smouldering barbecue and deal with the explosion of flames.
- Kick a soccer ball that turns out to be a bowling ball.
- Walk into a pole as you turn your head to flirt with someone attractive.

Challenge

Have individuals devise and present their own lazzo to the class.

Hint

If you have juggling or acrobatic skills you can include these in your development of comic scenes to add both excitement and humour.

> ### Write and Discuss
>
> 1. Give two examples of how you incorporated the skills you learnt in exercises 1 to 6 into the practice of lazzi.
> 2. Describe how you felt you used timing well in one lazzo.
> 3. Use examples of the lazzi you saw and comment on what you felt contributed to a successful lazzo, for example clear mime, facial expression and timing.

7.3 Character in Slapstick Comedy

Read Comic Characters

Characters in comedy can be represented in a variety of ways, from highly stylised to naturalistic. The circus clown often uses slapstick comedy and is an excellent example of a highly stylised character. In this unit we will look at creating stylised characters by using exaggerated movement, voice and costume.

In the following two sets of exercises you are required to adopt a character and improvise scenes as high-status and low-status characters. The first set of exercises explores how you may develop a comic character. The second set of exercises then looks at how humour can be created by establishing clear status relationships between characters. Your skills of improvisation will be required in these exercises (see Unit 2.2, pages 27–33).

Hint

It is best to practise the exercises before performing some for the class.

Exercise Creating Comic Characters

1 Personality Traits
Comic characters often have a dominant personality trait that is generally seen as a failing. Choose one of the following personality traits that you find appealing: greediness, silliness, laziness, clumsiness, cheekiness, bossiness, selfishness, vanity or enviousness. There may be other traits you can think of.

Walk through the room and find a way of communicating your trait through the way your character walks. As you walk, pause occasionally and find a pose that incorporates use of the arms, hands and facial expressions to communicate the character's personality trait.

Find a word or sound that expresses your character's personality and repeat this as you walk. Occasionally hold a pose.

2 Costume

The ability of a comic character to amuse can be enhanced through the choice of costume. Find items of costume to dress your character. Take into consideration their dominant personality trait. Mismatched items and ill-fitting clothes often add to a character's potential to amuse. For example, your character may wear a pair of pants that is too big, a very tight-fitting waistcoat and an enormous hat. You do not need to find a complete costume; sometimes just a hat or scarf will give enough indication.

Continue exploring your character but include a slip, trip, fall or combination of these, and explore the character's response.

Write and Discuss

1. Think of one or two of your favourite comic characters from film or television. Your comic characters may be real or animated. Write a short list of their main personality traits. Can you suggest why these traits make each character amusing?
2. Using the characters you have chosen, describe the costume they wear most often. Suggest how it adds to their comic potential.

Exercise Playing With Status

1 Status

The entire class moves through the room as though they are high status. It helps to imagine that you are the most important person in the room. You may look at other class members to convey your status, but you are not to speak or physically interact with them.

On the signal from your teacher, everyone becomes low status. It helps to pretend you are the least important person in the room. Once again, only eye contact is allowed as a form of communication.

Your teacher divides the class into two: half will be high status and half will be low status. Both groups move through the room and use only eye contact to communicate their status. On a given signal, the groups swap their status positions and continue moving through the room.

Status is the relative amount of power a character has or believes they have in relation to other characters. Their status may be established through wealth or lack of wealth, or through occupation, level of knowledge, experience, strength, and so on.

Episodes of the British comedy 'Absolutely Fabulous' are excellent examples of how the use of costume, human weaknesses and status relationships between characters create comedy.

Write and Discuss

1. What body language was used to communicate high status? Among other things, consider posture, mannerisms, eye contact, personal space and walk.
2. What body language was used to communicate low status? Again, include a consideration of the types of body language listed in question 1.

Hint

The term 'master' can apply to either a male or female character.

2 Master and Servant 1: Establishing Status

Divide into pairs. One person is high status (the master) and the other is low status (the servant). The characters can be any type of high-status and low-status pair, for example coach and athlete, builder and apprentice, employer and employee, or shop assistant and customer. In this exercise it is important that the low-status character always yields to the high-status character.

Improvise a situation in which the high-status character wants the low-status character to complete a task. Both characters should display a dominant personality trait. The high-status character may be a pompous explorer who wants to use a teaspoon to dig a tunnel through a mountain range, or a wealthy socialite who wants a huge banquet prepared to impress important guests. The low-status character is always willing to complete the high-status character's wishes. The high-status character does not necessarily have to be nasty or bossy; they may display other personality traits such as being benevolent or patronising.

Once you have completed the exercise, swap over so that each person has a turn at being either high status or low status.

3 Master and Servant 2: Undermining Status

In this improvisation, the master instructs the servant to undertake an activity, which the master will supervise. The servant makes mistakes, either deliberately or accidentally, and this complicates the situation. For example, the servant may deliberately drop things, break the only spade available, mis-hear information or creep away and fall asleep on the job only to be discovered by the master. When these accidents happen, the master's status is lowered momentarily because the servant is hindering progress. The master may then re-establish their status by reprimanding the servant or giving the servant a ridiculous punishment.

Hint

In exercise 3 it is important to balance the deliberate or accidental mistakes of the low-status character with moments where the master's wishes are met successfully. The low-status character tends to show their 'naughty' side when the master is not around or is unaware of the servant's actions.

4 Masters and Servants Meet

In this improvisation two masters and two servants meet for a reason you decide. For example, they may meet to discuss a merger of companies or to watch a football game. The two masters speak to each other, but instruct their servants to complete the range of activities required. The humour in this situation is

Dramatic Forms and Performance Styles

the inevitable status competition that develops between the two masters. Their competition to be 'top' master is usually played out through their servants. The comedy arises, for example, from the servants' failure to complete tasks properly and their attempts to be the 'best' servant.

5 Status Line

In this improvisation divide into groups of five. The members of the group are numbered 1 to 5. Number 1 is highest status and Number 2 is next in line, and so on. Numbers 2 to 5 can only speak to the character either immediately above them or below them. Number 1 is the foreperson, the leader, and can speak directly to any of the other participants. The participants all respect the status of Number 1 and the number immediately above them, but can be less courteous to the number below them.

The group completes a task, for example the packing of highly sensitive scientific equipment or canisters of smelly gas. As the work is passed down the line, Number 1 supervises proceedings and attempts to keep the others in line. Of course, accidents and problems occur and blame is passed down the line, with Number 5 always being blamed for everything. If the leader wishes he or she can sack participants and move them down the line. Participants can plead for mercy or bribe the leader to stay in their current position.

Write and Discuss

1. What improvisation skills do you need to employ in the Status Line exercise?
2. In what ways can the focus be maintained during an improvisation that has many participants? Did this occur in the scenes you improvised for exercises 4 and 5? What could be done to improve focus?

 ## Prepare and Perform a Comic Skit

Divide into pairs or into groups of four. Prepare a short skit that shows characters of different status in a situation of your choosing. You must include examples of some of the slapstick exercises covered in this unit and in Unit 7.2 (pages 131–6). You must also use costume to help make each character comic.

A 'skit' is a short, comic performance.

Write and Discuss

1. In your skit, how was the status relationship between characters established through the use of body language?
2. What slapstick skills were included in your presentation? What impact did these skills have on the success of the performance?
3. Imagine you are the director of one other group's skit. Make suggestions for how you could heighten the humour of their presentation. In your discussion, consider character, costume, timing and slapstick skills.
4. Choose one character from any of the skits you observed, or from your own. Comment on how their item of costume helped to add to their character's comic qualities.

7.4 Parody: Imitation and Exaggeration

Hint

In 'parody' the characteristics of a chosen person or group of people, or a written work or form of entertainment, is imitated for amusement.

Read An Overview of Parody

Parody is a form of comedy that uses imitation to create humour. The intention of parody is to make fun of identifiable situations and people we may normally take seriously. For example, a parody of an advertisement for a beauty product and its potential benefits may highlight the false claims being made and the amusing aspects of vanity. You will have seen many other examples of the use of parody in television comedy programs. People often use parody when they tell personal stories. They may act out people by imitating voices and gestures to increase the humour for the listener. It is important to use parody selectively in performance so that it does not judge or ridicule people unfairly.

Exercise: Parody

1 Imitating Character Through Observation

Choose a famous personality to imitate. They may be a movie star, politician, pop star or television personality. Before you begin to practise, use the chart below to make precise notes about how your chosen personality uses voice, stance, mannerisms and body language.

Practise being your personality exactly as they are presented by the media. Do not try to exaggerate their movements or voice.

Hint

It is helpful to work with a mirror when you practise imitating your chosen personality. By observing your use of body language you can make your imitation more accurate.

Name of personality	Description and explanation of how to imitate
Use of voice	Deep tone, speaks slowly, a bit posh, sounds educated. I would need to deepen my voice and speak more slowly. I would also have to get used to adding long pauses and the occasional 'little' cough.
Facial expressions	
Standing posture	
Seated posture	
Mannerisms	
Walk	
Hair and clothing	
Other important features	

2 Using Imitation and Exaggeration

Use the same personality that you prepared in the previous exercise. Now exaggerate some or all aspects of the use of voice and body language. For example, you may:

- emphasise some words they say in a certain way
- exaggerate a particular mannerism
- use repetition to heighten the effect of a physical movement or facial expression.

Challenge

Prepare a solo presentation in which your chosen personality is exaggerated in ways you choose. Examples of presentations include a short speech, a news announcement, an advertisement for a product or an interview.

Present: Newsflash

- Divide into groups and prepare a parody of a newscast by imitating and exaggerating the characters and features of a news program.

- When preparing characters, you may use more general representations. For example, to parody a newsreader you may use a style of delivery that is common to news presenters and include stereotypical movements, such as the shuffling of papers or answering calls from the producer. The same could apply to the representations of the reporters (such as weather, sports, consumer watchdog) and the characters they interview (such as angry consumers, politicians and pop stars).
- Include the use of exaggerated character traits and body language to heighten the humour.
- Include in your news presentation one news story where you cross 'live to air'.
- In the 'live to air' scene you are to parody a type of news story, for example a human interest story, sports report or the launch of a political campaign.

Write and Discuss

1. Describe the process you used to create your character. Include in your discussion any research and techniques you employed, including reference to any actual personalities you observed.
2. Evaluate the achievement of one other group member. Highlight two examples of how body language was used well. Consider their use of imitation and exaggeration.

7.5 Performance Task: Don't Slip on the Soap!

Read The Task

Soap opera is a very popular form of television that uses predictable character types and plots to engage audiences. The popularity of soap operas relies on the inclusion of highly dramatic and emotionally charged situations, often with the traditional 'good versus evil' plotline (see Unit 6.2, page 117). Dramatic tension is the key to soap opera episodes, and characters lurch from one emotional trauma to another to keep us on the edge of our seats. Although soap operas are written to create tension and excitement, they stretch the realms of possibility to achieve this goal.

In this task, you will parody soap operas by imitating the stock characters, situations and conventions of this form of television entertainment. By creating a parody of a soap opera episode you will highlight how the situations and characters in soap operas are often stereotypical and exaggerated.

In groups, you are to devise a parody of a soap opera episode. Your episode will include:

- a range of stock soap opera characters
- two or three story-lines that are emotionally charged
- three locations
- the convention of close-ups at the ends of scenes
- the convention of a cliffhanger ending
- exaggeration to add humour to character portrayal
- slapstick, including trips, slips, falls and collisions.

Prepare Creating and Making a Soap Opera Episode

- Refer to Unit 3.1 (pages 45–6), which covers the steps in playbuilding. Use the steps as a guide for your rehearsal process.
- Outline the two or three exaggerated story-lines you would like to include in your episode.
- Consider how slapstick and lazzi can be included to highlight and enhance comic moments.
- Consider how you may encourage the audience to focus on the character close-ups at the ends of your scenes, in the same way a camera draws our attention to close-ups at the ends of scenes on television.
- List typical soap opera characters, locations and situations.
- Choose recorded music to help add atmosphere to your performance.

Hint

The close-up at the end of scenes in soap operas helps the audience read the reactions of the character. Although you will not be using a camera, you can create the effect of a close-up by making the reactions of the characters more powerful and exaggerating facial expression.

Prepare ## Creating and Making a Soap Opera Character

- Create characters that are imitations of soap opera character types by using discussion and improvisation.
- Through improvisation, determine the status of each character and their status relationship to other characters.
- Consider the use of costume to help highlight the humour of your character.
- Consider the use of exaggeration, body language and voice to portray your character in a comic way.

This magazine cover highlights how soap opera story-lines appeal to audiences through shock and sensation.

144   Dramatic Forms and Performance Styles

Evaluate Performance Checklist

You and your teacher will evaluate your work individually, using a list of criteria. These criteria relate to your achievement in this task. Some criteria will relate to the achievement of the group. The criteria are listed on the evaluation sheet at the end of this chapter and will be used to evaluate your ability to:

- include imitation, status and exaggeration in the representation of your soap opera character
- include an appropriate and effective character voice for your character
- select and incorporate body language and movement to portray character
- sustain and develop character in performance
- research and prepare for your comedy performance
- effectively select and incorporate slapstick and lazzi to heighten comic moments
- select and link elements of your parody to create a coherent and polished performance
- include close-ups at the ends of scenes and a cliffhanger ending.

Hint

You can create the impression of a television close-up at the end of your soap opera parody scenes by incorporating the technique of the tableau. On the last line, or in the last moment of the scene, all performers freeze and simultaneously turn their faces to the audience. Facial expressions and body language should be exaggerated to show the characters' reactions in the final moment of the scene.

Write and Discuss

Arts Criticism and Aesthetics

1. Was your performance coherent? Give reasons for your success or lack of success. Offer suggestions for how you could improve in this area.
2. What was the climactic moment of your performance? How did you make this moment humorous for the audience?
3. Describe how well you felt you used imitation, status and exaggeration to portray your character.
4. Describe the moments where you felt you used slapstick well. Can you explain how timing or the reversal of status may have influenced this moment?
5. Did you manage your rehearsal time well? How could you improve your time management in future playbuilding activities?
6. Choose one group and evaluate how they used imitation, exaggeration and status to portray their characters.
7. Discuss one group's use of slapstick moments. Pick two slapstick moments you felt were particularly good and explain why.

Past and Present Contexts

8. Explain your understanding of the value and importance of comedy in performance. Include in your discussion examples of how comedy can be both entertaining and provocative. Your examples may come from your own work or the work of others, past and present.

Hint

Refer to Appendixes 1, 3 and 4 for help with your logbook entries. The appendixes provide you with guidelines for evaluating your own performance work and the work of others.

Evaluation Sheet — **Chapter 7 Comedy: It's All in the ... Timing**

Performance Task: Don't Slip on the Soap!

Student: .... Teacher: ....

Related Outcomes

By completing this task you should be able to:
- perform physical comedy, including a slip, a trip and a fall
- explore and demonstrate how the status relationships between characters create comedy
- utilise the skills of imitation and exaggeration to create parody
- explore and discuss ways in which comedy can contribute to performance work.

Criteria	Level of Achievement			
	Beginning	Consolidating	Mastering	Excelling
Exploring and Developing Ideas Have you prepared for your performance by: • considering and incorporating the plot conventions of soap opera? • recording all planning, rehearsals and decisions in your logbook? • recording your observations about soap opera character types? • completing Write and Discuss questions as required?				
Using Skills, Techniques and Processes Have you used skills, techniques and processes to structure a comedy performance by: • effectively incorporating imitation, status, and exaggeration in the representation of your soap opera character? • including an effective and appropriate character voice? • incorporating appropriate body language and movement to portray character? • including exaggeration to add humour to character portrayal? • effectively incorporating slapstick and lazzi to heighten comic moments? • sustaining and developing character?				
Presenting Have you rehearsed and presented a performance for a specific audience by: • structuring the drama into a coherent and polished performance incorporating effective scene transitions? • incorporating close-ups at the ends of scenes? • finishing your play with a cliffhanger ending?				

Comments: ....
....
....

© Mathew Clausen

Chapter 8

Mask: Disguising and Revealing

Why Study Mask?

Masks are a potent tool for the transformation of the performer. They have a distinctive influence on both portrayal of character and the style of performance. Masks in performance create a powerful experience for both the performer and the audience because the wearing of a mask simultaneously disguises the actor and reveals a character. In this chapter you will explore three different types of mask performance: neutral mask; half mask and chorus work; and African masks. The performance task at the end of the chapter will allow you to blend all three types of mask work and incorporate them into a performance.

This chapter is divided into the following units:

- **8.1** An Overview of Mask
- **8.2** Neutral Masks: Creating Individual Character
- **8.3** Half Mask and Chorus Work: Creating Group Character
- **8.4** African Mask Performance
- **8.5** Performance Task: Mask Ritual

Outcomes

In this chapter you will:
- apply the skills of performing with masks
- explore the creation of character through neutral mask
- interpret text to create masked chorus work
- appreciate the influence of masks in the performance work of a range of cultures and apply this knowledge to performance work
- devise and present a ritual that incorporates the use of masks.

8.1 An Overview of Mask

'Once a student understands the immense difference between controlling a mask and being controlled by a mask, then they can be taught.'

Keith Johnstone, Impro: Improvisation and the Theatre

Read Disguising and Revealing

The earliest indications of the use of mask in performance come from cave paintings in Africa. In these paintings, hunters wear animal skins and heads. It has been suggested that this use of mask was designed to help camouflage the hunters.

Masks were used in Ancient Greek religious festivals to help accentuate the features of characters. They also made the actors more visible to the audience.

Masked Italian commedia dell'arte actors use half masks to portray stock characters in improvised comedies. The exaggerated features of the commedia dell'arte masks highlight the comic qualities of the characters.

The dance–dramas of Asia, Southeast Asia, Africa and India feature the use of mask. The masked dance–dramas are a mix of religion, folklore and tradition. They use masks in performance to help bring their spiritual world to life. Ancestors and mythical beings interact with gods and mortals. The power of the mask to transform the actor into another character gives great power to the more ritualistic performances. In some of these performances it is believed that the wearer of the mask is actually possessed by the spirit of the mask. The masks used in these performances are considered sacred items. Only certain actors are permitted to wear them, and these actors have undertaken years of intensive training to receive the honour of wearing a mask in performance.

In each culture, unique conventions are observed in mask performances. For example, in Japanese Noh theatre only Shiite characters, gods, ghosts, women, animals and warriors wear masks.

In Nigeria, the Obuele and Abua Igbo peoples hold water spirit ceremonies to appeal for good fortune. The water masks are large and horizontal; they represent two parts—human and crocodile, shark or hippopotamus. The wearer walks in the water and the mask appears to float on the surface.

Masks have also been used in many countries in a more frivolous way, appearing in street parades, masquerades and carnivals, and at parties. Here the mask's appeal is not so much the character created by the mask, but the elements of mystery and intrigue created by disguising the identity of the wearer of the mask.

Hint

Noh is a highly ceremonial Japanese dance–drama. The plots are usually tragic dramas involving mysterious and supernatural characters and events. Most of the performers, who are all male, are masked.

8.2 Neutral Masks: Creating Individual Character

Practitioner Profile

Tony Kishawi
Mask Performer and Teacher

Born into a performing family, Tony's career includes solo, community and conceptual performance. He has consistently created immediate, spontaneous and interactive theatre. Tony performed in various guises, including puppet and object theatre with the Tasmanian Puppet Theatre, until he commenced studies at the Victorian College of the Arts. He is an original member of Theatre Works in Victoria, and has performed extensively throughout Australia, in Europe and most recently in Japan.

Currently, Tony is Co-director of Transient Company. His teaching focuses on specialist workshops for youth, community groups and professionals. He specialises in mask and mime, focusing on the tradition of commedia dell'arte following studies with teachers Antonio Fava in Italy, Philippe Gaulier in England, and Eves Marks and Clare Hagen in Holland. Tony's work has a consistent focus on the spirit of the mask and the complicity of the ensemble. It is founded on the belief that the social or political comment of this tradition must come from the game created by the interaction of the performer, rather than from some predetermined comment.

Read: Creating and Expressing Masked Character

Neutral masks are masks that are plain in colour and do not show a particular or distinctive personality. They are excellent to use when practising mask work because their neutral quality allows for greater freedom to create character. Neutral masks encourage the performer to be more expressive with their body because the performer cannot use facial expression or voice to communicate character personality.

Write and Discuss

1. Research different types of masks by finding pictures of masks in your library or on the Internet. Write a description of two masks, including their features, personality and the materials from which they are made. Report your findings to the class.
2. Discuss how the impact on a performer of wearing a neutral mask could differ from the impact of wearing a character mask.

Hint

As neutral, full-face masks prevent speech, you will need to use body language and mime to communicate (see Units 1.2 and 1.3, pages 6–13).

Hint

You will need to use neutral masks in these exercises. You will also need to use one or more mirrors to assist in building character.

Hint

Prior to a performance, a Noh theatre performer will use a mirror to look at their reflection wearing mask and costume. This helps the performer to 'see' and become more connected to the character they are playing.

Exercise Mask and Mirror

The exercises in this unit will take you through a process of working with neutral masks. Before you start the exercises, it is important to consider and remember these five guidelines for the use of mask in rehearsal and performance:

1. Only wear your mask when in character; remove your mask to talk to your teacher or another student.
2. Do not put your mask on when facing the audience.
3. Use a mirror to see your reflection when wearing the mask. Use the reflection to help develop the character.
4. Do not touch or refer to your mask once you are in character.
5. Do not touch or refer to another performer's mask.

1 Building Character No. 1

This exercise allows the group to observe the process of building a character using neutral mask and mirror work. Choose one volunteer to wear the neutral mask. Choose another volunteer to hold the mirror; or use wall mirrors if you have access to them. Your teacher will take you through the following steps:

- Stand opposite the mirror with your back to the audience.
- Put on the mask.
- Look at the reflection of the mask until you get a strong sense of character.
- Once you feel the character is established, turn away from the mirror and walk through the room. Explore the character's movement and use of body language. The person holding the mirror can move with you through the room to help you see the character's movements.
- Keep referring to the mirror to 'recharge' the character or to help you regain focus.

150 Dramatic Forms and Performance Styles

2 Building Character No. 2

This exercise is similar to exercise 1 but involves the whole class. You will need to set up mirrors around the room so that people can refer to them.

- Find somewhere to sit on the floor. Place your mask on the floor face up.
- Examine the mask.
- On a signal from your teacher, put on the mask and look into a mirror. Try to gain a sense of the character instinctively. Keep referring to the mirror until you feel a strong sense of character.
- When you feel the character is established, move away from the mirror and explore the character's walk, gestures and movements. Do not interact with other characters. Return to the mirror every time you feel you need to refresh the character.

Your teacher will provide side coaching to help you adopt your character. They may merely encourage you or they may ask the character questions. The character's replies are only communicated through the use of body language.

Use your skills of spontaneity, commitment and focus to help make your neutral mask work successful.

Write and Discuss

1. Describe your character.
2. Describe how you felt during the process of becoming the character. Why?
3. Evaluate your ability to remain focused and committed when wearing masks. Offer suggestions for how you can maintain focus and commitment.

3 Character Exploration

For this exercise you will need to have the basis of a character before you begin. The basis for your character could come from the work you completed in exercises 1 and 2. You will need to set up mirrors to refer to during the exercise.

On the signal from your teacher, put on your mask. Look into the mirror and adopt your character. Undertake a selection of the following activities:

- Go through the character's morning routine.
- Show the character engaged in their hobby or favourite pastime.
- Show the character in a situation where one small disaster leads to another.
- Show the character with their favourite possession.
- Show the character performing an activity they have been looking forward to.
- Show the character discovering something disappointing or annoying.

Show each other your work by dividing the class in half. One half of the group watches as the other half of the group performs one of the above activities.

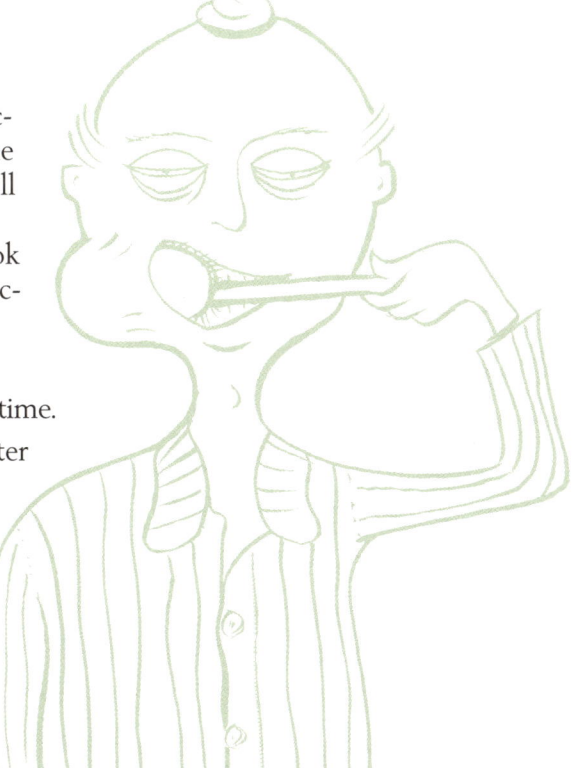

Write and Discuss

1. Comment on one character. Discuss the effectiveness of the performer's portrayal of their character. Refer to their use of body language.
2. Add to your character biography, incorporating any new information you have gained from the activities in exercise 3.
3. Create a point-form character biography that outlines any information about your character.

Present Character Interaction

Divide into pairs. Describe your character to your partner. Use your character biography to assist you. Devise a short situation in which the two masked characters meet and complete a mimed task.

In your preparation consider:

- each character's status in relation to the other
- creating a task that is involved, unusual or awkward
- how the characters will communicate through the use of body language.

Write and Discuss

Use the following tasks to evaluate your own work and the work of others.

1. Describe two memorable moments from one masked performance. Explain why you found the moments memorable.
2. Outline your situation and comment on the strengths of your performance.
3. Discuss how you felt you could have improved aspects of your performance.

8.3 Half Mask and Chorus Work: Creating Group Character

Read ## Masks and Voice

Half masks are cut across the lower half of the mask from one side to the other just below the nose. The half mask allows for the inclusion of voice in mask performance. In this unit we will use neutral half masks and will focus on the role of the masked chorus in performance. This will require you to focus not so much on individual characters but on a group character.

Hint

The half mask requires the performer to use their voice in a skilled way to create character and to suit the heightened style of acting that is encouraged by the wearing of the mask.

Exercise ## Running Exercises

To prepare for chorus work you will need to complete the following exercises. You will not need to wear half masks when you practise these exercises. Director Neil Cameron, in his book *The Running and Stamping Book*, developed running and stamping exercises to help actors develop coordination, fitness and a feel for rhythm. His research involved work with Indigenous Australians, particularly in the development of the stamping exercises (see page 159). These exercises are excellent training for developing your sense of working as a team.

1 The Snake

The class forms a line, with each person standing directly behind the next. The leader changes regularly throughout the exercise. The leader begins a swift jog around the perimeter of the room. It is important that you do not talk to each other because the group needs to concentrate in order to achieve a unified rhythm. In this exercise, the emphasis is on the group maintaining a rhythm and on each individual maintaining an exact distance between the person in front of them and the person behind.

Challenge

The line weaves through the room, but must not cross itself.

The Snake

Mask: Disguising and Revealing

Hint

The two lines weave through the room, but must never cross each other and must maintain the distances.

2 Parallel Lines

The class divides into two groups and forms two parallel lines. Each participant puts one hand on the shoulder of the person in front of them and another hand on the shoulder of the person opposite them in the other line. The two lines must maintain the distance between each line and the distance between the person in front and the person behind. The pairs drop their arms from each other's shoulders. The two leaders run around the outside of the room, maintaining the distances.

Parallel Lines

3 Chorus Line Turn

The class can work as a whole group or divide into smaller groups. Begin with the Snake exercise. Once a rhythm has been established, the snake is free to explore the room randomly.

- On a given signal, the line stops moving through the room and jogs on the spot, making sure each participant is evenly spaced one behind the other.
- On the next signal, each participant takes a quarter turn to create one line standing shoulder to shoulder.

Chorus Line Turn

Dramatic Forms and Performance Styles

- On the next signal, some participants walk forwards and some walk backwards so that the line rotates on the spot and completes one revolution.
- On the given signal, the participants make a quarter turn to stand one behind the other.

Exercise: Working as a Chorus

1 Cannoning

'Cannoning' is a series of movements that follow each other in quick succession, creating a wavelike effect. Audiences in stadiums around the world have witnessed the flowing effect of cannoning and felt the powerful impact of the effect, which has been loosely termed the 'Mexican wave'.

- Stand in a circle as a group.
- One person starts a movement that has a starting and finishing point. For example, you can raise your arm from your side, up above your head and then back down to your side.
- The person next in line copies the movement, but slightly after the first person has begun the first movement.
- The third person does the same, and so on around the circle.
- Make sure each person in the group has a turn starting, devising a different movement each time.

2 Rapid Cannoning

In this exercise you work as you did in the first cannoning exercise, but here all the movements are sudden and sharp. They need to be copied and passed around the circle at high speed.

- Once each person has had a turn at contributing a movement, go around the circle again.
- Repeat the same movement and add sound.

Challenge

In exercise 1 create a wavelike effect, but each person contributes a different movement rather than a copy of a movement. Add sound to the movement. The type of sound used must change with each new movement.

Challenge

In exercise 1 your teacher will divide the class in half. Each half of the class will work independently. The group members stand one behind the other. The wave is initiated by the person in front and is passed down the line. It may be arm movements or involve the whole body. An interesting spiral effect can be achieved when each person extends their arms and body to create a circular movement that starts at floor level, moves out and up to the ceiling and down the other side.

Challenge

In exercise 2 use moods or personal qualities to create shapes as you go around the circle. For example, you may use grief, arrogance or sensitivity. Choose the appropriate pace for each mood or personal quality.

Mask: Disguising and Revealing

Hint

The changes in direction in exercise 3 should initially be well spaced until the group gains confidence in responding to the changes quickly.

3 Fish

Divide into medium-sized groups. The participants of each group arrange themselves in a square formation. There should be enough space between each person to allow the group to move smoothly through the space. Each group will move through the room like a school of fish. You need to follow these rules:

- The group must always stay together, evenly spaced.
- Only the people on the outside of the group can initiate a change of direction.
- All changes in direction must be sharp ninety-degree turns.
- A change in direction can be initiated at any time.
- The whole group must try to respond as quickly as possible to the change in direction.

If members of the group become separated from the main group they must move through the room, following the above rules, until they connect with the main group again.

Challenge

Work in groups of five or six. Using ideas gained from the chorus exercises, devise a short movement performance with or without use of mask to present to the class. Your performance should demonstrate the ability of the group to control timing, rhythm and movement.

Write and Discuss

1. What did you enjoy about the chorus exercises? Why?
2. List four points you feel are important for group participants to remember when performing chorus work.

Read: The Chorus of Ancient Greek Theatre

The chorus of Ancient Greek theatre has its origins in the earliest form of theatre, which is known as the dithyrambo and was a drunken, dance–chant, fertility ritual. The dithyrambo festival changed over time into the more formalised, scripted performances of Ancient Greek theatre. By the fifth century, writers had created individual characters that were separate from the chorus. This development encouraged the chorus to act as a commentator on the actions of the main characters.

Hint

Revise the chorus skills you have covered in this chapter to help you complete this task successfully.

Present: Working as a Chorus with Half Mask and Script

Divide into large groups. Use the following script extract and prepare a chorus presentation of the material. Use half mask to help convey the group character. A brief synopsis of the play has been provided to help you with your interpretation. You will probably need two sessions to complete this task.

In your preparation, consider the following:

- What is the predominant role of the chorus in the extract? In what way is the chorus commenting on the action?

- Can you identify the predominant character of the group?
- What movements do you think would best communicate the ideas and emotions of the lines?
- How can you arrange the voices of the chorus to deliver the dialogue effectively?

Put the words of the extract on transparencies and using an overhead projector shine them on a wall. This will help you to rehearse the movements without having to hold your books.

The chorus in *Medea* represents the women of Corinth; a group character rather than an individual one. Performers in Ancient Greek drama were male and played all the female roles.

Read ## Synopsis of *Medea*, written by Euripides in 431 BC

Medea is the mother of Jason's two sons. She arrives in Corinth after helping Jason kill his uncle, who is his enemy, by using her 'witch' powers. After a time, Jason deserts Medea to marry the daughter of the King of Corinth.

Medea sets up a plan of revenge in two stages. The first stage of revenge involves sending to the King of Corinth and his daughter wedding presents that are poisoned with magic. The King and his daughter die, consumed by flames. Medea then deceives Jason and gains his trust. When his guard is down she kills their two sons, who are Jason's only heirs.

The following chorus extract occurs just after a powerful speech in which Medea commits herself to the task of killing her sons by putting aside her maternal feelings and reminding herself of Jason's treachery. At the end of this speech she exits through the rear doors of the stage and the chorus chants the following.

Chorus   Earth, awake! Bright arrows of the Sun,
Look! Look down on the accursed woman
Before she lifts up a murderous hand
To pollute it with her children's blood!
For they are of your own golden race;
And for mortals to spill blood that grew
In the veins of gods is a fearful thing.
Heaven-born brightness, hold her, stop her,
Purge the palace of her, this pitiable
Bloody-handed fiend of vengeance!

All your care for them lost! Your love
For the babes you bore, all wasted, wasted!
Why did you come from the blue Symplegades
That hold the gate of the barbarous sea?
Why must this rage devour your heart
To spend itself in slaughter of children?
Where kindred blood pollutes the ground
A curse hangs over human lives;
And murder measures the doom that falls
By Heaven's law on the guilty house.

Pitiable: deserving pity.
Fiend: monster, villain or murderer.
Vengeance: the desire for taking revenge.

8.4 African Mask Performance

Read An Overview of the Use of Mask in African Performance

Africa is a vast continent containing many different countries, each with distinct cultures and traditions. Mask is used widely in Africa and can be found in a performance form known as dance–drama. In African dance–dramas, masked performers enact tales and events to the accompaniment of rhythmic drumming. They contain exciting displays of acrobatics, movement, mime, dance, chanting, singing and magic. Dance–dramas are performed outdoors and use the performance space in a distinctive way. As the performance travels from one spot to another, the performance area changes shape. The audience is encouraged to move with the performance and may also participate in the action.

The story-lines of the dance–dramas vary greatly. They are often connected to significant moments of the past and present and they also look to the future. The dance–dramas also reflect the community's relationship with the land and the environment. For example, many African cultures have rituals that

158 Dramatic Forms and Performance Styles

celebrate the transition from childhood to adulthood and use images of animals to create symbols and add meaning to the ceremony. Dance–dramas have also been created to mark funerals, harvests, the change of seasons and heroic tales from the past.

The masks worn in performance are treated with great respect because they often hold great symbolic significance for the community. Performers are specially chosen and trained in performance skills. The masks used portray the faces of animals, spirits, mythical beings, gods and ancestors. They are made from a variety of natural materials, including wood, shells and grasses.

Write and Discuss

1. Research one African country and a cultural group within that country that uses masks in performance. Find out information that describes how and why masks are used in performance. Report your findings to the class.
2. Find pictures of African masks. Present these to the class and describe the characters the masks portray and their significance in performance.

Exercise: Stamping Exercises

1 Practise the Stamp
Before you can begin stamping you need to perfect the technique of executing the stamp. To do this correctly you firstly need to bend the knees slightly. Raise the knee in front of the body and bring the foot down flat on the floor. The heel and the toe should strike at the same time. The floor does not need to be struck hard.

Revisit the Running Exercises in Unit 8.3 (pages 153–5) and use some as a warm-up for these exercises.

2 Running to Stamping
The group begins running around the perimeter of the room in a line. This continues until a comfortable rhythm is established. After a short time the group forms a straight line, running on the spot. On the signal from your teacher, the line makes a quarter turn so that everyone is shoulder to shoulder. The run is gradually slowed down until it becomes a stamp. The group must establish a uniform rhythm.

African masked performances are accompanied by drumming and chanting. Try to incorporate drumming or another form of rhythmic sound into the practice of these exercises.

3 Two Lines Stamping
The class divides into two groups. Each group forms a line and stands facing each other at either end of the room. Both groups begin a slow, rhythmic stamp. On the signal from your teacher, include a sound to accompany the rhythm of the stamp. On the next signal, the two lines walk towards each other. As they get closer to each other, the volume of the sound is increased. Once the two lines have met, they both retreat, fading the volume of the sound as they return to their starting positions.

Repeat this exercise but use a focus on different emotions to change the way that each group stamps. For example, one group may approach the other communicating victory, while the other group communicates defeat.

Mask: Disguising and Revealing

Write and Discuss

1. Evaluate your ability to effectively combine running and stamping.
2. Evaluate the group's ability to effectively combine running and stamping.
3. What skills are needed, individually and as a group, to encourage consistency of rhythm?

Exercise Representing Nature

1 Animals

Find a space in the room where you can work on your own. You will begin by trying to create a physical representation of an animal. Use neutral mask or half mask to help establish the animal character. Begin to explore the ways in which your chosen animal moves, lies, eats and sleeps. On a given signal from your teacher, exaggerate an aspect of the animal's behaviour. For example, if it is an animal that is constantly wary of being attacked, you may highlight its sharp movements every time it senses danger.

2 Seasons Around the Circle

The group stands in a circle wearing half mask. The circle is divided into four sections. Each section represents one of the four seasons. The exercise commences at the starting point of any season. Each person provides a suitable sound and movement to represent an aspect of the season they are to portray. The next person in line copies the sound and movement, but adapts the sound and movement slightly to show the progression of the season. Continue around the circle several times without stopping.

Challenge

Your teacher will count slowly from one to four. Each number represents a transition from animal to human form. Although the physical shape changes, the essential traits of the animal are evident in the final human form.

Write and Discuss

1. Describe the animal you created using mask. Discuss how the mask assisted you in developing the character's personality.
2. Describe the movements you used to create the animal character. How did you alter these to become more 'human'?
3. Discuss the representation of seasons in the Seasons Around the Circle exercise. Identify strong use of movement and sound by individuals who you felt captured the essence of a season.

Present: Aboriginal Dreamtime

Divide into small groups. Use fabric, face painting, as well as neutral and half mask to devise a short movement piece that represents an Australian Dreamtime story. You may like to use the website listed at **hi.com.au/centrestage** to source your story.

Your presentation should attempt to represent locations and experiences that capture Australia's natural landscape.

Remember to follow the mask guidelines from Unit 8.2 (pages 149–52) when preparing your piece. Also consider the use of chanting, stamping, running and other chorus skills in your preparation.

Write and Discuss

1. Describe one group's movement piece and focus on retelling the steps in their story.
2. Discuss how the group used the following elements: mask, stamping, running, rhythm and fabric.
3. Are there any suggestions you would make to improve the group's performance?
4. Discuss what you have learnt from the exercises in this chapter. Comment on how you feel they have prepared you for your Aboriginal Dreamtime performance.

8.5 Performance Task: Mask Ritual

Read Rituals

Rituals are established and repeated practices that celebrate important moments in human experience. Some common rituals are marriages, funerals, the beginning of a New Year and honouring those who died in battle. Rituals can include the following elements: a blessing, cleansing, re-enactment, procession, crowning or prayer, chanting, or the powerful use of symbols.

The steps in a ritual can be divided into three phases:

1. **Introduction and preparation.** In this phase, the tone of the ritual is established, preparations are completed and any cleansing or blessing is undertaken.
2. **The climactic moment.** This is the moment of focus. The focus may represent a change or turning point for individuals and the community, be it overcoming evil, or a transformation from child to adult or from boy to warrior. This moment can be heightened with the use of symbol. For example, the initiated is adorned with a special item of clothing that is a symbol of their new status.
3. **Confirmation.** The ritual finishes by unifying the audience in a feeling of common understanding and awareness. This could be a sense of leaving the past and looking to the future. This section of the ritual may involve, for example, a procession, chanting, comic performance or feasting.

Hint

This performance task is especially challenging because it requires commitment from the performers and a strong use of focus to help engage the audience in the ritual. This does not mean that the ritual needs to be formal or serious. In fact some rituals are highly comic and festive.

Read The Task

You are to work in medium-sized groups and draw on your own research of rituals in different cultures to devise a masked ritual. You can adapt your research on rituals and place the ritual you devise in any place and at any time.

The ritual will show distinct phases and include use of symbol and chorus work. It will contain a distinct climactic moment. This point of focus will heighten the importance of the ritual to the community. The masked ritual will focus on one or more human characters experiencing a new understanding or achievement as the result of a difficult experience or test. The masked ritual will also include mythical characters, for example spirits and gods who will provide tests, guidance and advice.

The ritual will include the use of masks. These can be character masks, neutral masks, half masks or a combination of these.

Dramatic Forms and Performance Styles

The presentation of the ritual will be accompanied by the appropriate use of one or more of the following: acrobatics, stamping, running, music, drumming, percussion or chanting. The presentation will incorporate changes to the shape of the performance space, movement from one location to another and appropriate audience interaction.

Prepare: Creating and Making a Mask Ritual

This performance task requires you to devise a mask ritual that celebrates a significant moment. You need to research and consider the different types of rituals. Although your final presentation may be fictional, it is important that the group is committed to the purpose of the ritual. The performers' commitment will encourage commitment from the audience. The questions and tasks in the Write and Discuss section will guide you through the creative process.

Hint

Use the information you found in your research task at the beginning of Unit 8.2 (page 150) to give you ideas for your performance task.

Write and Discuss

1. Research rituals from different cultures either within Australia or from other countries. Identify the purpose and importance of the rituals you find in your research. Describe one ritual to the class.
2. Identify and explain the purpose of the ritual you devise.
3. Decide the event on which your ritual will focus. For example, it may focus on a birth, death, creation, coming of age or harvest.
4. What is the history of this ritual and why is it significant to the community?
5. What skills can be incorporated to make sure the presentation of the ritual flows smoothly?
6. What symbols can be used to heighten moments of the performance? Examples of symbols you may use are water, earth, precious metals, emblems and totems.
7. How could mask be used in a symbolic way?
8. What rhythmic sound can be incorporated in the ritual?
9. How can the audience be made part of the performance by altering and changing the shape of the performance space during the ritual? Can the audience be included in any parts of the ritual?

Hint

When considering how to include audience members in a performance you need to avoid embarrassing or intimidating people because this could undermine the success of your ritual.

Prepare: Creating and Making a Mask Ritual Character

- Who are the people in your fictional community that are allowed to perform the ritual? Why have they been chosen?
- What role or function will they play in the ritual?
- How can mask be incorporated to represent the characters?
- What are the guidelines that need to be followed when using mask in performance? Can these guidelines be built into the performance of your ritual?
- What aspects of the ritual will the chorus represent? For example, will they be the elements, the seasons or the spirits of the ancestors?

Evaluate: Performance Checklist

You and your teacher will evaluate your work individually, using a list of criteria. These criteria relate to your achievement in this task. Some criteria will relate to the achievement of the group. The criteria are listed on the evaluation sheet at the end of this chapter and will be used to evaluate your ability to:

- incorporate your research, knowledge and understanding into your performance work
- sustain and develop character and role in performance
- select and incorporate appropriate body language
- select and incorporate appropriate voice, if wearing half mask
- include the use of symbol in the ritual
- establish an appropriate mood and atmosphere
- structure your ritual into a coherent and polished performance incorporating effective scene transitions
- effectively include chorus work
- successfully include audience involvement.

Write and Discuss

Arts Criticism and Aesthetics

1. Outline the highlights of the rehearsal process and explain why you felt they were moments of success.
2. Evaluate the final presentation of your mask ritual. What were the strongest moments in your performance?
3. Discuss how individual groups made effective use of mask, chorus work, rhythm and movement.

Past and Present Contexts

4. Imagine you are teaching mask work to drama students. Outline a series of lessons that explores mask work from one other culture. Include practical activities in your lessons to help your students explore the topic.
5. Draw on your knowledge and understanding of mask work. Explain and describe how mask work can be incorporated into contemporary performance work. Include examples of how masks in performance can create powerful moments for the audience.

Refer to Appendixes 1, 3 and 4 for help with your logbook entries. The appendixes provide you with guidelines for evaluating your own performance work and the work of others.

Evaluation Sheet — Chapter 8 Mask: Disguising and Revealing

Performance Task: Mask Ritual

Student: .... Teacher: ....

Related Outcomes

By completing this task you should be able to:
- apply the skills of performing with masks
- explore the creation of character through neutral mask
- create masked chorus work incorporating use of half mask, movement, sound and text
- appreciate the influence of masks in the performance work of a range of cultures and apply this knowledge to performance work
- create and present a ritual incorporating use of masks.

Criteria	Level of Achievement			
	Beginning	Consolidating	Mastering	Excelling
Exploring and Developing Ideas Have you prepared for your performance by: • incorporating into your performance your understanding of rituals in different cultures? • focusing the climactic moment on one or more human characters who are experiencing a new understanding or achievement as the result of a difficult experience or test? • including mythical characters, for example spirits and gods, who will provide tests, guidance and advice?				
Using Skills, Techniques and Processes Have you used drama elements, skills, techniques and processes to structure a mask performance by: • incorporating mask to portray character and role? • incorporating body language and voice appropriately? • including the use of symbol in the ritual? • including the use of chorus work? • sustaining and developing character and role?				
Presenting Have you rehearsed and presented a performance for a specific audience by: • establishing an appropriate mood and atmosphere for the ritual? • effectively manipulating the actor–audience relationship through consideration of the performance space? • structuring the ritual into a coherent and polished performance incorporating effective scene transitions?				

Comments: _____

_____

Dramatic Forms and Performance Styles © Mathew Clausen

Chapter 9

Non-Realistic Theatre: Visions, Dreams and Symbols

Why Study Non-Realistic Theatre?

Non-realistic theatre covers a variety of early twentieth century styles, including Expressionism, Symbolism, Absurdism and Epic Theatre. (We will look at Epic Theatre more closely in Unit 10.2, pages 193–98.) The influence of non-realistic theatre can be found in performance work today. By studying non-realistic theatre you will learn about and acquire performance skills and theatrical techniques to help you create abstract, strange, symbolic and dreamlike performance works.

This chapter is divided into the following units:

- **9.1** An Overview of Non-Realistic Theatre
- **9.2** Dreams and the Subconscious
- **9.3** Expressionist Theatre
- **9.4** Performance Task: Non-Realistic Theatre

Outcomes

In this chapter you will:

- explore the influences that encouraged the development of non-realistic theatre
- select and incorporate stylised movement and voice in non-realistic performance work
- explore the origins, purpose and conventions of Expressionist theatre
- devise and present a non-realistic theatre performance.

Melita Jurisic in *Mourning Becomes Electra*, Sydney Theatre Company, 1998.

9.1 An Overview of Non-Realistic Theatre

Read The Development of Non-Realistic Theatre

Non-realistic theatre developed in reaction to the style of Realism (see Unit 4.3, pages 74–80). Non-realistic theatre is not confined to re-creating life on stage. It also seeks to explore the more elusive and intangible qualities of human existence. As well as heightened use of movement and voice, non-realistic theatre experiments with non-realistic sets, sound effects and coloured lighting to create effect. Some of the major developments of non-realistic theatre are listed below:

- During the 1890s, artists, poets and theatre practitioners reacted against Realism and developed a style known as Symbolism. A Belgian, Maurice Maeterlinck, wrote plays that included the use of non-realistic characters; sounds interspersed with long, static silences; and dreamlike colour combinations of lighting.

- In 1896, Alfred Jarry wrote *Ubu Roi*, a highly comic and physical play that explores the abuse of power. The production of this play caused great scandal for its unconventional performance style and use of vulgarity.

- The development of the study of psychology, and an increasing interest in the power of dreams and the subconscious, inspired artists, musicians, poets and theatre practitioners to explore human experience beyond day-to-day living.

Although Stanislavski is remembered for his contribution to the development of Realism, he also experimented with non-realistic forms of theatre later in his career.

- Vsevolod Meyerhold, a Russian director and a collaborator with Stanislavski, broke from the Moscow Art Theatre to create a non-realistic acting style known as biomechanic acting. This style was highly theatrical and incorporated abstract design and innovative use of the performance space.

- In 1911, Strindberg wrote *A Dream Play*, which incorporated memory, fantasy, absurdity and improvisation.

- Scenic designers, lighting designers and musicians designed sets, lighting and music to help create fantasy worlds.

Changes in theatre at the turn of the century closely mirrored changes in visual arts, music and literature.

- Increased use of machines in the workplace and the introduction of automated machinery were seen as a threat to the human spirit. Artists in Germany reacted to this change in society with a movement known as Expressionism.

- Antonin Artaud developed the Theatre of Cruelty between 1926 and 1933. Theatre of Cruelty is an often misunderstood term for performance work that abolished traditional actor–audience boundaries. Artaud was greatly influenced by the ritualistic and disciplined dance–drama work of Cambodia and Bali. Artaud promoted a theatre of the senses. The audience

was to be shocked and moved by images of great power and beauty.
- Bertolt Brecht, affected by the futility of World War I, wrote plays that not only reflected the world but also attempted to change it. He developed Epic Theatre, which is a non-realistic style of performance that seeks to provoke the audience to reflect on and consider political issues.
- In the late 1940s, the impact of two World Wars and increasing questioning about the philosophy of human existence encouraged the development of Absurdism. Samuel Beckett's Absurdist play *Waiting for Godot* caused outrage when it was first performed in 1953.

Write and Discuss

Research one of the following non-realistic theatre practitioners: Antonin Artaud, Jerzy Grotowski, Vsevolod Meyerhold or Gordon Craig. Make point-form notes on the distinctive conventions of their performance styles. Present your findings to the class.

9.2 Dreams and the Subconscious

 ## Dreams and Interpretation

In this unit you will undertake exercises that help create theatrical representations of dreams and the subconscious. There are many theories regarding dreams and the subconscious. Some theorists have suggested that dreams are an expression of our subconscious and are a process of 'sorting out' our issues and concerns. Others believe that dreams hold symbolic significance and that we need to interpret our dreams to understand their meaning. Another group of theorists believe that dreams are merely erratic electrical activity in the brain that triggers disconnected and unrelated memories and images as we sleep. These theorists maintain that dreams have no particular meaning.

The Austrian psychiatrist Sigmund Freud suggested that our concerns and anxieties come from a conflict between our conscious and the needs of the subconscious. Freudian psychologists believe that the subconscious is connected to our primitive and instinctive needs and urges. It is believed our conscious mind is often unaware of the influence of the subconscious.

These discoveries and theories influenced the art world and the ways in which characters and situations were expressed in theatre. Writers and directors played with characters, time and space, and created non-realistic stories that were often disjointed and disconnected.

Write and Discuss

1. Research art works from the Surrealist painters or Expressionist painters. Look for images that you feel express dreams and the subconscious. Find one painting to show to the class. Some artists from this period are Klee, Dali and Munch.

Exercise Dreams and the Subconscious

Challenge

Explore different combinations of high speed, slow motion and exaggerated movement in situations you devise.

1 Slow Motion, High Speed and Exaggeration

Manipulating movement is a very effective way to create non-realistic performance work.

Choose one of the activities below:

- eating large quantities of very soft and sticky toffee
- being trapped in a room with a venomous spider
- leaving the premiere of a movie you star in, to meet hundreds of your fans.

You will perform the chosen activity and explore the use of slow motion, high speed and exaggeration.

Slow Motion. Slow-motion movement requires the performer to give the impression that movement has been slowed to a minimum. The performer still needs to communicate effort and reactions, for example, but all in slow motion. Strong discipline and control are required for this exercise. Each time your teacher gives the signal, halve the speed at which you perform the activity until you have reached slow motion. Do not exaggerate the movements, only slow them down.

High Speed. Begin performing the activity at normal speed. Each time your teacher gives the signal, double the speed at which you complete the activity until you reach high speed.

Exaggeration. Exaggerated movement requires the performer to amplify the size of their movements. Repeat the chosen activity. Begin with normal movements. On a signal from your teacher, exaggerate your movements slightly. On each subsequent signal, continue to enlarge your movements until they take on giant proportions. Do not increase the pace of your actions as you exaggerate the movements.

2 Transformation

You will need coloured pieces of fabric for this exercise. Performers can use transformation as an effective technique in non-realistic performance. When you are practising this exercise, it is important to complete the transformations slowly. You can complete 'snap' transformations when you have gained confidence in this technique.

Try the following exercises:

- Work in groups of four. Choose a piece of fabric. Each person in the group of four must take a turn using the fabric as an object. The first person turns the fabric into an object, which is then passed to the second person. They transform the object that has been passed to them into a new object.
- Work in groups of four. Choose a piece of fabric. Decide on three objects. The group will use their bodies and the fabric to create these objects. Examples include a piece of furniture, a musical instrument and an antique clock. On a signal from your teacher, the whole group becomes the first object. On the next signal, the group transforms into the next object, and so on.

3 Sounds and Language

Sounds and language in dreamlike performances are heightened and stylised to add to the symbolism and atmosphere. The use of percussion instruments, recorded sound effects, atmospheric music, vocal sounds and stylised language adds to the non-realistic quality of the performance.

A Dream Play, Scene 3, by August Strindberg

It is we, we, the waves,
that rock the winds
to rest!
Green cradles, we the waves.
We are wet and salt;
we are like flames of fire,
we are wet flames.
Quenching, burning,
washing, bathing,
breeding, bearing.
We, we the waves
that rock the winds
to sleep!

Non-Realistic Theatre: Visions, Dreams and Symbols

Divide into small groups and use the extract from *A Dream Play* by August Strindberg (see page 171) to create a short movement and sound presentation. Be creative in the way you use movement and deliver the dialogue. Consider the use of multiple voices, repetition, long pauses, volume and pace to add impact to your presentation. Also consider how you may convey the contrast of fire and water in your performance work. If possible, include the use of percussion to enhance your performance work.

Write and Discuss

1. Describe how you incorporated the techniques you learnt in the Dreams and the Subconscious exercises into your interpretation of the extract.
2. What choices did your group make when deciding how to deliver the lines? Did you incorporate any special techniques for effect? Why?

The class divides into groups of five. Each group presents two of the listed dream states to the class.

4 Recreating Aspects of Dreams

Find a space in the room in which to work on your own. Explore how you may use your body in performance to represent the following common dream states:

- running but not getting anywhere
- screaming but not being heard
- floating
- falling but not hitting the ground.

Write and Discuss

Comment on the use of movement by two different groups to represent dream states. Discuss how their use of movement helped to make their presentation successful.

5 Recalling Dreams

Divide into pairs or small groups. Each person is to share a memorable dream they can recall. Although you can ask each other questions about their dreams, allow the person time to tell their dream fully before you ask questions. When you tell your dream, make sure you include details that describe the characters, time and place, focus, tension, atmosphere and mood.

6 Interpreting Dreams

Once each person has shared their dream, use the following table to help identify certain aspects of your dream. You are to make suggestions for how you may represent these aspects of your dream in performance.

Write and Discuss

An example of a dream has been provided in the table below. Use the table as a guide to help identify how the elements of drama will work together to communicate your dream.

Selected Element of Drama	Description	How do I show this in performance?
Characters and situation	• A talking elephant • Bizarre performers	• I follow an elephant into a circus tent • I observe peculiar circus acts on my way into the tent
Tension	• Comic • Bizarre • Hint of danger	• Elephant character will be funny • Create tension and anticipation of the tightrope walk using slow motion • Use sound effects and repeat the same piece of music
Focus	• I have to tightrope walk with the elephant!	• Use a line of chairs to create the tightrope, give the illusion of height and focus the audience's attention • Silence just before I step on the tightrope
Time and place	• Weird, old-fashioned circus	• Use a length of rope to show the performance ring of the circus • Use boxes for podiums
Language and movement	• Need to communicate the bizarre qualities of the characters • Need to communicate, through dialogue, information about the tightrope task	• Four people could be a non-realistic elephant; use four arms to create elephant's trunk; use some grey fabric • All speak at the same time in a deep, slow voice • Use heavy, slow movements • Other bizarre performers hold frozen, contorted poses in the background • The rope could transform from the circus ring to the tightrope
Symbols	• Tightrope = facing your fears • Elephant = wisdom • Colours: red (danger), black (fear) and yellow (success)	• Use red lights as I step onto the tightrope • People under a black cloth, beneath chairs, represent fear • Elephant gives me a yellow cloak as I cross the tightrope

Present Dreams and the Subconscious

Divide into groups. Each person will need to share the dream that they recalled in exercise 5. Choose one group member's dream to present in performance. As a group, document the breakdown of the aspects of the dream and how you will realise these in performance.

Performing dreams opens exciting possibilities for physical work. Include balances, carrying and lifts into your work if you can. Include the use of sound, lighting (if possible) and material, for example, to heighten the dreamlike quality of your performance. Consider how you can manipulate voice and movement to add to the non-realistic effect.

Hint

If you are attempting any physical work, make sure you first complete a physical warm-up. Check with your teacher that you are completing any heavy lifting or physical work safely.

Write and Discuss

1. How have the exercises in this unit helped you to make decisions about the ways in which you can present dreams in performance?
2. Describe one other group's presentation. In your description, highlight one aspect of the performance you felt was effective and explain how the group made the moment effective.
3. Based on your knowledge, research and experience, discuss why you feel non-realistic theatre is a valuable style of performance work.

9.3 Expressionist Theatre

Read Transforming Reality

Expressionism is an art movement that originated in Germany in the early 1900s. Artists and writers reacted to what they saw as the mechanisation of human society and produced non-realistic artwork to challenge the changes in society. Although this movement was shortlived, it has had an enormous influence on

Edvard Munch's *The Scream*.

modern art forms. It is directly linked to the development of Bertolt Brecht's Epic Theatre. The function and purpose of Epic Theatre are quite different from those of Expressionist theatre. However, the two forms of theatre do have a few similar features.

The creators of Expressionist theatre wanted to convey a heightened interpretation of the world through the use of stylised acting, including controlled physical movement and the use of concise and direct language. The features of Expressionist theatre are:

- transformation of reality as we know it into a dreamlike and fantasy world
- use of many varied characters and locations that build to a powerful climax
- communication of a political or social message
- use of fantasy and symbolism, with moments of realism
- use of generalised character names, such as mother, father and worker, to make characters representative of all mothers, fathers and workers, for example
- use of symbolic props and sets; the sets were often abstract and vast
- use, in some productions, of slides to help show the many locations and to help create mood and atmosphere
- use of coloured lights and shadows to create spectacle
- integration into the performance of music and sound effects, often at very loud levels
- use of masks and stylised make-up

- generally non-realistic movements that are, for example, rhythmic, slow, graceful or mechanical
- change of characters during performance, for example a character appearing as a robot in one scene and then moving realistically in a later scene.

Practitioner Profile

Barrie Kosky
Director

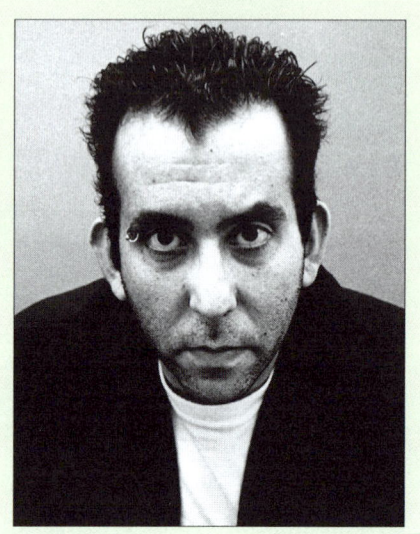

Barrie Kosky is recognised as one of the most exciting and creative directors in Australia; his productions span theatre and opera.

I am someone who believes in the power of tradition; if you don't have tradition then there is nothing to react against, nothing to transform. If you work in the theatre now you have to be sure of your ideas, technique and theatrical imagination. If you're not interested in design, if you're not interested in working with actors' bodies, if you're not interested in the use of light in space and you're not interested in the three-dimensional form, then you shouldn't be working in theatre.

Exercise Expressionist Theatre

1 Humans Become Robots

Your teacher will need a whistle for this exercise. As a class, walk through the room, maintaining an even distance from each other. On the first sound of the whistle, freeze and hold the freeze for about thirty seconds. On the second sound of the whistle, transform your character from human to robot. Alter your walk and movements so they become rigid and sharp. When the whistle sounds again, freeze and hold the freeze for about thirty seconds. Then, one by one, unfreeze and revert to your normal walk. On the final whistle, freeze and remain completely frozen for one minute. Repeat these steps.

2 Puppets

Divide into pairs. You will take turns at being both puppet and puppet controller. The puppet controller coordinates the puppet's movements by pulling on invisible strings that are connected to the puppet's limbs, head and body. The puppet yields to the pulling of the invisible strings and can be made to walk, sit down, pick up items and perform other movements. The controller can also control emotional responses from the puppet through verbal instructions.

Write and Discuss

Describe the differences between your use of body language and movement in human form and your use of body language and movement in either robot or puppet form.

3 Paper Chase

Divide into medium-sized groups. Improvise a short play in which a human is seeking approval for an important and urgent matter. For example, it may be a loan, a traveller's visa or an insurance claim. The human character must get the correct form signed in order to get approval.

During the improvisation, the human approaches an inhuman and impersonal world of machines and robots or puppets and seeks their advice as to how to get the matter approved. Each robot or puppet tries to thwart the attempts of the human by creating diversions, extra charges, more forms and so on.

Hint

If you choose to act as puppets for exercise 3, you may wish to include human controllers in the improvisation. If you do include human controllers, they should appear to be invisible to the human character seeking approval.

Write and Discuss

1. What kind of mood and atmosphere was created in the exercises where you played robots and puppets?
2. What reactions did you experience as you observed the human character and their dilemma in exercise 3? Why?
3. Describe an incident from your own personal experience that reflects the issues presented by the actions of the characters in exercise 3.

Present — Working with an Expressionist Script

The following extracts are from the US playwright Eugene O'Neill's *The Hairy Ape*. Once you have read both extracts and completed the written tasks, choose one of the extracts to present to the class.

Read — Synopsis of *The Hairy Ape*

Written in the 1920s, *The Hairy Ape* is a strong example of Expressionist theatre and explores the dehumanising of ordinary workers as they become slaves to industry. O'Neill's message is reinforced through the title of the play and the repeated use of the symbolic image of humans as primates in captivity.

The central character, Yank, who is tough and aggressive, works shovelling coal on a ship. He is attracted to and rejected by Mildred, who is the pale and pampered daughter of 'a captain of industry'. Yank seeks revenge for being rejected. His subsequent futile and violent search for Mildred symbolises the hopelessness of his existence. Despite his physical strength, he will always be a slave to industry. He is arrested, escapes and eventually goes mad and dies in a gorilla cage at the zoo.

The Hairy Ape conveys a lot of power and energy and has an important social message, even though it may seem a little peculiar to us today.

Read Extract A

Extract A gives the opening stage directions for Scene 3, where Yank first sees Mildred in the furnace room of the ship. The directions establish the atmosphere of the scene. Before Mildred arrives, Yank and the others are working stoking the furnaces. Yank's anger builds as he is provoked by his superiors. The tension is heightened by the use of the shrill sounds of whistles and other loud noises. As the scene builds to a climax, Mildred enters and sees Yank at the peak of his anger. This terrifies her and she hurries away under protection, referring to Yank as 'a filthy beast'. Note the ways in which lighting and sound are incorporated to add impact to the opening of this scene.

The Hairy Ape, Scene 3

(Scene. The stokehole. In the rear, the dimly-outlined bulks of the furnaces and boilers. High overhead one hanging electric bulb sheds just enough light through the murky air laden with coal-dust to pile up masses of shadows everywhere. A line of men, stripped to the waist, is before the furnace doors. They bend over, looking neither to right nor left, handling their shovels as if they were part of their bodies, with a strange, awkward, swinging rhythm. They use the shovels to throw open the furnace doors. Then from these fiery round holes in the black a flood of terrific light and heat pours full upon the men who are outlined in silhouette in the crouching, inhuman attitudes of chained gorillas. The men shovel with a rhythmic motion, swinging as on a pivot from the coal which lies in heaps on the floor behind to hurl it into the flaming mouths before them. There is a tumult of noise—the brazen clang of the furnace doors as they are flung open or slammed shut, the grating, teeth-gritting grind of steel against steel, of crunching coal. This clash of sounds stuns one's ears with its rending dissonance. But there is order in it, rhythm, a mechanical regulated recurrence, a tempo. And rising above all, making the air hum with the quiver of liberated energy, the roar of leaping flames in the furnaces, the monotonous throbbing heat of the engines.)

Write and Discuss

1. Describe how O'Neill creates mood and atmosphere using the following elements: lighting, sound, movement and rhythm.
2. Describe how the performers in this scene of *The Hairy Ape* would need to use movement and body language to communicate their status as well as the atmosphere of the location.

Read Extract B

Extract B is from Scene 5. Yank is on Fifth Avenue in New York. O'Neill indicates an abstract setting of shops selling overpriced jewels and furs. His stage directions indicate, 'The effect is of a background of magnificence cheapened by commercialism.'

The selected extract occurs at the end of the scene. A crowd of wealthy people is leaving a church and Yank attempts to accost them to avenge his wounded pride at being rejected by Mildred. In Yank's mind, all wealthy women represent Mildred and all wealthy people represent those who keep him working in subhuman conditions. The wealthy people's desire to buy monkey fur in this scene symbolises how Yank and others like him are regarded as products rather than people. This particular moment further infuriates Yank and reminds him of how Mildred rejected him.

O'Neill used masks for the wealthy characters in performance and described them as moving like 'A procession of gaudy marionettes, yet with something of the relentless horror of Frankensteins in their detached, mechanical unawareness'.

If you choose to perform extract B of *The Hairy Ape*, use the script detective steps outlined in Unit 4.3 (pp. 64–70) to assist you in your preparation.

In extract B, Yank punches a gentleman but the punch has no effect. To achieve this in performance you should practise 'pulling punches'. This means you deliver a punch with full effort to make it appear real, but 'pull' the force of the punch away from the object you are punching just before you make contact. It is suggested you practise pulling punches before you perform this extract.

The Hairy Ape, Scene 5

(Yank is in the middle of abusing the wealthy men and women as they leave the church.)

Yank *(He turns in a rage on the wealthy men, bumping viciously into them but not jarring them the least bit. Rather it is he who recoils after each collision. He keeps growling.)* Get off de oith! G'wan! Look where yuh're goin', can't yuh? Git out a-here! Fight, why don't yuh? Put up yer mits! Don't be a dog! Fight, or I'll knock yuh dead!

The People *(But, without seeming to see him, they all answer with mechanical affected politeness.)* I beg your pardon.

(Then at a cry from one of the women, they all scurry to the furrier's window.)

The Woman *(Ecstatically, with a gasp of delight.)* Monkey fur!

(The whole crowd of men and women chorus after her in the same tone of affected delight.) Monkey fur!

Non-Realistic Theatre: Visions, Dreams and Symbols

Yank *(With a jerk back of his head back on his shoulders, as if he had received a punch full in the face—raging.)* I see yuh, all in white! I see yuh, yuh white-faced tart, yuh! Hairy ape, huh? I'll hairy ape yuh!

(He bends down and grips at the street kerbing as if to pluck it out and hurl it. Foiled in this, snarling with passion, he leaps to the lamp-post on the corner and tries to pull it up for a club. Just at that moment a bus is heard rumbling up. A fat, high-hatted, spatted gentleman runs out from the side street. He calls out plaintively: 'Bus! Bus! Stop there!' and runs full tilt into the bending, straining Yank, who is bowled off his balance.)

Yank *(Seeing a fight—with a roar of joy he springs to his feet.)* At last! Bus, huh? I'll bust yuh!

(He lets drive a terrific swing, his fist landing full on the fat gentleman's face. But the gentleman stands unmoved as if nothing had happened.)

Gentleman I beg your pardon. *(Then irritably.)* You have made me lose my bus. *(He claps his hands and begins to scream.)* Officer! Officer!

(Many police whistles shrill out on the instant, and a whole platoon of policemen rush in on Yank from all sides. He tries to fight, but is clubbed to the pavement and fallen upon. The crowd at the window have not moved or noticed this disturbance. The clanging gong of the patrol wagon approaches with a clamouring din.)

(Curtain.)

Write and Discuss

1. What does Yank's inability to affect the passersby symbolise?
2. Describe how you could incorporate skills you have learnt in the Expressionist theatre exercises to achieve O'Neill's description of the wealthy people.
3. How would you create the impression of Yank bumping into and hitting the wealthy people without them being affected?
4. Why does Yank react as though he has been punched when the crowd choruses 'Monkey fur!' How would the actor playing Yank perform this moment?
5. What sounds could you incorporate into this scene to heighten particular moments? How do you create these sounds?

9.4 Performance Task: Non-Realistic Theatre

The Task

Devise a non-realistic theatre performance. Divide into groups and appoint one person as stage manager/technical operator. Your group must choose option 1 or 2 (see below) as the basis for your playbuilding.

In your performance you must use:
- a variety of non-realistic locations
- realistic and non-realistic characters
- stylised movement and voice
- effective and appropriate scene transitions
- recorded sound and/or lighting to establish mood and create effect
- at least one distinct symbol
- extended moments of stillness
- mask and/or stylised make-up for some of the non-realistic characters.

Option 1 'To Sleep, Perchance to Dream'

Create a dream story in which one or more characters move from one dreamlike location to another. During the dream, the central characters confront aspects of themselves, experience memories, confront hidden fears or phobias, are tested, witness a prophetic event or are given advice.

Option 2 Humans, Machines and Technology

Create a story in which one or more characters show the effects (positive and/or negative) of a world that is run by machines and technology. Your performance should resemble our world but incorporate some of the features of non-realistic theatre and Expressionist theatre to accentuate the issues and concerns of your performance.

Hint

Refer to the playbuilding steps in Unit 3.1 (pp. 44–5) to assist you in preparing your performance task.

Prepare ## Creating and Making a Non-Realistic Expressionist Performance

- Use research on dreams or the impact of technology to provide material for your performance.
- Use improvisation and movement to explore bizarre, odd, dreamlike and ridiculous situations.
- Consider how voice and language can be used to create atmosphere. Consider the sort of language that characters may use, for example poetic, colloquial, informal or formal. Can you incorporate repetition, chanting and multiple voices, for example?
- Explore how the use of transformation of objects and fabric, for example, can help to create different environments.
- Consider how you can include moments of stillness. Describe the effect you want to achieve.
- Consider how lighting and recorded sound can be incorporated into your performance.
- Consider the possibility of incorporating overhead projections, slides, video and data projection into your performance.
- Prepare a prompt copy (see Unit 4.2, pages 72–3) that has provision for action, sound and lighting cues. The prompt copy should be prepared as a series of annotated blocking diagrams if your script is a description of action rather than dialogue.

Prepare ## Creating and Making a Non-Realistic Character

- Explore and document how your character or role will move and will use body language. Create different and distinct gestures to communicate particular emotions and attitudes.
- If you play more than one character or role, consider how you can use body and voice to distinguish one character or role from the other.

Evaluate ## Performance Checklist

You and your teacher will evaluate your work individually, using a list of criteria. These criteria relate to your achievement in this task. Some criteria will relate to the achievement of the group. The criteria are listed on the evaluation sheet at the end of this chapter.

As a performer, the criteria will be used to evaluate your ability to:

- sustain and develop character or role in performance
- select and incorporate vocal dynamics to portray character or role

- select and incorporate movement and gesture to portray character or role
- incorporate at least one distinct symbol
- select and link elements of your non-realistic drama into a coherent and polished performance.

As the stage manager/technical operator, the criteria will be used to evaluate your ability to:

- effectively incorporate one or more of the following: sound, lighting and audiovisual
- provide sound tapes, for example, at rehearsals and the performance
- blend technical operation with the performance.

Appendixes 5 and 6 provide lighting and sound cue sheets that you can use in preparation for your performance.

Write and Discuss

Arts Criticism and Aesthetics

1. Evaluate your own group's performance. Analyse the elements that you felt were successful. What factors contributed to this success?
2. Describe how one other group created a powerful moment through the use of either slow motion or stillness.
3. Offer suggestions for how one group could further improve their performance. Identify the particular areas you feel could improve, and describe the approach you would take.

Past and Present Contexts

4. Imagine you are speaking to non-realistic theatre practitioners from the past. Explain to them your understanding of the influences that encouraged the development of this style. Include in your discussion the relevance of this style to performers and audiences today. Include in your explanation examples from your own performance work.

Refer to Appendixes 1, 3 and 4 for help with your logbook entries. The appendixes provide you with guidelines for evaluating your own performance work and the work of others.

Non-Realistic Theatre: Visions, Dreams and Symbols

Evaluation Sheet — Chapter 9 Non-Realistic Theatre: Visions, Dreams and Symbols

Performance Task: Non-Realistic Theatre

Student: .... Teacher: ....

Related Outcomes

By completing this task you should be able to:
- select and incorporate conventions of non-realistic theatre
- select and incorporate stylised movement and voice in non-realistic performance work
- devise and present a non-realistic theatre performance.

Criteria	Level of Achievement			
	Beginning	Consolidating	Mastering	Excelling
Exploring and Developing Ideas Have you prepared for your performance by: • utilising improvisation and movement to explore bizarre, odd, dreamlike situations? • considering how vocal dynamics and recorded sound can be used to create atmosphere? • exploring how the use of transformation of objects and fabric, for example, can help create different environments? • preparing a prompt copy that has provision for action, sound and lighting cues?				
Using Skills, Techniques and Processes Have you used the elements of drama, skills, techniques and processes to structure a non-realistic performance by: • selecting a variety of non-realistic locations and characters? • incorporating stylised movement and voice? • incorporating recorded sound and/or lighting to establish mood and atmosphere? • including at least one distinct symbol? • incorporating extended moments of stillness? • remaining focused in performance?				
Presenting Have you rehearsed and presented a performance for a specific audience by: • establishing an appropriate mood and atmosphere for the chosen topic? • effectively manipulating the actor–audience relationship through consideration of the performance space? • structuring the drama into a coherent and polished performance incorporating effective scene transitions?				

Comments: ....
....

Chapter 10

Playback Theatre and Documentary Drama: Interpreting True Stories

Why Study Playback Theatre and Documentary Drama?

This chapter explores how true stories can be incorporated into performance work. Playback Theatre uses personal stories from the audience and employs improvisation and elements of realistic and non-realistic theatre. Documentary Drama re-enacts historic events using the performance conventions and techniques of Epic Theatre. Exploring these performance forms demonstrates how our own true stories can be powerful and provocative material for performance work.

This chapter is divided into the following units:

10.1 Playback Theatre
10.2 Documentary Drama
10.3 Performance Task: Documentary Drama

Outcomes

In this chapter you will:

- draw on personal stories and historical events as the basis for performance work
- utilise skills of listening, interpretation and improvisation to 'playback' personal stories
- explore both realistic and non-realistic acting styles in Playback Theatre exercises and performance work
- examine and explore how Brecht's Epic Theatre has influenced Documentary Drama
- devise a performance using the techniques and conventions of Documentary Drama.

Julie Forsyth in *The Caucasian Chalk Circle*, Company B Belvoir, 1998. Photograph by Heidrun Löhr.

10.1 Playback Theatre

Practitioner Profile

Jacque Robinson
Practitioner with the Melbourne Playback Theatre Company

Jacque is a founding member of the Melbourne Playback Theatre Company. She has worked both as conductor and performer with the company.

Melbourne Playback Theatre Company was founded in 1981. There are Playback companies working in many parts of the world, including Japan, the United States of America, Finland and France. Melbourne Playback Theatre Company is the longest-running Playback Theatre company in the world. We perform in a variety of educational settings, as well as in the corporate, community and government sectors.

The Playback form is not only exciting and fun to do but it can also be a useful tool for developing a myriad of skills, including improvisation, storytelling, working with metaphor, movement, voice, ensemble work, listening skills, constructing narrative and developing an understanding of the levels of meaning in stories.

Read The Power of Personal Stories

Playback Theatre is an original form of improvisational theatre. It was first created in 1975 by Jonathan Fox, Jo Salas and the original Playback Theatre Company in the Hudson Valley of New York. In a Playback Theatre performance, audience members tell stories from their lives, and watch them enacted on the spot.

As a Playback Theatre performance progresses, the audience becomes involved in sharing stories. This experience of sharing creates an atmosphere of recognition and understanding because participants relate to each other's experiences. The performance does not seek to solve people's problems by giving answers, rather it provides an opportunity to reflect. Some of the conventions of a Playback Theatre performance are provided on page 187.

The stories can include simple events, events from the past and dreams. The story must belong to the storyteller because this makes the Playback Theatre performance more engaging for the storyteller and the audience.

Non-realistic acting techniques are used to help heighten particular moments, for example to portray an audience member's (storyteller's) dreams or to draw out deeper issues in the stories.

An open performance space is used. There are no special sets. The conductor sits with the storyteller to one side of the performance space. The actors sit on chairs in a line against the back wall of the performance space.

Realistic acting techniques are used to help portray characters and real life situations truthfully.

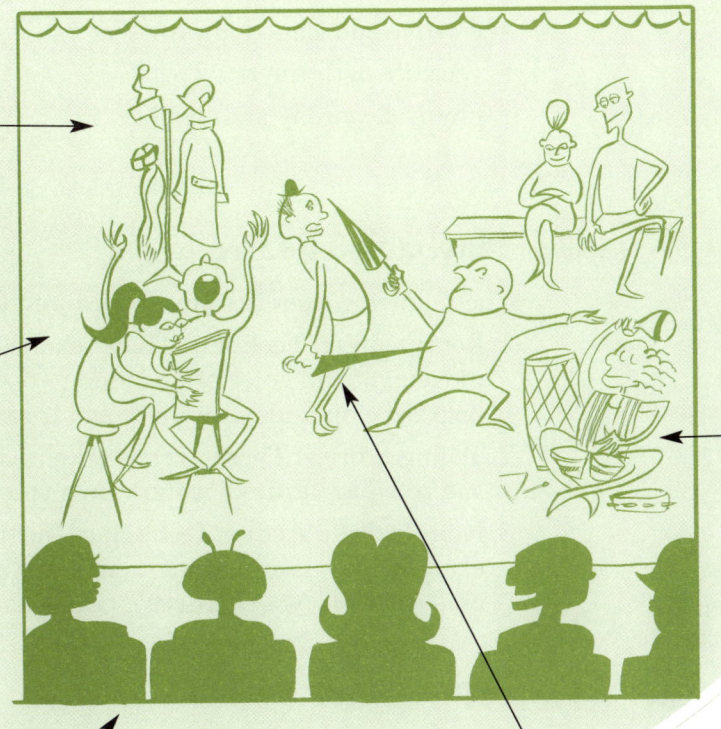

The performers wear uniform, neutral-coloured costume and suggest character through the use of simple items, such as hats, scarves and material. This also allows for quick character changes.

A 'conductor' acts as master of ceremonies. The conductor's role is to guide the proceedings and establish an atmosphere of trust to encourage audience members to share their stories.

A percussionist or other musician is included to add atmosphere and sound effects during performances.

All performance is improvised from the stories told by audience members. The performers aim to represent the stories accurately and provide some insight by 'playing back' the stories to the audience.

The performers incorporate transformation of objects to help suggest locations and objects as well as to create symbols.

Write and Discuss

1. List some of your favourite family stories and share them with a partner.
2. Imagine you had to pick people in your class to play the characters in your story. Who would you choose? Why?
3. Who would you choose to play you? Why?
4. Imagine you have been chosen to play the role of another class member in their story. What acting skills would you need to utilise to perform the character truthfully and sensitively?

Read: Playback Theatre Actor Training

Playback Theatre requires the performer to listen to, interpret and perform the stories of others with little or no preparation. Playback Theatre performers undertake regular and extensive training. They need to be:

- careful and sensitive listeners
- creative and skilled improvisers
- versatile performers
- physically strong and flexible.

Exercise: Playback Theatre

The following exercises are divided into three sections:

1. **Representing Feelings.** These exercises help explore how movement and voice can be used to portray feelings. They also help develop a sense of unity and trust within the group.
2. **Telling Stories.** These exercises help you practise listening to and retelling stories both in words and in performance.
3. **Non-Realistic Acting Techniques.** In these exercises you will explore how non-realistic acting techniques can be incorporated into Playback Theatre performance work.

Representing Feelings

1 Recalling and Reflecting Feelings

As a group, stand in a circle. On a signal from your teacher, everyone makes a sound and movement that expresses how they feel in the following situations. Each response must be truthful:

- breaking up for holidays at the end of last year
- waking up on your last birthday
- getting your school report at the end of last semester
- a sporting match that your team lost
- how you felt when you came into the room.

Hint

It is advisable to revise the improvisation skills in Unit 2.2 (pages 27–33) in preparation for the Playback Theatre exercises.

Hint

Take time working with the Playback Theatre exercises. Your teacher will work as a conductor and will offer side coaching and advice to help you in your work.

Hint

In these exercises you need to be spontaneous and trust your instincts about the best decisions to make in your performance work.

Challenge

In exercise 1 each person chooses one response to perform to the group. The group plays back the response by copying the movements and sounds exactly.

Write and Discuss

List some actual situations in which members of the group have experienced conflicting emotions. Use these as material for exercise 2.

2 Mixed Feelings

Often we are in a situation where we experience conflicting emotions. In this exercise you and a partner will each represent an emotion. For example, you may feel happy that your friend won a scholarship to study overseas, but also feel disappointed that they will be leaving. To represent these two emotions, stand one behind the other. The person in front completes a movement, sound, word and/or phrase to represent one of the two emotions. Once the person in front has completed their representation they crouch down. Then the person behind reveals themselves and uses movement and sound to portray the emotion they represent.

Write and Discuss

Describe how one pair used body language, movement and sound to portray the conflicting emotions they represented.

Hint

Feelings are abstract. Using sound, words and movement can help give physical representation to how we may be feeling in a situation. Be creative and imaginative in the ways you represent feelings.

3 Multiple Emotion Machines

As a group, choose two of the following situations. Discuss the range of emotions you may experience in these situations. Create a group machine that represents these emotions. Each person who joins the machine contributes a repeated movement, sound, word and/or phrase to help sum up the experience. The situations to choose from are:

- being called to the principal's office
- winning the lottery
- being asked out on a date
- seeing your best friend trip and fall just before the finish line in a race.

Write and Discuss

Imagine you are teaching a drama group how to make an emotion machine that uses rhythm and movement. List five reminders you would give to the group to help make the machine work effective.

It is important to remember that, as a Playback Theatre performer, you are looking for the key moments and issues in each story. These should be highlighted in your playback of the story.

Listening is easier if you actively engage yourself in the story by imagining what it would be like to 'be in the shoes' of the storyteller. This requires an effort of concentration. Ensure that you do not interrupt your partner when they tell their story. If you want to ask questions for clarification, do this once your partner has finished the story.

Not everyone needs to be part of the machines in exercise 3. Sometimes it is helpful to observe so that you develop a sense of when a machine seems complete.

Telling Stories

1 Telling and Listening

Divide into pairs and take it in turns to tell a personal story to your partner. The story must be true and can be about any situation at any time. Listen to your partner's story. Once they have finished, repeat the story to your partner; try to recall all the details as accurately as possible. Once you have retold your partner's story, check with your partner to see how accurate you were. Some ideas for stories are embarrassing moments, a memorable holiday, the greatest achievement or the biggest disappointment.

2 Telling, Listening and Performing

Find a new partner. Each person will tell the other a story. Once you have heard your partner's story you will playback their story by acting out the story in mime. In the playback of the story aim to be as accurate as possible. Once you have finished, check with your partner to see how accurate you were.

3 Machine Playback

For this exercise you will need to use an actual story from the group. Your teacher will guide you through this process so that all elements of the story are represented in a machine.

One person tells a personal story to the group. Your teacher discusses with the group the different aspects of the story. Each group member contributes a repeated movement, sound, word and/or phrase to the machine to help represent an aspect of the story. For example, if the story is about dropping a bottle of drink in the supermarket, the machine will show the dropping of the bottle, the feeling of embarrassment, the giggles of onlookers, the repeated sound of crashing glass, and so on.

Volunteers continue to add to the machine until the group senses instinctively when the machine is complete, at which point the group must simultaneously stop the action of the machine. Once the machine has stopped, the participants look to the teller of the story. The conductor checks with the storyteller that the machine is an accurate representation of the story.

4 Story Playback

For this exercise you will need to work in groups of six. This exercise is excellent preparation for a Playback Theatre performance. Each group member will have their story played back by the other members of their group. Each person takes a turn telling a short personal story. They then pick the members of their group whom they would like to play the essential characters. The group members then playback the story. It is important to remember to playback the group member's story as truthfully and accurately as possible. You should not attempt to give your point of view or embellish the story.

Write and Discuss

1. What did you enjoy most about seeing your story performed?
2. What skills did you feel were tested when you listened to and performed others' stories?

Non-Realistic Acting Techniques

1 Incorporating Non-Realistic Acting Techniques

When playing back a story, sometimes it is important to magnify the important moments. These are usually the climactic moments or moments of greatest tension in the story. You can use some non-realistic acting techniques to help draw out these moments for the storyteller and the audience. These techniques can include slow motion, exaggerated movement, exaggerated sound, mechanical movements and the transformation of objects. Try each of the following:

- work with a partner and represent the fear that someone may be feeling as they search for an intruder
- work with a partner and represent the disappointment someone feels when their date fails to turn up
- work in groups of three and show the anxiety someone may be feeling as they realise they have been caught lying.

As a group, share actual moments from personal stories and re-enact them, incorporating non-realistic acting techniques.

2 Non-Realistic Techniques and Playing Back Stories

Form groups of six. Each person needs to share a personal story that is either a dream, daydream, eerie occurrence or bizarre situation. The group chooses one group member's story to playback. The group must use one or more of the following non-realistic acting techniques in the playing back of the story: slow motion, exaggerated movement, exaggerated sound, mechanical movements or transformation of objects.

Rehearse your chosen story and present it to the class.

3 Character Thoughts

Often when audience members tell their stories they will include moments where they reveal what they were thinking at the time, or the story may be a situation where the storyteller spoke infrequently or not at all. In this case, the playback will focus on feelings and thoughts rather than words.

Form groups of four. Devise a fictional situation in which we hear the thoughts of two characters. The situation may be someone plucking up the courage to ask another person out on a date or it may be a couple having an argument at a restaurant and then refusing to talk to each other for the rest of the meal. The performers playing the characters' thoughts 'shadow' the character by standing just behind them and speak the character's thoughts aloud at suitable moments.

For exercise 3 use an actual story from your group. Choose volunteers and spend twenty minutes rehearsing a playback of the situation, which you will perform to the class. Include the use of character thoughts.

The improvisation skill of yielding (see page 30) is particularly important to the success of exercise 3.

Hint

Although your stories may contain more characters than you have people, it is a good challenge for the performers to find ways of picking the important characters and moments rather than including every small detail.

Write and Discuss

1. Explain how non-realistic techniques can draw out aspects of a personal story. Provide an example to illustrate your ideas.
2. Evaluate your group's ability to incorporate characters' thoughts into the performance. What skills are needed to include this technique successfully?
3. What impact do characters' thoughts have on the audience?

Read Steps in a Playback Theatre Performance

- The conductor welcomes the audience and explains Playback Theatre, including the procedure of a Playback Theatre performance.
- The conductor starts a warm-up activity to encourage the audience to share their personal experiences. The audience is asked to share, for example, their feelings about their day, and words that sum up a particular event.
- Performers create a machine, using repeated sound and movement that incorporates the suggestions of the audience.
- The conductor invites an audience member (storyteller) to share a story. The storyteller sits with the conductor to one side of the performing area.
- The storyteller tells their story to the audience. The type of story can vary. For example, it may be simple or complex, humorous or moving.
- The Playback Theatre performers listen carefully to the details of the story.
- The conductor asks the storyteller questions to help them express all the important aspects of the story, especially feelings and reactions.
- The conductor invites the storyteller to choose performers to play the characters in the story.
- The performers who are not selected are free to participate as background characters or as a chorus using abstract movement and sound to portray feelings, mood and atmosphere.
- The performers then playback the story.
- At the end of the story the performers look at the storyteller to 'give back' the story.
- The conductor then asks the storyteller their opinion of the playback, including its accuracy and any insights they had.
- The storyteller is thanked for their contribution and a new volunteer is chosen.

Dramatic Forms and Performance Styles

Present ## Playback Theatre

Invite an audience to the Playback Theatre performance. Your audience may be another drama class. Your teacher or a student in your class can act as conductor of the performance. Follow the steps for a Playback Theatre performance, as outlined on page 192.

> ### Write and Discuss
>
> 1. Recount your experiences in the Playback Theatre performance.
> 2. Describe two moments you found important or valuable in the performance.
> 3. Reflect on the performance and list three or four points that you feel are important to remember for your next Playback Theatre performance.
> 4. What dramatic techniques and/or performance styles do playback performers have available to them when performing in front of an audience? Discuss how some of the performers in your class effectively used these strategies.

10.2 Documentary Drama

Read ## Encouraging Audiences to Question

Documentary Drama evolved in Germany in the 1960s. It re-enacts historic events by incorporating the techniques and conventions of Epic Theatre; and it aims to provoke audiences to think about important issues. When devising Documentary Drama performances, writers use transcripts, letters, oral histories and other documents as material for the performance.

Documentary Drama uses distinct theatrical techniques and conventions to establish a non-realistic style. Although the performance is about a true incident, the performers want to remind audiences that what they are watching is a play in a theatre not a

Hint

Brecht wanted his actors to understand their characters rather than emotionally connect with them. He required his actors to represent character types and their feelings, rather than adopt a Stanislavskian approach, which requires actors to become emotionally absorbed in the characters.

real-life situation. This approach encourages the audience to be more objective about the issues in the performance rather than to become emotionally involved in them.

Documentary Drama performances incorporate the techniques and conventions of Epic Theatre to achieve the purpose of 'distancing' the audience so that they can think critically about the issues in the performance. Bertolt Brecht, the creator of Epic Theatre, wanted his audiences to listen to and think about issues. He wrote many plays that dealt with issues of good and evil, justice and injustice, and how the pressures of society can affect the way people behave. Brecht deliberately created a non-realistic style of performance by using conventions and techniques that made Epic Theatre performances seem 'strange'. He was greatly influenced by Expressionism (although he rejected Expressionism early in his career), Asian theatre and the writings of Karl Marx.

Read The Influence of Epic Theatre

Documentary Drama utilises the following Epic Theatre techniques and conventions.

Play Structure

- Many scenes have self-contained episodes, each of which are linked to the same subject. This creates the impression of a journey that covers a long period of time. It is also a device to prevent the audience from becoming too emotionally involved in the performance.
- A narrator speaks directly to the audience. This convention links scenes and breaks the 'fourth wall' barrier between actor and audience. The narrator also reflects on the action and presents questions to the audience.
- Songs that carry a political message are included. Often scene changes are bridged with songs. Songs in Epic Theatre often comment on the action and provoke the audience to question the issues being presented in the performance.

Staging

- Signs, placards and graffiti, for example, are used to give each scene a title.
- Historical film footage is used to point out the current relevance of the issues to the audience. This is also known as the technique of 'historification'.
- Sets are non-realistic. Platforms, scaffolding, film, slides and half curtains are used.
- On stage, in view of the audience, characters change costume to become different characters
- There is an occasional use of masks.
- Minimal props and furniture are used. This allows locations to be suggested, rather than re-created.

Write and Discuss

1. Choose three of the techniques and conventions of Documentary Drama. Explain how you think these elements would encourage an audience to think rather than be involved emotionally.
2. Revisit Unit 9.3 (pages 174–80) and see if you can find any similarities between the techniques and conventions of Epic Theatre and those of Expressionist theatre.

Documentary Drama Performance Skills

An actor needs to be energetic and versatile in a Documentary Drama performance. They need to be able to:

- play a variety of characters
- work effectively as part of an ensemble to strengthen the impact of chorus work and background characters
- use heightened movement and voice to represent characters and their responses.

Performing in Documentary Drama

1 Character Movement

Performers in Documentary Drama are not restricted to realistic movements. Try the following character types:

- Imagine you are a soldier carrying a weapon. Walk in a menacing way, with heavy, slow, rhythmic steps.
- Imagine you are a dishonest, no-good drunk. You are trying to get money from passersby as they flee from an invading army.

- Imagine you are a member of a greedy and selfish royal family. Use stylised gestures and mannerisms to convey your high status.
- Imagine you are a simple, honest person struggling to get by. You are on a long journey through a war torn country and are carrying a weak and injured person. As you move through the room, try to convey an illusion of travelling a great distance over a long period of time.

2 Chorus Work

One of the many techniques used in Documentary Drama is chorus work. The use of a chorus is a powerful technique as it can create atmosphere, establish location and represent points of view. The chorus may perform synchronised, controlled or stylised movements, or may play various roles, in order to background the main action.

The following extract is from the play *Wild Rice* by Huong Nguyen, Phi Hai, Pat Rix and Geoff Crowhurst. In this play a rebellious teenage boy named Sonny runs away from home to escape the strict rules of his father. The play is a Documentary Drama as it draws on the stories of Vietnamese Australians, and also employs the techniques and conventions of Epic Theatre.

This extract is from a scene in the play that is a re-enactment of the memories of Sonny's sister, Phuong. In the extract Sonny is recalling his family's perilous journey from Vietnam to Australia. The memories are heightened because of the fact that Sonny was very young at the time the family escaped. Toan, Long, Anne, David, Kim, Dale and Craig are the names of some of the performers who made up the chorus.

In groups, prepare a performance of this script extract. Consider ways in which the techniques of narration and chorus can be used effectively.

Hint

The playbuilding task at the end of this chapter requires you to use an actual historic event as the basis for your performance. You are encouraged to use a combination of realistic and non-realistic language. This will help to emphasise certain ideas and will also distance the audience from the performance.

Wild Rice

Banner 4: 'Precious jade'

(Sonny enters.)

Sonny Escaping was the best part. It was really exciting. It was around midnight, I think …

(The rest of the Chorus come on one by one as if secretly meeting at night. Throughout this escape sequence they show us the story with their movements.)

Toan Ten o'clock …

Long Two a.m. …

Anne Four in the morning …

Sonny	…when Mum woke me up. She started putting three to four pantses on me along with four or five jumpers. Man, I thought she was going nuts. Then out of the blue she gave me a hug, kissed me on the cheek … strange … and I was dragged away by my older sister. The moon was high, the night quiet. I mistook the little river that ran behind our house as a path and stepped into it, pulling my sister along with me. She screamed.
David	Ssssh!
Kim	Shut up!
Anne	Do you want us to get caught?
Toan	Giu su Maria Giu se. Cái gì đó (*Jesus, Maria, Jesus. What is it?*)
Dale	I thought it was the Communists.
Craig	Here! Grab my hand.
Dale	They're all wet!
Long	Sssssh! (**Long** *gives* **Dale** *a clip around the ears.*) Sorry!
Sonny	Man, I was cold! We climbed onto this fishing boat and were led down under the deck of the boat and told to sit down and be quiet.
Dale	There's not enough room in here.
Anne	It's too dark. How long do we have to stay in here?
Toan	Two days? Where's my children?
Dale	What reeks?
Kim	Get off my foot.
Long	Who farted?
Dale	I wanna go up on deck for a pee.
Toan	You can't. We've got to stay below. We don't want to look suspicious.
David	Who's been eating garlic?
Craig	How long? Two days.
Kim	Two days!
Dale	Hey! We're moving.
All	At last.
Sonny	As the night wore on I began to miss my mum and dad and cried.
Long	Shut that kid up!
Sonny	I must have annoyed a hell of a lot of people but my sister was so gentle with me. She cradled me in

her arms and put me to sleep soon afterwards.

The next morning she told me that Mum and Dad were still at home and that we had managed to escape.

It was two days and nights under the deck until we were supposedly out of danger and were allowed to go up on top.

Anne I can stretch at last.

David Fresh air at last.

Dale I can have a pee at last.

Long Look. Dolphins!

Dale I feel sick.

Craig Finally.

Kim It's too bright!

Toan It's all water.

Sonny Bloody hell. By that time my body was covered in rashes from the sea water so my sister took all my clothes off to ease the pain. Man.

Stark naked at six.

On the fourth day we ran out of water, food and petrol. We just drifted for two days. I was so thirsty …

… and hot. My sister put me in a cooking pot full of sea water to keep me cool. Maybe that's how I ended up this colour!

Just kidding. Anway, one kid, my age, started to scull sea water. He died. We found him in the morning all bloated like a puffer fish. His sister went crazy.

(*Some of the* **Chorus** *begin to pray while others pick up the dead boy*.)

The older men wrapped him up and threw him overboard.

(*He is thrown overboard*.)

But there wasn't much we could for his sister.

(*The prayer stops*.)

Write and Discuss

1. What is the mood or atmosphere of this extract? How did your group establish an appropriate atmosphere in performance?
2. Describe how your group used timing and rhythm to effectively create chorus work. What suggestions would you make to improve your creation of chorus work in future performance tasks?

10.3 Performance Task: Documentary Drama

Read ## The Task

Divide into groups and devise a Documentary Drama performance that explores an issue. Your performance aims to encourage the audience to think about an issue by examining and re-creating aspects of an historic event. Use an actual historic event as the basis for your performance. The incidents of the historic event can be intertwined with fictional scenes that are set at other times and involve other characters or roles. You will incorporate and utilise a selection of non-realistic, Epic Theatre techniques and conventions to highlight the main issues and concerns.

Your performance must include:

- An actual Australian or world historic event.
- Narration.
- Documentary Drama acting style, including heightened voice and movement as well as chorus work.
- Signs to title scenes and to point out issues in your performance. For example, you may write a famous quote on a banner and hang it above your performance space or reveal it at a point in your performance. The signs can be projected, graffiti or placards, for example.
- Use of minimal props, furniture and costumes. Changes to role or character are to be made in view of the audience.
- Consideration of interacting with and addressing the audience to highlight the issues of your drama.

Your performance may include projected film and/or slides. It may also include songs to make political points.

Prepare ## Creating and Making Documentary Drama

- Research a historic event that is of interest to you. The event may have occurred in the distant past or recently.
- Determine the issue that the historic event highlights. For example, it may be injustice, racism, poverty, dishonesty, discrimination or violence.
- Decide how your performance can include newspaper articles, interviews and/or oral histories, for example, that relate to the historic incident.
- Incorporate improvisation in rehearsals to explore stylised movement and voice to portray your characters or roles.
- Consider how you can make quick and efficient costume changes on stage.

- Consider how your group can use skills of mask work and chorus work (see Units 8.2 and 8.3, pages 149–57) in your performance.

Evaluate — Performance Checklist

You and your teacher will evaluate your work individually, using a list of criteria. These criteria relate to your achievement in this task. Some criteria will relate to the achievement of the group. The criteria are listed on the evaluation sheet at the end of this chapter and will be used to evaluate your:

- degree of focus and commitment
- ability to use vocal dynamics appropriately and effectively
- ability to use movement appropriately and effectively
- successful inclusion of the techniques and conventions of Epic Theatre
- effective adaptation and interpretation of the historic event
- ability to establish an appropriate mood and atmosphere
- presentation of a well-rehearsed and polished performance
- effective manipulation of the actor–audience relationship to highlight the issues of the drama.

Hint

Refer to Appendixes 1, 3 and 4 for help with your logbook entries. The appendixes provide you with guidelines for evaluating your own performance work and the work of others.

Write and Discuss

Arts Criticism and Aesthetics

1. Outline the strengths of your group's performance. Explain why you felt these aspects of your performance were effective.
2. Outline the strengths of your own performance. You may comment on your use of movement or vocal dynamics, your ability to play a variety of characters or your ability to work effectively as part of an ensemble.
3. What areas of your own performance did you feel needed improvement? Why?
4. Choose another group's performance and discuss the following:
   - the overall flow and cohesion, making special reference to how scene changes were achieved
   - the effective use of Epic Theatre techniques and conventions.

Past and Present Contexts

5. Choose Playback Theatre or Documentary Drama. Discuss the value and purpose of either form. Include in your discussion examples of the ways in which particular performance techniques and conventions are incorporated to influence the audience's perception of the characters and the story.
6. Find out more about Bertolt Brecht and about Epic Theatre.

Performance Task: Documentary Drama

Student: .... Teacher: ....

Related Outcomes

By completing this task you should be able to:
- draw on personal stories and historic events as the basis for performance work
- devise a performance using the techniques and conventions of Documentary Drama and Epic Theatre.

Criteria	Level of Achievement			
	Beginning	Consolidating	Mastering	Excelling
Exploring and Developing Ideas Have you prepared for your performance by: • researching a historic event that is of interest to you? • including in your performance newspaper articles, interviews and/or oral histories, for example, that relate to the historic incident? • using improvisation to explore and develop character or role?				
Using Skills, Techniques and Processes Have you incorporated a Documentary Drama acting style by: • selecting and incorporating appropriate body language and movement? • using voice to effectively communicate character or role? • using reported speech? Have you used skills, techniques and processes to structure a Documentary Drama performance by: • incorporating narration to the audience? • incorporating signs to title scenes and to point out issues in your performance? • using minimal props and furniture to suggest locations? • making costume changes in view of the audience? • sustaining and developing character or role?				
Presenting Have you rehearsed and presented a performance for a specific audience by: • effectively interpreting and adapting an historic event? • effectively manipulating the actor–audience relationship to encourage the audience to think about the issue of your drama? • structuring your drama into a coherent and polished performance incorporating effective scene transitions?				

Comments: ....

© Mathew Clausen

Chapter 11

Physical Theatre: Roll Up, Roll Up!

Why Study Physical Theatre?

This chapter explores the techniques and conventions of physical theatre. Physical theatre is a unique dramatic form in which the performers focus upon the movement of their bodies to create meaning. Physical theatre is often visually powerful, and may rely upon the power of symbolism to achieve a dramatic effect. By exploring and discussing physical theatre you will appreciate and understand the ways in which this dramatic form can create powerful and engaging theatre.

This chapter is divided into the following units:

11.1 Legs on the Wall: A Physical Theatre Company
11.2 Physical Theatre Exercises
11.3 Performing a Physical Theatre Script
11.4 Performance Task: Physical Theatre

Outcomes

In this chapter you will:

- identify the techniques and conventions of a physical theatre performance
- develop movement skills to create counter balances and contact roles
- apply a process to create, record and perform a physical theatre performance
- create, perform and evaluate a physical theatre performance.

Performers from the Legs on the Wall theatre company. Photograph by Daniel Bereholak.

11.1 Legs on the Wall: A Physical Theatre Company

'Our whole body must adapt to every movement no matter how small. If we pick up a piece of ice from the ground, our whole body must react to this movement and the cold. Not only the fingertips, not only the whole hand, but the whole body must reveal the coldness of this little piece of ice.'
                    Polish theatre director Jerzy Grotowski

Read Company History

The Legs on the Wall theatre company began in 1986 with the primary aim of creating a performance style that uses circus skills to tell stories as emotional journeys. The company also wanted to understand how visual images affect people emotionally and how 'intention' adds meaning to a physical skill.

The group has evolved from performing cabaret in a community hall to being recognised as a world-renowned performing arts company, which today receives continuing invitations to perform. Legs on the Wall has regularly toured Australia and has consistently been part of the international circuit, touring to Scotland to perform in the Edinburgh Fringe Festival, as well as to Germany, Brazil, New Zealand, Columbia, the Netherlands and Brussels.

Read Creating Australian Performance Work

The work of Legs on the Wall is characterised by the willingness of the company to take risks, both in the physical performance of the actors and in the look, style and design of performances. The company's aim is to communicate Australian stories to a broad audience using ideas and feelings in radical yet accessible theatrical contexts. Legs on the Wall achieves this by making theatre that breaks down the barriers between circus, theatre and dance, as well as between literal and metaphoric narrative.

Beginning with a thematic, text, physical or site-based idea, the company uses strong physical language as a primary source for the building of narrative. Each production is a reaction to what is happening in the world at a personal or global level. The company regularly works with new directors, which allows for fresh perspectives and approaches to physical theatre performance.

Hint

In the 'metaphoric narrative' of a performance, the dramatic action works symbolically to establish atmosphere and communicate themes and issues. For example, a performance features an actor who uses a suitcase as a prop. The suitcase contains heavy and dark objects. The character never speaks and is very attached to the suitcase, taking it everywhere, sleeping on it and refusing to let others take it away. The metaphoric narrative of the dramatic action is that the character is unable to let go of their 'emotional baggage'.

Read A Performance: *Homeland*

Legs on the Wall performed *Homeland* in Sydney (1999 and 2000); Brisbane (2001); Manchester, United Kingdom (2002); and Berlin (2003). The staging requirements for the show included a structure that was a minimum of twenty storeys in height and had a width of twelve metres; one face of the structure would preferably be without windows. *Homeland* was originally performed on a skyscraper. It was created as a site-specific performance, using a wall of the AMP building at Circular Quay, Sydney, in New South Wales; the audience stood to watch the performance from the Customs House Square nearby. The site and the building were central to the development of the thematic content and the 'aerial language' of the performance.

Thematically the show responded to Australia's white immigration history. It explored the journey that thousands of people took from Europe to Australia, having little knowledge of their destination. The performance also addressed the concerns of present-day asylum seekers: their strong links to the homeland, their courage and desperation.

The four performers worked in harnesses using mountaineering rigging techniques to descend and ascend the wall. The choreography explored notions of caution and unknown territory; searching and exploring; and the celebration of newfound freedom. During the show huge images of passports, refugees, suitcases and windows were projected onto the building. The performers interacted with the images as part of the choreography.

Hint

To see images of *Homeland* and other Legs on the Wall productions visit the company's website at: hi.com.au/centrestage.

Write and Discuss

1. Refer to the description of *Homeland*. The performance addressed the topic of the immigrant's journey to a new country. How did the choreography of *Homeland* help to communicate the themes and issues of the performance?

2. Research circus as a performance form: its origins, features and history. Your research may examine the circuses of China, Russia and Canada, as well as those of Australia. As part of your research focus on the development of acrobatics as a form of entertainment.

3. Using your research on circus and your knowledge of Legs on the Wall, list the similarities and differences between a Legs on the Wall performance and a circus performance.

11.2 Physical Theatre Exercises

Exercise: Warming Up

Before undertaking physical exercises you should make sure you adequately stretch and relax your muscles. Some other exercises that may be useful in your study of the physical theatre form can be found in Chapter 1, Units 1.1, 1.2 and 1.3.

Hint

Connecting the inhalation and exhalation of breath with your stretches helps to extend the stretch and establish focus. Inhale when you stretch and exhale when you relax.

1 Align Posture

Stand with your eyes closed. Check your posture so that your stomach is pulled in slightly, your shoulders are relaxed, your feet are under your hips and are parallel. Check your head is not tipped forward or backward.

2 Spine Rolls

Complete four spine rolls—one over eight counts, one over four counts, one over two counts, and one in one count. Repeat three times. Remember to keep your shoulders and neck loose. (Refer back to page 5 if you need a description of how to perform a spine roll.)

3 Neck Stretch

Stand with a relaxed and aligned posture. Bring one arm up above your head. Drop the arm from the elbow so that the hand is on one side of your head. Leave your other arm by your side but push down with the heel of the hand while raising the fingers upwards. As you push down with the heel of one hand, simultaneously pull your head gently to one side to stretch your neck. Relax, and repeat using the opposite side.

4 Wrist and Shoulder Warm-up

Begin by waving both hands from the wrist so they are loose and floppy. Place your left hand on your left shoulder and your right hand on your right shoulder so that your elbows point forwards. In this position, loosen your shoulders by rotating your arms five times in each direction.

Now hold both arms out to either side. Raise your hands from the wrists, then relax them. Drop your hands even further so that they hang down lower. Repeat this sequence quickly six times, then relax.

5 Cat Stretch

On all fours form a table shape. Make sure your wrists are under your shoulders and that your middle finger is pointing forward. Turn the inside of your elbows slightly to face each other. Keep your hands flat and push down into the floor with your fingertips. Make sure your thighs are under your hips and your knees are not too close together. Keep your stomach firm. Using the full motion of your spine, slowly arch your back up like a cat and hold for a moment. Return to the table position. Now arch down by dropping your stomach and raising your head to look at the ceiling. Hold for a moment and return to the table position. Slowly look over your left shoulder behind you and repeat on the right-hand side. Relax.

6 Claw

Staying on all fours, stretch one arm out to one side and form your fingers into a claw position with the fingertips digging into the floor. Rest your other arm on the elbow with the forearm out along the floor. Simultaneously push the elbow into the floor and attempt to draw the clawed hand towards you. Relax. Swap sides and repeat.

7 Downward Dog

From your position on all fours, push your toes and hands into the floor while lifting your hips high into the air. Keep your chin to your chest and relax the neck. Simultaneously press your heels down while pushing your hands into the floor.

8 Touching Toes

Sitting down, stretch your legs out in front of you. Flex your feet toward the body and away from the body. Lean forward from the hips. Relax the upper body. Gently slide your arms down your legs to a stretch that is comfortable for you. Gently grasp your lower legs. Breathe in and exhale as you count to five. Breathe in and then gently reach forward. Only reach as far as you find comfortable.

Read Counter Balances

The basic principles of counter balance can be applied in a wide variety of contexts, from partner balance and acrobatics, to contact improvisation, and the creation of controlled movement.

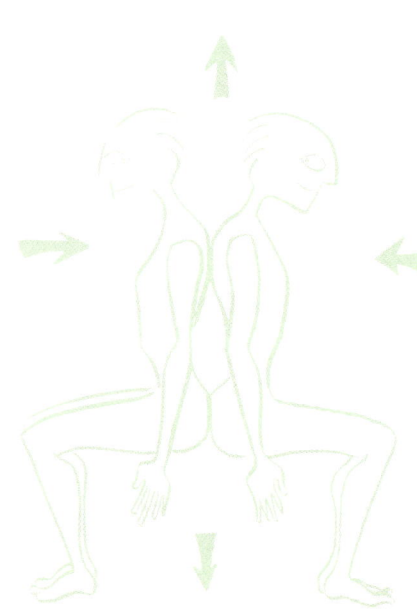

> ### Write and Discuss
>
> While attempting the following exercises focus on the shapes that are being created. What do these shapes remind you of? How do they make you feel, both as an audience member and a participant? Whilst executing and analysing these exercises try to remain open to the feelings or stories that the shapes evoke.

1 Leaning In

Leaning Sit

Stand back-to-back with a partner, with your hips and shoulders touching. Lean into each other, and while maintaining contact with your hips and shoulders, walk your feet outwards so that you arrive in a sitting position supported by your partner. It is important here that you maintain pressure between the contacting points of the body. Remember that this is a 'counter balance'—your partner should be in balance with you and the weight should be evenly distributed between both of you. The angle of balance will vary slightly for different couples.

From this position try lowering yourselves to the floor by bending your knees and pressing into each other. Then, while maintaining contact with your partner, try standing up.

Variations on Leaning In

Following on from the standing up position described above, try to shift the point of contact to a different part of the body, whilst staying in contact with your partner.

Try rolling sideways onto your shoulder so that you and your partner are both facing the same direction. Continue rolling onto your fronts so that your chests are touching, with your heads on each other's shoulders.

From this position change the point of contact to the hands, so that you are leaning into your partner hand-to-hand with straight arms (you may need to walk your feet out further to achieve this). Now try shifting your hands to different parts of your partner's body while still leaning into your partner (you may have to bend your arms and legs, or alter the height and angle of your body).

From this position you can also change the points of the body that are in contact. Try locking shoulders and pushing against each other (as in a rugby scrum). Finally try returning to the back-to-back position without using your hands.

2 Leaning Out

Stand facing your partner with your feet close together. Hold each other's wrists in a 'monkey grip'. Lean yourselves backwards, keeping your legs straight, so that you are both balanced outwards and sharing the distribution of weight.

From this position try lowering yourselves to the floor by bending your knees and pulling away from each other. Then try standing back up again maintaining the counter balance. Now try this exercise with one of your hands holding your partner's, and the other hand free.

Variations on Leaning Out

- Alter the position of your body while pulling away from your partner. Try one person crouching down low, and one standing tall. Try turning side on, or even turning away from your partner.
- Holding one hand, walk in a circle around your partner. Now, try one person lowering their bottom to the floor, while the other person continues to walk around them pulling. The person on the floor should spin around. You can then use a counter balance to stand up again.
- Now try leaning out using body parts other than your hands. For example, try the exercise using your feet, your knees, or your elbows.

3 Devising with Leaning In and Leaning Out

Here are some starting points for creating set pieces of choreography with counter balances.

Hint

In counter balances, always move slowly so that your partner can anticipate your movement and respond accordingly. Always stay in complete control of your movements to protect yourself and your partner. Try to breathe in unison with your partner to establish a common rhythm. This will also help you and your partner to sustain focus.

Hint

In these exercises it is important that you maintain complete focus. This will create a safe environment for you and those you work with.

Hint

It is best not to talk during your practice of these exercises. Learn to negotiate the changes in position in silence.

- Create a sequence using five leaning-in and five leaning-out movements.

    Try to connect (the) movements so that the transition from one to the next occurs seamlessly. Conversely, you could include two changes where the pace or intensity of the movement alters dramatically.

- As a solo, devise a sequence using leaning-in movements against a wall. Experiment with ways of contacting the wall (with your back, front, hands, feet, hips, head, shoulder, fingers, and so on). You could also include moments of peeling yourself off the wall, and returning to it. Also, try to focus on the texture and feel of the wall, and let this affect the way you make contact with it.

- Repeat the above exercise using one or more people as a 'wall'. For example, you could use their backs, fronts, or individual body parts (legs, arms, hands or stomach) as a solid surface to respond to and move against.

4 Contact Rolling in Kneeling Position

In this exercise you and your partner begin kneeling on all fours next to each other. You take turns to contact roll across each other's backs.

- Kneel on all fours side-by-side next to a partner who is in the same position. Make sure that your wrists are directly beneath your shoulders and that the insides of your elbows are turned to face each other. Check your knees are directly beneath your hips (hip-width apart), and that you are in contact with your partner (hips, sides, shoulders and arms touching). You should also lean slightly into your partner's body, so that there is pressure between you. Keep your back straight; don't arch it. The shape you make should feel very solid.

- Push your toes into the floor and straighten your legs while maintaining contact with your partner who remains in the original position. Keep your hands and feet on the ground for a moment.

- Lift your outside arm and roll onto your partner's back so that you are looking at the ceiling and lying on your back.

- Continue to roll to the other side of your partner's body, ending in the kneeling position from which you started, but on the opposite side. Your partner then repeats the contact roll over your body, and the movement travels across the space.

Variations on Contact Rolling in a Kneeling Position

- Roll onto your partner's back so that you are lying facing the ceiling. Sit up so that you are positioned on their hips (as if you are sitting on a chair). Now carefully experiment with different ways of balancing your body on your partner's back. Try lying on your side in a foetal position, so that your head is near your partner's and your hips are on their hips. Try sliding slowly off your partner's back, feet first onto the floor.

- As you contact roll across the space, make the last point of contact with your partner into the place from which the next roll is initiated. For example, if your partner ends up kneeling next to you with only their arm touching you, try a contact roll that begins from the arm. While exploring this exercise you may find that you do not end up kneeling in full contact with your partner. This is fine as long as some part of your body is in contact. You should also try to finish each roll on all fours in a stable position for your partner to then roll across.

5 Arena

Work with a partner. Imagine you have a circular performance area to work in. When you stand outside the circle you are 'offstage'. When you step into the circle you are 'onstage' and need to provide the appropriate level of focus and energy. One of you enters the arena and creates a strong shape. The other person enters the arena and connects with their partner by creating a gentle lean or a counter balance. Hold this for a moment, and then, finding your own weight, exit the arena. Repeat with each person alternately offering a starting shape.

6 Mirror or Complement

Using the concept of the arena, the class sits in a circle. One person enters the arena and creates a strong shape. One at a time, four or five others enter the arena and create a shape that either mirrors or complements the shape of the first person. Look for ways to create interesting tableaux using physical shape, space and levels.

7 Moving as Text

In a physical theatre process text can act as a starting point for creating action. Here are some methods for devising movement from a text. The text can be anything from a monologue in a play, to a passage in a novel, or an article in a newspaper.

- Read the text first. Look for the rhythm of the text, including pauses. Also identify significant images and metaphors.
- Underline the verbs in the text. Create a physical movement for each verb (for instance, a star jump for the word 'catch', or a swinging of the arms for the word 'write').
- Link the movements together to form a sequence. Consider how you will create transitions from one movement to the next.
- Now analyse the sequence in view of the text from which it was created. What does the sequence express? Is it similar or completely different to the themes of the text?
- Choose an aspect of your chosen text that appeals to you and use this as the basis for creating a short sequence. For instance, how does the text make you feel? If it fills you with wonder, create some movement based on this sense of wonder. Try to be lateral in your thinking. For example, you could create a movement for each letter of the word 'wonder' and link the movements into a sequence.
- Memorise your chosen text. Devise a counter balance sequence using one of the suggested methods listed above. Now recite your text while performing your counter balance sequence, allowing the physicality of your sequence to affect the way in which you recite your text. What does the movement do to the text? Is it easier or harder to speak text while moving? What new meaning, if any, does this combination of exercises create?

A 'metaphor' is a figure of speech in which one thing is identified with another. For example, 'She was a tower of strength during the crisis'. In drama an object or effect can be a metaphor, or symbol, representing something other than itself.

As you rehearse your text interpretation, be aware of how the use of breath, pauses and silences affects the rhythm of your performance.

11.3 Performing a Physical Theatre Script

Exercise: Interpreting Text Using Physical Theatre

Divide into groups of six. Use the following poem as the basis for a physical theatre performance. You may choose to perform all or only part of the poem. Use the guidelines for interpreting text outlined in the Moving as Text exercise on page 209. In your preparation consider how your performance might incorporate an effective use of space, levels, movement, counter balances, contact rolls, dialogue and vocal dynamics.

> **Solitude**
>
> Right here I was nearly killed one night in February.
> My car slewed on the ice, sideways,
> into the other lane. The oncoming cars—
> their headlights—came nearer.
>
> My name, my daughters, my job
> slipped free and fell behind silently,
> farther and farther back. I was anonymous,
> like a schoolboy in a lot surrounded by enemies.
>
> The approaching traffic had powerful lights.
> They shone on me while I turned and turned
> the wheel in a transparent fear that moved like eggwhite.
> The seconds lengthened out—making more room—
> they grew long as hospital buildings.
>
> It felt as if you could just take it easy
> and loaf a bit
> before the smash came.
>
> Then firm land appeared: a helping sandgrain
> or a marvellous gust of wind. The car took hold
> and fish-tailed back across the road.
> A signpost shot up, snapped off—a ringing sound—
> tossed into the dark.
>
> Came all quiet. I sat there in my seatbelt
> and watched someone tramp through the blowing snow
> to see what had become of me.
>
> Tomas Transtromer
> *(translated from the Swedish by Robert Bly)*

Write and Discuss

Evaluate one group's performance of the poem *Solitude*. Comment on their use of movement, space and vocal dynamics to realise the intention of the poem. In your evaluation describe two specific moments that helped establish tension for the audience.

Practitioner Profile

Conrad Page
Physical Theatre Teacher, Director and Actor

Conrad Page studied theatre at the Victorian College of the Arts. He also trained with Circus Oz and the Fruit Fly Circus. Conrad has performed with the Sydney Theatre Company, Belvoir Company B and State of Play; he has toured the world with self-devised physical theatre shows. Conrad has taught theatre skills at the Corrugated Iron Youth Theatre in Darwin, the Australian Theatre for Young People and Theatre Nepean at the University of Western Sydney.

I believe that the use of physical movement is an essential tool for every performer when exploring character, text and ensemble work. The performer learns to explore text from a 'visceral' (emotional) base by grounding the body and connecting to the action. This allows the performer to push boundaries and welcome new possibilities. A connected body means a connected audience.

Physical Theatre Script Extract

A physical theatre script extract has been provided as an example of how you might record a physical theatre performance. The extract is from the Legs on the Wall performance of *Runners Up*. It contains examples of the techniques and conventions used in physical theatre. As you read through the extract identify the techniques and conventions that have been used, for example the use of minimal dialogue. To do this ask yourself the following questions.

- What makes the performance realistic or non-realistic?
- How does a physical theatre performer use movement, body language and gesture? Is the use of movement realistic or non-realistic? In your evaluation consider rhythm, energy, control and facial expression. How is this use of movement different to a performer's use of movement in other dramatic forms?

- What is the actor–audience relationship in a physical theatre performance?
- Have you seen any forms of theatre that are similar in performance style to *Runners Up*? What are the similarities? What are the differences?

It is recommended that you do not perform the *Runners Up* script without the appropriate training, rehearsal and precautions.

Write and Discuss

Read through the script extract from the Legs on the Wall performance of *Runners Up*. Choose one scene that you enjoyed reading. Use a pencil to sketch a storyboard of the action in your logbook. You will need to divide the scene into key moments. You only need to draw simple shapes and figures.

Read *Runners Up* Script Extract

In the following scene from *Runners Up* the central character is an 'armchair athlete', whose fantasy, to become his sporting hero, is played out on and around his armchair. The three other characters are his mates real and imagined. They are dressed in singlets, which like jockey silks have individual colours, and black shorts.

After a hard Saturday morning at work the main character comes home to watch the football final. He is glued to the TV as are his mates. As they watch the game their passion for sport and the highs and lows of the competition are symbolically represented and heightened through physical theatre.

The players use their own names: Kerry (KY) is the main character, and the others are Telford (T), Rowan (R) and Kirk (K). In the production the armchair was reinforced to support the choreography and protect the performers. It was located in a central pool of light, and at points in the show the players would disappear into the surrounding shadows.

Armchair Athlete

KY *(Brings out the armchair as he enters from upstage centre; he is muttering but becoming clearer.)*

This is it … Today's the day … the big one.

(He places the chair in the centre of the stage, walks forward toward the audience and mimes pushing the button on the television.)

That trophy's ours …

(Walks backward to the chair.)

Yes …

(He takes off his suit jacket, swings it around his head and throws it behind the chair as he says ...)

... Eighty minutes of ecstasy ...

(Loosens tie, sits and sings ...)

Hear the barrackers shouting, like all barrackers should ...

(He moves through three sitting positions, never taking his eyes off the television. On the third position he leans forward.)

Enough of the dancing girls—bring on the men! Gird the loins for battle, boys ...

KY, T, K and R   *(together)* Gird the loins for battle!

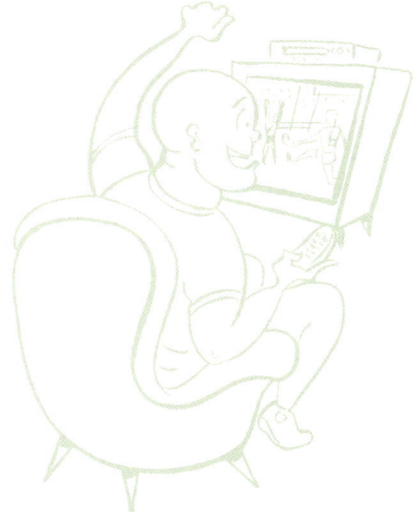

Play #1

       *(**KY** leans back in the chair.)*

T   *(Runs in front of chair right to left; stepping off arm of chair.)*

KY   Kicks off ...

K   *(Runs in front of chair left to right.)*

KY   ... takes it up ...

R   *(Dive rolls over front of chair.)*

KY   ... bunnies ...

*(**T** runs diagonally downstage to upstage; steps on arm of chair, then places one foot on **KY**'s head and leaps over the back of the chair.)*

KY   ... like a ballerina.

*(**R** steps off **KY**'s head too.)*

KY   Elegant.

*(**K** steps on arm of chair, balances as **KY** grabs his leg in a frozen running shape.)*

KY   Hold the line.

Play #2

KY   In there.

*(**T** and **K** run from behind to jump on arms of the chair in a squat; **T** comes from right side, **K** from left side. **R** runs in to stand behind chair.)*

KY   Get in there.

T   Get in there.

*(**R** supports **T** around the belly. **T** reaches behind **KY** and turns upside down.)*

KY   Get in there.

T	Get in there (*one leg bent, one leg diagonally up*).
K	Get in there (*holds* **T**'s *leg, stands on arm of chair*).

(**R** *is supporting* **T** *around the belly;* **T**'s *legs frame his face.*)

KY	Get in there.
T	Get in there.

(*Getting faster and more intense.*)

K	Get in there.
R	Get in there.
All	Get in there.

(*Pause, hold the moment, then melt down in disappointment.*)

Aagggghhhh …

(*Return to original position.*)

T	… aagggghhh …

(**KY**, **K** *and* **R** *all look at* **T** *who stops the extended 'aghh'.*)

KY	(*exploding after returning to television*) Noooo (*his arms hit the others*).

(**T**, **R** *and* **K** *leap off the chair.*)

Play #3

KY	(*Stands on the chair.*)

Bring him down … Go for the legs … he can't run without his legs … round the ankles … take his … (*He sits into the back of the chair.* **T** *runs from downstage, body slams* **KY** *and chair is tipped over backwards.*)

… bloody head off!

(**KY** *is on his back with* **T** *on top with chair under both on its back.*)

R	Stacks on. (*Runs in leaps and dives on top.* **K** *steps on* **R**'s *back, then onto chair, standing it up.*)

Play #4

K	(*sitting in chair*) Make a decision, mate. If you can't think 'n' chew, spit it out.
KY	(*Dive rolls over* **K**, *steps to television, then backward shoulder rolls and sits on top of* **K**.)

Pin him down.

K	(*pushes* **KY** *to one side*) Get off him. (*Wiggles in front of* **KY**.)

KY	(*pushes* **K** *back behind him*) Pin him down.
	(**T** *and* **R** *do 'the whizzer' behind the chair.*)
R	(*chanting the nickname of a footballer*) Telf, Telf, Telf.
T	Round, round, round.
R and T	Down, down, down.
K	Off him.
KY	Down.
K	Nooo (*as* **KY** *pushes* **K** *out of the chair to left, reclaiming his territory*).
T and R	Oooohhhh (*like a crowd noise, with hands around mouths*).

Exercise Unpacking *Runners Up*

1 Interpreting Role

After you have read the script extract, choose one role you like and one line that belongs to this role. On the signal from your teacher, adopt a pose showing your interpretation of the role. Make sure the shape you create and the energy conveyed are both strong. On the next signal from your teacher, make a substantial change of physical shape and say the line belonging to the role. Divide the class into thirds. Each group performs their role interpretations for the rest of class.

2 Comic Strip

Divide into groups of four. Allocate the roles of Kerry, Telford, Rowan and Kirk. Using one group member's storyboard (see the Write and Discuss section on page 212), re-create a tableau for each frame of one scene. If the scene you have chosen contains any inversions (in which a performer is upside down) change this position so that the performer is safer. Control your use of movement, rhythm and timing to find smooth transitions from one frame to another. Once you have completed your tableaux, add a moment of sound or dialogue to each one.

Write and Discuss

1. What messages and ideas about people and sport are communicated through the action of the script?
2. Explain how the style of physical theatre performance is effective in communicating the messages and ideas of *Runners Up*.
3. What messages about the character KY are conveyed through the performer's use of physical shapes and actions?
4. Imagine you are a physical theatre company performer. Outline the steps you would take to prepare for and devise a physical theatre performance.

11.4 Performance Task: Physical Theatre

Read The Task

You are to prepare a four- to six-minute physical theatre performance. Your performance is to explore one day in the life of a character you create. Your performance may be comic or dramatic. You may choose to start the performance at a particular point in the day or from when the character wakes up. The events of the day need to be part of an overall journey for the character. The style of this performance allows for group members to represent objects, feelings or thoughts, as well as other characters. Some ideas for performances are listed below.

- Murphy's Law
- The Wedding Day
- Moving House
- The Twenty-First Birthday
- Blind Date
- The Waterskiing Lesson
- The Job Interview
- Animal Farm
- The Detective

Your performance can include:

- dialogue
- music, either live or recorded
- projected images
- sound effects, either live or recorded
- dance.

You are also required to script your physical theatre performance. Your script can be made up of illustrations or sentences, or be a combination of both.

Prepare Creating and Making a Physical Theatre Performance

- Research ideas for your physical theatre performance. You will need to create an interesting central character.
- Decide on a central focus and intention for your performance.
- Devise the events in the character's day.
- Consider how dramatic techniques such as minimal dialogue, projected images and mime can be incorporated into your performance.
- Consider integral and efficient ways of creating scene transitions.
- Use improvisation in rehearsal to workshop your performance.
- Use appropriate preparation and safety procedures for all physical work.

Evaluate: Performance Checklist

You and your teacher will evaluate your work individually, using a list of criteria. These criteria relate to your achievement in this task. Some criteria will relate to the achievement of the group. The criteria are listed on the evaluation sheet at the end of this chapter and will be used to evaluate your ability to:

- create an original and engaging physical theatre performance
- incorporate physical theatre techniques and conventions
- demonstrate a high level of energy and control in the use of movement
- incorporate an effective and appropriate use of vocal dynamics
- create interesting and appropriate characters
- manipulate the elements of drama to establish tension and to create atmosphere
- incorporate the use of symbol where appropriate.

Write and Discuss

Criticism and Aesthetics

1. Recount the process of developing your physical theatre performance. What problems did you encounter and how did you overcome them?

2. Evaluate your physical theatre performance. In your evaluation comment on the ways in which your piece effectively incorporated the techniques and conventions of physical theatre. For example, an evaluation might read:

   'Our physical theatre performance was great fun to do. We decided to only use four lines, one for the start of each scene. We also worked on our timing so our synchronised movements were perfect. We incorporated lots of energy in our movement to make the performance exciting. In the running scene we controlled pace and rhythm to build tension.'

3. Evaluate one other group's physical theatre performance. In your evaluation discuss how successful the group was in using movement to communicate character and role. Consider how effectively they chose dramatic form to suit their intention.

Past and Present Contexts

4. Research the work of the Canadian theatre company Cirque de Soleil. Compare their work with the work of Legs on the Wall. Look for similarities and differences between the two companies.

5. Look up the Circus Oz website at: **hi.com.au/centrestage**. Read the company's newsletter *Oily Rag*. Prepare a brief report on the company. In your report identify the key features of the company.

Hint

Refer to Appendixes 1, 3 and 4 for help with your logbook entries. The appendixes provide you with guidelines for evaluating your own performance work and the work of others.

Physical Theatre: Roll Up, Roll Up!   217

Evaluation Sheet — Chapter 11 Physical Theatre: Roll Up, Roll Up!

Performance Task: Physical Theatre

Student: .... Teacher: ....

Related Outcomes

By completing this task you should be able to:
- identify the techniques and conventions of a physical theatre performance
- develop movement skills to create counter balances and contact rolls
- apply a process to create, record and perform a physical theatre performance
- create, perform and evaluate a physical theatre performance.

Criteria	Level of Achievement			
	Beginning	Consolidating	Mastering	Excelling
Exploring and Developing Ideas Have you prepared for your physical theatre performance by: • researching ideas for your performance? • selecting a central focus and intention for your physical theatre performance? • using appropriate preparation and safety procedures for all physical work?				
Using Skills, Techniques and Processes Have you incorporated elements of dramatic form, techniques and conventions by: • incorporating physical theatre techniques and conventions? • demonstrating a high level of energy and control in the use of movement? • incorporating an effective and appropriate use of vocal dynamics? • creating interesting and engaging characters through an effective use of focus, energy and belief? • manipulating the elements of drama to establish tension and to create atmosphere? • incorporating the use of symbol where appropriate?				
Presenting Have you completed your physical theatre performance task by: • structuring moments of your physical theatre performance into a coherent and polished performance incorporating effective scene transitions? • establishing an appropriate actor–audience relationship?				

Comments: _____

_____

_____

_____

Chapter 12

Scripted Drama: Writing Australian Plays

Why Study Scripted Drama?

This chapter explores the role of the Australian playwright in creating scripted drama. By exploring and discussing the work of the playwright, you will appreciate and understand the ways in which this theatre practitioner examines and reflects our society. You will also undertake exercises and activities to help you write your own Australian script.

The chapter is divided into the following units:

- **12.1** Exploring Australian Culture and Identity
- **12.2** Hannie Rayson: An Approach to Script Writing
- **12.3** Aboriginal Scripted Drama
- **12.4** Writing Your Own Scripted Drama
- **12.5** Script Writing Task: Australian Drama

Outcomes

In this chapter you will:

- recognise how theatre and drama reflect and explore aspects of Australian society and human experience
- apply a process to create, write, edit and publish a script that explores aspects of Australian society, politics and history
- identify and explain how the playwright incorporates dramatic form, dramatic techniques and dramatic conventions for a specific purpose.

Geraldine Turner as Maureen in the Melbourne Theatre Company production of Hannie Rayson's play *Inheritance*. Photograph by Jeff Busby.

12.1 Exploring Australian Culture and Identity

Read: Theatre as a Mirror

Theatre and drama are integral parts of society. They not only provide entertainment, but encourage us to reflect. Theatre and drama allow us to consider both life experiences that are familiar to us and that are not so familiar. The shared experience of theatre provides us with a valuable opportunity to examine ourselves, so theatre can lead to powerful changes both for individuals and for the community.

Theatre and drama reflect the significant changes occurring in society, politics and history. Through their work, playwrights can explore one or more of the following:

- Social concerns—The play may invite the audience to examine and explore individuals, communities, groups, the way we interact, social classes, racial tension, youth, the elderly, interpersonal relationships or living conditions.
- Political concerns—The play may invite the audience to examine and explore the ways in which power in society is exercised. For instance, the play may comment upon the politics of gender, issues of equality, human rights, our laws, economics or our interaction with other countries of the world.
- Historical concerns—The play may invite the audience to examine and explore the ways in which our past has shaped us. For instance, the play may focus upon significant historical events, or consider what we can learn from our history and how it might help us shape our future.

Write and Discuss

1. What are some important social or political issues that concern you at the present time? Write these down and explain your concern. Share your work with a partner.
2. Recall one play or performance you have seen recently. Consider the social, historical and political concerns listed above. Identify which of these was the most dominant concern of the performance.
3. Visit the Australian Bureau of Statistics website at: **www.hi.com.au/centrestage**. Gather as much information as you can regarding population distribution, racial groupings, family structures, and so on. Choose one piece of information which you find particularly interesting or which you feel challenges people's preconceptions about Australia. Share this piece of information with the class.

Exercise: Australian Culture and Identity

The following exercises allow you to explore your own perceptions of Australian society, politics, history and culture. It is important to remember that all opinions and ideas are useful. Our society is diverse so there will be many different points of view. Keep logbook entries of your work in these exercises as they will provide a useful resource for the performance task at the end of the chapter.

1 True Blue?
Work in groups of three. Write a list of as many things you can think of that are distinctly Australian. These might be particular examples of people, places, events, objects, animals or expressions. There is no need to edit or alter your list. Include everything you can think of. Try to group your words and ideas into categories. Share your ideas with the class.

2 Map of Australia
As a class use the entire area of the classroom to create a map of Australia incorporating movement, vocal dynamics and levels. On your map include cities, natural landmarks and other features you feel are important. As you become a city, landmark or feature, consider how you might use your physical shape and vocal dynamics to express the idea or object you are representing.

3 Tableaux of Australian Society
Divide into groups of six. Prepare two or three tableaux that represent an issue of concern you have about Australian society or politics. Present your tableaux to the class. Make sure each tableau represents as many aspects of the issue as possible.

4 Fair Dinkum!
In this exercise you will create a brief performance that explores three perspectives:
- how Australians think they are seen by others
- how Australians would like to be seen by others
- how Australians really are.

Divide into groups of five. Brainstorm ideas about the three different perspectives and then prepare a montage presentation that shows the three viewpoints. Incorporate an inventive use of movement, vocal dynamics, repetition and space. Also consider how you can control movement and timing to transform from one scene to another so there are no breaks in your performance.

Refer to page 48 for an explanation of a montage performance.

5 Mateship
The concept of mateship is a significant aspect of Australian culture. Mateship embodies certain values, including equality, loyalty and determination. Divide into groups of four and prepare a short performance that examines the strengths and weaknesses

of this code of loyalty. Spend some time in your group discussing the positive and negative aspects of mateship. Your performance may be linear or montage in structure, and include the use of narration, tableaux, symbols or freeze frames. Present your performance to the class.

6 The Australian Natural Environment

The Australian landscape has a powerful influence on our perception of our country and what it means to be Australian. Our relationship with the environment has been explored in many Australian plays and films.

- In large groups prepare a movement-and-sound-scape that shows two contrasting landscapes or seasons we experience in Australia.
- Prepare a role-play in which the natural environment is a central feature. Two or three people should play characters who respond to the environment; the others should create the environment. Some suggested environments to present are an ocean beach, a bushfire, the desert, a rainforest, the mountains or the underwater world.

Write and Discuss

1. Write a logbook entry that discusses your perception of what it means to be an Australian. In your entry refer to the performance work you have seen in class.

2. Research and create a list of four Australian plays or films in which the Australian landscape has been a dominant feature. Discuss the ways in which the environment is symbolic in the play or film.

3. Choose one of the exercises you participated in. Evaluate the ways in which you and your group used body language, movement, vocal dynamics and the elements of drama to achieve an effective performance.

12.2 Hannie Rayson: An Approach to Script Writing

'[Some playwrights] talk as if the power of one's own personal experience and imaginings is enough. It rarely is.'
Hannie Rayson

Read ## Australian Playwrights

One of theatre's key practitioners is the playwright. Australia has many successful playwrights whose work has been produced both nationally and internationally. Australian playwrights have written plays in a variety of dramatic forms. For instance, playwright David Williamson has written many successful realistic plays. Other playwrights have also used Realism as the core dramatic form but have explored other dramatic techniques including narration, symbolism and flashback.

In this unit we will look closely at the work of Hannie Rayson, a contemporary Australian playwright. Then in the following unit we will focus upon the work of some indigenous Australians, in particular the Aboriginal playwright Dallas Winmar. Looking more closely at these writers will provide you with an opportunity to examine contemporary Australian theatre in more depth. You will read about some different approaches to scriptwriting, the use of dramatic form, and the incorporation of dramatic conventions and techniques. Script extracts have been provided to help illustrate the playwrights' intentions. You can also read, discuss and perform these extracts.

Write and Discuss

1. Research one the following Australian playwrights: Nick Enright, Beatrix Christian, Tony McNamara, Louis Nowra, David Williamson or Dorothy Hewitt. Alternatively, choose an Australian playwright of your own. Find out biographical information. Also give examples of the dramatic forms they write in, as well as the dramatic techniques and conventions they use. Present your findings to the class.

Practitioner Profile

Hannie Rayson
Playwright

Hannie Rayson is co-founder of the Melbourne-based company Theatreworks. She has served as writer-in-residence at the Mill Theatre, Playbox Theatre, La Trobe University, Monash University and the Victorian College of the Arts. Her theatre credits include *Please Return to Sender* (1980); *Mary* (1981); *Leave It Till Monday* (1984); *Room to Move* (1985), which won the Australian Writers' Guild AWGIE Award for Best Original Stage Play of 1985; *Hotel Sorrento* (1990), which won an AWGIE award, as well as a New South Wales Premier's Literary Award and Green Room Award for Best Play of 1990; and *Life After George* (2000), which opened at the Melbourne Theatre Company, and went on to win the Victorian Premier's Literary Award in 2000, the Green Room Award for Best New Australian Play of 2001, and the Best New Australian Work at the 2001 Helpmann Awards. Hannie's plays have been performed extensively around Australia and a number have been produced overseas.

Read *Inheritance*

Researching a Play

As a playwright, Hannie Rayson believes that research is essential. As preparation for writing the play *Inheritance* Hannie travelled to the Mallee region of Victoria fifteen times to meet the people who lived there and to listen to their stories. She wanted to get to the heart of the discontent that was a feature of life at this time for many people living in regional Australia. The director and cast of *Inheritance* travelled to the Mallee region with Hannie to help develop their understanding of the characters and the issues of the play.

Here are some statements from Hannie about what she discovered during her research in the Mallee:

- 'I went into these country towns and talked to these people in pubs, libraries, everywhere, and asked: "What's on your mind? What are the key things?" And they usually said, "Inheritance. Who gets the farm?"'

- 'Such tensions become worse as society changes. The recognition of women and minority groups disrupts the traditional lines of succession. For some time now wives and daughters have demanded their fare share.'

- 'Other challenges confront the owners of farms. Farming methods are changing; there are still the threats of drought, flood, fire, disease and pests, not to mention the decline of small towns and their essential services.'

Plot and Story

Inheritance was first performed by the Melbourne Theatre Company at the Playhouse in the Victorian Arts Centre on 1 March 2003. The play is set in the Mallee in Victoria. In the play the Myrtle twins, Dibs Hamilton and Girlie Delaney, are turning eighty. As the family gathers to celebrate speculation grows as to who will inherit the family property Allandale when the ageing Farley Hamilton, Dibs's husband, is gone. Lyle Delaney and his wife Maureen live and work on the Hamilton farm. Although they are related to the Hamiltons, they do not have ownership of the land. William Hamilton, his sister Julia and her son Felix, who have arrived from the city, provide an opportunity for the divide between bush and city to be explored.

After Farley Hamilton dies there are rumours that he has left the farm to his adopted son Nugget who is Aboriginal. Although a loved member of the Hamilton family, Nugget is viewed as an outsider. The tension in the play increases as various family members vie for their share of the farm.

Characters

The characters in *Inheritance* are as follows.

The Hamiltons
Dibs Hamilton, aged eighty (Girlie's twin sister)
Farley Hamilton, aged eighty-three
William Hamilton, aged fifty-two, eldest son
Julia Hamilton, aged forty-four, William's sister
Felix, aged nineteen, Julia's son
Nugget Hamilton, aged thirty-eight, adopted Aboriginal son

The Delaneys
Girlie Delaney, aged eighty
Lyle Delaney, aged forty-eight, her son
Maureen Delaney, Lyle's wife
Ashleigh Delaney, aged sixteen, their daughter
Brianna Delaney, aged fifteen, her sister

Themes and Issues

Inheritance comments upon many topical issues. It is structured and written to encourage us to consider not only the actions of individual characters but the concerns, fears, problems and joys of our Australian society. Some of the themes and issues in the play are:

family loyalty, land ownership, reconciliation, the Stolen Generation, the divide between the city and country, greed, suicide, intolerance.

Dramatic Form and Dramatic Techniques

Although *Inheritance* is realistic in style certain dramatic techniques are used to create memories of the past. The use of direct narration to the audience, and the appearance of characters from the past, helps the audience understand the family history of the Myrtle twins and how ownership of the farm came to be in Dibs's hands. In one significant scene the character of Nugget interacts with the spirit of his deceased adoptive father, Farley. In this scene Nugget reveals how as a youth he was torn between being with his white adoptive family and his own people. In this scene, breaking the style of Realism allows the audience to learn more about the characters, particularly as we are able to hear their private thoughts.

Elements of Production

The Melbourne Theatre Company's production of *Inheritance* was performed on a proscenium stage. The set was suggestive of the farm houses belonging to the two families, the Hamiltons and the Delaneys. Upright wooden beams, floorboards and rustic furniture were used to represent the interiors of the two houses. A floodlit cyclorama was used to create a distant, changing skyline. Moments of flashback were created with the use of lighting and sound. At certain moments in the play a wooden wall with two central doors was moved from the wings to centre stage. These doors helped to add an element of surprise to certain moments, such as when the hanging of Norm Delaney, who was the father of Girlie and Dibs, is revealed. A moving track in the upstage and downstage floor allowed large set items such as cars and trucks to be moved on- and offstage.

Costumes were designed to represent the characters in a realistic style. Differences in costume design were made to establish the past and present, the city and the bush, and the different generations.

Recorded music was incorporated to establish atmosphere.

Exercise Exploring the Themes and Issues of *Inheritance*

You have read about the themes and issues that are exposed in the play *Inheritance*. The following exercises provide an opportunity for you to explore some of these. You can read the *Inheritance* script extracts on pages 228–34 either before or after completing these exercises.

1 Country and City Characters

Find a space in the classroom to work on your own. On the signal from your teacher adopt a frozen pose as a character you would find in a country town. On the next signal from your teacher walk through the space as your character. Interact with other characters, and find phrases or greetings that help indicate the personality of your character. On the next signal from your teacher change your frozen pose to become another character from a country town. Repeat the exercise until you have played three or four characters. Then try becoming characters you would find in a major Australian city.

2 Point of View

One class member starts off as the performer in this exercise. He or she must take on the character of a person that might be found in a country town. This person does not like cities or people from them. Using the 'hot seat' technique the rest of the class asks questions to explore the character's views about the differences between life in the city and life in the country. Repeat the exercise, but this time a new performer becomes a character from a major Australian city. This character has never visited the country and has no desire to. Using the 'hot seat' technique again explore this character's views about life in the city and the country.

3 Country Hospitality

Divide into groups of four and prepare a short scene in which a person from the city is stranded in a small country town when their car breaks down. Your role-play should show some positive and negative aspects of this experience.

Write and Discuss

1. Recount your experiences of one of the exercises. What themes and issues did the exercise explore?
2. Discuss the relevance of the themes and issues you described above to today's world.

Exercise *Inheritance* Script Extracts

The following scenes are from the play *Inheritance*. Work in groups to prepare a rehearsed performance of one or more script extracts.

Write and Discuss

1. Read through the following script extracts. Identify the social, political and/or historical concerns in each extract.
2. Identify the objective and motivation of the character you will play.
3. Identify the tension and climactic moment of each scene by dividing the script into units of action (See Chapter 4, Unit 4.3).
4. Highlight three or four words, phrases or actions used by the character you will play. Explain why these are important to your understanding of your character.
5. Prepare a character biography for the character you will play.

Hint

When rehearsing a script it is important to identify the subtext, or the meaning behind the words of the character. By doing this you will more easily identify character motivation and objective. This understanding will add dimension to your character.

Scripted Drama: Writing Australian Plays

Act One, Scene Nineteen

Characters: Lyle, Maureen, Brianna, Ashleigh and William

In this scene Lyle and his wife Maureen discover that their cousins, the Hamiltons, intend to sell the farm that Lyle has spent his life working on but does not own. The scene begins with Lyle talking to his two daughters, Ashleigh and Brianna. They have heard rumours that the farm they live on is to be sold.

(Lyle *enters the kitchen.* **Ashleigh** *is doing her homework.*)

Ashleigh Dad. My friend Anne Cogsley told me that the Hamiltons are going to sell their farm.
(**Brianna** *enters*.)
Lyle Isn't she a sticky-beak.
Ashleigh Her Dad's their financial counsellor.
Lyle Cougar Cogsley. Jesus Christ.
Ashleigh She told me not to tell.
Lyle That's crook. Spreading your private business all over the district. Bloody hell.
Brianna Would we be able to buy it off them?
Lyle You wouldn't get me within a hundred mile of one of them, financial counsellors.
Brianna Would we?
(He laughs sourly.)
Lyle Got three million dollars, have you? No. If they sell Allandale we're up shit creek.
Brianna But it's our farm.
Lyle Our farm, Bri. But their land.
Brianna What about Cromies'? That's ours, isn't it?
Lyle It's only fifteen hundred acres. You can't feed a family on fifteen hundred acres.
(**Maureen** *enters.*)
Maureen Get a wriggle on, girls. You'll be late for choir.
Ashleigh It's at St Mary's tonight.
Maureen Can you take them? I've got a Progress meeting, then I've got to get down to the CFA to get signatures for the petition.
Lyle The Hamiltons are puttin' Allandale on the market.
(Beat.)
Maureen I knew this'd bloody happen. I'm going to the solicitor.
Lyle I said no.
Maureen They're walking all over you, Lyle. It's not fair.
Lyle Who says life is fair? Life is not fair.
William (*offstage*) Yoo-hoo.
Maureen Oh, Christ. It's the Pansy Boy.
Lyle He's come for the trestle tables.
William (*offstage*) Hello?

Dramatic Forms and Performance Styles

Lyle	We're in here.
William	(*entering*) G'day, Maureen. Lyle.
	(**Lyle** *goes to the fridge and gets out two tinnies. He pulls the tops off and hands one to* **William**.)
Lyle	Hear you're selling the farm.
Maureen	I just wrote you people a cheque for six thousand dollars—to run our sheep on land which should be ours.
William	What land is that, Maureen?
Maureen	You know damn well.
Lyle	Maur—when Nanna Myrtle gave the farm to Aunty Dibs, she gave Mum and Dad ten thousand quid to set them up in the pub.
Maureen	Big deal.
Lyle	That was a lot of money sixty years ago.
Maureen	The farm is worth two million dollars.
Lyle	And the rest. What with the two houses and the machinery …
Maureen	Three million, then.
William	Maureen, what has this got to do with you—?
Maureen	Lyle has put in more tractor hours than all of youse put together. Every school holiday, every Christmas, every weekend. And you walk back here after thirty years expecting just to clean up.
William	Maureen. It's my family's farm.
Maureen	Mate, the land belongs to the people who work it. Not to the banks. Not to the multinationals. And certainly not to a pampered city boy who turned tail because he couldn't hack it.

Act One, Scene Twenty-Six

Characters: *Girlie and Maureen Delaney, Julia, William and Felix*

In this scene William Hamilton, and his sister Julia and her son Felix, who are visiting from the city, bump into Girlie and Maureen Delaney in town. Maureen and Girlie are seeking signatures for a petition to open a rural transaction centre in the local milk bar as the bank and post office have been closed down. They are suspicious of Julia, her brother William and her teenage son Felix, because they believe the three are trying to persuade Dibs Hamilton, Girlie's sister, to sell the farm.

Julia	Hey, is that Maureen up there?
William	Quick. Nip down here.
Julia	No! We can't. She's seen us.
William	Shit!
Julia	(*waving*) Hi, Maureen!
Maureen	Hi! (*To* **Girlie**) It's whining Julia and the Pansy Boy.

Scripted Drama: Writing Australian Plays

Girlie	Is that Felix? He's a weedy-looking bloke, isn't he? I see what you mean. He does look like a fairy.
Julia	Hi, Aunty Girl. How are you? Felix, you remember Aunty Girl, don't you?
Felix	Hey.
Maureen	Hello, youse. Come to sign our petition, have you?
Julia	What is it?
Maureen	We're trying to get a rural transaction centre in the milk bar.
Girlie	Since we've lost the bank and the post office. How are you, Will?
William	Well, thanks, Aunty Girlie.
Maureen	They reckon we're too small, but we'll see about that.
Girlie	They all go into Swan Hill o' course. Do their business in there.
Maureen	(*pointing*) Poor ol' Archie here.
Girlie	Everyone shops at Safeway in Swan Hill.
Maureen	And on the way home, with two hundred bucks worth of groceries in the boot, they realise they've forgotten bread or milk or something—so they stop at Archie's and put it on the tab. It's not right.
Girlie	He can't keep going.
Felix	That's globalisation for you.
Girlie	She's going into politics, you know.
Julia	Mum said.
Girlie	Can't be any more stupid than Roly Pigget.
Felix	Who's he? Your local member?
Girlie	There was a time when you could've put a chook in the National Party and people round here woulda voted for it. But not anymore.
Maureen	So what's happening about Allandale? Any more news?
Julia	What about?
Maureen	Doesn't she know?
Girlie	What?
Maureen	William?
William	I don't know any more than you do, Maureen.
Julia	What's this?
Maureen	It's all over town.
Julia	What?
Maureen	Your mother's putting Allandale on the market.
Girlie	Over my dead body she is.
Julia	I think you might have got the wrong end of the stick.
Maureen	I hope so. I really hope so. Otherwise things might get very nasty around here.

Act Two, Scene Two

Characters: Maureen Delaney

Maureen Delaney gathers support for her political campaign. In this scene she arrives on the back of a ute at an agricultural show to give a speech.

(The Rushton Agricultural and Pastoral Show [A & P Society Show]. There are all the sound effects of fairground music, children squealing on the ferris wheel and a muffled loudspeaker announcing missing children, the results of the sheepdog trials and the preserves display in the pavilion. The Grand Parade will be at 3 p.m.)

Public Address (*voice-over*) Could someone please bring the results of the showjumping to the stewards' stand in the middle of the arena. Thank you. And now, ladies and gentlemen, here's a little lady with a lot to say for herself. They're calling her the 'Mouth of the Mallee'. Please welcome the Independent candidate for Murray—Maureen Delaney.

*(The back doors roll open. Accompanied by triumphant music, her campaign song, **Maureen Delaney** rides in on the back of a ute which rolls down the stage towards the audience. She is waving to the crowd of enthusiastic supporters who clap and whistle and stamp their feet [on the sound track]. A large banner reads: 'Vote One Maureen Delaney Putting the Mallee First'.)*

*(**Maureen** addresses the assembled crowd.)*

Maureen Thank you. Thank you. Thank you. Ladies and gentlemen. I was born in the Mallee. I went to school here. I got my first job at Dobsons' in Swan Hill. This is where I've raised my family. And I know what it means to work my guts out. I know Mallee people and I'm telling you right now, we've got a problem.

Do you know why some of us can't get the phone to work? Why we drive every day on roads that are not safe? Why our children are being educated in second-rate schools? Do you? I'll tell you why. We're too bloody nice. That's why. We're too decent. Let's get one thing straight. You deserve—your kids deserve—the same basic facilities as city people take for granted. But have you got a problem sticking up for yourself, or what?

Let me tell you a true story. One night, a gang of bikies come hooning into Rushton. Stirring up trouble, making a helluva racket. I had this young fella working with me in the pub and he says to me, 'Maureen,' he says, 'they're gonna trash this place.' And I thought, 'Bugger that. I am not going to be intimidated by a band of thugs.' So I march over to this big hairy bloke in a leather vest with tatts all over him and I say 'Out!' I say, 'You heard me. On yer bike. Now!' He stares at me long and hard, this creep, and then he says, 'Yes, ma'am.' And he gives me a little bow and they get on their bikes and ride out of town. True story.

My friends, we made this country. And we're not about to be bullied by foreign interests who are no different to those bikies. I'm talking about the multinationals. I'm talking about the foreign-owned banks. And I'm talking about every Asian, Moslem and Hottentot who come here and refuse to sign up to the Australian Way of Life. There are women who come to this country who are not prepared to show their faces. Well I say, 'Don't show your face around here.' My friends, this is Australia, where people say g'day to each other in the street and lend a hand when they see a mate in trouble.

You know me. I'm Maureen Delaney. On Election Day—put the Mallee first. Put a '1' beside Maureen Delaney.

Act Two, Scene Six

Characters: *Dibs, William and Nugget*

In this scene William and his mother are in the bedroom of her deceased husband. They discuss the will he has left behind and who will inherit the farm. They are interrupted unexpectedly by the arrival of Nugget who is also looking for the will. He believes that his adoptive father has left the farm to him.

(The Hamiltons' bedroom.)
(Dibs enters to find William rifling through his father's writing desk.)

Dibs What are you doing?
William I'm looking for the will.
Dibs It's with the solicitor.
William Uh-huh.
Dibs We made one about ten years ago.
William Mm-hmm.
Dibs I can tell you what's in it.
(William seizes upon an envelope. He opens it deftly with a letter opener.)
Dibs William! Please!
(William examines the contents carefully.)
William *(reading)* 'I hereby revoke all former wills and testamentary dispositions (*made by me*) and declare this to be my last Will and Testament.'
(He turns the pages to note the date and the witnesses.)

	(*Reading*) 'Dated this day Monday 26th April 1999. Witnessed by Frederick Barnard and Frank Scott.' (*Pause.*) Who are they? Mum?
Dibs	(*quietly*) Airforce chums. Bunty Barnard and Wing-Commander Scott.
William	He must have gone down to Melbourne. Did you know about this?
Dibs	Must have been Anzac Day.
William	(*reading*) 'After payment of my just debts, testamentary and funeral expenses, and any taxes or duties payable as a result of my death, I give my entire remaining estate to my son Neville Hamilton, known as Nugget.'
Dibs	Let me look at that.
William	(*reading*) 'I do hereby devise and bequeath the old house block … matrimonial home and garden … motor vehicle … money held in my name, Commonwealth Bank, Swan Hill, to my spouse Elizabeth Hamilton, known as Dibs.'
Dibs	Give me that.
William	My son, Neville Hamilton. Known as Nugget. (*Silence.*) What are we to understand from this?
Dibs	He didn't have anywhere else to go. So we adopted him.
William	But who's his father. Who is Nugget's father?
Dibs	Unknown. It was 'Unknown' on his birth certificate. Give me that. (**William** *hands her the will*. **Dibs** *rips it up.*) This is not Farley's farm. This is my farm. And I will decide how it's to be operated from now on. No-one gets anything until I say so. (**Nugget** *enters.*)
William	Haven't you heard of knocking?
Nugget	Get real.
Dibs	What is it, Nugget?
William	Did you want something? (*Pause.*)
Nugget	Farley reckoned there was something in his desk.
William	What sort of something?
Nugget	None of your business.
William	If my father said there was something in his desk for you, then I'd like to know what it is.
Nugget	It wasn't for you, mate. It was for me.
William	What is it? (*Pause.*)
Nugget	His will.
William	His will is with the solicitors in Swan Hill.

Nugget It's in the third drawer.
William Take a look.
(William and Nugget stare at each other.)
Nugget Farley left me the farm.
Dibs We've done everything we can for you, Nugget.
Nugget He left it to me.
Dibs You don't seem very grateful for what we've done.
Nugget Grateful?
William Yes.
Nugget Grateful.
William Frankly, this fantasy you've dreamt up—I find it quite an affront. I mean, who do you think you are?
Nugget Farley's son.
William That's a lie. Your father was a rabbito.
Nugget That's bullshit, mate.
William You conniving little cheat.
Nugget I'm not taking the farm off you.
William You're dead right, you're not.
Nugget I'm keeping it in the family.
Dibs You're not family. I'm sorry. But you're not.
(William pulls the drawer out to show Nugget.)
William There's nothing in here for you.
(Nugget exits, slamming the door behind him.)
Dibs He's not family. He's not.

Write and Discuss

1. Discuss the reasons why you think Hannie Rayson has chosen Realism as the core dramatic form for *Inheritance*. In your answer consider how Realism impacts on the actor–audience relationship.

2. Evaluate one group's performance of their script extract. Comment on their interpretation of the extract, including use of space, control of tension and the effectiveness of character interpretation through the use of movement and vocal dynamics.

3. Identify two key moments from the script extracts and explain how the playwright has used dramatic action and language to create tension.

12.3 Aboriginal Scripted Drama

Aboriginal performance and ritual began many thousands of years ago. Indigenous Australians use dance, singing, chanting and storytelling as a means of sharing and passing on experiences, knowledge and culture. Over the last thirty years a new form of Australian theatre has evolved that combines aspects of traditional Aboriginal culture with Western dramatic forms.

During the period of the 1960s and 1970s many Western societies experienced a significant change in attitudes to issues of equality and human rights. In Australia the influence of this social change encouraged Aboriginal Australians to express their concerns about how their own people lived in a post-colonial era. One famous Aboriginal playwright from this period is Jack Davis. Jack was born in Perth in 1917 and is a descendant of the Nyoongarah people of south-west Western Australia. He became an activist on behalf of his people, and from 1967 to 1971 he was director of the Aboriginal Centre in Perth. Jack's plays include *The Dreamers* (1983), *No Sugar* (1985) and *The Honey Spot* (1986). The plays are largely set in the past and are written to show the world from an Aboriginal perspective. Although they deal with oppression and conflict between whites and blacks they also encourage indigenous people to be self-empowered.

Current Aboriginal playwrights include Jane Harrison (*Stolen*, 1996), Wesley Enoch and Deborah Mailman (*The 7 Stages of Grieving*, 1996), Leah Purcell (*Black Chicks Talking*, 2002) and Dallas Winmar, whose work is explored in greater detail below. The following table outlines some of the features of contemporary Aboriginal theatre.

Contemporary Aboriginal Theatre

Dramatic Form	Thematic Concerns	Dramatic Techniques and Conventions
Non-linear narrative	Grief	Direct audience address
Eclectic and fragmented	Kinship/family	Symbolism
A combination of the styles and traditions of Western performance with aspects of indigenous language and culture	Relationships	Visual metaphor
	Identity	Storytelling
	The Stolen Generation	Dance and music
	Assimilation	Multi-media
	Racism	Indigenous language
	Reconciliation	Political oratory
	Connection with the land	Presentational acting
	Interactions with the law	Stand-up comedy
	Effects of the past on the present	Realism

Practitioner Profile

Dallas Winmar
Playwright

Dallas Winmar was born in Perth, Western Australia. In 1999 she was asked to write *Aliwa!* for the Yirra Yaakin Noongar Theatre in Perth. In the same year she attended the National Playwrights Conference in Canberra. From that experience she was also commissioned to write *Skin Deep* for Kooemba Jdarra theatre company in Brisbane.

Dallas was invited back to attend the National Playwrights Conference in Brisbane in 2000. Both her plays were also performed in that year. *Skin Deep* was performed in Brisbane at the La Boite Theatre, and *Aliwa!* was performed at the Hole in the Wall Theatre in Subiaco, Perth. In 2001 *Aliwa!* was performed in Sydney's Belvoir Street Theatre. The play was short-listed in the Script Category of the Western Australian Premier's Book Awards of the same year. *Aliwa!* was also a winner of the Kate Challis RAKA Award for Drama in 2002.

Read *Aliwa!*

Plot and Story
The title of the play *Aliwa!* comes from the indigenous language expression 'Aliwa Wadjella', which means 'Watch out! There's a whitefella about!' *Aliwa!* is about the plight of the family of Jack Davis, the well-known playwright. The play shifts between the past and present to tell the story of Jack's three sisters who are returning to Yarloop, a small town about 100 kilometres south of Perth in Western Australia, in order to show the youngest sister, Jude, the location of the family's past. The journey of the sisters in the present is paralleled with the journey and hardships of the Davis family in the 1930s. In particular the play focuses on Alice Davis's struggle to keep her family together despite ignorance and discrimination.

Characters
Actor 1—Young Dot, Old Dot, Mrs Pivot, Mrs Crawford
Actor 2—Young Ethel, Old Ethel, Teacher
Actor 3—Mum, Young Jude, Old Jude, Giddeon, Eddy, the Cowboy
Two musicians

Aunty Dot sat on the sidelines improvising comments on the action. The letters were read by the actors.

Themes and Issues

Aliwa! explores the following themes and issues:

racism; the importance of family; the need to resolve the past; interactions with the law and authority

Dramatic Form and Dramatic Techniques

One of the most powerful techniques used in the Belvoir Street production of *Aliwa!* was the inclusion of Aunty Dot, who is in reality a descendant of the Davis family. She acted as narrator and master of ceremonies for the play. Her presence gave the performance a special dimension as it was her life represented on stage. At times she would interact with the performers in an informal and improvised manner.

Certain techniques were used to move the action between the past and present. For example, actors transformed objects to create new locations, or characters narrated to the audience. This also helped to create an intimate and informal atmosphere. To establish the historically factual basis of the play, primary source letters from the Chief Protector of Aboriginal People to the Davis family were read out at various points.

Elements of Production

The production at the Belvoir Street Theatre used a minimal set. The family's journey and locations of scenes were suggested through the use and transformation of a small number of props. To one side of the stage were an old couch and some other furniture used at different points in the performance. The walls of the stage were layered with roughly painted wood and pieces of corrugated iron. It was important that the performance space allowed for the changes between the past and present. The live band added to the informality of the performance. Members of the band interacted with the performers and took on minor roles in certain scenes.

Exercise: *Aliwa!* Script Extracts

The following scenes are from the play *Aliwa!* Work in groups to prepare a rehearsed performance of one or more script extracts.

Write and Discuss

1. Read through the following script extracts and identify the social, political and/or historical concerns.
2. Identify the dramatic techniques used in the *Aliwa!* script extracts. Use the table on page 235 to help you. Discuss how these techniques will affect the actor–audience relationship in particular scenes.
3. Read the cast list for *Aliwa!* Identify the challenges for a performer acting in this play. Offer suggestions as to how a performer might deal with these challenges.
4. Explain how you will achieve effective scene transitions. Give examples.

The Picture Theatre—Yarloop (The Past)

(**Young Ethel** *is outside the house in Yarloop.*)

Ethel (*narration*) In the summer time we'd sit outside, under the bower shed that Dad built with his own hands. It had a great big table, stools to sit on and no matter how hot the day got, it was always cool under there. Tea time was family time. We would laugh and talk about the day we had. Mum would always have a big meal spread out. And jugs of her special home-made ginger beer. We were never short of a feed. Dad would go out hunting and bring back kangaroos, duck and parrots. So our cupboards were always full. In the winter time Dad played for the local football team, even trained and coached. Mum helped out working with the ladies' club, making scones and jam. We were the Davis family of Yarloop.

The Water Tower (The Past)

(**Young Dot** *and* **Young Ethel** *are both looking up.*)

Young Dot Go on then, you first.
Young Ethel I'm a bit puffed at the moment.
Young Dot You orright? Up you go.
Young Ethel It's very high, isn't it?
Young Dot Come, follow me.
Young Ethel I dunno, Dot.
Young Dot It's easy, come on.
Young Ethel (*taking one step*) It's a long way up.
Young Dot Just don't look down.
(*The actors improvise climbing—with music.*)
Aunty Dot (*To one of the musicians*) Cut it out, Wayne.
Young Dot Grab my hand and I'll help you up.
Young Ethel Oooo … ahhh.
Young Dot See, we're touching the sky.
Young Ethel Stay still, you're making it shake.
Young Dot You can see for miles and miles.
Young Ethel There's Dad.
Young Dot Where?
Young Ethel Over there. (*Shouting*) Dad!
Young Dot I see him. Ruffy's with him too.
Young Ethel He looks so small.
Young Dot Hey, Ruffy! Ruf, Ruf, woof, woof!
Young Ethel Ruffy, Ruffy! Woo, woo, woo, woo! Can we go now?
Young Dot No, wait until we can't see Dad no more. (*Shouting*) Dad! Dad!
Young Ethel He can't hear ya.

Young Dot	(*tearing herself, shouting loudly*) Dad!
Young Ethel	I think he might have heard that.
Young Dot	Dad! Bring back some good tucker! Love you … Dad!
Young Ethel	Love you, Dad!

Late in the Evening—Outside the Davis House (The Past)

(**Mum** *looks through the trees and then sits down.*)

Young Ethel	Mum, I can't sleep. I keep hearing this strange bird outside my window.
	(**Mum** *looks at* **Young Ethel** *and doesn't answer. She changes the subject.*)
Mum	Nothing to be scared of. It's only a bird.
Young Ethel	Shall I put Dad's dinner in the oven?
Mum	He'll be home soon.
Young Ethel	He's taking a long time. Isn't he?
Mum	It's late. Go to bed. Give me a kiss.
Young Ethel	Can you get him to tuck us in, when he comes home?
Mum	Yes, Ethel.
Young Ethel	Goodnight, Mum.
Mum	Goodnight, darling.
Young Ethel	(*narration*) When I came home from school the next day the house was silent. Mum was sitting with her head in her hands. When I got closer I could hear her crying. It was then I knew what that bird meant.
File Note	Fifth of September, 1932. Re: Death of William Davis—Half-Caste Aborigine. Constable O'Brien advised by phone this morning that half-caste William Davis met with his death yesterday whilst out hunting. With regard to the family of deceased, who left a wife and ten children, ages ranging from twenty years to seven months, it appears to me that something will now have to be done in connection with them. The children are in constant association with the white boys and girls of Yarloop and I do not think that it is in the best interests of either the white children or the Davis children, that this association should be permitted to continue. I am of the opinion that they should be sent some place where they will be able to mix with persons of their own race … A. O. Neville, Chief Protector of Aborigines.

The Cemetery—Yarloop (The Present)

(Jude, Ethel and Dot are now elderly.)

Old Ethel (*reading the name on a tombstone*) Noorn. May Bell. 1902 to 1903.

Old Jude She was only one, poor baby.

Old Ethel This one was only five.

Old Jude What's on his tombstone?

Old Ethel No tombstone. Just a number.

Old Jude Can you remember where?

Old Ethel I think it was … somewhere near a gum tree. Towards the back.

Old Dot Do you know which grave is his?

Old Ethel Don't know exactly, too long ago.

Old Dot What's important is that we are here.

Old Jude Feels like he's with us.

Old Dot Like his spirit is. Aye?

Old Ethel I remember the day it happened, Dot. We'd climbed up that bloody water tower.

Old Dot It was the last time we ever saw him.

Old Ethel He turned and faced us. His hand raised above his head.

Old Dot I waved that little hanky till he disappeared from sight.

Old Ethel Yarloop was never the same after that.

Old Dot Dad was out hunting when it happened, Jude, crossing old George's paddock. This bloody bull chased him. He tripped, fell, broke his neck. For years afterwards, I'd lay on my bed with my hand over my ears and hear that roaring and running. But it was only the beat of my heart, thumping through my eardrums.

Old Jude You right, sis?

Old Dot Yeah, I'm fine.

Old Ethel This is the first time we've been back since it happened.

Old Dot We came with Mum by horse and cart. This time we came in a flash car.

Old Ethel She was the last one to place a flower on the grave.

Old Dot She just stood looking down, not saying anything.

Old Ethel First time I saw her cry like that.

Aunty Dot After Dad died, the struggle really began. It was the middle of the Depression. While the whitefellas got what was called sustenance, us blackfellas got rations.

Write and Discuss

1. Evaluate one group's performance of a selection of script extracts. Focus your discussion on the use of effective scene transitions. Include consideration of how the transitions added to the atmosphere of the performance.
2. Evaluate one group's performance of their script extract. Comment on the ways in which the group effectively incorporated dramatic techniques in the performance.
3. Evaluate one performer who portrayed a character both in the past and present or a performer who played more than one character. Discuss the ways in which the performer manipulated vocal dynamics, body language, energy and focus to effectively present two or more different characters.

12.4 Writing Your Own Scripted Drama

So You Want To Be a Playwright?

When we go to the theatre and see a scripted drama performed it is important to remind ourselves that what we see is the end product of a long and rewarding process. It is unlikely that a playwright would be happy with the first draft of a script. It is a process of refining ideas, exploring them in rehearsal and re-drafting the script that creates the best work.

So where do you start? When writing a script it can be helpful to follow certain important steps as outlined below.

Read **Step 1 Define Your Idea**

This is the most important step in creating a script. You need to be clear about the intention of your script. This is similar to defining the purpose of a playbuilt performance. Ask yourself the following questions.

Hint

Visualise your play as you write. See the characters, costume, lighting, and setting; hear the sounds. Sketch any strong images down or record them on your script draft as stage directions. This helps establish the world of the play and defines the atmosphere you wish to create.

- What point do I want to make?
- What am I exploring in my script: relationships, society, politics or power?
- How can I make my play interesting through manipulation of language, action, character, tension, contrast and style?
- How long do I want the performance to be?
- What type of performance space will the script be performed in?

Read ## Step 2 Research Your Idea

It is crucial that you research the ideas for your play. Without substantial research your situations and characters can become clichéd or stereotyped. Often interviewing people or finding true stories can help give your writing a freshness and originality. Ask yourself the following questions.

- What do I need to know about my topic?
- Where can I access information?
- How do I record the information so it is useful to me when I write?
- How do I interpret the information?

Hint

Dramatic structure is the term used to describe the order and placement of scenes and acts.

Read ## Step 3 Plot the Journey

Once you have researched your idea you can begin to establish your dramatic structure and the dramatic action of your script. At this stage you can record your dramatic structure and dramatic action as a brief written description, or synopsis. You may also choose to prepare your synopsis as a storyboard with some explanatory notes rather than full descriptions. Initially you will need to think about dramatic form and the elements of drama. Ask yourself the following questions.

- What form or style will my play be performed in? Will it be realistic or melodramatic; or will it perhaps be realistic but with influences from other forms?
- What impact will the choice of form and style have on the actor–audience relationship?
- Is the dramatic structure that of a linear narrative or a non-linear narrative, or is it a montage structure? What is the best way to tell the story and present the ideas?
- Who is/are the protagonist/s? Who is/are the antagonist/s?
- How will the tension of the piece be established and built? What is the climactic moment of the piece? Will there be one or more climactic moments? When will they occur?
- What locations will be used? How will the locations be established using performers and the elements of production?

Dramatic Forms and Performance Styles

Read ## Step 4 Develop the Scenes

In Step 3 you completed your dramatic structure and synopsis. Your scenes then spring from this overview. Each scene explores a new development of plot or idea, like paragraphs in an essay. Each scene has its own particular point. All the scenes are linked together in a particular order to help establish the intention of the play. As the play has a climactic moment, so will each scene. Make sure you are clear about the significant moment or line in each scene, and how each scene contributes to the whole script. Ask yourself the following questions.

- Are all the scenes necessary?
- What is the climactic moment in each scene and is this moment clear?
- What is each scene's relationship to other scenes?

Once you have developed your dramatic structure and have a synopsis of the dramatic action it is possible to use performers to help develop scenes through improvisation. This approach may assist you in refining both plot and characters.

Read ## Step 5 Decide on Your Characters and Roles

Each character needs to have a crucial part in the telling of the story. Remember that both roles and characters are important. A good place to start creating character is through character biographies (see Chapter 3, Unit 3.5). Ask yourself the following questions.

- What are the roles and characters in my play?
- Why is each role or character important?
- Who is/are the protagonist/s and antagonist/s?
- What is it about each role or character that gives it dimension and complexity?
- What message do the actions of the roles or characters give to the audience?
- What are the character's objectives and motivations?

The Voice of the Role or Character

Each character or role needs to have a unique voice. The language they use will reflect their social class, personality and status. Finding character voice requires consideration of not only how the characters sound but how the characters move as well. Their physical appearance and use of body language will influence the use of vocal dynamics by the performer.

Exercise ### *Finding Character Voice*

Create three characters of your own imagining. Make each character distinctly different from the others. The differences might be in background, status, confidence, education, country of birth or personality, or due to other reasons. Imagine each character must give the first three minutes of a speech, for example at a twenty-first birthday, a funeral or a wedding. As you write the speech try to adopt the character's voice. Present your speeches to the class.

Hint

Make sure you bring a copy of your script and a pencil to your script workshop. Make annotations and notes as your script is read or performed by the performers.

Read ## Step 6 Workshop the Script

After a period of writing it is a good idea to have your script workshopped. Having actors read and perform your script will help you discover new ideas. The actors do not need to rehearse for the workshop. A reading of the script will help you work out the overall running time, develop the build of tension, improve scene transitions and fine tune character. It is also a good idea to invite a few people to see your script performed for the first time. Ask yourself the following questions.

- What were the strengths of my script?
- What did the performers enjoy?
- What improvements can I make?
- What did the performers find difficult to follow or understand?

Read ## Step 7 Edit the Script

Using the material you have gathered throughout the workshopping process edit your script. Make adjustments, delete lines, add lines, and so on.

Read ## Step 8 Perform a Reading of the Script

It is now time to revisit the rehearsal room. This time you will give your performers time to read the script and prepare their characters before a rehearsal. You may also give the performers some specific directions in terms of character interpretation, movement, entrances and exits, and so on. You might ask a friend who likes directing to rehearse with the performers. Invite a small audience to your performance. Sometimes it is helpful to invite some of the same audience members from your workshop reading, as they will have comments about the changes you have made. Once again you are looking not only for flaws but for ways to improve your script.

Read ## Step 9 Produce a Final Script

Once your play has been written up as a final draft it is ready to be performed. A director will create his or her interpretation of your play, and bring a directorial concept to the work. This is often an interesting time for the playwright as they are seeing their work interpreted by others.

12.5 Script Writing Task: Australian Drama

Read

The Task

You are to write a five-minute scripted drama for two to four characters that explores an aspect of Australian society, politics or history. You are encouraged to experiment with a range of dramatic forms, techniques and conventions in the writing of your piece.

You will present a final published version as a typed script which incorporates the following script conventions:

- a title and title page
- a cast list with brief role and character descriptions
- scene descriptions, including information about set, lighting and sound if appropriate
- role or character names in the left-hand margin of the page
- indented dialogue lines
- stage directions where appropriate
- double-spacing of the print.

You will also include a statement of three hundred words that explains your intentions as a playwright, the themes and issues you wish to explore, and the reasons for your choice of dramatic form, techniques and conventions.

You and your teacher will decide on whether or not to rehearse and perform the final script.

You may choose one of the following suggestions as a starting point for your script.

- The Lucky Country
- Island
- 'The strength of a nation lies with its people.'

You may also choose to set the action of your play against the background of a significant Australian day, or event, such as one of the following. This can add symbolic meaning to your script.

- Australia Day
- Sorry Day
- A protest march
- Anzac Day
- New Year's Eve
- Christmas Day
- The Melbourne Cup

Scripted Drama: Writing Australian Plays   245

Prepare: Creating and Making Australian Drama

- Research aspects of Australian society, politics and history that are of interest to you.
- Decide on a central focus and intention for your scripted drama.
- Choose a narrative structure to frame your scripted drama.
- Devise characters or roles.
- Consider how dramatic techniques such as narration, projected images or mime can be incorporated into your scripted drama.
- Consider integral and efficient ways of creating scene transitions.
- Use improvisation in rehearsal to workshop your script with other members of the class.
- Make notes of your observations of your scripted drama in performance. Adjust the draft of your script accordingly.
- Refer to Unit 12.4 for more detailed guidance.

Evaluate: Performance Checklist

You and your teacher will evaluate your work individually using a list of criteria. These criteria relate to your achievement in this task. The criteria are listed on the evaluation sheet at the end of this chapter and will be used to evaluate your ability to:

- establish an effective, original and clear intention as a playwright
- devise an effective and engaging setting and situation
- create interesting and appropriate characters or roles
- establish tension
- establish an appropriate atmosphere
- incorporate dramatic techniques appropriate to the style and purpose of the scripted drama
- publish a final script that incorporates formatting conventions
- explore an aspect of Australian society, politics or history.

Write and Discuss

Arts Criticism and Aesthetics

1. Recount the process of developing your scripted drama. What problems did you encounter and how did you overcome them?
2. Evaluate the reading of your scripted drama. In your evaluation comment on the ways in which the weaker aspects of your script could be strengthened.
3. Evaluate one other class member's script. In your evaluation discuss the playwright's intention. Consider how effectively they chose dramatic form to suit their intention.

Past and Present Contexts

4. Research one of the key periods in Australian theatre history. Present a short talk that outlines the features of the chosen period. In your presentation include the performance of a script extract from a play written during the period.
5. Imagine you are running a course in writing Australian drama. Explain the important steps you would take in the process of writing an Australian play.

Script Writing Task: Australian Drama

Student: _____ Teacher: _____

Related Outcomes

By completing this task you should be able to:
- recognise how theatre and drama reflect and explore aspects of Australian society and of human experience
- create, write, edit and publish a scripted drama that explores aspects of Australian society, politics or history.

Criteria	Level of Achievement			
	Beginning	Consolidating	Mastering	Excelling
Exploring and Developing Ideas Have you prepared your scripted drama by: • researching an aspect of Australian society, politics or history of interest to you? • establishing an effective, original and clear intention? • preparing written drafts of your scripted drama?				
Using Skills, Techniques and Processes Have you incorporated dramatic form, techniques and conventions by: • choosing the most appropriate dramatic form(s) for the intention of your piece? • selecting dramatic techniques and conventions for a specific purpose? • manipulating the elements of drama to establish tension and atmosphere? • incorporating improvisation to explore and develop role or character, and dramatic action?				
Presenting Have you completed your scripted drama ready for performance by: • structuring moments of your scripted drama into a coherent and polished performance incorporating effective scene transitions? • presenting an appropriately formatted and published copy of your scripted drama? • creating an appropriate actor–audience relationship?				

Comments: _____
_____
_____
_____

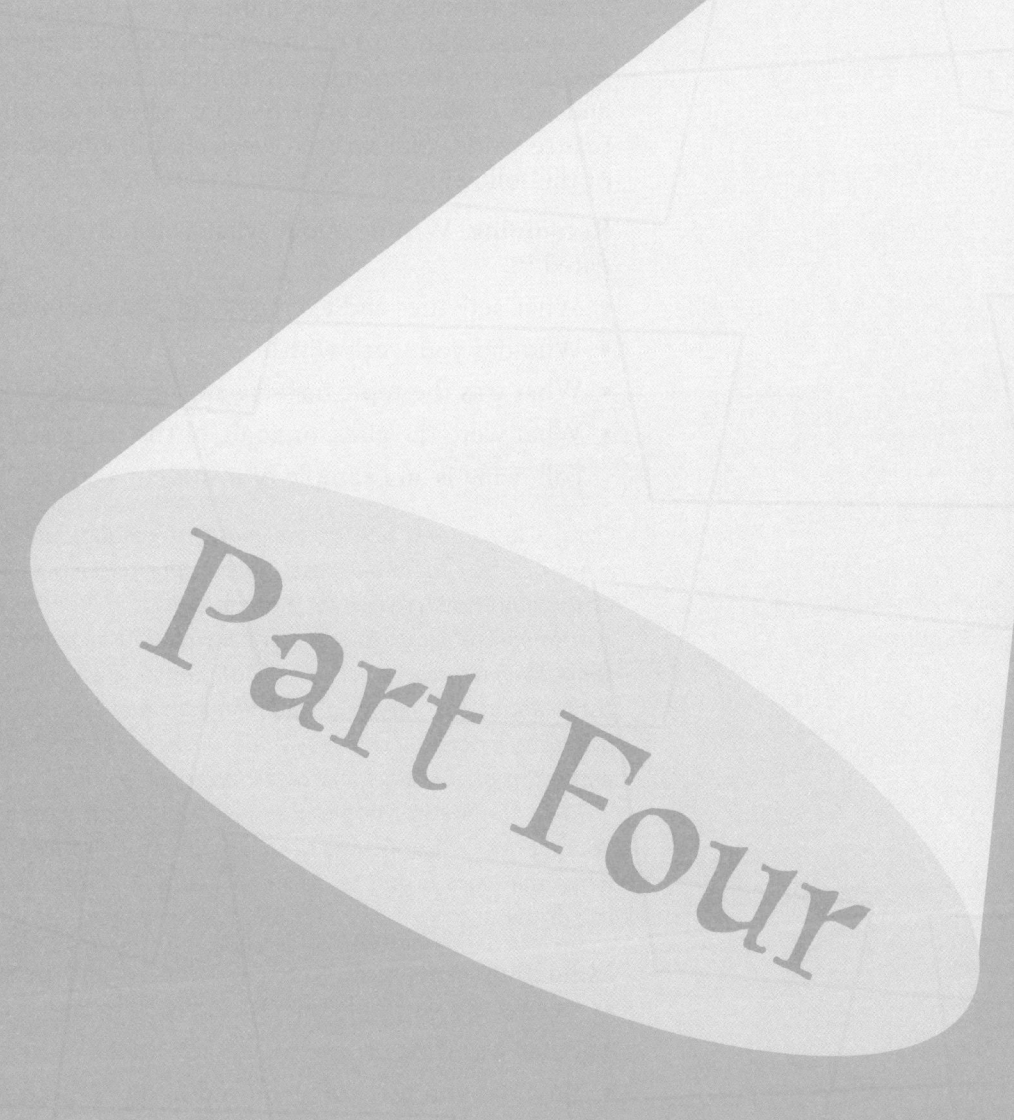

Appendixes

Appendix 1 The Logbook

Appendix 2 Rehearsal Log Sheet

Appendix 3 Performance Self-assessment Sheet

Appendix 4 Audience Evaluation Sheet

Appendix 5 Lighting Cue Sheet

Appendix 6 Sound Cue Sheet

Appendix 7 Make-up Design Sheet

Appendix 8 Costume Design Sheet

Appendix 1 The Logbook

To make the most of your drama work you should keep a logbook as an ongoing record of all your lessons and performance experiences. Your written entries should be submitted on a regular basis and will be used by your teacher when evaluating your performance work. Your written work should consist of a combination of the following.

Recounting. Writing about what you have observed and participated in.

- What activities and exercises did you undertake?
- Who did you work with?
- What was the topic or focus of the lesson?
- What were the aims, or goals, of the exercises, or the class?

Following is an example of a student's recount:

Today's lesson was one of the most interesting yet. We were played a piece of music that had these really interesting lyrics. They told the story of this guy and his search for good fortune and luck. We then had to make shapes and tableaux to represent words that were from the lyrics of the song. Then we read an article about gambling and some pretty awful statistics about the impact of gambling on families. We then divided into groups to prepare a role-play about luck. We started brainstorming ideas and will probably start improvisations next lesson.

I like the idea of doing a series of different scenes where the word 'luck' or 'lucky' is only used once. Maybe we could freeze for three counts when the word is said to help emphasise it. I'll discuss it with the group tomorrow.

Evaluating. Analysing your experiences and performance work, as well as the work of others.

- What was the purpose of the activities?
- How did you feel you achieved in different activities?
- How did you find working with others?
- Think critically about the activities. What worked? What did not work? Why?
- How successfully did you achieve the aims, or goals, of the lesson? Why?
- What suggestions could you make to improve your own work?
- What constructive criticism can you offer to improve the work of others?

Here is an example of a student's evaluation:

I really enjoyed today's lesson. The practical activities were fun but exhausting. I didn't realise you needed to be so fit to be a performer. I must go to gym like I promised myself last year.

I love tableau work. It was great to see how each group was able to capture the meaning of the words so well. I think Carla's group did a fantastic interpretation of the word 'opportunity'. Their use of levels, body language and facial expression really communicated how exciting an 'opportunity' can be, especially Will's face. It's like it's made of rubber!

Our group got some great comments. It was a shame the audience couldn't see Pip and Sarah because they were hidden by the table. They were important to the overall impact of our piece because they were the element of danger. Next time one of us has to remember to stand back from the tableau and have a look from the audience's point of view to make sure everything is okay.

PS I'm getting much better at holding a freeze. I only lost concentration four times today!

Researching. Investigating topics or areas of interest.
- What extra information can you find about the topic?
- How can you extend on the tasks you have been asked to do?

An example of a student's research is as follows:

I talked to my brother about luck and he wasn't much help because he said it didn't exist. Dad told me that he knew a friend who always won at the races; but then he said he had never heard about the times he lost. It made me think about how easy it would be lose everything. I wonder what makes people want to take that risk?

I also borrowed a book from Waheed. It has pictures of symbols and of objects that people have used as good luck charms.

Your written work can include other material that helps to explain and explore your ideas. Some other material could include:
- brainstorming charts
- tables, checklists and lists of ideas
- aerial drawings showing the placement of set items and the movements of actors
- sketches of characters, settings, costumes and make-up designs
- magazine and newspaper articles and pictures.

The following pages contain some sample logbook extracts. These were written by members of a group as part of the process of creating a playbuilt performance. The group studied the dramatic form of documentary drama, and then devised their own performance, which incorporated sound, lighting and multimedia. The selection of logbook entries gives a snapshot of a process, including the introduction of the topic, research, rehearsal and an extract from the final script.

Recounting and Researching

WEEK TWO:

We have begun "Documentary Drama" in class. Our assignment has been handed out and everyone has been deep in thought about an issue or an event to focus on. We found out our groups after nominating several names. My group contains: Lucy Jordan, Felicity Dinopoulos, Rebecca Douglas, Isabella Slawinski and me. Before the groups came together, I was having my own thoughts about what I wanted to do. I nurse a rather passionate collection of feelings for political turmoil. I was thinking along the lines of Stalin-operated Russia or the fall of the Berlin Wall. However, after we met with the group we decided to address what we felt was a very grim issue: domestic violence. We chose this because it is an issue that is prejudiced to particular areas and lifestyles. It applies to every social class and every region of the world.

At home, I decided to make it more definitive, as inspiration for arising ideas:

The Concise Macquarie Dictionary states:
DOMESTIC (adj.) 1. of or pertaining to the home, the household or household affairs. 2. Living with a man: tame.
6. (colloq) an argument with one's spouse.
VIOLENCE (noun) 1. Rough force in action. 2. Rough or injurious action or treatment. 3. Any unjust or unwarranted exertion of force or power, as against rights, laws, etc.; injury; wrong; outrage.

I came to the conclusion that before reading this I was rather naive when it came to my understanding of what "domestic violence" really meant.

I originally thought of it as battered women, who hid their bruises from their alcoholic husbands. It is a much more complex issue. It ranges from physical violence, and down to emotional violence. Emotional violence? Physical sounds worse, right? Wrong. In my research I quickly discovered that smarter men emotionally abuse their wives for long periods of time. If one is told that "you're ugly, you're fat, you're ignorant" over and over again, all they do is believe it. The emotional bruises take longer to fade than the optional physical ones. Our group does want to avoid at all costs turning this drama into a male-bashing issue.

We are holding many ideas between us. We came up with a few for a brainstorm. It contains ideas, theories, thoughts, facts, feelings and any other pieces that add to the development:

✶ Bruises   ✶ Social differences   ✶ Ignoring
✶ Emotional violence ✶ Drugs   ✶ Worthless
✶ Men vs. Women   ✶ Alcohol   ✶ Useless
✶ Children   ✶ Dysfunctional families ✶ Hard to let go
✶ Pain   ✶ Monsters   ✶ Happiness
✶ Secrecy   ✶ Masked fears   ✶ Change
✶ Abusive childhoods ✶ Paranoia   ✶ Anger
✶ Politics   ✶ Propaganda   ✶ Confusion

WEEK 6.

We began the week by showing the scripts we wrote over the weekend.

Felicity wrote the Anti-feminist scene which has 2 snobs criticising feminists and those trying to stop Domestic Violence. Also in the scene is a representation of what they really think e.g. their conscience.

The audience will learn that the women don't really believe a word they are saying and that they have suffered from domestic violence themselves. Whenever a conscience speaks the other woman and her conscience freezes so that attention can be focused on the reaction of the woman to what the conscience is saying to her. This scene is intended to be comical but at the same time it is sad. The audience should ask themselves questions like 'If women are not going to support the fight against domestic violence then who will?'. The conscience also mainly asks questions that the audience can think about. This scene has no link to the central story line.

Amanda wrote a duologue with the mother and social worker. And it is evident in this scene that neighbours have reported about the terrible fights they hear coming from the house. The mother shows no signs of wanting to change. We will display an image of a 'normal' suburban house for this scene to give the impression that the house is nice and normal but horrible events take place inside - Domestic violence can happen anywhere.

Bella wrote 2 brilliant scenes. The first is the mother on the phone to the father. The father has finally been jailed and he is calling to ask his wife to bail him out. He is in there for harming her (domestic violence). Throughout the play the mother's path to freedom is followed and in this scene she breaks free. She tells the husband she is not going to bail him out. The group recommended a change for the script - instead of ending with 'goodbye' it should stop at 'Don't tell me you love me, it disgusts me'. Then she hangs up. The phone rings again and she walks away which I think is a great end to this scene because it is the last temptation.

The second scene Bella wrote involved the husband/father/batterer describing to the police why it is he continues to beat his wife. He does not completely understand

Evaluating

Evaluation:

Group Performance: Lucy Jordan, Felicity Dimopoulos, Rebecca Douglas, Amanda Lian and Isabella Slowinski.

We felt, as a whole group, that on the night it was definitely our best. After being on stage we felt positive about our performance and felt that the audience had responded well to everything. They had laughed in uncertain places; however, they kept us in focus, and we were particularly impressed at the level of maturity from our own form...

On the night of the performance I was extremely nervous before. I was becoming confused with my social worker scene; I found the lines hard to remember and arduous to say. Every time I said a particular line I had a tendency to lose focus and lose grip of the character. This loss of character caused me to panic and I would more often than not forget my next line and stare helplessly. Amanda and I revised the scene about six or seven times before the performance, and on the night it was totally different to the one that we had first created several weeks prior. This change was due to the fact that Amanda changed the personality of her character frequently, from a woman in denial, to a woman in despair, to one who was rude and hostile, and finally, to the quiet, submissive housewife Grace. I think I agree with Amanda's final portrayal. It made my lines easier, because I then had a solid purpose and objective to the scene. My objective was to assume the role of Michelle, the social worker, who has a personality that everyone opens up to. Grace I had to feel was a challenge to me, and I was gently coaxing her into telling me her problems. Grace remained timid and shy; however, at the end of the scene, is made to realize that "before she can get help, she needs to help herself". This scene ran smoothly on the night, and I didn't skip any lines. I felt the audience could hear me (projection and articulation had been two of my major problems). The only problem I felt this scene held was the fact that it dragged on slightly, and I was worried about the audience becoming restless. We played it quite rapidly on the night; however, it wasn't too fast, just more charged and energetic than it had ever been.

Our movement part in Scene One was well received apparently. I was told by friends in the audience that the torchlight was extremely effective and the music was symbolic (heartbeat). I used to worry about not getting the movement right (I am definitely not a dancer). On the night, we were very well timed. Felicity said her lines very well, and it felt like a chill ran through the audience, the words literally hung in the air.

Our scene transitions from one to two worked brilliantly. I felt casual as I donned the coat and shoes, and attempted to even walk in a different manner. I'm not entirely sure that it worked, but it was more the thought that helped build my confidence.

Scene Three was interesting. The audience was laughing when Lucy and Bec walked on, probably due to the fact Bec was wearing leg warmers and Lucy had on a t-shirt saying "MEN ARE PIGS". It was a fun scene to write. However, prior to the performance it lacked energy and impulse. On the night, however, we were very energetically charged, and had converted our nervous energy into producing a charged performance.

I was really happy with that scene, it was worked very well and the audience reaction was strong. My small piece was well projected I felt I was particularly impressed with Bec she was slightly worried about it and felt she slowed the scene up, but on the night she was snappy and recited her lines perfectly she was vibrant and portrayed an energy that caught on to all of us. Our scene change from three to four was also very smooth.

I was not in Scene Four but commendations should be made to Bec and Amanda as they made a fantastic appearance on stage Bec was particularly good she added in lots of mannerisms and intonations that made her extremely believable in performance. Amanda was good again. She's a very talented actress. Her portrayal of

Researching

WEEK 7

Domestic Violence

We decided to focus on domestic violence as our issue.
There are many reasons for this choice. It is an issue that is worldwide, extremely common and it is left in the shadows. Domestic Violence destroys people's lives and it often goes unnoticed by the community.
We felt we could relate to the issue because it is mainly women who are the victims of domestic violence. We hope our performance is powerful + leaves the audience in thoughts about our issue.

THE FACTS

Domestic Violence is the leading cause of injury to women aged 15-45, more than rape, muggings + automobile accidents <u>combined</u>.

97% of victims are women.

On Average women will leave the abuser 7 or 8 times before making the final break.

Why do batters get away with it?

Shattered LOVE Broken LIVES

Sound and Lighting Ideas

daddy and mummy

Light: flashing blue + red lights

Sound: Music: '97 Bonnie and Clyde by Tori Amos

Action: Changing defensive positions every 8 seconds

Script Draft

Final Script Extract

ACTION	SOUND	LIGHT
SCENE FOUR		
(Daughter storms onto the stage where the mother is folding laundry)		
Daughter: Why are David's suitcases in the hallway? I thought he was gone for good this time.		• Light fades up downstage right
Mother: Your father, as you are to call him, is back because he is going to change. We had a long talk last night.		
• Amanda enters carrying a basket		
• Mother is folding laundry downstage right		
Daughter: So just because you have one argument without a fist involved you think he has transformed! Do you have no concern for my life let alone your own?		
Mother: Samantha how can you even ask me such a question?		
Daughter: (exasperated) How can I ask you! I know how much he hurts you emotionally and physically as much as you try to hide it.		
(Silence. The mother continues to fold washing as if she has not heard the daughter)		
I hate him		
Mother: You do not hate him. He is your father.		
Daughter: And I hate you. You are pathetic. He is not going to change. You'll see he will hit you soon enough but I won't be here for him to get me. I'm going to go and live with Gemma. (The daughter walks angrily out of the room. The mother at first appears oblivious to what has just happened).		
• Daughter exits		
• Mother throws tea towel		
Mother: (Very softly) Samantha don't leave me (calls out) Sarah come back! you dare close that door Samantha		
(sound of door slamming. The mother cries out and throws the folded laundry onto the floor. She collapses sobbing)		
He says he loves me! He will change because he loves me!	• Music	• Blue light
• Mother exits		• Light fades out
Time: approx. 1min and 10 seconds		• Blackout

Appendix 1

Appendix 2 Rehearsal Log Sheet

Name:

Rehearsal number:

Date:

Working title:

Option:

Agreed aim for the session:

Research activities or research used in the session:

Time management:

What was achieved:

What needs to be done:

Time left to performance:

Activities undertaken:

Detail and polishing achieved:

Appendix 2 Rehearsal Log Sheet (cont.)

Diagrams of blocking or stage choreography:

Technical or design ideas arising from the session:

Agreed changes made from last session:

Development of role/character:

Appendix 3 Performance Self-assessment Sheet

Name:

Date:

Title of piece:

Brief description of the piece of work:

Description of role/character/function:

Vocal skills used:

Volume

Pace

Pitch

Tone

Accent

Pause

Emphasis

Overall vocal evaluation

Physical skills used:

Movement

Posture

Gesture

Stillness

Mannerism

Facial expression

Body expression

Use of space

Overall physical evaluation

Creation of mood and atmosphere:

Relationship/interaction with the audience:

Quality of group work in the performance:

Rehearsal ideas/techniques that worked in performance:

Successful elements or moments in the performance:

Areas to develop in the next performance or piece of work:

Appendix 4 Audience Evaluation Sheet

| Name | Date |

| Others in the group |

| Title of piece |

Brief description of the story or narrative as you understood it:

Description of the roles/characters:

Evaluation of vocal skills used:

e.g. Volume Pace Pitch Tone Pause Accent Emphasis

Evaluation of physical skills used:

e.g. Movement Posture Gesture Facial expression
Stillness Mannerism Use of space

Copyright © Pearson Australia 2009

Audience Evaluation Sheet **263**

Appendix 4 Audience Evaluation Sheet (cont.)

Did you feel that a sense of mood and atmosphere was created in the piece?

Successful moments of tension/comedy/suspense/tragedy/climax:

Evaluation of dramatic conventions and theatrical techniques used:

e.g. Chorus   Counterpoint   Flashback   Monologue   Narration   Physical theatre   Repetition and echo   Slow motion Synchronised movement

Evaluation of the overall impact the piece made on you:

Areas that you would suggest for development:

Appendix 5 Lighting Cue Sheet

Sheet number														
Requirements:	CUE													
	INTENSITY													
	FADERS/AREAS													
	DURATION													
Name Title of performance Operator	ACTION													
	CUE NUMBER													

Appendix 6 Sound Cue Sheet

CUE NUMBER	ACTION	DURATION	TITLE	VOLUME	CUE

Sheet number

Requirements:

Name
Title of performance
Operator

Appendix 7 Make-up Design Sheet

Name:

Date:

Performance:

Character:

Relevant details of character to be considered:

Base:

Highlights:

Shadows:

Eye:

Mouth:

Nose:

Cheek:

Powder:

Hair:

Prosthetics:

Additional notes:

Appendix 8 Costume Design Sheet

Name:

Date:

Performance:

Character:

Actor:

Relevant character details to be considered:

Front

Back

Torso:

Legs:

Feet/hands:

Head/hair:

Accessories:

Extra notes:

268 Appendix 8

Glossary

Absurdism A theatrical style that evolved after the Second World War. It explores a world without purpose or meaning. Famous Absurdist playwrights include Eugene Ionesco and Samuel Beckett.

advance An improvisation term that is used to instruct performers to move the plot forward.

amplifier The power source for a sound system.

antagonist The character who forces the protagonist into action.

articulation The use of the lips, teeth and tongue to create sounds.

aside A theatrical technique in which something is spoken by an actor that is intended to be heard by the audience, but not by the other characters on stage.

atmosphere An element of drama. The atmosphere of a performance is the mood created by means such as the plot, the use of the elements of production, the use of symbol, or the behaviour of the characters and roles.

audience engagement An element of drama. The quality of an audience response depends on the drama maker's control of the actor–audience relationship in context of the chosen form or style and performance space. The type of audience engagement that occurs during a performance will also be dependent upon the purpose of the performance; and will contribute towards making the dramatic meaning of the performance clear.

barn doors A metal frame that slots into the front of a theatre lamp. It has four moveable, hinged panels that can be arranged to control the beam of light.

block An improvisation term for a performer's failure to yield to an offer; 'blocking' is also a term used to describe a rehearsal process in which the director and performers make decisions about the moves of the performers.

Boal, Augusto The South American theatre practitioner who founded the Theatre of the Oppressed. Boal believes that theatre is a powerful instrument for change. Theatre of the Oppressed performances feature the use of audience members as performers to explore social problems and issues.

body language The messages communicated by movement, facial expression, poses and gestures.

breathing exercises Exercises that relax the performer and increase lung capacity; essential preparation for voice work.

Brecht, Bertolt The German playwright who created Epic Theatre. He saw theatre as a powerful tool for making audiences think about issues.

bump in The move into a theatre of sets, lighting and sound equipment, props and costumes.

centring The process in which a performer undertakes a series of exercises to improve concentration and focus.

character Characterisation involves the playwright and/or performer creating a complex character with a personal history, intention, status and attitude. A character's complexity can be developed through interaction and relationships with others. Character is an element of drama.

character biography A written record of all aspects of a character and his or her life.

chorus Originally a convention of Ancient Greek theatre. The chorus moves as a group; it can be representative of a point of view when it addresses either the protagonist in a play or the audience.

climactic moment The moment of greatest tension in a play or scene; the high point.

commedia dell'arte A theatrical style that evolved in Italy in the fifteenth century. It employs the use of half masks, stock characters and improvisation to create slapstick comedy and satire.

control This term is used to describe the degree to which a performer is effectively able to harness and manipulate focus, energy, movement and voice.

cue The indicator or signal that instructs the performers and crew to complete an action or task. A cue can be aural (heard) or visual (seen).

curtain call The appearance of performers at the end of a theatrical performance to acknowledge applause.

cyclorama The white wall or curtain in the upstage area. It is usually used for washes of coloured light.

diaphragm A dish-shaped muscle located above the abdomen that helps the lungs work to draw in air. It assists the performer to control the rate of exhalation.

director The person who guides the actors through the process of rehearsal to performance.

directorial concept The directorial concept is the director's vision for the performance of a play. The directorial concept will take into account the themes and issues of the play, and consider staging and the manipulation of the elements of production, as well as approaches to rehearsal and background research.

Documentary Drama A theatrical form that developed in the 1960s and utilises Epic Theatre techniques and conventions to interpret and present true historic events.

dramatic convention A dramatic convention is an identifiable feature of a dramatic form. For example, an aside is a convention used in the dramatic form known as melodrama.

dramatic form A recognisable type of dramatic or theatrical performance which uses certain structures, techniques and conventions.

dramatic meaning An element of drama. This is what is communicated between the performers and the audience to create an actor–audience relationship.

dramatic technique A device used in a performance for a specific purpose; for example, slow motion or mime.

dramaturge The person who provides support to the director and perfomers by researching a play to find useful insights and resources. The dramaturge also offers advice and suggestions for interpretation of the script.

dress rehearsal The final rehearsal. It is considered to be the first performance.

elements of drama The essential ingredients needed to create performance work.

elements of production Set, costume, lighting and sound.

emotion memory A Stanislavskian exercise that involves a performer drawing upon their own experiences to help play their character truthfully.

emphasis Refers to an aspect of vocal dynamics; to create emphasis the performer places stress on particular syllables, words and sentences.

environment An audience–actor arrangement in which the performers are among the audience.

Epic Theatre A theatrical style created by Bertolt Brecht. Epic Theatre employs a number of conventions and techniques to distance the audience and discourage them from becoming emotionally engaged in the performance.

episodic The quality of a performance composed of a series of loosely related scenes.

evaluate A student of drama will evaluate their own work and the work of others using criteria that help to establish both strengths and areas for improvement.

Expressionism A theatrical style that developed in reaction to Realism. Expressionism distorts reality and draws on the world of dreams and the subconscious as inspiration for performance work.

expressive skills The voice and movement skills of the performer. An effective use of expressive skills involves the performer manipulating and controlling vocal and movement dynamics.

extend An improvisation term for the performer's ability to make the most of a particular moment in the action of an improvisation.

flashback A dramatic technique used to show the audience events that happened in the past. The use of flashback is intended to progress the plot and may help to build tension.

flat Canvas stretched across a wooden frame. It can be painted and used for scenery.

floodlight A light that does not have a controlled beam.

fly bar A bar suspended from the roof of the stage by cables. Scenery attached to a fly bar can be raised into the fly tower or lowered onto the stage using a system of weights, pulleys and ropes.

focus This can refer to controlling a beam of light. It can also refer to the point of attention for the performers and the audience. When a performer is focused in performance they are using their skills of concentration to remain in character.

fresnel A theatre lamp that creates a spread of light with a soft edge.

front of house This term encompasses the duties and services provided by ticket sellers, bar staff and ushers.

given circumstances A Stanislavskian term for the information given in a script; for example, information about place, time and season.

gobo A perforated piece of metal that is inserted into a profile lantern in a gobo holder. The perforations create patterns in the area where the beam of light falls.

headset The headphones that the stage crew uses to communicate with one another during a performance.

historical context The conditions and circumstances of the past that are relevant to the play.

house lights The lights used in a theatre before a performance starts. These lights are usually dimmed to settle the audience before the performance.

improvisation The spontaneous creation of performance work.

Lazzo A comic moment that is extended.

lighting bar A metal bar from which stage lanterns are hung.

lighting rig The arrangement of metal bars (rigging) and lanterns used for a performance.

lighting desk The lighting desk is where lighting changes are operated from. Some are manual and some are automated. They have rows of faders, which are used to control the levels of different theatre lanterns.

linear narrative A narrative that tells a story in chronological order; it has a beginning, a middle and an end. Events happen sequentially and have a cause and effect.

'magic if' A Stanislavskian exercise in which a performer uses their imagination to try to put themselves in the character's position and understand the way the character would react or respond.

mask A covering of the face and/or head. It is used to create character.

melodrama A Western theatrical style that flourished in the nineteenth century. It employs stories of good versus evil, stock characters and sensational scenery.

mime A dramatic form or dramatic technique in which controlled movement is used to create the illusion of objects and locations.

moment An element of drama. Key moments in the performance are fundamental to the pacing of the dramatic action. They encourage the audience to focus on a particular atmosphere, a shift in plot or character reactions.

montage A playbuilding structure in which there are a number of scenes not linked by cause and effect but linked by theme or subject.

morality play A medieval theatrical style in which biblical stories were performed on wooden wagons in front of churches.

motivation The reason 'why' a character wants to achieve their objective.

movement Movement is created by the performer in order to physically express character, role, atmosphere or symbol. Movement can be literal or abstract. Types of movement include body language and mime.

movement dynamics The dynamics of movement are dependent upon the performer's physical control, pace, rhythm and energy.

narration The telling of the story of the play by one or more of the actors.

Noh An early Japanese theatrical style that is sombre, mysterious and employs the use of mask to create character.

non-linear narrative The story-line of a play or performance in which the sequence of events does not follow a chronological order.

non-realistic Non-realistic theatrical styles do not try to re-create life on stage. Absurdism, Expressionism, Surrealism and Epic Theatre are all non-realistic theatrical styles.

objective What a character wants to achieve or gain.

offer An improvisation term to describe what a performer contributes to the progression of the action. An offer can be verbal or physical.

pace Pace is dictated by rhythm and is linked to tension. The use of a slower pace will create and build tension in a different way to the use of a faster pace.

pang, provocation, penalty The ingredients of a melodrama plot.

pause A pause occurs when the action of the performance stops momentarily. Pause can be effectively used to create focus or to establish a significant moment; it can also be used to interrupt or change the pace and rhythm of the performance.

pitch In voice work pitch refers to how high or low the sound of your voice is. For example, you may pitch your voice so that it is either very deep or falsetto.

Playback Theatre A theatrical form that uses true stories from the audience as the basis for performance work.

playbuilding The process of using resources, ideas, improvisation and rehearsal to create a performance.

political context The aspects of government, power and laws that are relevant to the play.

profile spot A theatre lamp that uses polished lenses and metal shutters inside the lamp housing to focus a beam of light to a precise area.

projection The ability of the performer to be heard from a distance without shouting.

prompt The person who assists performers to recall their lines. A prompt is useful during rehearsal to help performers learn their lines more quickly.

prompt copy The copy of a script that contains all the sound, light and action cues, as well as lists of props, costumes and pre-show settings.

proscenium arch The frame around a stage that hides the backstage area from the audience.

protagonist The central character of a linear narrative.

Realism A theatrical style that attempts to re-create life on stage through the use of realistic sets, lighting, sound and acting.

rehearsal The process of developing and polishing a performance.

rhythm An element of drama. Rhythm is important in maintaining pace and tension in a performance. The rhythm of a performance is established by the performers through their interaction with the audience. An understanding of the power of rhythm helps a performer develop a sense of timing. He or she becomes aware of the internal patterns within the performance.

role An element of drama. A role is often a representation of a type of person; an actor may play a role having only general information about it. Characterisation is the development of a role into a character.

Sensation Melodrama A melodrama performance involving a spectacular moment using stage technology.

situation An element of drama. The situation of the play is the circumstances the characters find themselves in. Characters and their relationships are shaped by the situation. The situ-ation is created as a consequence of the intentions, or motivations, of the characters.

slapstick Visual comedy usually involving accidents and mishaps.

social context The aspects of society that are relevant to a play.

sound-mixing desk The operating desk used to blend music, sound effects and public address into performance work.

spontaneity The ability of the performer to act without hesitation.

stage manager The person who is responsible for running a performance. The stage manager ensures that all is ready for the performance and calls cues.

Stanislavski, Constantin The founder of Realism and the Moscow Art Theatre. He is best known for developing the System, which is a series of exercises designed to achieve truth in performance.

status The relative position or power of one character compared with another.

striking the set Removing all props and set items from the stage.

standby cue The warning cue given before the actual cue.

Symbolism A dramatic form that emerged during the early twentieth century. Symbolism also refers to the use of symbols to create meaning and focus in drama; symbols are sometimes understood by the audience on a subconscious level. Symbols can be evident in the text of the performance, in the movement or gesture of the performers, in the use of objects during the performance, or as elements of the design or staging.

tableau An arrangement of actors in a frozen pose resembling a painting or photo.

technical rehearsal The rehearsal that focuses on the technical aspects of a production, such as set changes, as well as lighting and sound cues.

tension Tension is created in a number of ways; it engages the audience and creates anticipation and excitement.

thrust A thrust stage pushes out into the audience. The audience is seated on three sides of the performing area.

tone The tone of a voice is the quality of its sound and the way in which it communicates meaning. For example, the printed words of a script might indicate that a character is happy, but an actor might deliver the words in a tone that suggests the character is sad.

transformation A dramatic technique developed by Grotowski in which actors use an object to represent different things.

unit A section of the script or action that contains a particular idea and/or moment of action.

volume The indication of how loud or soft a voice is. A performer will manipulate volume to establish character, tension and atmosphere. Volume is different to projection. A performer must be able to project his or her voice no matter what its volume; in other words, the voice must be heard and understood by the audience whether the volume is loud or soft.

warm-up A series of physical, vocal and mental exercises designed to ensure the performer is fully prepared for performance work.

wings Angled curtains or wooden flats to the sides of the proscenium arch stage that disguise the backstage area.

yield An improvisation term that refers to a performer saying 'yes' to the offer made by another performer.

Useful Resources

Chapter 1
- R. Benedetti, *The Actor at Work*, 2nd edition, Prentice Hall, New Jersey, 1990
- C. Berry, *The Actor and His Text*, Harrap, London, 1987
- K. Linklater, *Freeing the Natural Voice*, Drama Book Publishers, New York, 1976
- A. Pease, *Body Language*, Allins, London, 1984
- J. Sabatine, *Movement Training for the Stage and Screen*, Backstage Books, New York, 1995

Chapter 2
- P. Bernardi, *Improvisation Starters*, Betterway Publications, Whitehall, Virginia, 1992
- B. Haseman and J. O'Toole, *Dramawise*, Heinemann, Melbourne, 1996
- K. Johnstone, *Impro: Improvisation and the Theatre*, Methuen, Sydney, 1997
- L. Pierse, *Theatresports® Down Under*, ImproCorp, Sydney, 1993

Chapter 3
- E. Bray, *Playbuilding*, Currency Press, Sydney, 1991
- C. Tarlington and W. Michaels, *Building Plays*, Pembroke, Canada, 1995

Chapter 4
- D. Carey, *The Actors' Audition Manual*, Currency Press, Sydney, 1985
- M. Carpenter, *Basic Stage Lighting*, University of New South Wales Press, Sydney, 1996
- M. Greenslade, *All On Stage: Book 2*, Samuel French, London, 1995
- E. Jones and J. Marlow, *Duologues for All Accents and Ages*, A&C Black, London, 1993
- B. Keyte and R. Baine, *Exits and Entrances: A Drama Workbook*, Thomas Nelson, Melbourne, 1992
- NIDA and University of Wollongong, *Stage Struck: Discover Australian Performance* (CD-ROM), NIDA and University of Wollongong, 1998
- D. Redler, *Stage Lighting* (CD-ROM), Danor Theatre and Studio Systems, Ramat Hasharon, Israel, 1996, Fax: 972-3-5490751
- T. Woollams, *Scenes for Young Actors: A Scene Study Resource Book*, Currency Press, Sydney, 1999

Chapter 5
- J. Gadaloff, *Australian Drama*, The Jacaranda Press, Brisbane, 1991, pages 193–7
- State and Territory newspapers

Chapter 6
- J. Brown (ed.), *The Oxford Illustrated History of Theatre*, Oxford University Press, Oxford, 1997
- B. Burton, *Three Hisses for Villainy*, Hanbury Plays, London, 1982
- E. Irvin, *Australian Melodrama*, Hale&Iremonger, Sydney, 1981
- M. Kilgarriff (ed.), *Three Melodramas*, Samuel French, London, 1970

Chapter 7
- W. Harmer, *It's a Joke Joyce*, Currency Press, Sydney, 1994
- H. Szeps, *All In Good Timing*, Currency Press, Sydney, 1996

Chapter 8
- G. Dickinson, *Mask Making*, Quintet Publishing, London, 1995
- K. Johnstone, *Impro: Improvisation and the Theatre*, Methuen, Sydney, 1997
- S. Pern, *Masked Dancers of West Africa*, Time Life, Amsterdam, 1982
- D. Sensier and A. Earl, *Masks: Traditions Around the World*, Wayland, East Sussex, 1994

Chapter 9
- R. Benson, *German Expressionist Drama*, Macmillan, London, 1984
- A. Strindberg, *A Dream Play*, University of Washington Press, New York, 1975

Chapter 10
- S. Cooper and S. Mackey, *Theatre Studies*, Stanley Thornes, Cheltenham, UK, 1995

Chapter 11
- Jerzy Grotowski, *Towards a Poor Theatre*, Methuen Drama, London, 1991

Chapter 12
- Veronica Kelly (ed.), *Our Australian Theatre in the 1990's*, Rodopi, Atlanta/Georgia, 1998
- Dennis Carroll, *Contemporary Australian Drama*, Currency Press, Sydney, 1995
- Hannie Rayson, *Inheritance*, Currency Press, Sydney, 2003
- Dallas Winmar, *Aliwa!*, Currency Press, Sydney 2003
- Judith Gadaloff, *Australian Drama*, The Jacaranda Press, Queensland, 1991

Index

Aboriginal Dreamtime exercise 161
Aboriginal playwrights 235–6
Aboriginal scripted drama 235–41
    Aliwa! (script extract) 236–40
    conventions 235
    dramatic forms 235
    techniques 235
    themes 235
actor–managers 71
advancing 32
African mask performance 158–61
Aliwa! (script extract) 236–40
Arena Theatre Company 88
Armfield, Neil 71
Aronson, Linda 98
Artaud, Antonin 168, 169
articulation 17–18
asides 49, 123
Audience Evaluation Sheet 263–4
audience seating arrangements 58–61
Australian culture and identity 220–2

Beckett, Samuel 169
blocking 72, 73
Boal, Augusto 12
body language 9–13
breathing 15
Brecht, Bertolt 169, 175, 194 *see also* Epic Theatre

cannoning 155
Carbins, Jenni 92
centring exercises 5–6
character biography 56–7
character objectives 79
character types and status, in improvisation 33–5
characterisation 56
characters
    building 79–80
    creating 56–8
chorus work 153–7
Circles of Attention exercise 83
Clausen, Sophie 74
comedy 129–43
    characters 136–7, 141
    lazzi 135
    parody 140–2
    skit 139
    slapstick 131–6
    soap opera 143–5
commedia dell'arte 26, 49, 131, 148
concentration 83
Costume Design Sheet 268
costume designer 91
Cranney, P. P. 94

Dana and Lee (script) 76–8, 84
dance–dramas 158–9
Davis, Jack 235, 236
designers 86, 89–92
Dinkum Assorted (script extract) 98–101
director 71–2
directorial concept 85–8, 89
Documentary Drama 193–8
    performance task 199–200
    performing in 195–6
    techniques and conventions 194–5
    see also *Wild Rice*
Double Take exercise 134
downstage 61
dramatic conventions 49
dramatic forms 48–9
Dream Play, A (script extract) 168, 171
dreams and the subconscious 169–74

elements of drama 35–8
elements of production 85–8, 107
emotion memory 81, 82
Enoch, Wesley 235
environment, audience arrangement 60
Epic Theatre 175, 193–5
Euripides 157
evaluation
    in the student logbook 250–1, 254
    of performance 84, 106–8
exposition 106
Expressionist Theatre 174–80
extending 32

feelings, representing 188–9
focus 31, 50–2
fourth wall 75
Freud, Sigmund 170

Grotowski, Jerzy 53, 55, 169, 203
group character 153–7

Hairy Ape, The (script extract) 177–80
Hallett, Bryce 104
Harrison, Jane 235
historical concerns 220
Home (script extract) 94–8
Homeland 204

imitation and exaggeration 140–2
improvisation 25–43, 168
    and elements of drama 38–40
    character types and status 33–5
    ideas for improvisations 40
    performance task 41–3
    skills of 27–33
Inheritance 219, 224–34
    (script extract) 228–34

Jeziorny, Richard 89
Johnstone, Keith 27, 148

Kishawi, Tony 149
Kosky, Barry 176

Lake, The (poem) 20–4
Legs on the Wall 203–4
lighting and sound designer 90–1
Lighting Cue Sheet 265
Lilley, Chris 130
linear narrative 47
living objects 18–19
logbook 250–8

MacGregor, Gayle 91
'magic if' 81, 82
Mailman, Deborah 235
Make-up Design Sheet 267
making offers 29
marketing 92
mask 147–66
    half-mask and chorus work 153–7
    in African performance 158–61
    neutral 149–52
    overview 148
    ritual 162–6
McGough, Roger 20, 21
Medea (script extract) 157

Melbourne Playback Theatre Company 186
melodrama 114–28
   acting style 119–24
   asides 123
   character and voice 122–3
   characters 118, 121
   conventions 116
   history 115–16
   in Australia 115–16, 125
   performance task 126–8
   plot and dramatic structure 117
   sensation melodrama 125
   staging 124–5
Meyerhold, Vsevolod 168, 169
mime 6–9, 49
montage playbuilding 48
Morrochesi, Antonio 121
motif 55
Myers, Rosemary 45

Noh 148
non-linear narrative 47–8
non-realistic acting techniques 191–2
non-realistic theatre 167–84
   development of 168–9
   Dream Play, A (script extract) 171
   dreams and the subconscious 169–74
   Expressionist Theatre 174–80
   performance task 181–4
Nowra, Louis 86

objective 79
Obozarnec, Gideon 10
offers, improvisation skill 29
O'Neill, Eugene 177, 179

Page, Conrad 211
pangs 117
parody 140–2
penalty 117
Performance Self-assessment Sheet 261–2
performance style 50
performing scripts 81–3
physical theatre 202–18
   exercises 205–9
   performance task 216–18
   Runners Up (script extract) 211–15
Pierse, Lyn 27
Playback Theatre 185–92
   actor training 188
   history 186
   non-realistic acting techniques 191

overview 186–9
representing feelings 188–9
steps in a performance 192
telling stories 190
playbuilding 44–68
   creating a character 56–8
   performance tasks 61–8
   process of 45–6
   scene transitions 52–4
   stage spaces and the audience 58–61
   structures 47–9
political concerns 220
projection 15–17
prompt copy 73
props list 73
proscenium 60, 61, 75
provocation 117
publicity and marketing coordinator 92
Purcell, Leah 235

Rayson, Hannie 223–4
Realism 75
recounting 250, 252–3
Rehearsal Log Sheet, 259–60
rehearsals 81–2
relaxation 3–6, 82
representing feelings 188–9
researching 224–5, 251, 252–3, 255
review
   of a live performance 104–5
   sample 110–11
   structuring a 106–8
   writing a (performance task) 109–12
ritual, mask 162–6
Robinson, Jacque 186
role 56, 243
Romeo and Juliet, Instant, exercise 28

Sabatine, Jean 6
scene transitions 52–5
script detective work 74–80
scripts
   building characters 79–80
   rehearsing and performing 81–4
   unit breakdown and sub-objectives 79
   writing 223–44
sensation melodrama 125
set designer 89–90
Side Fall exercise 133
slapstick 117, 131–40
   characters in 136–40
   status in 137–9
Slip exercise 133
snap transformations 53

soap opera 143–5
social concerns 220
Solitude (poem) 210
Sound Cue Sheet 266
sound, shaping of 17–18
Soundscapes exercise 18
spine rolls 5, 205
spontaneity 27–8
stage left 59
stage manager 72–4
stage right 59
stage spaces and the audience 58–61
stamping 159
Stanislavski 71, 75, 168
Stanislavski's System 74–80, 81–3
status 33–5, 137–9
stock characters 26, 118
Strindberg, August 168, 171–2
Summer of the Aliens 86–8
Sunny South, The 114, 125
Swift, Gavan 90

Tempest, The (review) 110–11
Theatre of Cruelty 168
theatre spaces, types of 58–61
Theatre Works 59
theatre-in-the-round 60
thrust stage 60
transformation 53–5, 171
Transtromer, Tomas 210
Trip exercise 132

upstage 61

vocal dynamics 17–18
voice, training the 14–19

warm-ups
   centring exercises 5–6
   physical exercises 3–4
West, Jennifer 14
Wild Rice (script extract) 196–8
Winmar, Dallas 235, 236

yielding, improvisation skill 30–1